EXOTIC GOTHIC 5

VOLUME I

Exotic Gothic 5

Volume I

Edited by **Danel Olson**

2013

Exotic Gothic 5

Volume I

Copyright © 2013 Danel Olson

Front and Back Cover Art

Copyright © 2013 Marcela Bolívar

First Edition

This edition is limited to 300 numbered copies, 201–500.
200 special slipcased two-book sets numbered 1-200 are also available.

129

This is copy

ISBN 978-1-848636-18-7

Design & Layout by Michael Smith

Printed in England by the T.J. International

PS Publishing Ltd
Grosvenor House
1 New Road, Hornsea
East Yorkshire, HU18 1PG
England

e-mail: editor@pspublishing.co.uk
website: www.pspublishing.co.uk

CONTENTS

LOCATIONS

PREFACE

DANEL OLSON

In Carl Jung's theory of character, every vice and every virtue, every interest and every mood, can be found in every single one of us. Everybody is capable of anything. What attributes we choose to display is what we are about. But everything is potentially there, in that room that we call our soul . . .

In a place with few or no distractions [a Cistercian monastery in the Vienna Woods] . . . I wrote. To the eerily soothing sounds of Gregorian chants, I discovered the lecherous corrupt politician in myself, turned myself into a prostitute working exclusively for the Secret Police, turned into an actress whose spirit has been broken by the injustices of dictatorship—and of course, into my protagonist, the ideologue who gradually realizes that he can't disown his humanity. All these people were there within me, waiting in some dark place to be discovered.

At the end of the six weeks, I had a pretty scary self-portrait on 130 pages. But the most interesting discovery was . . . you will not find it in you completely to condemn your villains. In the process of writing . . . you are your own villain. You will not condemn the character you have created completely because you would be condemning yourself.

—Florian Henckel von Donnersmarck,
Writer/Director of *The Lives of Others* (2006)

MY FAVORITE GOTHIC STORY ALWAYS DISCLOSES THE MOST monstrous revelation of all: that we are the beast. Terrifying self-recognition always scared me more than the dark whatsit at the threshold, the beast in the corner, or the re-animated remains up in the attic. In these thirteen unlucky new tales you may end up staring into the dim depths of your own soul, and you may "pity the monsters," as Robert Lowell wrote in his poem "Florence". Even if the story should have no mirrors or glimmering waters, you may see yourself. It was Alfred Hitchcock who admitted that the "more successful the villain, the more successful the picture," and I find that to be true for these stories. There are other secrets I cannot whisper here, as they are the stories' revelations, but a great one is already told above: "You are your own villain." In these tales' uncertain nights and days, you fixedly appear. Does that trouble you? As a story-catcher, I have to hope so, or else what's a Hell for?

This collection with its fully rendered characters, involving conflicts and moral dilemmas has many other discoveries for you, too. It has the seven dark shadows of the traditional Gothic. We witness damning cover-ups and curses, evil that is somehow alluring and louche personalities whose misuse of power seduces, bad and absentee parenting, unknown or weak heirs—and as we remember from David Mitchell's 2004 exotic Gothic-infused masterpiece *Cloud Atlas*, "The weak are meat, the strong do eat" (503)—a human coldness that shocks us, disputes over legacies and land, antiquated places with secrets from late or the long ago which drain visitors psychically or physically, and hauntings that take so many forms (from ghosts, to transformed beings, to viruses) all showing in unsolved crimes, or in violated taboos that will explode before everyone's eyes. And through it all rank decadence, of which "decay" is of course the rotted root word, a spoliation that the victim takes part in. Everything is dissolving here; everything moves us to ruin. Before the reading is all over you may find yourself blue enough to agree with the *Graham's Lady's Magazine* review of a new novel (back in 1848), when the novelist's identity was still unknown . . . "How a human being could have attempted such a book as the present without committing suicide before he had finished a dozen chapters, is a mystery. It is a compound of vulgar depravity and unnatural horrors." The novel in question? *Wuthering Heights*. And should these stories' manipulations of you truly offend, you may chime in with Clifton Fadiman in his *New Yorker* judgment of a Southern Gothic that came along 88 years later: "Seriously, I do not know what to say of this book except that . . . this is a penny dreadful tricked up in fancy language and given a specious depth by the expert manipulation of a series of eccentric technical tricks. The characters have no magnitude and no meaning because they have no more reality than a mince-pie nightmare." The book scrutinized? *Absalom, Absalom!*

Now if the living writers in *Exotic Gothic 5* risk a critical flaying as suffered by these distinguished dead interpreters, they show no visible fear of it. By continuing the grandly desolate tradition started either with Thomas Leland's *Longsword, Earl of Salisbury* (1762) or Horace Walpole's *The Castle of Otranto* (1765)—which of these two is the earliest full-credentialed Gothic novel is of debate—they reinvigorate the Gothic in ways Leland or Walpole could scarcely foresee, taking even more double-dares with the reviewers. Our writers of eleven nations in Volume I also set the Gothic flag outside of its home territories of the UK and Ireland. Their tales grapple against the closing of the imagination in their dislocated and transgressive fictions. This is Gothic at its brutal best, the well-wielded crowbar prying locked psychic doors, getting us comfortable with being uncomfortable, opening up what is long hidden, and then gasping! Wander into the Gothic dreamland they conjure and you may identify with the victimizer one moment, and the victimized the next, sometimes with the monsters, and sometimes with the dead too. As Taryn Simon's 2012 photo exhibit at MOMA (*A Living Man Declared Dead and Other Chapters I–XVIII*) declared so well, "we are ghosts of the past and future . . . we are pieces of the dead."

In this fifth collection of original Gothic trials, we experience North America and Europe in a genre-bending way. Fantasy embraces and kisses history, mystery walks off with philosophy, and myth slips off to mate with reality. What offspring all this fornication produces is the stuff of nightmare, and just the kind of terror we have not experienced before—like ambling into a truly ancient castle on the swampy outskirts of Princeton, New Jersey. That's impossible, of course, yet it is something which will happen in this volume, written by arguably the greatest Gothicist of our lives. What beckons now from these stories is a romance of moral wilderness and every fatal danger.

All these stories reach their arms out to you. However, as the Chilean poet Violeta Parra wrote in "Teneme en Tu Corazon", ". . . And someone always dies of love, love, love" (loosely translated by the singer Elvis Perkins). And you are their burning bride or the combustible groom. More than any other one, they want you in their world. Why will you say No? I have been smiled at by my college classes for saying so, but Gothic stories that stay freshly odd (like these originals) are to me love stories. Yes it's rough love, all right. It's love hungry... lurid, feral, incendiary, joker-mad, abhorrent, feline-eyed, fanged, & bloody. But isn't hunger the sincerest kind of love? And have you not had such cravings? I say it is true as Jung said, that everything done is doable by all of us. Don't we all go a little mad sometimes? These neo-Gothic stories will show us just how mad we can go.

Readers will see what is coming, and then they won't. The protagonist and the most entrancing character won't always be one. Plots will rupture with vanishings and horrid disclosure. Children or lovers will disappear, a murder will occur with a family member apparently to blame, and people will transform into something else unrecognizable. We will have dreams in the water as we wander into Deborah Biancotti's Venice and Simon Clark's Bruges. We shall know lost women in Georges-Olivier Chateaureynaud's France, Theodora Goss's Budapest, and Anna Taborska's Poland. All will tense over the fates of endangered children in the America of Gemini Wahhaj, Nick Antosca, and Joyce Carol Oates. And we will wait for men to make their terrible decisions in that same country from the new fiction of Stephen Susco, Sheri Holman, Camille DeAngelis, Nancy A. Collins, and D.E. Cowen.

> *"Saddest fact: women are never surprised by misogyny though some men seem to be."*
> —Joyce Carol Oates on *Twitter* (25 November 2012)

Reaching to farther lands to find contributors for both volumes, I have Gothicists contributing from Australia, Bangladesh, England, France, Hungary, India, Mexico, South Africa, Sudan, USA, and Wales. Most satisfying to me, for reasons about to be explained, thirteen of the stories are written by women, and thirteen by men; one of the covers was completed by a woman, one by a man.

It is a paradox that the most ironic and unsettling aspect of recent speculative/dark mystery/horror/Gothic fiction is not what happens inside the stories but upon the table of contents. A study of Canadian, American, and British horror anthologies from 2010 by Peter Tennant in the British journal *Black Static* showed that "disappointingly six of the seven titles in which women are least represented are British." Out of 177 new stories produced from UK collections during 2010, only 37 of the tales (or 21%) were by women. One highly regarded anthology series out of Britain featured fourteen stories by men and only one by a woman that year. In 2012, Tennant determined there were only four English-language dark fantasy anthologies (and they were from the USA, Canada, and Australia), out of a review total of thirty-six, with gender parity, where the number of female contributors listed in the table of contents ranged from 45-58%. But the UK sat at the very bottom of the reviewed for featuring both genders with any measure of equality. Among six prominent anthologies out of the UK, here are the ratios of women writers to men in their table of contents . . . 3:27, 1:11, 1:12, 2:28, 0:10, 0:12. How would any respectable editor or press in the 21st Century defend this? How do you grow readers if you continue to ignore half the world? How can one legendary British horror novelist and anthologist keep saying, "only the work matters, not the gender," if so few women are invited to his anthologies in the first place? In a field made intriguing, irresistible, and profitable from Mrs. Radcliffe and Mary Shelley and the Brontë sisters, from Shirley Jackson and Angela Carter and Joyce Carol Oates, we have to decry the blindness of not inviting Gothic sisters in fair numbers. Looking at recent dark anthologies in 2012, Tennant found only 62 stories out of the 330 were composed by women (or a piddling 19%).

After looking on with shock at how writers (who happen to be women) are severely underrepresented in many British genre anthologies, I cannot neglect noting the disproportionately low numbers of women to appear in many esteemed, non-genre American journals (in terms of women contributing short stories and features, getting reviews, and serving on editorial boards). The survey "Women in Literary Arts" shows a large number of pie charts which should cause distress at the continued alarming gender imbalance at some of the best venues in the USA, including: *The Atlantic, Boston Review, Harper's, The New Republic, The New York Review of Books, The New Yorker, The New York Times Book Review, The Threepenny Review, The Paris Review,* and *The Nation* (http://www.vidaweb.org/the-2011-count). For instance, in 2011, according to the same survey, *The New York Review of Books* had 201 male reviewers, and 53 female reviewers; in turn, this journal reviewed 293 works by men in 2011, but only 71 by women.

So why are editors and publications cheating themselves and readers in this way? How can any of us face our daughters if we keep doing this, or letting it be done? Let us not be our own villains. May shame rouse us. These discouraging numbers can change if we as editors, agents, scholars, publishers, writers, and readers want them to. If we write enough honestly searching letters to the editor of each publication that we worry has become a de facto men's club, and ask them if they see any problem with the slant of these statistics, we will discomfort them enough to eventually face what appears to be the most illogical bias and discrimination. Eventually some of these letters of ours will be published. Blandishment after blandishment may be offered by the journal or book, and if the statistics above are questioned that's a good: I await clarification. It would please me if any of these statistics were wrong or somehow skewed. But after the last excuse from an embarrassed publication falls in like the eyeball of a 3rd grader's still-wet papier-maché mask, then we may see the eye of truth peering back behind the absurdity. We may find explained the mystery behind such corrosive misogyny. In 2012, some dictionaries of English widened the definition of misogyny to include not only hatred of women but also "entrenched prejudices against women." Can anyone say that unfairness is not what we have here?

For the good of this anthology and to make the most basic attempt at fairness, I made the commitment early and clearly to encourage gender balance. I feel from my shivers it is the best in the Series yet. PS now presents a UK anthology not afraid to scare, one which does not spurn the madness, and one that is brave and fast enough to run with wolves and even with women.

Horror and the Gothic are typically dismissed as conservative sub-genres. Stephen King has shown convincingly in *Danse Macabre* (as many others have in their criticism) how slow these fields are to break out of patterns, how obsessed with the same cycle of broken taboos and certain retribution, how drowsily in love with the status quo. That is probably true most of the time. But they are also sub-genres of destruction and, frankly, they fancy nothing more than to break things. They go *smash*. Smash. SMASH. *SMASH!* And I love them for that. So I extol you, ungentle reader: in whatever capacity you have, let us take sledgehammers to glass ceilings, and let us break them every one.

EXOTIC GOTHIC 5

VOLUME I

Remembering
RAY BRADBURY
(22 August 1920–5 June 2012)

Who made wine out of words.

EUROPE

All the Lost Ones

Deborah Biancotti

"Ah, but no? You have not moved into a house of the Lombardi?"

"Temporarily," Francesca explained, "while my husband finds a residence."

The air in the cavernous salon of the Contessa Rossi was warm and dense with humidity, and the furniture was at once plush and sharp. Ornate gold arms were fixed to plump black chairs, and heavy drapes blocked the sunlight. It smelled of the ocean as much as of the fat, perfumed candles that stood unlit and uneven in the candelabra around the room.

In the midst of it, Francesca in her simple blue silk felt almost infantile. Her hair was plain and dark and pinned back with none of the clasps of the Contessa's tresses, and she lacked for rouge and powders on her face, being too modest to buy such fineries. She admired the heavy lace and crinoline of her hostess's dress. She was as elaborately regal as the porcelain figurines that seemed to pin the room to its floorboards.

"*C'est bon à savoir,*" Contessa Rossi replied. She beat the air with a white, silk fan, a tracery of trees distorted by its folds. "It is not an adequate address."

"I have heard about some houses in Venice . . . " Francesca hesitated. She did not want the Contessa to think her entirely foolish. "I've heard many are haunted?"

The Contessa's eyes widened and the fan rose to cover the indelicate smile on her face.

"*Alors!* It is true."

"Really?" Francesca leaned forward.

She'd been in this salon for less than an hour, with its heavy, closed air. She looked forward to breathing fresh air again. But the stories of the Contessa Rossi were proving too much of a delight to move.

"They call the city *La Serenissima*, but how serene is she?" the Contessa asked. "Have they told you, for example, of Biasio?"

"Did he live in the house of the Lombardi?"

"*The* house? *Mais, non.*" Rossi shook her head and sent her careful curls bouncing.

It was almost impossible to guess Rossi's age under the heavy rouge. Her hair—her wig—was carefully colored a deep, unconvincing red and her décolletage was gently hidden behind fine lace.

"Who is he, then?" Francesca asked in a rush.

"A butcher."

"Is that all?"

Contessa Rossi waggled a finger. "The *murderous* butcher of Venice."

"Here?" Francesca leaned forward. "Now?"

"*Ah*, centuries ago. He served the finest meats in Venice. He was a favorite of the sailors of Venice, and his pies were much sought after. Until one—" here she leaned forward and whispered conspiratorially, with her fan to one side of her face, "one sailor discovered in the sausage he had bought, the tiny finger of a little child."

"No!" Francesca whispered.

"*Oui!*"

It took Francesca a moment to recover, to hide her face with her hand, since she lacked a fan, and to lean back into the awkward settee.

"What happened to this monster?" she asked.

"They cut off his arms," Rossi smiled, leaning in. Her voice dropped a full octave. "And they took him into *la Piazza San Marco* so they could behead him."

"Good," Francesca heard herself mutter.

"And they hung the pieces of his body from the four corners of the city."

"*Mon Dieu!*"

"*C'est vrai!*" Rossi leaned back with a satisfied look. "And then they named a street after him, can you believe? *La Riva di Biasio.* Where even the priests fear to tread."

"Also as a reminder?"

Rossi shrugged and clucked her tongue. "Who knows? The Italians! And they think us the savages."

"I see."

"This is Venice," Rossi sighed. "No place for innocence. Do you have children, Madame Branscombe?"

Francesca bit back on the gnawing sorrow that had followed her from London. There was something about the Contessa's bluntness that drew her in, after the mannered parties and dull dinners her husband liked her to attend. There was something about Venice, too, all that jeweled finery and the easy grace of her people.

"We did," she said. "But . . ."

She gestured, and Rossi nodded her understanding.

"Lost," the Contessa said. "So many lost. Mothers waking to stillness. Do you know, children have been snatched from Italy for many years."

"But, why?"

"To serve evil masters as slaves and street peddlers. Some go as far as England, even the Americas. You might have seen them in London?"

"Perhaps." Francesca nodded.

She'd seen those sad, unsmiling children, dark-haired ghosts obscured by layers of grime from the streets. She'd had them beg her for coins and offer to play incongruous melodies on harps and horns and violins that were bent and old, tucked beneath the points of their small chins. The sight of them had made her cry even before her own lost child.

"It is the scandal of Italy," the Contessa continued. "Garibaldi and his man, this Generalissimo—"

"Menabrea?"

"Si, they shall have to deal with it if they are to build a united Italy."

"Will they, do you think?"

Contessa Rossi shrugged and gestured to the heavens hidden behind her dark ceiling. "What is the future of Italy without her children?"

When Francesca's baby had been lost, it had left something behind. She could feel it, restless, tugging at her. Sometimes when she was alone, she thought the child spoke to her. She tried never to be alone.

The Contessa must have caught in her expression some of the grief she felt.

"Yes, yes," Rossi said in her deep, brooding tone. "I understand."

The Contessa seemed to forget Francesca was there for a moment, her gaze lost to the patterned walls.

"The house?" Francesca prompted her.

"Oui?"

"You were saying it was not appropriate?"

"Ah! The Lombardi have several other houses, it is the height of rudeness to put you in such a place."

"It is close to the *Ponte di Rialto*," Francesca replied. "I thought it quite fashionable."

"The *fashion* of the Lombardi is not in doubt." Rossi was almost crooning, waving her thick, silk fan in front of her, the tassel bouncing against her forearm. "It is because we are French, you see? And foreign, they give us the dreadful places. Venice is so unforgiving."

Francesca couldn't think what to say, so she stayed silent and rocked in her oversized chair and tried not to look at the Rossi family portraits that hung sternly above her. The salons of Venice, Francesca was finding, were at least as dangerous as the streets.

"It is better for me," Rossi continued. "At least I married an Italian."

"That must be a relief," Francesca muttered, more to herself.

"And to think! The Italians, they took Venice from Austria in this war of theirs. I ask you, why? Other cities would do better."

"Contessa," Francesca interrupted, "If it is not the fashion of the Lombardi house that is at issue, then what?"

"Oh, *ma chère, ma chère petite.*" Rossi's fan thumped the heavy air. "It is because of the child who haunts it."

Francesca rose from the sheets, heavy linens twisted with sweat and sleeplessness. There was, she thought, a terrible energy in the house tonight. The dark chewed through everything. It turned the red of the rugs to black and made the marble fireplace gape like a maw. The heavy magenta curtains were held back from the windows in the hope of breeze, but whatever breeze was out there only travelled along the canal this evening and not up.

In the gloom, she tripped on the brocade bed cover they had kicked to the ground. She stumbled and stifled a cry.

Francis' voice was clear. "Have you hurt yourself, *mon amour?*"

"My pride, only," she muttered. "I thought you were asleep."

Francis sighed and stirred and kicked off the thick sheets. "I might never have slept. I feel I might not have slept in my entire life."

"You exaggerate so," she replied.

The air was damp with canal water. Strands of hair stuck to her neck and forehead. She pulled at her long nightgown. The lacemaker had assured her it was wrong for the season, but the lacework was so delicate—like rose-buds against spider's web—that she'd declared she must have it. And the lacemaker, shrugging, had wrapped it for her and then tried to sell her others that were, he proclaimed, just as fine. Nightgowns, he declared, you would be proud to wear even to your grave.

Francesca had thanked him sourly. But now she saw fit to curse him. Lace fell like a rash along her chest and lace clamped wetly around her wrists.

"Why did you agree to purchase this wretched nightgown?" she asked.

Francis twisted to look at her. "You insisted—"

"*Cette m'ennuie*," she cut him off.

"I think it was this stifling Venetian air, it does things to one's mind."

"How is your fever?"

"Still as wretched as ever."

Francesca sighed. She crossed to the tall, arched window and stood side-on against the curtain, wrapping it around herself like a shroud. Outside, Venice hung with its spires reaching towards Heaven, its colors like a muted carnival, all pink and grey and blue with cascades of flowers that were, by daylight, bright yellow and red. There was still a buzz of activity, even this late. People were walking along the embankments, moving slowly, the best to show off their evening finery. The *gondole* that populated *il Canalasso* fluttered like black moths on the water. If she pressed the side of her face to the cool window glass, she could just catch a glimpse of *il Ponte di Rialto*.

"It's only April," she said.

"Yes?"

"Already so warm. What will July be like?"

"Warmer, I should think." His tone was flat.

She rubbed her wet cheek on the sleeve of her nightgown. "There are still people outside."

"What are they doing?"

She gestured, the heavy lace dripping from her wrist. "Walking, mostly."

"Well, this is Venice."

She turned from the window and faced him. The moonlight gave him a ghostly pallor and his shadowed eyes seemed sunken in his head.

"You say that like it explains things. What does it explain?"

Francis sat up from the crumpled bed. He sighed. "They sleep in the after-noons. In the evenings, *loro fanno un passeggere*. They walk."

She turned back to the window. "Contessa Rossi says I should have married an Italian."

"I don't see why, half the people in Venice aren't Italian."

"When are we leaving, Francis?"

"The house? Or the city?"

"The house would do," Francesca replied. "I can't sleep here."

"The heat will be the same all over the city."

"It's not the heat, it's the ghost."

"Ah," Francis sighed. "That foolish Rossi woman, she tells you stories of make-believe for what reason? Perhaps she despises the Lombardi and seeks to get back at them—"

Rossi was an old woman, and bored, and perhaps she had invented the stories to save herself from more boredom. But Francesca didn't believe it.

"You weren't there," Francesca said. "She was convincing."

"You were convinced, you mean," he corrected her. "You do love these sordid stories the locals tell. You listen and then you let your imagination run away with you. And you don't sleep. This Rossi, she sounds grotesque."

"She is quite macabre," Francesca replied, with feeling. "And honest, in her way. I like her. And anyhow, what about those drawings I found? The ones the servant Marzio snatched away."

"So you assume the drawings you found were done by a child who died, but you base that on nothing."

The servants were so forbidding that Francesca had taken to spending her time in the two rooms assigned to her for sleeping and dressing. She'd been admiring the furniture, running her hands along the deep, lacquered wood, pulling out drawers and opening wardrobes. They were all empty and she assumed the rooms had been unoccupied a long time. There was a sense of wilting to them, of the neglect that comes from an empty space. She noticed, too, that the servants hadn't bothered to clean the rooms for their arrival. Now and then she'd find a scattering of dust and the marks where covers had been left on furniture haphazardly, exposing a corner to the thick air.

It was the wardrobe she'd been inspecting when she'd found them. They were pressed up against a back corner, looking as if they'd been wedged there, perhaps behind whatever had been evacuated from the wardrobe when she'd arrived. Two little pages in a child's hand, all thick, colorful pencil and smiling figures in what appeared to be pink gowns and lace caps. Images of Venice, she'd realized, the broad buildings behind the figures unmistakable with their repetition of windows, the doors so vast that smaller doors had to be cut into them so a person could come and go without three others to help open the door. The buildings in the drawings sat not on the ground but seemed to float on the dark, blue water that ate into their foundations. They were cheerful images, except for the consuming waves. The pictures were yellowed on one page, but the other, having fallen behind its partner, had remained better protected.

"You assume," she said, "that the drawings were *not* made by that child. But why else hide them away in a wardrobe?"

"If they were hidden," Francis sighed. His face was ashen with fatigue. "If they weren't, perhaps, simply forgotten. And this ghost, this child died how?"

"The Contessa wouldn't say."

"She didn't know."

Francesca shrugged and pulled back her wet hair. "Quite possibly. She doesn't seem the kind to hold back a detail like that."

"I should think she's not the kind to hold back on any detail."

"She's been kind to me, in a way. She's invited me to her house. She's the only one."

"Give it time."

"Do you think we'll find somewhere to live as grand as this?" she asked.

"We might find it, but we couldn't possibly afford it. I have heard of a modest place nearer the university."

"Beside *il Canalasso?*"

"I'm afraid not. But possibly there is some place other than the Grand Canal to take your heart away from me."

She smiled. "Is it far from the Rialto Bridge, then?"

"Nowhere is far in Venice," he said.

"Will there be other people there? Foreigners, like us?"

"Ah, you're lonely, my dear. That's all."

He held out a hand and she crossed to him, moving through the dark and the light of the window. She sat with her back to a bedpost and pulled her feet up under her.

"I didn't expect it to be so . . . different," she said.

"To France?" he scolded.

"Yes, to France, to home."

"*Ma chère,* all of Europe seems different to me, from England. And different, again, each city from every other." He clasped her hand with both of his. "Soon enough the offers from other Venetian ladies will arrive, the calls to private salons, the exhibitions, the . . . well, whatever it is you'll find to be of interest. There is music, art. The glass and the lace—"

"Come for a walk with me," she said.

"At this hour?"

"Why not? All of Venice is doing it. We may as well fit in."

She didn't add, *and get outside this accursed house.*

Francis raised a weary hand. "I have a meeting in the morning with the Generalissimo."

"*Bien sûr*, sleep, then, if you can." Francesca got to her feet. She pressed the back of her hand to his temple to feel the heat of his skin. Beneath her wrist, his eyes were heavy and dark.

"Perhaps I'll see if there's any cool water to be had in the kitchen," she said.

"I'm fine," he said roughly. "If you want something, call for one of the servants."

Francesca snorted. Her husband liked to pretend—if he had not forgotten—that it was not long ago she was a servant herself, and a scandalous woman for stealing a Lord's heart.

"I don't want to wake them," she said.

"You think they're sleeping?" Francis lay back on the bed. "They're probably all outside, taking a walk."

She tiptoed into the hallway with her dressing gown pulled tight around her, lending heat and weight to her progress. The house was huge, designed for a large family and all their attendant servants. A hall ran its length, rising through two stories, so that Francesca could grasp the balcony outside her bedroom and gaze down to the marble floor that led to the front door. She liked the unfamiliar openness of the place. But even here the air was stifling and clammy and the marble balustrades shone wetly in the gloom.

She left the hallway and crossed to the room adjoining the bedroom, where her trunk had been deposited. The servants hadn't unpacked it, but rather left it standing on its end with its contents crowded and falling. The dress she'd travelled in two days earlier was still laid on the bed where she'd left it. In the gloom it looked like someone had fallen there, angled across the bed in an attitude of neglect.

She moved to the trunk and pulled out a simple, grey gown. But she decided it was too heavy for the climate, even this late at night. She swapped it for a lighter gown in green, where the sleeves finished at her elbows. She dressed by candlelight and then slipped from the room towards the stairs.

She wouldn't go far at all, she promised herself. She would stand with her back to the front door and watch the people who walked the embankments. She would take in the air that ran the length of *il Canalasso*.

All the way down the stairs she had to steel herself against the sound of her stiff silk dress and the whispers she was sure filled the air. She thought the stones of the building were talking amongst themselves. When one step creaked, she thought she could hear soft crying. She moved forward, through the dense air and the noises of sorrow.

The closer she got to the bottom of the stairs, the worse the whispering became. It was almost chanting, a soft susurration of noise that rose and fell, holding her up and bearing her down. Her heart thudded in unison. She felt she might be enclosed in the lungs of something warm and wet and alive. She would have turned and run back to the room where Francis lay, probably still awake and fitful, except then she would have to explain to him her dress and why she'd been heading outside alone. The darkness at her back was worse than the gloom of the hall in front of her, so she kept moving though her hand stiffened on the railing and she had to drag herself forward.

In the well of darkness at the bottom of the staircase, she hesitated. The chanting had stopped, fallen away with a choking noise. Instead, a sound hung in the air around her, a kind of hushing, hissing noise. More than a rush of wind through a half-closed window or the ocean against stone foundations. The skin of her temple prickled and something seemed to crawl up her spine.

Something watched her in the dark.

She spun, fast enough that the candle she was holding faltered and almost went out.

"Hello?"

Her voice was sharp and too loud. In the cavernous space of the central hall she heard it echo. No answer. She waited with her heart pounding, hoping Francis wouldn't rise and find her, dressed to go out in the wide hallway.

A face caught on the edge of the candle's light.

"Who's there?" she whispered hoarsely.

"Scusa, Signora."

It was only one of the servants. She felt the relief roll from her temple to her toes, though her heart seemed to beat all the harder.

"Marzio?"

He loomed out of the darkness and stepped towards her. *"Prego."*

"Why are you here in the dark?"

But it wasn't quite dark, and as he moved, she glimpsed a triangle of light behind him. It was coming from one of the sitting rooms, where a heavy brocade curtain had been pulled aside.

"Who gave you permission to light the lamps in that room, Marzio?" she asked. "That is not for servants."

She moved to go around him and Marzio blocked her.

"Pardon!" she cried. "You do not dictate where I may go in this house."

Marzio sneered and for a moment Francesca quailed and might have turned away, back towards the relative safety of the stairs. But then behind her she heard a door open and Francis' voice calling. She turned, humiliated, and watched him come down the stairs in his nightshirt and dressing gown. His hair was untidy and he looked as far from a lord of any manor as she had seen. But she was glad he was there.

"What the devil?" he asked. "And who are those people in the sitting room?"

Francesca realized he was right, there were people in the sitting room. Seven of them, wedged together around a dining table, their hands linked, their skin shining from the light of the lamps. Francesca recognized one of them—another servant, Knaus, a young man with pale skin and dark eyes. The rest were strangers. An old couple caught her eye, their skin the deep olive of the south. The old woman's face was red and puffy with tears that still stained her cheeks.

"What is this?" Francis asked. "Marzio, explain yourself."

"Permesso." Marzio bowed stiffly. "We gather in honor."

"In honor of what, blast it?" Francis asked. "For the duration of our stay, I am the master of this house and I will give you permission or otherwise."

Tall as he was, Marzio seemed to cower.

Francis moved to the sitting room and she followed. In the room, the strangers dropped their hands and turned with expressions of contrition or contempt. Gathered on the table in front of them, Francesca saw something familiar, a child's drawings of Venice.

"Where did you get these?" she asked.

Marzio turned to her stiffly.

"The family," he began, "the Lombardi, in their absence, we may borrow this room."

"They allow it?"

Marzio gestured with his hands, but he didn't quite nod.

"You should know your place," Francis said.

To her horror, Francesca felt the eyes of all the servants turn to her. She looked down to the table, her face burning.

"These drawings," she said. "These are the ones I found in the wardrobe."

The mournful look on the face of the old woman changed to something between wonder and horror. Her hands rose, twisted together in something akin to the shape of prayer.

"You see?" the woman asked. "You see?"

Francis interrupted, "I see that whatever you're doing here is unchristian. You must desist at once. Kindly leave."

At first the gathered people sat still like they'd collapsed there, wilting in the heat. But then the oldest man stirred. He rose to his feet, bobbing his head and uttering strange, accented apologies. The others followed, making their way to the front door of the house where Marzio bowed to each of them as they left.

"Francis," Francesca whispered, "They were trying to speak to the dead child."

"Oh, hang the child," Francis muttered.

She reeled. "Francis!"

His face twisted and something rose in his eyes, something hot like the air. But then he righted himself with an effort.

"I'm sorry, *chérie*," he said. "The fever. And the servants! Where did Marzio go? I would speak with him first."

"I didn't see. Perhaps to the kitchens. Go," Francesca said. "I'll take some air."

"Not alone."

"Knaus will accompany me," she said.

"See that he does. A house empty so long they think they own it, not just serve it. It's not decent."

Francesca wanted to say that the house wasn't empty, that even without the fact of the servants, something moved in here, wetly, through the hot air. But she let Francis return to the bedroom and watched his candle narrowing in the darkness of the vast hall. Then she took a seat in the room where the drawings of the unknown child still lay on the table. Knaus had also remained behind, putting out the lamps with a slow methodicalness. Darkness took over the room, spreading with slow certainty.

"Knaus?"

"*Si?*"

"Your name isn't Italian. You're from Austria?" she asked.

"My family," he shrugged.

He shrugged like an Italian, she couldn't help thinking, that careless grace she was growing used to.

"These drawings are very old."

"*Si*, they are from a long time ago."

"Do you know of a ghost in this house?"

Knaus chuckled. "Only one?"

"Then there are ghosts here?"

"This is Venice." He gave that shrug again.

"Yes. This is," she said. "Who were you trying to contact?"

Knaus frowned. "What do you mean?"

"During the séance, what spirit were you hoping to raise?"

His frown lifted into something that looked like a grin. "You think we contact the dead?"

He threw his head back and laughed.

"Then, what?" Francesca insisted.

"That is not for me to say," he grinned. "How you say, a *séance?*"

"What, then?" Francesca gestured with both hands towards the tall ceiling. "Wait, don't tell me. That is not for you to say."

Knaus might have shrugged again, but by then she was on her feet.

"Come with me," she said, with as much insistence as she could manage.

Knaus looked at her as if she were mad. But he followed when she marched to the front door, through the dark, the candles neglected on the sitting room table. She pulled open the heavy door and stepped out, and turned once to make sure he followed.

She found the old couple boarding a *gondola*. From this distance it looked like a floating coffin on the dark waters of *il Canalasso*. She rushed towards them, crying out in what Italian she could manage. She pulled at Knaus' sleeve and urged him forward. The old man only looked confused, but the woman with the sad eyes, she stopped and watched and waited until Francesca joined them at the water's edge.

"I should like to know," Francesca breathed, "about the child."

"The child?" the old man muttered.

She could feel Knaus' stare burning into her back. Away from the over-heated rooms of the Lombardi house and the overheated salon of Contessa Rossi, she didn't feel so afraid. Outside where the air moved and she could breathe at last. The breeze was cooling her skin, soothing the strange ideas the house had put into her head. The *Ponte di Rialto* sat in canopied splendor across the Grand Canal.

The *gondolier* spoke to Knaus in rapid, staccato Italian. Too fast for Francesca to understand. She clambered into the *gondola*, feeling it rock under her feet. It was lacquered black, like they all were save for the official boats of the papacy. The small cabin where the old couple now sat was embossed with curlicues and shapes like swirling vines. Thin blinds let in slants of light across the couple's faces.

She turned to Knaus. "Please tell *signore il gondolier* that I should like to be returned here when we deliver this couple to their home. And I will pay him handsomely."

Knaus sneered, but he spoke to the *gondolier* and from what she could gather, the man agreed.

They slid through the canal and the dark night. Francesca felt the air swell around her, cool and smooth, but still dense with seawater. She settled into the rock of the boat, the push as the *gondolier* levered the oar into the water from the stern was soothing, a steady press of boat through water with the night-calmed city around her. Most houses featured a window or two where light still showed, but they seemed stilled, their broad facades and evenly-spaced windows calmer than the day. Even the spires didn't pierce, and the arches only beckoned. She realized she could surrender to this Venice, this softer place of night and dark.

"*Il mio nome è* Francesca," she said.

"*Signore Neri,*" said the old man, "*e Signora.*"

Francesca felt her way forward, as much into the language as the topic. "Tell me about the child."

The couple exchanged a glance. For a long while, no one spoke. Francesca thought of Contessa Rossi's stories. She thought she should like to pay the woman back with stories of her own.

"I found drawings," she prompted, "in a child's hand. Drawings of Venice. Would you know anything about them?"

The couple was silent, immobile as stone. As if they had been painted to the inside of the lacquered cabin.

"We used to work for the Lombardi," the old woman said at last.

Her voice issued hollowly from the cabin. The light from the blinds lit her brown cheeks and left her eyes dark.

"Yes?" Francesca asked.

"Our daughter would play in the rooms of the Lombardi. They indulged her. We thought they were . . . kind."

"*Celto,*" Francesca said. "Where is she now?"

"She is lost."

The old woman's voice broke and with it, something inside Francesca seemed to break, too.

"I lost a child, too," she said, in earnestness. Venice, she thought, could have all her secrets. "My child died."

"She did not die."

"*Excusez-moi?*"

The old woman leaned forward, out of the cabin and into the light. Her hair was silver and dark grey, and the lamp that swung from the bow of the *gondola* lit her face into masks of the *carnivale.* She gave Francesca a piercing stare. "Our daughter was taken from us."

"Ah!" Francesca said. "Is it so? What took her?"

Above her the sky was bright with stars, and the water dark at her sides. She thought perhaps plague or cholera had claimed the girl, perhaps this was some great family tragedy from which the Neri, servants of the Lombardi, had never recovered. She thought, too, she could repay Contessa Rossi handsomely with this story.

"What, indeed?" the old woman continued. "She was *bellissima.* All who saw her could not resist. And so, they took her from us."

"They?"

"The Lombardi," she said.

"The . . . ?"

"The family," the old man interrupted, "who own the house you stay in. They took our *nipotina* to raise as their own."

"But then," Francesca hesitated. "Why does she haunt the house?"

The couple reeled and turned to each other, their hands entwining in a motion that was practiced and perfect. Light bounced on the lacquered black finish either side of them, light slid along the carvings of vines that looked like serpents.

"Haunt the house?" the old man said. "She does not! She lives."

"But," Francesca replied, "I was told a child haunts the house."

"Her memories," his wife explained. "They haunt us, all of us."

"They took her . . . alive?"

"*Si.*"

"Where is she now?"

The woman gestured as if it were all the same to her. "Innsbruck."

"Ah." Francesca was still. "But it's not the same. *Non*, it is not the same at all."

She was ashamed of her disappointment. The child lived, after all. She lived. Francesca wanted to explain that a child being raised in wealth and the semblance of honor was not a dead child. Not truly lost if she lived. But when she thought of all those lost children, the ones sent from Italy to beg, she wasn't sure herself if that was true. Too many children had never found their ways home. To a parent, a missing child was a loss that broke them in half.

"My child died," Francesca said. "She *died*."

The old man eased back into the cabin, waving a dismissive hand in Francesca's direction. "She was chosen by God to return to Heaven."

Francesca didn't answer. All lost children should be mourned, she knew, but not all lost children vanished in the same way.

She caught the *gondolier* frowning at her, so she turned to watch the progress of the houses and the people making their *passeggere* in the lamp-lit streets.

"So, there is no ghost?" she asked softly.

Signore Neri let out a noise that might have been a sigh of disgust. "You long for ghosts? Life is hard enough."

"Life is very hard," she corrected him. "So I would like to know, for sure . . . if there is something more. For our children."

No one replied.

The *gondolier* made a sharp left into a canal. They drifted past a white house with red roof and a cluster of short trees, their foliage black in the evening light, limned with moonlight at their untidy tops. He pulled the *gondola* to a halt beside a modest square and the old couple moved to depart. The old man alighted first, so he could turn and offer a hand to his wife.

Signora Neri leaned forward and squeezed Francesca's wrist. "You must leave the house. Bad things happen there."

Francesca felt a hollow open up in her stomach. She nodded and looked away quickly so the old woman wouldn't see her tears. She heard the *Signora* heave herself from the *gondola* and felt the sway of the narrow boat as the other woman left. Francesca did not watch them go.

The canal was too narrow to turn in, so the *gondolier* navigated backwards to the entrance where it joined *il Canalasso*. He gestured at Francesca, almost like he was waving her away.

"You leave here," he said.

"I do not," she replied. "The understanding was I return to where you collected me."

"You leave here," he repeated, his voice neither insistent nor harsh.

Two men lumbered towards the *gondola*, greeting the *gondolier* like an old friend. They stepped into the *gondola*, sending it rocking, and only then did they seem to catch sight of Francesca.

"You travel to Murano?" one asked.

"No, I return to *il Ponte di Rialto*."

"It is the other direction," the second man said.

"We had an agreement—" she began.

The *gondolier* waved her off. From here, she figured she could walk back to the Lombardi house within half an hour. From the island of Murano, there would only be the *gondolier* to return her. She stood and made for the embankment, ignoring the hand of the man who tried to help her alight. They sniggered as she tripped and nearly fell, and then with a splash the *gondolier* pushed off.

Francesca watched them go. She stood under the darkness of the trees on the embankment and tried to quell the anger that rose in her. This would never happen in France, she was sure, never would a young woman alone be dumped onto a dark and empty street. And then she realized that everyone who'd been out walking had, as if by agreement, disappeared to their houses. The windows here were dark and empty, the houses looked abandoned. Toys floating in a dark bath. The canal where the Neri had exited was between her and home, and there was no bridge. Even if there had been a bridge, the house on the other corner took up the whole block. There was no place to walk. It was the same when she tried to move from the trees and up the canal to her right, the house blocked her.

Francis spoke often of how easy it was to lose oneself in the serpentine streets of Venice. Now she knew the truth of it. The only direction she could take was away from home, in the hopes she might find another bridge like the Rialto to carry her towards the other side and then, hopefully, home. She marched as fast as she could, looking for a way back in the right direction. She had no idea where she was, had never travelled this far alone, and the houses that had looked so cheerful in the daylight now loomed tall, almost bending beneath the sky.

It was quiet, and her footsteps were too loud against the paved embankment. She began to tiptoe, watching her feet.

"*Aiuto!*"

Francesca froze. The voice came again, *Aiuto! Aiuto!* Someone was calling for help. Softly, like they were far away. The sound echoed off the water and stone of Venice.

"Hello?"

Aiuto!

Francesca froze. The sound was coming from the canal she'd just left. She turned, but saw nothing except the shadows of the trees, almost solid under the moonlight.

The voice was fading, but something even worse than that occurred to her then. The voice was the voice of the child. She stood, listening for it over her heavy pulse. The night was silent, even the breeze along *il Canalasso* seemed to have died.

Aiuto!

It wasn't a voice, she realized. It was a group of voices, crying in unison. It wasn't an echo. It was children.

"Where are you?" she cried.

She ran along the embankment, pulling at her skirts to free her knees, but even then she had a tottering gait, the dress clinging to her damp skin. She ran away from the sounds of the cries, away from home. She almost cried out herself, but she was afraid of rousing whatever was behind the blank Venetian glass of the windows around her. She slipped, and skidded over the embankment. She hit the canal with a splash and for a moment the moon was obscured by dark water. It was warm, warmer even than the air. Warm like something alive. Long skirts carried her down and she gulped water. She kicked off her thin shoes and grabbed for a mooring sunken deep and hauled herself up. The stars danced in blurred patterns above her. She kept her head up, out of the water.

Something in the dark canal seemed to wrap around her, pinning her green dress to her, something hooked around her ankles, something pulled on her toes and knees and dragged her down. Something was in the water with her, its small hands pulling her under.

"Help!" she called. She choked and coughed and spat sour water. "Help!"

No one was there to help her. It was as if the whole city of Venice had emptied out.

With a lunge, she made for the embankment and dragged herself, dripping, onto land. Her elbows shook as she raised herself from the water. For a moment there was a tug-of-war between her hands and the hands that held her to the water. Francesca pressed her palms to the stone and leaned forward until just her feet were in the water. Then with a roar she pulled her feet free of the water and rolled onto her side. She spat up canal water and laid her forehead to the cold lettering of the street name embossed in the stone.

The cries she'd heard were gone. The hands she'd felt—Francis would never believe her. All was quiet now. She lay for a while in the cool of the dripping water and the cold moonlight. Then she lifted her head and read the words embossed into the street.

And then she cried for all the lost children for whom this street—*Riva di Biasio*—had been named.

DEBORAH BIANCOTTI (*b. Cairns, Queensland, Australia, 1971*) *is native to the fierce rainforests of northern Australia, where a diaspora of Italians like her great-grandparents settled after fleeing the rise of European fascism. In Italy, several ancestors worked vineyards, but in Australia they grew sugar cane and raised wild, olive-skinned children. Deborah fell in love with Italy on her first visit, finding in the faces of the Italians a kind of familiarity that felt like a homecoming. She still carries the surname she was born with—unlike many sisters and cousins who have shrugged it off—and this means Deborah still receives missives from people commemorating the times the Biancotti family inhabited Villa di Tirano and surrounds. Though nowadays, the missives mostly appear via Facebook.*

Lately, Deborah has been reading about the military unification of Italy in the 1860s, the scandals of General Giuseppe Garibaldi's affronts to the Catholic Church, and the political struggles of Italy's first Prime Minister, Luigi Garibaldi, to address the "lost children" forced into beggarships in far-flung, foreign countries.

Deborah's first short story won the Aurealis Award for Best Horror Short Story, and her first collection was nominated for the William L. Crawford Award for Best First Fantasy Book. Her 2011 novella in the Ishtar *anthology,* And the Dead Shall Outnumber the Living, *was nominated for a Shirley Jackson Award. She is currently working on a novel series and planning a book set in Italy in 1867.*

Commentary on "All the Lost Ones": *In his 1851-53 treatise,* The Stones of Venice, *leading art critic John Ruskin opined that Gothic architecture was identi-*

fiable not by any single features, but by the relationships of features. Under the heading "Savageness," Ruskin wrote, "I am not sure when the word 'Gothic' was first generically applied to the architecture of the North; but I presume that, whatever the date of its original usage, it was intended to imply reproach, and express the barbaric character of the nations among whom that architecture arose. It never implied that they were literally of Gothic lineage, far less that their architecture had been originally invented by the Goths themselves; but it did imply that they and their buildings together exhibited a degree of sternness and rudeness."

Despite that—or perhaps because of it—Ruskin was a fan of the architecture, though he saw Venice as a place in moral decline. The unrestrained architecture bore a relation to the expression not just of the individual builders but the entire community and society. (Ruskin's chapter "The Nature of Gothic," from Volume II, was later re-published in its entirety—but without the rest of the text—by William Morris, in an elaborate and Gothic-inspired manuscript, full of detailed page ornamentation.)

It is the abundance of events in the days leading up to the unification of Italy— not just the events themselves, but their wildness, their relations to each other—that fascinate me about the Venice of this period. It is the power and culture of Venice— and her ghost stories—that draw me back. And so, into the most particular city of Venice I have pitted two characters against the most ghastly of stories in Venetian history, Biasio the Butcher, whose abode truly did offer up the bodies of children and whose meats were found, at one time, to encase the finger of a child.

The Open Mirror

Georges-Olivier Châteaureynaud

Translated by Edward Gauvin

WITH FERVOR, TWENTY-FIVE YEARS OF AGE, AND ENOUGH NAIVETÉ to redeem the foible of having too much faith in himself, Germinal—his real name hardly matters—had picked his pen name. It pleased him, with its air of promise. He had an editor who believed in him, and his first novel, though fantastical in nature, had gotten notice. To finance the second, the young hopeful was led to a writing residency like a horse to a stall, a few months in a country manor deep in the heart of a wood. The word "manor" had done as much to seduce the young man as the stipend. He'd pictured a façade crimson with Virginia creeper, a staircase of noble aspect, high windows peering in on dark rooms, formal gardens with a fountain and stone nymphs, even a workspace, walls lined with books from floor to ceiling, atop a little tower . . . and he'd been right. With the exception of the tower, the manor where he'd spend the next three months looked exactly like the image he'd seen in his mind's eye, down to the very last cliché. There was indeed Virginia creeper, and woodwork bathed in shadows; there were gables, and as you came round a bend in a garden path by the mossy fountain, a stone nymph better admired from afar, since years of hail and weather had scarred her face and body like a pox.

The master of the house matched his manor to a tee. His feet propped up on a bedwarmer (for with night a penetrating damp emanated from the woods), wearing a bathrobe of Pyrenees wool and a brimless side cap like Sainte-Beuve, he welcomed the new resident from beneath a portrait of his grandfather in hunting garb. Germinal had never met anyone so old. The baronet's hands—God knew why he bore that English title!—were mere bundles of twigs where bulged veins not blue but green. From the ascot that hid his neck brace emerged a chelonian visage with lips downturned at the corners and flaking skin, the nose almost nonexistent. But his gaze was lively and tinged with slightly caustic goodwill. His voice betrayed barely a creak, his careful elocution recalling a time when men articulated each and every syllable, omitting not the slightest syntactic expletive.

In theory, the manor was meant to host several authors at once. A complicated partnership between the ministry of culture and councils regional and municipal financed the stipends and footed the heating bill. But for now, due to budgetary restrictions, Germinal found himself alone.

"I trust you enjoy seclusion," the baronet said after serving tea. "We have no television, and the nearest inn is six kilometers distant. In the past, your peers would form merry little bands. In the evenings, after a day of solitary labor, they would convene for dinner, and then play Parcheesi, or launch into deep literary discussions. Between myself—I tend to retire early—and my housekeeper, who has the conversational skills of a horse, I do hope you won't feel too lonely."

Germinal protested that he wished for nothing more than to be alone, to cut himself off from the world and bury himself in his novel like a minor in the bowels of the earth.

"In that case, you won't be disappointed," said the baronet. "You'll find the atmosphere here most conducive to such interment. Your writing tends toward—how shall I put it—the fantastical, I believe?"

"Indeed," Germinal nodded. "Though fantastical isn't quite the right word. It's usually associated with horror and evil, the manifestation of irrational and destructive forces. But I'm not the least bit interested in that kind of thing. There's something childish about such a limiting notion. A fantastical tale for adults can do quite well without fear and evil. That's what I'm working toward."

"The notion you condemn doesn't seem so silly to me," the baronet replied. "An experience that gives the lie to reality as we live it every day would surely provoke horror."

"Probably, but who said anything about living? All you have to do is imagine it and write it," Germinal objected. "The world in its reality conforms to the vision of an atheist policeman. Ghosts, striges, ghouls, and all those creatures only exist inside me. Should they escape the mental crypts where they're confined, that would only mean I was fit for an asylum. But if I've got enough talent, there's nothing keeping me from bringing them into the light of day and parading them like a lion tamer."

The baronet greeted these plans with a trembling little laugh. "You impress me with your confidence. However, as you descend into the depths, have a care to hold on to reality's banister."

Seizing a little silver bell, he rang for the housekeeper. "Hestia will show you to your chambers. If there's any equipment you need, please speak to her; she's the soul of this house. As for you and me, it is unlikely we shall see each other often, for my habits are those of an old man."

He rose with the help of his cane. Germinal took his leave, and followed Hestia.

The baronet hadn't been lying: when it came to informing the young man about household arrangements, the housekeeper proved almost brutally laconic, which she made up for with the briefest of smiles before taking her leave. Once unpacked, Germinal considered his domain more carefully. No tower, but the room was vast, with an almost dizzyingly high ceiling, a massive bed, and one of those ancient armoires big enough to hold the costumes—every last crinoline—for an entire troupe of actors. Hestia had seen to the fire, which lit the room most impressively, and provided heat; the adjacent bathroom left nothing to be desired; but what most delighted Germinal was the desk. A writer's desk is the vessel of his stationary journeys, the caravel of his inner voyage. This one was huge and black, its leather shiny with age. Its flanks concealed countless drawers deep as a galleon's hold. Germinal adopted it at once. Near the bed, a heavy wall hanging of Genovese velvet drew his attention. He pulled it aside, expecting to find an alcove. Instead, he found himself before a tall mirror. At least ten feet tall and freestanding, it touched the floor, so he could see himself from head to toe without taking a step back. Or he could have, had it not been for a wrought iron grille whose every bar was thick as a finger.

Ever fond of strange things, Germinal was charmed by this discovery. His imagination was even more greatly moved when, upon examining the grille more closely, he noticed it was not part of the wall, but rather a door that could, in theory, be opened, since it was outfitted on one side with hinges, and on the other, a large lock with a frankly carceral look to it. For a moment, Germinal was lost in conjecture as to the reason for such a device. He went so far as to grab the bars and give them a shake to test it. The results were conclusive: the grille was solid and locked. With his fingers fully outstretched, Germinal could almost touch his own reflection, marred here and there with russet blossoms of tarnished backing. Had someone in the past once been so afraid of mirrors? Germinal vowed to question the baronet about it.

That night, he took his first meal alone. An inscrutable Hestia served him. Without conversation to keep up, he didn't hesitate to spy on the housekeeper as she busied herself about him. She was a woman in the prime of her life. Her face, severe at first, would briefly, unexpectedly light up. Germinal's gaze was not entirely innocent. He took a moment to fantasize over the maidservant's slightly heavyset figure and brown complexion, which made her the exact opposite of a certain elfin blonde he'd met not long ago, who occupied his thoughts, though he was unsure she felt the same. He chided himself. Given how little boldness he usually showed, there was little chance that any intimacy would develop between himself and Hestia. He finished his dinner, folded the embroidered napkin, and stole meekly away.

Back in his room, he reread the first few pages of a recently sketched-out story that was slow to take shape. But his day on the train had tired him. He wasn't in a mood to work. He undressed, performed a few quick ablutions, turned out the light, and got in bed. He hadn't pulled the wall hanging back over the mirror, or drawn the curtains on the window across from him. The skies were clear, and from his bed, he could see the pale crescent moon reflected in the mirror gridded with iron. Suddenly, as his eyelids were lifting one last time before falling for good, he thought to see a female figure press itself to the grille. He came to his senses abruptly, like a swimmer surfacing with a splash. There, close by, a captive creature was reaching out to him, a rounded shoulder glowing in the moon's silver light, breasts crushed against the bars. He was dumbfounded for a moment. His heartbeat had sped up in an unreasonable, vulgar way, as if he were watching one of those silly horror movies he saw as a sign of contemporary bad taste. But soon he was convinced his imagination—a faculty he prided himself on having in spades—was playing tricks on him. He threw off sheet and comforter, left his bed, and ran to the mirror. Was this another illusion? Terrified by the abruptness of his reaction, the captive had pulled away from the grille and was retreating. Now he was the one clinging to the bars, the better to search the mirror's depths, which the reflection of a cloud momentarily darkened. He hesitated to commit the incident to paper, and closing his notebook, went back to bed. This time, sleep caught him in its toils. He only emerged ten hours later. Sunlight, flooding through the window, struck the mirror with its innocent rays. At the memory of the intriguing hallucination from the night before, the young man vowed to give some thought to what literary use he might make of it, but for now, his mind was mostly occupied with thoughts of coffee, and toast with jam. He dressed quickly and went down to the dining room.

That afternoon, as he was pacing his room and waiting for inspiration as one might on a station platform for a train, an old vase on a mahogany half-moon caught his eye. Restless as he was, he stuck his hand inside and pulled out a heavy, dusty, rusted key. Intuition struck at first sight: the key opened the grille on the mirror! It wasn't just the likely size that made him think so. The key's shape and substance, ironwork and ornament, reminiscent of pseudo-medieval smithery, all led him to believe it. He was astonished by its weight, as if it were made from some metal even denser than lead. He crossed the room, unveiled the mirror, and stuck the key in the lock. The bolt cleared the keep without a sound; he didn't need to force it at all. The grille swung silently open. Leaning forward, Germinal found the iron hinges hirsute with the dusty down that gathers, over time, on oiled metal parts. All he could deduce from these observations was that someone—the baronet? Hestia?—had taken care to oil lock and hinge relatively recently. Germinal swung the grill open wider, and felt the smooth, cold surface of the mirror, brushing with his fingertips the spatters that blurred it in places, as though to assure himself of its existence. Finally, with a shrug, he turned away, leaving the grille cracked open with the key in the lock.

He dined alone, just as he had the night before, with Hestia serving. He hadn't seen the baronet all day. He almost asked the housekeeper about the grille. He couldn't shake a native shyness that had weighed on his childhood and adolescence. He told himself he'd have all the time in the world to ask questions. Besides, there were other thoughts on his mind. It had seemed for some hours now that the sails of his becalmed novel were stirring once more in the light breeze of inspiration. But once he was back in his room, no matter how he clung to scraps of phrases that occurred to him, none pleased him. Piqued, he gave up. He opened *The Manuscript Found in Saragossa* and read a few pages, breaking off twice to sneak a glance at the mirror. Both times, he felt a vague desire to get up, lock the grille, and pull the wall hanging back across. Both times, he did nothing. His bed, which Hestia had warmed as in days of yore, was too cozy to leave for even a few seconds. And what was the point? There was no draft, no banging shutter to be feared.

He fell asleep, and dreamed that he woke to the sound of footsteps— light ones—on the oaken floorboards. A bright shape approached his bed, slipped under the covers, and pressed up against him. He wrapped his arms around its warm, shivering nakedness . . . What man hasn't been visited by a dream like that one night or another? For some, it leaves regrets crueler than any real embrace can. Shortly before dawn, the visitor placed one last kiss on Germinal's lips and fled toward the mirror. The young man dreamed he fell asleep again. He woke a few hours later, and as he was dressing, pacing the length and width of his room and recalling the spendthrift joys of the night, he suddenly stopped, speechless, before the wide open grille. He could have sworn it was almost closed when he went to bed last night. He closed it now, turning the key several times, first one way, then the other. Finally, perplexed, he went back to the bed, the key in his fist. The disorder of the bedclothes bore witness to an active night. There were even a few stains he blushed to think Hestia might find on changing the sheets. Hastily he made the bed, left the key on the half-moon, and went down to the dining room. Germinal greeted the baronet, just finishing his breakfast, and sat down across from him.

"I was just wondering," he began, buttering a piece of toast, "about the big mirror in my room . . . "

"Yes?"

"Well . . . a grille protecting a mirror—that's strange, isn't it?"

"Do you think so?"

"Yes. I mean—what's it for?"

The baronet lifted his gaze to the heavens before settling it on Germinal, who detected a glint of irony in his eye. "A bit unusual as fixtures go, I'll admit. I found it that way myself, a long time ago, in my youth, when that room was mine. What of it?"

Germinal blushed. Telling a stranger, just like that, what you were up to in an erotic dream that might not have been a dream at all, that might in fact, you suspect, have some connection to a mirror and a grille left open . . . rather than look like an idiot, Germinal dodged the question.

"Oh—nothing. Just odd, that's all."

"Odd," the baronet echoed. "Troubling, even. But isn't that the kind of thing an imaginative sort like you could make use of?"

The irony in the old man's eyes was shining almost fiercely now. Germinal nodded, to save face.

"I'll certainly give it some thought."

Luckily, at that moment the baronet rose and waved for Hestia to clear his plate. Turning to Germinal, he excused himself. He was using the time he had left to reread Madame de Sévigné. Ah, the marquise! What a marvelously obtuse mind, free of the slightest poetic concern, like her entire century!

Germinal had a sudden desire to get away for a few hours. Going for a walk in the woods, breathing in the smells of sodden humus and rotting timber would do him a world of good, he thought, spreading homemade preserves on his toast.

Night came, as it always does. At bedtime, Germinal grabbed the key almost despite himself and threw the grille wide open. He left the key in the lock just as he had the night before, but this time on purpose. To his own irritation, he seemed almost to be looking on as he did so, like a movie actor dismayed at his performance in the day's rushes. He felt like he was standing wrong, walking wrong, even breathing *wrong*. He doused the light and ran to hide in his bed, burrowing deep like a clam in the sand, and closed his eyes.

When she curled up against him, he opened his arms in welcome. It was her, all right. He recognized her soft skin, her silky hair, her perfumed body. She sought his mouth with the same childish eagerness. Later, he lay listening to her breathe. When he was sure she was asleep, he disentangled himself from her embrace with infinite caution. He crossed the room on tiptoe. As gently as he could, he closed the grille, turning the key twice in the lock, then dropped it in the vase and went to bed.

A howl of pain, fury, and horror tore Germinal from slumber. He sat up on the bed, frozen. He saw her from behind, naked in the pale dawn, clinging to the bars of the grille with both hands, trying in vain to tear or hurl it aside. Her spine was bent so far it seemed about to snap. The muscles of her back, her shoulders, her buttocks, tensed and twisted with effort, had shed the softness and tenderness of the night, and recalled instead the cruel, shocking precision of an anatomical cutaway. She howled again, and turned to him. Her eyes burned with the fire of madness, her nostrils flared convulsively, and from the lips she bit with rage blood ran down her chin and neck, all the way to her breasts, heaving with tormented breathing. Germinal wanted to calm her. He didn't know her name, or if she even had one. They'd exchanged nothing but sighs and moans. But in her state she could hear nothing, understand nothing. In her eyes, he glimpsed a spark of possibly murderous madness and hastily retreated, until between them stood the obstacle of the bed whose disarray still testified to their frolics. It was the right choice. Grinding her teeth, letting out screams alternately horrifying and heartrending, she began to devastate the room. Unable to reach Germinal, she scratched at chairs and tables, overturning them, lacerated cushions, hurled anything that fell beneath her hand against floor and walls. As he despaired of making her listen to reason, he spotted the still intact vase. He ran for it, grabbed the key, and dashed toward the mirror. His hand trembling, he unlocked the grille and threw it open. With a cry of deliverance, the captive shoved him aside and dove into the frame as if into a corridor yawning before her. Germinal seemed to glimpse walls covered in ivy, or maybe seaweed, but the vision faded in a milky fog. Soon there was nothing more in the mirror than his own reflection, naked and shivering.

Germinal left the manor that very day, in an ambulance. Aware it was impossible to explain to anyone's satisfaction the deplorable state in which he'd left his room, he let it be believed he'd suffered a nervous breakdown. In addition to the charges incurred, he got off with a few months' rest in a sanatorium. Strangely enough, his second novel, even more fantastical than the first, advanced more smoothly in that residency of another genre altogether.

GEORGES-OLIVIER CHÂTEAUREYNAUD *(b. Paris, France, 1947) is widely known in his native France and has been honored over a career of almost 40 years with the Prix Renaudot, the Prix Goncourt de la nouvelle, and the Grand Prix de l'Imaginaire at Utopiales. His stories have appeared in* Postscripts, Fantasy & Science Fiction, Podcastle, Subtropics, Conjunctions, The Harvard Review, The Southern Review, AGNI Online, Epiphany, Eleven Eleven, Sentence, Joyland, Confrontation, The Brooklyn Rail, *and* Café Irreal; *another is forthcoming in a Penguin anthology edited by Kate Bernheimer. His volume of selected stories,* A Life on Paper *(Small Beer, 2010), selected from over one hundred stories in eight collections and chapbooks, won the Science Fiction & Fantasy Translation Award* *and was shortlisted for the Best Translated Book Award. The first volume of his memoirs,* La vie nous regarde passer *[Life Watches Us Go By], came out in 2011 from Grasset, which will release his newest collection of stories in November,* Les amants sous verre *[The Lovers Under Glass]. He is at work on his tenth novel."*

Author's Commentary: *I wrote "The Open Mirror" on commission from* La Croix, *the leading Catholic daily, as part of a short story series in summer 2008. I no longer remember if rules, or a theme, had been imposed on us. At any rate, had there been, it would have been the author's duty to subvert such a theme, or appropriate it in some intimate fashion to produce a more personal work. As it happened, I was working on a set of stories about writing residencies; "The Open Mirror" wound up being the middle tale in a triptych of such pieces published in 2011 by Éditions des Busclats with the appropriately grim title* Résidence dernière *[Final Residence]. As far as subversion, I intended the tale as something of a playful wink at the conventions of the classical fantastical tale, and the primacy of fear in that genre I have practiced for so long.*

EDWARD GAUVIN, *Translator (b. Atlanta, Georgia, USA, 1976), a graduate of the Clarion Workshop, has received fellowships and residencies from the National Endowment for the Arts, the Fulbright program, the Centre National du Livre, and the American Literary Translators' Association. He won the 2010 John Dryden Prize for his translation of André Pieyre de Mandiargues'* "The Red Loaf". *Other publications have appeared in* The New York Times, Tin House, World Literature Today, Quarterly Conversation, *and* PEN America. *The contributing editor for Francophone comics at* Words Without Borders, *he translates comics for Top Shelf, Archaia, Lerner, and Self Made Hero. He writes a bimonthly column on the Francophone fantastic at the VanderMeers'* Weird Fiction Review. *A fiction writer under the name H.V. Chao, his work has appeared in* Epiphany, The Kenyon Review, *and* Brèves, *and is forthcoming in* Birkensnake *and* Strange Tales IV.

Translator's Commentary: *"The Open Mirror" is taken from a chapbook of three stories all set at writing residencies. They are, like much of Châteaureynaud's work, meditations not only on the nature of the supernatural, but on the writer's life: pos-*

terity, purpose, and pretensions. In addition to his usual themes of loneliness, temp-tation, and fate, we find such recurring preoccupations as sphinxes and concentration camps. The title story, "Final Residence", was first published in Issue 14 of Subtropics *(Spring 2012).*

In "The Open Mirror", Châteaureynaud examines the persistent grip of hoary trappings on our imagination, and his wicked, ironic fable, with its early quibbles over labels, becomes quite literally, in its final line, a commentary on the genre that traditionally leaves the reader between the psychological and supernatural. What we believe cliché can turn out terrifying, and our pride protects us as little as disbelief dispels. When we tarry with monsters, which way lies madness?

L'Amour est Mort

Simon Clark

First Verse

Midnight in Bruges. As I step into the boat I hand the ferryman the price of the journey to see the "the Blessed and Blighted Poet". Ghosting into town from the bleak fields of Flanders is a cold, misty rain that softens the once sharp geometry of the old buildings that line the canal.

As the ferryman dips his oars, and begins to ease the boat along the darkened waterway, which runs alongside Coupure, I tell myself the perfect music for such a voyage through the Venice of the North at dead of night would be the melancholy strains of an accordion. However, without any sense of occasion, rap music from a nightclub nearby beats like a massive heart. The accelerating heart belongs, perhaps, to someone experiencing life at its most astonishing and visceral—a ferocious, sexual excitement pounding out through this, the witching hour.

When the man takes our little boat round a bend in the canal the music fades. Soon there is silence apart from the light splash of oars.

"Mon Dieu!" the ferryman tells me. "He will not see you."

"He asked me to come. I have a letter."

"Madame. Everyone who goes to see him have letters. He always turns them away."

"Why?"

Instead of answering my question, the ferryman grimaces as we pass beneath an old stone bridge. "I hate this part of the canal. Terrible . . . an awful place." He shudders. "This is where my father drowned himself."

That's the kind of memory which is difficult to comment upon. Should I express sympathy? Change the subject? Or remain silent? I choose the latter. So I gaze at those phantom shapes that are the houses. The buildings themselves form the edge of the channel, the pale yellow stonework plunges down beneath the surface to the canal bed. Many windows lie just a foot or so above the water itself. If they wanted to, the occupants could open a window, and reach down to dabble their fingers in that Black Blood that runs through the veins of Bruges. Most of the houses are in darkness. Tonight, this sombre quarter of Bruges is a ghost town.

At that moment I ask myself if my journey from Paris is a wasted one. That morning I'd sat at the computer to print out the recording contract with a great sense of anticipation and optimism. I'm going to bring back to life Christian De Guerre, I told myself, I'm going to revive his career. His songs will make him rich again. Me, too.

And all because I'd bought a moribund record company for little more than a fancy supper in Ezelstraat. That adroit acquisition included what is quaintly known as "phonographic rights" to twenty songs by Christian De Guerre, one of the most famous Belgian singer-songwriters of the twentieth century. Considered as the musical successor to the legendary Jacques Brel, De Guerre's star burned brightly for a single decade. Known romantically, and possibly even *without* Gallic irony, by the press as the Blessed and Blighted Poet, he triumphantly sold out theatres across Europe. His concerts were heart-wrenching, they were uplifting, they were never forgotten. Those lucky people who witnessed the man sing still talk in awe about the night they were there. Music critics must have been swooning at their desks as they strove to outdo one another in their praise for De Guerre's ability to hold an audience spellbound: PROFOUND. ELEGIAC. AURAL CASTLES OF ENCHANTMENT. FOR THREE MAGICAL HOURS DE GUERRE CARRIES OUR SOULS TO HEAVEN. THERE WE WISH TO DIE AMONGST THE STARS, BECAUSE NOTHING WILL EVER SURPASS THE POWER AND THE GLORY OF HIS VOICE. And now I own twenty of his songs (admittedly only a modest portion of his songbook). They haven't even been available on CD, let alone as MP3 downloads. The last time they were heard in European homes and boulevard cafes they were enshrined in vinyl.

I've heard tantalizing rumours that after the accident, which killed De Guerre's career, the master chanteur began to record again in secret. I want those hidden songs. I want his music out there in the world again, touching hearts and uplifting souls—and no, it really isn't all about the money, even though there will be money. Genuinely, I adore the man's music. This is more about the love of his art than anything else.

The ferryman's grunt rudely tips me out of my golden day-dream. "We're here. You're wasting the time, though. The man's insane. He'll laugh at you and send you away."

"He won't. I have something he wants."

"What he wants is far and away beyond what you can give him." He mutters these mystifying words as he allows the boat to glide toward the immense stone wall of a house that looms over the canal. Dear God. What a forbidding, dark castle of a place.

I frown. "Why can't I give him what he wants?"

The man laughs softly and does not reply; his thick fingers catch hold of an iron ring beside a door, which opens directly onto the water. Then I had been told that the only access to De Guerre's house is from the canal itself.

I grab the man's arm. "Tell me. Why can't I give him what he wants?"

He scowls. His bulging eyes are staring at the canal's surface beneath the door. The water looks exactly like cool black glass: perfectly flat, and reflecting the stonework that towers above us. "This is where I found my father." His features tell me he's recalling that grim moment of discovery. "Floating there, face up, eyes open, like a dead fish. He always told my mother that this part of the canal owned his soul." He gave a shake of his head. "Merde! I hate this place. I hate its stinking water and its rotten walls."

When he falls silent, well . . . that's when the accordion does begin to play. I should grin at what should be risible cliché; however, the plaintive voice of the instrument conjures the melancholy spirit of the canal—this narrow channel is a dreary and silent grave for dead water. The mist comes ghosting in once more from Flanders fields that saw hundreds of thousands of soldiers die in World War One. My ferryman has become a statue, an inert sculpture wrought from skin, meat, bone and enduring sadness. He's staring into the water as if his own soul is being drawn into its blackness. As the poignant melody of the accordion dies away, the door to the house slowly opens, and I step from the boat into the home of the Blessed and Blighted Poet.

Chorus

My name is Christian De Guerre. And my best friend makes a home with my wife.

Here in Bruges I watch them pass my house every day. Their merriment is yet one more ghost that laughs me to my lonely bed. Such contemptuous laughter; it haunts the hours of darkness until dawn. Sleep is rarer than pearls in cow dung. L'amour est mort: Love is dead.

Second Verse

Walking along a gloomy passageway toward the inner sanctum, I've arrived at the home of De Guerre. Behind me, the door to the canal swings shut. Electrically powered, I guess. An automatic door that admits only the rare few into his lair of music—a man who has been a recluse for over twenty years. The ferryman has been shut out. Faintly I hear the oars splash and splash. Not that his furtive departure concerns me, he's done what I've paid him to do. He has no reason to stay.

Music plays softly from somewhere inside this house on the canal. A melody shimmers along cool, stone walls. Soft piano music. Possibly Debussy's *Deux Arabesques*, although too faintly to be certain.

Am I really at journey's end? In my shoulder bag is the contract. I also have a surprise for Monsieur Christian De Guerre. I hope this surprise will be pleasant enough to encourage him to accept my proposition—that I intend to resurrect his career. The first phase of my strategy will see the release of those twenty songs that I acquired when I purchased the record company. The second phase will consist of TV and press interviews followed by judicious live performances in the most intimate of venues. What's more, I plan to persuade him to let me hear the music that he's rumoured to have been composing during those years of solitude.

"*Hello? Monsieur De Guerre?*" My voice sounds so small in this gloomy void. "I'm Ruth Pearson. You agreed to meet with me. Hello?"

The chilly air of the canal has followed me down the stone slabs beneath my feet. As has the unpleasant smell of its water, a spiky combination of aromas suggestive of spilt fuel oil, ditch water and burnt human hair. I recall the ferryman telling me that his father drowned out there in that "Black Blood" of Bruges. How many other people have lost their lives in those liquid thoroughfares? How many bones lie in its old cold mud?

Maybe I have come all this way for De Guerre to turn me away. Perhaps this is some perverse hobby of his. You're invited to venture so far—then no further. But if the canal is the only means of access to the property, how can I actually leave?

"Monsieur De Guerre. You invited me. It's not at all well-lit. You would-n't want me to fall and hurt myself, would you? I am on heels." I raise my voice—polite yet firm, very firm. "I insist you open the door, Monsieur."

The first door I reach I try to open. And open it does. I step through the doorway to find a remarkable scene. I enter a room full of water. By that, I mean that instead of a floor there is an expanse of dark liquid—and this dark liquid is perfectly still. A dim lamp on the wall casts an equally dim light. The room is the size of a large domestic garage and to my surprise I realize that it contains a portion of the canal. So is this a boathouse? Gates at the far end of the chamber appear to afford access to the canal. There is a boat in here; however, it lies submerged. I can only just make out the ves-sel's shape beneath the surface. Running along the far wall, is a narrow walkway. I begin to feel scared, but I tell myself that this must lead into the house itself.

As I hobble onto the walkway I find that I can see down through the water. The lamp reveals moving objects beneath the surface. Fish? Eels? In any event, there are living things in the boathouse pool. They glide, to and fro. Restless, predatory shapes. I wonder if the reclusive owner of the house feeds them. Now they have grown large on the food he casts into the water. Surprising that fish as large as this, even GIGANTIC as this, live in the urban canals of Bruges. The atmosphere of the boathouse is worrying for some reason. I don't like it here. The first signs of panic display themselves, with a painful tightening of my chest that makes breathing difficult.

The Debussy still plays, yet I can hear scratching from the shadows. Per-haps De Guerre also leaves food here for the water rats, and their hairy bodies have grown bloated on Belgian cheese and morsels of spicy meat.

"Monsieur De Guerre!" I hurry along the narrow walkway. The water is just a slip away beneath my feet. Thoughts of plunging into that black canal alarm me more than I can adequately say. I reach the far side of the boat-house, a door is opening. I don't hesitate. In no time at all, I'm through a corridor—this one pleasantly well-lit, the music is louder, there are woollen rugs in differing shades of orange and yellow on the floor. Behind me there are loud splashes. Fish leaping from the water? Or something large and lum-bering? Attempting to heave itself out of the pool before dropping back in again? That does it. I run along the corridor. At this point, the reason for being here isn't important; it isn't important at all. In fact, all that does matter is that I get away from that grim tomb of a boathouse with its fright-ening, if unseen, tenants.

I fly through the building, arms outstretched in front of me, hair flying out, cursing that I've allowed myself to become so scared.

Then! Round a bend in the corridor and—bang!—I slam into a figure. He grabs hold of my arms. A face seems to rush at me. The face is ruin. The face is destruction. The face is horror. I yell at the gargoyle. Then there is no strength in my body. I've no control over my legs. All sense of balance is gone, and I'm falling into an expanse of darkness every bit as black as the pool in the nightmare boathouse.

CHORUS

My name is Christian De Guerre. And my best friend makes a home with my wife. Here in Bruges I watch them pass my house every day. Their merriment is yet one more ghost that laughs me to my lonely bed. Such contemptuous laughter; it haunts the hours of darkness until dawn. Sleep is rarer than pearls in cow dung. L'amour est mort: Love is dead. And so, one day, will they be: my faithless wife and my former friend.

THIRD VERSE

When I wake there are no drowsy questions of "Where am I? What happened?" I know my location with absolute precision. I'm in the house of Christian De Guerre. Beyond its walls, the black canal. Beyond that, the midnight streets of the old city of Bruges. I know exactly what happened to me: I fainted because I saw the face.

That face, which is slish-slashed this way and that with scars, harbours two glittering eyes that stare at me. Those scars form a series of X-shaped patterns on the face. Strange that in text we use an X to represent a kiss. In a surrealist fashion, the man's face is covered with X after X after X. A surfeit of kisses so violently planted. Kisses that must have been the epitome of agony. *Stop that.* The mutilated face is making me so dizzy that my thoughts are turning slippery and bizarre. *Don't you dare faint again,* I tell myself. Swooning is for weak girls in fairy tales.

I stand up from where I've been lying on a black leather sofa. My eyes sweep round a room that is furnished with Sixties-style modernist furniture. Low armchairs that are the colour of burnt orange with vast, flat cushions. Lights shine from angle-poise lamps. There are rugs of sharp geometric patterns: trapezoid, rectangle, triangle and diamond. Debussy's music flows from a sound system that would be state-of-the-art thirty years ago. Gorgeously lyrical piano notes dance around this striking room.

The only object in the room that isn't beautiful is the man with scars. He stands there, dressed in a black business suit with an open-necked white shirt. Those eyes that glitter so brightly are fixed on me.

In a firm way that conveys my strength I tell him, "You don't frighten me."

He continues to stare, as if it is *my* face that is the most unsettling face in the room.

"I never faint," I continue speaking in that forceful way. "I haven't eaten since this morning. Now I wish to see Monsieur De Guerre."

"You are seeing him."

His voice is very gentle. More a sigh than speech.

This is such a shock. The man with the ruined face is De Guerre? No. Impossible. He was one of the most strikingly handsome men to appear in the concert halls of Europe. So this must be an imposter. I know that if I take control of events here I can quickly establish the truth. What's more, I am adamant that I will not allow my mission to fail. I have travelled from Paris to Bruges for a reason. De Guerre *will* sign the contracts in my shoulder bag. I pick up the bag from beside the sofa and pull out a file.

"I have an appointment with Monsieur De Guerre."

"No."

"I have a letter, confirming the date and the time right here." I flick open the piece of paper with all the confidence of a police officer producing a search warrant. "I am to present myself at Christian De Guerre's house on March 3 at thirty minutes past midnight. It is now 12.29. I'm never late for appointments. Invariably, I'm early."

"I am De Guerre." He lightly touches his right cheek. Two criss-crossing scars paint a vivid red X against his bone-white skin. "Glass. More than the pain, I remember the way the glass sounded when I shattered it."

My heart pounds with such force as he tells me this. *Embarrassment has made him a prisoner here.* Already, I start to change my plans. But my mission hasn't failed. Far from it. De Guerre's facial condition becomes that unique selling point. When I release the songs of his that I control, and then re-launch his career, everything will work. He will be famous again. I will be the one who restored him.

"Monsieur De Guerre, I am in awe of your work. And I am here with an exciting proposition."

"Non."

"You invited me here so we could discuss the rights to the songs that I acquired when I bought—"

"Non . . . no, no."

"But you will allow me to explain my plans for the Flamandes recordings?"

"There's no point."

"Why not?" I'm getting angry now. "Why isn't there any point?"

"What's the point in conversing with ghosts?"

"Monsieur?" I can't believe what he's just said. "What ghost? Are you playing a game with me?"

"You, madame, are a ghost." The eyes in the ruined face are melancholy. "Madame, you died exactly one year ago tonight."

CHORUS

My name is Christian De Guerre. And my best friend makes a home with my wife. Here in Bruges I watch them pass my house every day. Their merriment is yet one more ghost that laughs me to my lonely bed. Such contemptuous laughter; it haunts the hours of darkness until dawn. Sleep is rarer than pearls in cow dung. L'amour est mort: Love is dead. And so are you, my long lost and tragic friend.

FOURTH VERSE

I adore the music of Christian De Guerre. His songs mesmerize me, just as they mesmerized millions of fans. His lyrics seamlessly weave timeless stories of love, betrayal, madness and death. De Guerre is a genius. I admire him so much. Yet I cannot stand here in his house and not refute that absurd statement.

"Monsieur," I begin with some heat, "believe me when I tell you this fact: I am not a ghost!"

"Oh, but you are."

"You say that I died twelve months ago?"

"Yes. This is the anniversary of your death."

De Guerre is not a well man. This much is obvious. Seclusion encourages him to muddle dreams with reality.

"I can prove to you that I'm no ghost," I tell him. "Touch my hand."

Very slowly, he shakes his head.

"Then I'll touch you." I squeeze his fingers between my fingertips. His skin is much cooler than mine. "You felt that."

"I don't hold conversations with ghosts." He sits in a swivel chair. "It's the equivalent of speaking to one's self. A one-sided conversation. The same as debating with a person in a dream."

The Debussy tape has finished. He replaces the vintage cassette with another, presses a button and Vaughn Williams' *Fantasia on "Greensleeves"* flows from the speakers. A stately melody full of courtly grace. The Blessed and Blighted Poet closes his eyes. There are even X-shaped scars on his eyelids.

"I am not a ghost," I insist. "Why won't you let me prove that I am a living woman?"

"Legions of ghosts pass through this house. *Legions.* They're here all the time. The ghosts of Jacques Brel and Serge Gainsbourg. They all want to talk. They strive to persuade me that they're alive, with beating hearts and warm blood in their veins, just as you're trying to now."

"Feel my pulse."

Without opening his eyes, he shakes his head. "Ghosts manipulate the senses. When I see a phantom it's because the image is imported into the visual receptors of my brain. My eyes play no part in the illusion. The optic nerve is directly bypassed. If I took your pulse I'd no doubt feel a steady beat there, but it's a felt illusion. Ghosts feed the mind with convincing deceptions."

"You're saying that a ghost is like a computer virus? That they reprogram our thoughts?"

"A computer virus? Use the comparison by all means."

"I am real."

"You are as real as a dream."

"What if I stripped off my clothes and you made love to me?"

"An erotic delusion. Nothing more."

I cross the room and grip the man's hands in mine; he opens his eyes when I lift them to either side of my face and hold them there. "Of course, I am real. You feel skin against skin, you feel my breath on your face, you can smell my perfume. So tell me that I'm a ghost now."

"Would a living woman visit a stranger's house at midnight?"

"I'm no ordinary woman."

"I agree. You are images flickering in my brain."

"But this letter invites me to the house." I step back from him. "If I leave it right here on the table and if it's still here in the morning then . . . "

"It won't. The letter will have vanished—just as you will vanish."

I lunge at him, kiss his face, and with my lips I feel the ridges of skin that are his X-shaped scars. "There! That is real." I kiss him on the mouth. "You must taste my lips, just as I can taste yours."

"In dreams, other people seem real, absolutely real, until we awake, then *fffтt.*" He flutters his fingers as if imitating rock doves flying away.

I sit on the sofa. I can see my reflection in the glass that covers a framed gold album. More importantly, I see myself there. Dark eyed. Hair falling about my shoulders. I move. I breathe. I live. *De Guerre is playing games with me. Nasty, twisted games.*

Suddenly, he begins to speak as he sits there in the chair. He's not addressing me. He's speaking aloud to himself. "I've done everything humanly possible to stop the ghosts. Come what may, they still haunt me. I see every kind of jaded phantom in this house. I see the people who occupied the building before me. I even see the ghosts of animals that roamed here before Bruges existed. *Before any town existed.* Big, snarling brutes that have been extinct for a million years." He turns to me and speaks as though it pains him to do so. As if he knows he's indulging a fantasy; he's as shamefaced as the atheist that feels obliged to pray to God. "Night after night the ghosts come. Sometimes they are of my old friends: Brel and Gainsbourg. Other nights, I see the dead from the First World War filling the house with a dark fog. Then the ghosts of those roughly formed beasts will come lumbering through this room again; they snort, their eyes dart this way and that; maybe they are searching for animals to kill, or maybe they are looking out for animals that will kill them. I'm visited by the souls of artists, ferrymen, criminals and saints. I've seen the ghosts of influenza viruses—they paint the walls with such a dazzling light that I can't bear to keep my eyes open. I'm stared at by the spirits of my dead mother and father—and let me tell you, I've even seen the ghosts of dead gods." He takes a deep breath, leans forwards, and looks directly into my eyes. "But do you want to know a surprising fact? I have never seen the ghosts of my wife and my best friend."

CHORUS

My name is Christian De Guerre. And my best friend makes a home with my wife. Here in Bruges I watch them pass by every day. Their merriment is yet one more ghost that laughs me to my lonely bed. Such contemptuous laughter; it haunts the hours of darkness until dawn. Sleep is rarer than pearls in cow dung. L'amour est mort: Love is dead. And so is all hope of redemption from Him, the maker of souls.

Fifth Verse

"Madame Ghost," he speaks softly. "Will you hear my confession?"

"Perhaps you should confess to a priest," I tell him, "or the police?"

"But that won't cease these visits from the dead."

De Guerre is insane. That fact is plain to me. He will never tour again. Perhaps there are still recordings of new songs, though? My optimism and the music of a madman. Ah, *Songs of Psychosis.*

So humour him. Play along.

"Of course, I'll listen to your confession," I tell him. "And I'll do whatever I can to get these shades out of your life."

He gives a tired smile. "I wonder if I'm being tested. If I confess my crime to enough of you then maybe I'll be spared any more of these nocturnal visits. I've made this confession a thousand or so times before to your fellow spectres."

"Go ahead, Monsieur De Guerre," I say gently. "Make your confession . . . In the hope that your confession will make us ghosts go away." I catch my breath and laugh—a nervous laugh it has to be said. "See? You almost had me believing that I really am dead."

"Perhaps we're both closer to the truth of our natures than we realize."

I squirm uncomfortably on the sofa and squeeze my knee in my hand to check that there really is firm flesh and bone there. When I'm reassured I nod to him. "You promised me a confession, monsieur."

"Ah, Madame Ghost, I confess as follows. For ten years I enjoyed too much success throughout Europe. Sell out concerts. Millions of album sales. My own TV show was seen by tens of millions from France to Siberia. I felt myself fortunate to have a best friend, who was also my manager. I married one of the most beautiful women on Earth. Rosa's charisma and looks had the force of a tropical storm. Rosa blew men down with a single glance." He gives a sad smile. "Figuratively speaking of course. We had more money than I thought we could spend and fame. We dined as guests in the royal palaces of Europe. But somehow it wasn't enough for Rosa. She started to blame me that I wasn't able enough in providing what she wanted. Though what she did want I'm not exactly sure. True, she was angry with me for not being a star in the United States. Her dissatisfaction with me became a hairline crack in our relationship. That hairline crack grew over the months into a fracture. Within five years it was a gaping chasm.

"We had a daughter—the loveliest child I could imagine. I was so proud to be her father. I cherished my little Co-Co. And yet Rosa grew bored of her own daughter. As soon as she could, she sent her away from home to a private school in Switzerland. My little Co-Co sleeping in a dormitory in a foreign land? Ah, the memory still breaks my heart."

"Where is Co-Co now?"

"Grown up and married to a schoolteacher in New Zealand. I never have contact with her. I would love to speak to her but she believes it was me, not Rosa, who sent her away to school. She hates me."

De Guerre runs his fingernails down his scarred face. At that moment I really do believe that he wishes the pain from the injury would return in order to mercifully obliterate the memories that rise up to torture him. He's a father deprived of his child. That hurts him beyond my powers to describe.

"I confess, I confess," he murmurs. "I failed to realize that my wife was driven by immense ambition. At some point, Rosa decided, in what must have been a cold, calculating way, that she'd only find true happiness if she could achieve two goals. The first goal: to remove me entirely from her life. The second goal: to take possession of all my wealth." He shrugged. "There you have it, she wanted me to disappear, and she wanted my money. Compromise never featured in her world. You see, if she divorced me she'd have to agree to taking only a share of my assets. No, not good enough: she wanted to own everything. So she set out to kill me."

"You mean she tried to murder you?" I gaze at the scars; those XXX marks.

"Rosa's monstrous self-importance was too high to risk being sent to prison. Because being incarcerated would mean she'd lose control of her life. No, she decided to force me to commit suicide."

"She couldn't succeed in persuading you to kill yourself, surely?"

"Remember, Rosa is driven by ambition. In her, it is an irresistible force. Oh, she didn't say anything as trite as 'Christian, why don't you poison yourself today?' No, Rosa possesses the same strength of ambition as the builders of the Egyptian pyramids. She was prepared to invest years of her life into achieving her goal. My self-inflicted death. So she belittled my every achievement. When royalty statements arrived and I proudly showed her sales of a hundred thousand records, she'd give a dismissive shake of the head and ask why they weren't a million. She'd constantly compare me to other popular singers of the day. Needless to say, she managed to convince me that I was inferior to my rivals. Rosa was smart. She never tried to deliver body blows. She spoke softly—always in a disappointed tone—focusing on my faults real or imagined in nothing less than forensic detail. She had become the soft rain that very slowly, very subtly, and very destructively erodes the once proud statue. Year by year, Rosa succeeded in lowering my self-esteem. Perversely, as my bank balances increased so my sense of self-worth plummeted." His soulful eyes lock on mine. "The perfect crime, yes? Murder by suicide. Because it's the victim that delivers the lethal blow—not the assassin."

"How did she . . . "

"How did she drive me to this?" De Guerre touches his ruined face. "After five years of her relentless corrosive scorn I shouted back at her one day, 'I've a good mind to kill myself.' She laughed in contempt. 'You? Kill yourself? Christian, you haven't got the guts!' She was right. I hadn't. Another fifteen months passed. Fifteen months of criticism. Fifteen months of Rosa convincing me that I'd become so inferior to every other songwriter and performer that I was an embarrassment. Such was her charisma that I paid no attention to audiences and how they applauded me and shouted, *Bravo!* If Rosa said I was garbage then garbage I was. So . . . " He sighed. "Fifteen months after the first time I threatened to kill myself I drank a bottle of brandy and stepped from a hotel window. A second later, I crashed through a glass canopy. That reduced the impact speed on the ground below, so I survived. The shards of glass, however, cut my face to pieces. Surgeons did the best they could." He shrugged. "Even so, I am as good as dead. Naturally, I stopped recording and retreated into my own world where nobody would ever see my face. Even the press, who can be so intrusive, were good to me. They praised my legacy and reported I was leaving show-business for quiet retirement; graciously, they begged my fans to leave me in peace. No photograph of my face was ever published."

"You left your wife?"

"No, she left me. She moved into the home of my best friend who, as I've already told you, was my manager. A shrewd move, because George had persuaded me to sign contracts that were extremely favourable to him, not me. The pair seized control of all my songs and my recordings, with the exception of the rights to the twenty songs that you acquired."

Oh yes, Christian De Guerre is insane. Nothing less. He dwells in his own world of ghosts and paranoid delusion. Even so . . . I will not yield.

"Monsieur De Guerre. I acquired the rights to the Flamandes recordings. I control those twenty songs of yours. I intend to release them as downloads. I can offer you a thirty thousand euros advance against royalties as a gesture of goodwill on my part. I'm not obliged by the contract to do this, but I want to prove to you that our business relationship will benefit you immediately. There are also rumours that you have been recording new songs since your . . . retirement. If you sign the contract I have here I will pay you fifty thousand euros tonight, simply to have the opportunity to hear the recordings and be granted an option to release an album twelve months from now."

"Ah . . . you ghosts make such sweet promises." His smile is one of deep sadness. "I wish you were real. I wish we really could make exciting plans for the future. Alas, even though you are as wonderful as a happy dream, that's all you are. In the next few minutes you'll have vanished. Your place will be taken by the next spirit."

I calculate my chances of having the effect I desire and say quickly, "But you have never seen the ghosts of your wife and your best friend. Why?"

"That will be a vital element of the curse. If I saw their ghosts I could ask their forgiveness."

"Forgiveness? Why must you ask for their forgiveness?"

"For being responsible for their deaths."

"What did you do?"

"You should know, madame, you were there."

Before I can yet again insist that I am not a ghost, nor part of this occult drama that he believes he is embroiled in, I hear a woman's scream. It doesn't come from outside the house. It comes roaring up the passageway from the depths of De Guerre's home. The echoes distort and manipulate the sound into a banshee shriek.

He turns the volume of the music down. "What did you hear?"

The scream pierces the walls of the house again. Its sheer volume hurts my ears. A man starts shouting: panic, fear, desperation. Oh, yes, I hear those emotions.

"A woman screaming, and there's a man shouting . . . " I turn to him in astonishment. "Surely, you heard them?"

His face pales; those X-shaped scars turn from red to white. The man's gaze appears to turn inward; he's recalling events that fill him with horror.

"De Guerre," my voice rises over the yells of the man and the woman. "Two people are shouting for help. We must find them."

"I know where they are." He grips my arm to hold me there in the room. "They are in the boathouse."

"Why are you holding on to me? Something awful's happening down there."

"It is. They are dying."

In total shock, I stare at him. The man's words have knocked breath from my lungs.

"What did you say?"

"Rosa and George are already dead, my dear. And so are you."

"No!"

"Unlike you, I can't hear their screams. I can't see their ghosts."

"Dear God, you need help . . . "

"You don't remember what happened a year ago tonight, do you? You arrived here to discuss those songs you acquired. And, just as we have been doing now, we'd been in this room, with the music playing, and talking. Then came the screams. Just like now."

"So you do hear them?"

Gravely, he shakes his head. "As I've just explained: I never hear Rosa and George, I never see their ghosts."

"That sound is terrible. Half of Bruges must be hearing it."

He continues speaking . . . confessing . . . baring his tortured soul . . . this elegant man known as the Blessed and Blighted Poet . . . "Only you ghosts hear the sound."

"I'm going to help. If we stand by and do nothing, it's murder!"

He doesn't release his grip on my arm. "I know your body lies in a tomb. But I wish I had held you like this twelve months ago . . . you would have been spared. I liked you."

I struggle, trying to break free. But the moment he begins speaking in that gentle voice that flows with melancholy I become still and listen to the final part of his despairing confession.

"We discussed the contract you'd brought. I poured another glass of Pernod. Then the screams began. I later discovered that George and my Rosa had rowed a boat along the canal and had secretly entered the boathouse, and closed the doors behind them. Rosa must have kept a key to the padlock. Why were they here?" He shrugs. "To try and persuade me to sign this house over to her, perhaps; I wouldn't be surprised to discover that she planned to deprive me of my home. Then she'd have everything. So . . . as we sat here one year ago, the screams began. We both ran downstairs to the boathouse to discover that Rosa has fallen in the water. There is so much debris in there, including the wrecks of old boats. One of her feet had become wedged into the rotting timbers lying at the bottom of the boat-house pool. George had jumped in to help. Because of the depth he had to grip Rosa beneath her arms in order to hold her face above the water so she could breathe. He couldn't leave Rosa to fetch help, otherwise she'd drown. So both of them shouted—they were shouting for their lives. The sound was immense. It echoed through the house."

I begin to feel even colder. At that moment, I realize I can smell wet soil. It is very close. As if the wet earth is just inches above my face. Even though I become suddenly lightheaded, I make myself speak. "First, we must find out who's in the boathouse, after that I'll telephone for a doctor. You are very sick, only you don't realize—"

"No! You must hear what happened to you! Then you might remember—even though it was your last movements on Earth. Only then might you be content to lie quietly in your grave." He isn't holding my arms now, though I don't recollect him releasing me. "Ruth, that night twelve months ago, you moved so fast. You were a blur. The instant you entered the boat-house you saw those two poor people struggling in that cold, black water. To help them, to save them! That's what dominated your mind. You ran onto the narrow walkway. And that's when you slipped. Everything happened in a matter of three or four seconds. Yet when I recall it, everything is moving so very, very slowly. Your feet slip from under you on the walkway. You fall backwards—there's a shocking sound. Almost like a very loud pop. That's the sound of your head smashing onto a stone slab. The next second you're in the water. And I know you're dead. There's so much blood. Your eyes are open. Unblinking, staring. The light of your life is extinguished. There is nothing I can do." His voice becomes whispery. "Rosa and George are still in the water. They're shouting. George roughly shoves your body away when it drifts too close to the love of his life, my beloved Rosa." He shakes his head. "Her foot is still trapped in the debris at the bottom of the boathouse pool. I return to this room. The music is still playing and I turn up those merciful decibels. I turn them up more until I can't hear their screams. Nobody would hear them from outside—the walls are more than a foot thick and the gates to the canal are made of solid timber. They faced certain death: the water in March is very cold. My old friend was utterly devoted to Rosa to the last—if he'd abandoned her to certain death he could have saved himself. Yet he stayed with her and doomed the pair of them. Hypothermia made Rosa and George lose consciousness. As soon as their heads sank beneath the surface they would have drowned."

I stare at him. My heart is pounding. However, I am frightened to rest my hand on my breast just in case the awful truth of the matter is this: that I am only remembering what a fierce heartbeat is like. The smell of wet soil fills my nostrils again; the rot of the grave. Fear . . . a bloated and malignant fear at that... worms its way into my trembling body. Meanwhile, Christian De Guerre, the Blessed and Blighted Poet, closes his eyes.

The awful braying screams still pierce the air. I yell at the man: "I'm going to check the boathouse for myself! Someone needs help!"

"The Chief of Police explained to the coroner that there had been a dreadful accident. Three people had recklessly attempted to visit me by boat late one night. A tragic accident and nothing more. The press were kind to me yet again. No real detail was given, other than a boat had sunk near my house."

The screams become an irresistible force. Of course, I must run toward them. Those are the screams of a man and woman in terror. Enough of De Guerre's insane lies! Enough of his deluded fantasy! There are two human beings in trouble and I'm determined to save them.

The walls of the corridor are a blur. I race down the steps to the boathouse door. A second later I crash through into the vaulted chamber with its waters a lagoon of black blood.

There, in the dim light of the lamp, I see the horror . . . I do not breathe. There, below me in the water, are three people. A man struggles to hold a woman's head above the surface. Their eyes are fixed upwards, as if they long with all their hearts to rise clear of the canal. Their expressions are becoming blank as the coldness overwhelms their bodies. They are dying: hypothermia shutting down vital organs. Yet they still have the strength to scream—their mouths are stretched wide into a yawning O. Each mouth is a red cavern framed by white teeth and pale lips. Then there is me, Ruth Pearson: the woman lying face down in the centre of the boathouse pool. Blood streams from my head. Crimson blooms pattern the water.

Rosa and George sink beneath the surface. Ripples gradually subside, leaving a body of water that is absolutely still. A deathly silence fills this cold and lonesome chamber.

So it's all true: ghosts do flow through the house of Christian De Guerre. Perhaps he dreams them here, the spirits of the dead. Suddenly, here they come, flooding through the walls, phantoms of which I am but a single one. Here they are, gushing through the boathouse. The ghosts of bacteria and viruses by the billion—they paint rainbows of supernatural intensity across the stonework. Now the shades of primordial animals lumber into view, those tusked and shaggy beasts, which dwelt here long ago when Bruges was still a swamp. Those are followed by souls wrenched free of flesh in the Belgian killing fields of World War One. And, all the while, yet more phantasms join the torrents of the dead: those men and women who breathed their last breath in Bruges, this Venice of the North. Yes, I'm now part of that soul river, which flows from the grave to who knows where. In a heartbeat, I'm borne away towards whatever comes hereafter.

Christian De Guerre remains behind—no doubt condemned to haunt this house by the canal. A living ghost eternally brooding over the deaths of his wife and former friend. Two people he loved. Not anymore, of course. *L'amour est mort: Love is dead.* But even a dead love can haunt us, and hold us prisoner for ever more.

SIMON CLARK *(b. Wakefield, West Yorkshire, England, 1958) was raised on tall tales of mysteries, ghosts and battlefields, of which there is a rich supply in his native county that has seen many peaceful migrations as well as violent invasions by Romans, Vikings and Normans—all of which have left their mark, either archeologically, genetically or culturally. He is the author of over twenty novels, including* Nailed by the Heart, Blood Crazy, Vampyrrhic, Death's Dominion *and* The Midnight Man. *Simon's latest novel,* His Vampyrrhic Bride, *is set in present-day Yorkshire, yet draws on Nordic folklore, and the notion of spurned gods determined to punish humanity.*

Commentary on "L'Amour est Mort": *In Bruges, I was dramatically swept along by excited crowds, rushing toward the 13th century Church of Our Lady. Was there a fire? A riot? A famous film star posing for photographs? No, I discovered that the second most famous bell-ringer in Belgium had arrived at the church. Bruges is a town of unusual appetites; unusual to many of us, that is. This ancient Belgian city is home to quaint buildings, soaring towers, fabulously potent beers, and choco-*

late of such dizzying varieties. There is also another Bruges, a watery labyrinth of black canals, bridges and waterside buildings that are centuries old. This second Bruges has the air of a hidden realm. Its canals were once busy thoroughfares in their own right. Low doorways open directly onto the water to admit amphibious visitors. This mysterious Bruges threaded with canals became the inspiration for "L'Amour est Mort". The title is taken from a Jacques Brel song, and that Belgian singer of darkly twisted and troubling anthems to love, betrayal and death also had a big part to play in establishing my after-midnight mood when I wrote the story.

Elena's Egg

Theodora Goss

IT SEEMED AS THOUGH ELENA HAD BEEN SITTING IN THE HALLWAY a long time. Across from her, on a wooden bench, the kind you see in old churches, sat a man in a worn gray suit holding a potted geranium on his lap. Next to him, but not too close (she was not his daughter, thought Elena) sat a girl in what looked like her Sunday best, with a blue ribbon holding her hair out of her eyes. On her lap was a kitten. She was kicking her heels methodically against the bench, but the man did not seem to notice, or at least to care. Elena gave up trying to share a look of annoyed sympathy, and instead gave an annoyed sigh. He sat looking down at his geranium, and once in a while he wiped the sweat off his brow with a crumpled handkerchief.

Elena looked down at the egg. It sat in the nest she was holding, an intricate construction of twigs and bits of string and down, leaning a little to one side, the large chip where the bird had come out visible on top. It was the delicate, pale blue of a robin's egg. Elena shifted—the wooden chair under her was uncomfortable. There were several wooden chairs on her side of the hallway, but hers was the only one occupied.

She glanced at her watch again, but it was still only two o'clock, and when she held it up to her ear, she realized that it had stopped. She was about to ask the man with the geranium what time it was when the door next to the bench opened and the secretary emerged, holding a clipboard.

"Mr. Schmidt, won't you come in, please?"

Everything about her, from her short blonde hair, to her crisp cream-colored blouse and low-heeled, immaculately polished shoes, whispered efficiency. She was young, probably just out of university, thought Elena, conscious of her own shoes, which were old and scuffed, and the wisps of hair coming out of the bun at the back of her head. She was fairly certain that she had a ladder in her stocking.

Mr. Schmidt followed the secretary into the office, and the door shut behind him.

Next, it was the girl's turn. The kitten mewed when she lifted it to her shoulder, and it looked back at Elena with large blue eyes as the girl walked through the doorway. By leaning to her right, Elena was able to catch a glimpse of a set of French doors with a bookshelf beside it before the door closed.

Elena looked at her watch, although she knew what it would say. Two o'clock.

Finally, the door opened again. "Elena Kovács," the secretary said. Elena rose, holding the nest carefully in both hands, and followed.

The office was filled with sunlight. Through the French doors, she could see a garden with a sloping lawn bordered by shrubs and flowers. Along the walls were bookshelves, filled with books and *objets d'art*—vases, small statues. At one end of the office was a desk, where a woman sat writing. At the other end were a sofa and two armchairs around a low table. Wherever there were no bookshelves, there were paintings of landscapes or still lifes with flowers and fruit spilling out of bowls. The room looked old, comfortable, as though it had been inhabited for a long time. And yet it was clearly a workplace as well—the desk was covered with piles of papers, and through an open door to the left, Elena could see a more utilitarian room filled with metal file cabinets. Before, Elena had been impatient; now, she wished she were still sitting in the hall.

"Mrs. Moth?" said the secretary. "This is Elena Kovács. She is the last for today."

"Excellent," said the woman at the desk. "Miss Kovács, won't you have a seat on the sofa? Much more comfortable than those wooden chairs. I keep asking for cushioned ones, but you know how it is. As long as they still work, why change them? After all, they're only for the waiting area. Bureaucracies are inherently conservative and unwilling to innovate—even in the matter of cushions! But I do apologize for the wait. It's been a busy day."

Blinking in response to the sunlight, which seemed particularly bright after the darkness of the hallway, with its electric lights, Elena sat on the sofa. She set the nest, with its egg, carefully on the table in front of her.

"Would you like some coffee?" asked Mrs. Moth. "I've already been through your file, so we should be able to proceed quickly." She closed the file folder she had been looking through, but brought it with her as she walked across the room to where Elena was sitting. She sat in one of the armchairs across from the sofa.

"Yes, please," said Elena.

Mrs. Moth nodded. "Hyacinth, two coffees. Cream and sugar, I think?"

Elena nodded, assuming the question had been meant for her.

The coffee was very good, probably the best she had ever tasted. Without asking her, Mrs. Moth had added milk and three lumps of sugar, which was fortunate because Elena would have been ashamed to ask for more than two. But she liked her coffee sweet.

"Now," said Mrs. Moth, when Elena had taken a few sips of her coffee and the secretary was sitting in the other armchair, with a notepad on her knees, her pen poised. "Tell us about the egg." When Elena started to speak, the secretary—Hyacinth—started to write in the loops and whorls that Elena recognized as shorthand.

The incident had happened when she was a child.

One day, as she and her father were walking in the park around the Némzeti Muzeum, across the street from her parents' apartment, they found a nest under one of the linden trees. It had obviously fallen from its branch. Inside it, still intact, was a single egg. They took the nest home, and her father, who had grown up on a farm, put it under a light bulb.

Day after day, Elena watched the egg, until one day—it hatched. Oh, what a hard time they had then! Just keeping that baby bird fed. Elena would go to the park with her tin pail and pick up all the insects she could find. She would even dig for worms. Then she would chop them up and feed them to the baby bird with a pair of tweezers. Even Elena's mother helped, although she complained loudly about the mess Elena was bringing into the apartment. It was summer and Elena was not in school, or she could never have spent so much time being a mother bird. Each evening, when her father came home, he checked on the bird and said that it was growing nicely. "It's a robin," he told her. "Robins are lucky. Taking care of this one will bring you good luck all your life."

Elena's father had told her that the bird might not live, that birds were delicate. They died easily without their parents. But the bird lived. As summer passed, it grew larger and stronger—and bolder. Elena's father constructed a cage for it out of a wooden frame covered with pantyhose. Elena went around to all the women in the apartment building, asking them for pairs of pantyhose that were so laddered they could no longer be mended. The women laughed but gave her their old pairs, and Elena's mother sewed them together to cover the wooden frame. Despite Elena's mother's objections, the robin was allowed to fly around the apartment so it could strengthen its wings. It would fly to her, perch on her shoulder, and eat directly from her hand. Then, it would allow her to put it back into its cage. Afterward, Elena had to clean up whatever mess it had made.

"It thinks you're its mother," her father would tell her. While the robin was pecking at her fingers, she would stroke its feathers, so soft and brown, and its red breast. At dawn, it would wake her up with its chirping and twittering.

She thought she would be its mother for always, but one day, when her mother had left the windows overlooking the park open, Elena noticed a tear in the pantyhose. The cage was empty. She looked everywhere, but the robin was gone.

Elena cried and cried. Her father told her that it was for the best, that a bird belonged in the park, not in a cage. Her mother told her that she was losing patience with her, and to go play outside. Elena walked around the park aimlessly, until she heard what she thought were its particular cheeps. She looked up, and there it was—at any rate, she was convinced it was her robin. For years afterward, she was convinced that there was a particular robin in the park that was hers, that came back every summer and, when it spotted her, would follow her around from tree to tree. She could see it looking down at her, from among the linden leaves. But it would never fly down to take bread crumbs from her hands, although she tried to coax it.

While Elena told this story, the secretary took notes in her notebook. Mrs. Moth simply sat and listened, nodding once in a while. When she was finished, Mrs. Moth opened the file folder on her lap and said, "You've been recommended for work in our aviary. We have a large variety of birds, some quite rare, that need to be fed and cared for. The Great Auk, I understand, has a respiratory infection and needs to be given medicine every couple of hours, and the Passenger Pigeons get lonely. There used to be so many of them, and we have only a small flock. Reading to them is often helpful. Based on your qualifications and experience, I agree with the recommendation. Hyacinth, can you telephone Dr. Pál and tell him that we've found him a new assistant? And then, can you show Miss Kovács where to go? It's been very nice meeting you, Miss Kovács. And I hope you enjoy your new position." Mrs. Moth held out her hand.

"Wait," said Elena. "Is that it? I mean, that's a single incident from my childhood. It happened so long ago."

"That's all we need," said Mrs. Moth. "I've been in this position a long time, Miss Kovács. I pride myself on knowing where our new arrivals will be most useful, and I hope most content."

"But you don't know me at all," said Elena. "You don't know—once, I did something horrible. If you knew—"

Mrs. Moth closed the file folder and looked at her with only a hint of impatience. The secretary sat, with her pen poised over the notebook. They waited politely.

It happened while I was in art school, said Elena.

My father had warned me that the life of an artist is difficult. But my secondary school teacher had told me that I had talent, and I was determined to use it. While other students were kicking a football in the school courtyard or sitting on the stairs smoking cigarettes and talking about their favorite rock bands, I was drawing. I always carried my sketchbook. On the weekends, I would go up to the Castle Hill and sketch tourists for a few hundred forints a picture. It was how I made my spending money.

I was fortunate enough to be admitted to the art school at the university. My first year, I was put in a drawing class with Antal Andrássy. He was a famous artist, in those days. He had designed that monument—you know the one, it used to stand beside the building everyone knew was the headquarters of the secret police. He had been given a medal by the government. He was one of the art school's most respected professors.

In class, he would walk around the room, a piece of black chalk in his hand, frowning and running his fingers through his hair. He wore it long, down to his collar—which was considered long in those days. Some of the students said it was affected, as though he were posing for a picture of an artist, but I thought it made him look romantic. If he felt that our drawings were not good, he would correct them—with a thick line, some shading. He was not kind—"The model is leaning on that arm. It's supporting the weight of her torso. It needs to have tension. You've made it look like a cooked noodle." But he almost always made our drawings better.

At first, I thought he did not like me. "No, Elena!" he would say, standing behind me so that I had to look nervously over my shoulder. "Are you trying to insult me? Where do those shadows under her shoulder blade come from? Identify your light source. Have you listened to any of the things I've taught you?" I thought that I was the worst in the class, that I should quit art school. Finally, I went to his office. I could not help it—tears came to my eyes as I told him that I had lost confidence in myself, that I was considering leaving.

"Elena," he said, leaning back in his chair, "why do you think I'm so hard on you? Harder than on anyone else in the class? It's because you're the most promising, the one with the most potential. If I didn't believe in you, I wouldn't waste my time trying to teach you, to correct your technique." I was so startled that I did not know what to say. "You're also quite beautiful," he added. "I was thinking of asking you to model for me. I'm working on a mural for the Ministry of Agriculture. I need a model who looks exactly like you—with your coloring, and that expression you sometimes have, as though you were looking at distant mountains."

I stammered that of course—if he wished to paint me, of course I would be willing to model for him. I would consider it an honor.

"Good," he said. "Come to my studio, on Ráday Utca. Can you begin on Saturday?"

The mural was going to be in the lobby of the ministry building. He wanted me to pose for a series of preparatory sketches. On Saturday, I posed for hours with a basket on my arm. At the end of the session, my arm ached, but Antal was pleased with the results and asked me to pose for him again. I went the next Saturday, and the one after that. When I looked at his sketches, some in pencil, some in colored chalks, I could see the mural begin to take shape: in the foreground was a peasant girl, her braided hair in loops the color of wheat, holding a basket of wheat sheaves. Behind her were fields of wheat, a barn, a tractor, men harvesting—all the elements of a prosperous cooperative farm. I asked what the peasant girl was doing, exactly, but Antal said she was allegorical—she represented agriculture itself. She was looking off into the distance, toward a prosperous future.

Posing for him was not easy. When I got tired, when the basket began to weigh on my arm, I would shift, and he would get angry, telling me that I was ruining his painting, that I did not care sufficiently for art. So I would try to stay still as long as I could, despite the pain in my arms or legs. One day, I posed for him so long, and I was so tired, that I simply fell. In a moment, he was beside me, kneeling on the ground. He took me in his arms and said, "Beautiful Elena. I am a monster, torturing you like this. I never wish to hurt you, not even for my art. Tell me you're all right, my darling." I had never expected to hear words like this from him. Tears sprang to my eyes. He smiled down at me and kissed them away. "You know that I'm in love with you, don't you? You must have guessed, from how I look at you, how I draw you."

Of course I had not guessed, although over the weeks of posing for him, of having him correct my drawings, I had come to think of him as the greatest man I had ever met. I still think of him that way. To be loved by him—I could not imagine a greater happiness.

"I have always longed for a muse, a woman who could represent art to me," he said. "You inspire me, Elena—as no woman ever has." He leaned down and kissed me.

We did not become lovers that day—but the next time I posed for him, he threw down his pencil and said, "I can no longer draw you. I'm too madly in love with you, Elena. Either I must have you, and still this madness that is in me, or you can never pose for me again." He looked so desperate as he said it, so filled with anger and longing and fear, I could not deny him. Of course I knew that he was married, but he had told me that he and his wife were together only for their daughter's sake. If she had not been ill, they would have separated long ago.

I have to admit, I was jealous of all the women I saw in the sketches and paintings in his studio. They had posed for him too—had he loved them as he loved me? He assured me that they had been models, nothing more. That even if he had felt something for them, it was nothing like what he felt for me. That I was the muse, the woman, for whom his soul had always longed. Can you imagine how happy I was? How I lived to be with him, to help him fulfill the artistic destiny for which he was so clearly meant? I stopped focusing on my own art, but I did not care. I only wanted him to be content, to be as productive as he wanted to be. When he touched me—

when we made love on the mattress he kept in the studio, for nights when he needed to work late—I felt as though I was one of his sculptures, being molded into a more perfect image of myself. An image that showed me the way he saw me—as I had never been seen before by the boys I had gone out with or awkwardly made love to. I was being touched by a master's hand.

After the sketches for the mural, he asked me to pose for another project—a magazine cover, he told me. I was supposed to wear a long dress and hold a staff. "What is the staff for?" I asked him. The pose did not make much sense to me. But he said it did not matter what it was for, that all I needed to do was stand still and look into the distance with that same expression, as though I were peering into the future. I had become used to posing, by this time. My legs no longer cramped, and I was able to stand still for hours at a time.

One day, while he was taking a cigarette break on the balcony and I was walking aimlessly around the studio, I found out what the staff was for. I looked through a pile of recent sketches and saw the design for the magazine cover in colored chalk. It was rough, but I could already tell what it would be: a woman in a long white dress, across which she wore a red, white, and green sash. From the staff she was holding hung a banner, on which was the old shield of Hungary, with the crown of St. István. At the top of the sketch was the name of the magazine: *The White Hart*. I dropped it as though I had been burned. Why was Antal designing the cover for what everyone knew was right-wing monarchist propaganda? Surely he was not a monarchist himself? I did not know what to think.

I wanted to ask him about it when he returned to the studio, but he was in one of his moods: abrupt, almost angry, wanting to return to work. I knew it was not a good time to ask him anything. But it bothered me, as I lay in my bed at night, in my parents' apartment. I told myself that I would go ask him, that surely he would have a reasonable explanation. I had never gone to his studio unless he asked me, but he loved me—surely he wouldn't mind.

The next day, a Sunday, I went.

Another tenant was going in as I arrived at the building, so I did not need to ring for Antal to let me in. I walked up the three flights of stairs to the studio. I paused at the top—those three flights always put me out of breath, although with his long legs he ran up them easily, despite his smoking.

The door of the studio had swung open several centimeters: it was old, and needed a new bolt. Through it I could hear two voices. One was his. The other was a woman's.

"Who is she?" the woman asked, angrily. "Another one of your students? I promise you, Antal, if I find you've slept with her, I will leave you. I can't stand it anymore. I can't stand the way you treat me—or the way you treat them!"

"Márta, please," he said. "How can you think I would want anyone but you? You're my muse, the woman for whom my soul has always longed. If I lost you, I would be a dead man. I would throw myself off the Szabadság Bridge. Don't you know that I love you, and only you?"

I could not listen anymore. I ran down the stairs, not caring whether they heard the clatter of my heels. I was so hurt, so angry. At him, and at her, for the words he had said to her, for being the woman he had said them to. I wanted to hurt him somehow, but I felt so powerless. I wandered around the streets, not caring where I was going, until I came to the Danube. There was the Szabadság Bridge, and for a moment I considered throwing myself off it, as he had just said he would. I even looked down over the railing into the swirling green waters. But the impulse passed. Instead, I walked along the river for hours, with my arms wrapped around me as though holding myself together, trying to wipe away the tears that kept streaming down my face.

Finally, I thought, I can't just keep walking. I must go home. And that was when I saw it: his famous statue, in front of the building everyone knew was the headquarters of the secret police. It was the statue of a woman, larger than life, arms raised to the sky. Was it her—was she the one who had modeled for it? I wondered what it was an allegory of.

All those women, all those sketches, always representing something other than themselves.

I walked into that building and denounced Antal as a monarchist sympathizer.

Elena sat silent, looking down at her hands. Mrs. Moth waited.

"He was more than a sympathizer; he was one of the leading members of the monarchist party. When they searched his studio, they found magazines, letters, lists of names. He was so stupid, so confident he would not be caught, that he had hidden them under the floorboards—just where the secret police would look. First, he was made to denounce the other members of the organization. And then, he was sent away. Not just him—his wife Márta, even the little girl. They said his wife was complicit because she had posed for some of the covers. I wonder if she knew what they were for . . . "

Again she paused. Then, she looked up and said, "I could not draw after that. I left school, went to work in a factory like my father. When my supervisor learned that I had been in an art program, he asked me to design a logo for a shampoo. He liked the logo I created, and after that, I was moved to the unit that designed product labels. I have made packaging for chocolate bars, cigarettes, face cream. When the political system changed, the factory closed, and I went to work for a German company with an office in Budapest. There, I created advertising campaigns. That is what I do—or what I did, until I retired last year. Once the files became available, I was able to find out what had happened to them. The girl died that winter—she had a heart condition, and she could not survive the cold and privation of the prison camp. Her mother hanged herself shortly after. I was not able to find out what had happened to Antal. His file was missing."

Elena looked at Mrs. Moth. "So, you see . . . " She did not finish the sentence, but seemed to be waiting.

"Yes," said Mrs. Moth finally. "Thank you for what has been an interesting and informative story. I'm sure the events you describe must have caused you much grief. Now, if you follow Hyacinth, she will show you the way to the aviary."

"Come with me, Miss Kovács," said Hyacinth, rising.

Elena rose. She felt tired and bewildered. Was that it, was that all there was to it? Not knowing what else to do, she followed the secretary to the French doors. Hyacinth opened them and pointed down the sloping lawn.

"Just follow the path," said Hyacinth. And there it was, at the bottom of a lawn: a path bordered with flowers, winding off into the distance. "It will take you to the right place. When you get there, just tell the Professor that Mrs. Moth sent you."

Elena stepped outside, into the sunlight, and followed the path.

Mrs. Moth sighed and took off her sensible pumps. It had been a long day.

"Why do they always want us to punish them?" asked Hyacinth.

"Because they don't realize how effectively they do it themselves," said Mrs. Moth. "I'm curious: could you bring me the files for the Andrássys?"

"I've already pulled them," said Hyacinth. "Here is the wife, Márta, and the daughter, Judit. Antal's is not yet closed."

"And?" said Mrs. Moth.

Hyacinth opened the file folders on her lap, glanced through them quickly, and said in her efficient secretary's voice, "Márta and Judit Andrássy arrived together. They were sent to the children's section. She had been a primary school teacher, so she worked with the children while she was here. When Judit was old enough, they were sent on. There are pictures of a party that was given for them, with chocolate and raspberry cake. Everyone was sad to see them go."

"And Antal?"

"He escaped from the prison camp. That explains why his file was missing: who would want to admit that a prisoner had escaped? But of course our files are complete. He made his way to England, where he took a different name. He has become a celebrated artist, part of the Trash Art movement. He has married twice since." Hyacinth looked up at Mrs. Moth. "That doesn't seem fair."

"We are not in the business of justice, my dear," said Mrs. Moth. "I'm sure we'll encounter Antal Andrássy eventually, and I'm sure he'll tell us his story. Would you mind putting away the nest before you go?"

"Of course," said Hyacinth, rising. "I'll put it on one of the back shelves. Anything else?"

"No, thank you," said Mrs. Moth. She poured herself another cup of coffee, leaned back into the armchair, and looked out into the garden, where the roses were blooming. As they always were.

THEODORA GOSS (b. Budapest, Hungary, 1968) *is the author of the short story collection* In the Forest of Forgetting *(2006);* Interfictions *(2007), a short story anthology co-edited with Delia Sherman;* Voices from Fairyland *(2008), a poetry anthology with critical essays and a selection of her own poems; and* The Thorn and the Blossom, *a novella in a two-sided accordion format. She has been a finalist for the Nebula, Locus, Crawford, and Mythopoeic Awards, as well as on the Tiptree Award Honor List, and has won the World Fantasy and Rhysling Awards. Her work has been translated into Czech, Polish, Serbian, Russian, and Japanese. She lives in Boston, where she teaches writing and literature at Boston University.*

Commentary on "Elena's Egg": *I wrote it in Budapest, at a desk in the apartment that had once belonged to my grandmother, where I had played as a child. My mother escaped from Hungary when I was only five years old, and I grew up in the United States, but I always remembered the apartment, with the large windows that look out onto the park around the Hungarian National Museum. I returned there this summer to write, and it became Elena's apartment in the story. When I was asked to write a gothic story set in an unusual locale, I immediately thought of Hungary and the Communist era. I wanted to write a story that would not rely on the usual gothic tropes. I had recently completely a doctoral dissertation on the gothic, so I was steeped in mysterious passages, significant portraits, and ancient sins. I wanted to write a story that, rather than having the trappings, was deeply gothic at its heart. For me, the heart of the gothic is the carceral; its central horror is the realization that the universe you inhabit is a closed system from which you cannot escape. This idea of the gothic comes from Eve Kosofsky Sedgwick's* The Coherence of Gothic Conventions, *in which she argues that the central trope of the gothic is live burial, and from Franz Kafka. We are no longer afraid of vampires, but we still fear entrapment and loss of meaning. In my story, I wanted to write two stories: the one Elena tells, which involves more obviously gothic motifs of illicit sexuality and betrayal, and the larger story in which she arrives, is judged, and is sent on—all in ways and by standards she does not understand. In that larger story, the story she tells does not have the same meaning. She is part of a universe with standards different from ours. I did not make that universe explicitly horrific—that would have been too easy, and perhaps too much in the lineage of Kafka. Instead, it appears to be pleasant, although bureaucratic—but what happens in it is beyond our understanding. It is a closed system, like the Communism from which my mother escaped. But its files are complete. No escape is possible. That, I think, is more horrifying than vampires.*

THE GIRL IN THE BLUE COAT

ANNA TABORSKA

So it's our last day together. You've been a good listener. And thanks to you I'll have a voice—albeit a posthumous one . . . I'm sorry—I've made you feel uncomfortable. But I believe that's what you wanted to cover today—my thoughts on my imminent demise. Well, we can do that, but first I want to tell you a story. I've never told it to anyone, but then again you're not really anyone—are you? Please don't be offended—you know I value your work, and one day you'll be a successful writer in your own right and under your own name. But today you're just the extension of a dying old man.

The painkillers they're giving me have stopped working; the pain is becoming unbearable, and soon I'll be on morphine. The doctors tell me I'll be hallucinating and delusional, and nobody will believe the ranting of a cancer-ridden old man . . . Is the Dictaphone working? Good . . . As you're my ghost writer, the story I'll tell you is most appropriate because it's a ghost story—at least, I think it is . . . Do I believe in them? Perhaps once you hear the story, *you'll* be able to tell *me*. I don't know. It all happened long ago . . .

I'd only been working at *The History Magazine* for four months, but they were pleased with my research skills, and I was the only person on the staff who spoke Polish. It was my second job since leaving university, and I'd already cut my teeth on an established, if somewhat trashy, London daily. So when the powers that be decided to revisit the Holocaust, the Senior Editor chose me to go to Poland.

I'd been to Poland before, of course. My mother's family hailed from the beautiful city of Krakow, and I'd been taken there fairly regularly as a boy to visit my aunt and cousins. But this time I was to travel to Międzyrzec—a small and unremarkable town, the name of which caused considerable hilarity among my colleagues, and which I myself could scarcely pronounce.

"You'll be going to My... Mee... Here," said my boss, thrusting a piece of paper at me with a touch of good-natured annoyance at the intricacies of Polish orthography. Foreign names and places were never his thing in any case. He seemed happiest in his leather chair behind his vast desk in the *Magazine* office, and I sometimes suspected that the furthest he'd been from Blighty was Majorca, where he'd holiday with his wife and children at every given opportunity. And nothing wrong with that; nothing wrong at all—I thought—as I drove my hire car through the grey and brown Polish countryside, trying hard not to pile into any of the horse-drawn carts that occasionally pulled out in front of me without warning from some misty dirt side track.

I'd done my homework before driving the eighty miles east from Warsaw to Międzyrzec. Before the outbreak of World War II there had been about 12,000 Jews living in the town—almost three-quarters of the population. The town had synagogues, Jewish schools, Jewish shops, a Jewish theatre, two Jewish football teams, a Jewish brothel and a Jewish fire brigade. I wondered idly whether the Jewish fire brigade was sent to extinguish fires in Christian homes too, or just in Jewish ones. I figured it was the former, as by all accounts the Poles and Jews got on like a house on fire—excuse the pun—and most of the town's inhabitants worked happily side by side in a Jewish-owned factory, producing kosher pig hair brushes, which were sold as far afield as Germany. In fact, commerce in Międzyrzec flourished to the degree that the envious, poverty-stricken inhabitants of surrounding towns and villages referred to the place as 'Little America'... Does prosperity render a man better disposed towards his fellow man? I don't know. Certainly, during the course of my research I read of various acts of generosity—big and small—which were extended to others regardless of background, so that, for example, when a film such as *The Dybbuk* came to town, the cinema owner would organise a free screening for all the citizens of Międzyrzec, and the queue stretched half way down the main street.

As with any positive status quo, the good times in Międzyrzec were not to last long. When war broke out in September 1939, the town was bombed, then taken by the Germans, before being handed over to the Russians, and finally falling into German hands once more. The horrors that followed were fairly typical for Nazi-occupied Poland. The Polish population was terrorised, while the Jews were harassed, attacked, rounded up and either murdered on the spot or sealed in a ghetto, from which they were eventually shipped off to death camps. Nothing new there, I thought, as by now I was becoming—not jaded by all the atrocities I'd read about, but something of a reluctant expert on Nazi war crimes and the pattern they followed in the towns and villages of German-occupied Poland. And yet something about the destruction of this surprisingly harmonious community—not just the murder of people, but the annihilation of a functional and thriving symbiotic organism formed from thousands of disparate souls—added to the customary level of distress that I'd somehow learned to live with since being assigned to the Second World War project.

Finally the countryside gave way to ramshackle housing, and the dark green and white road sign confirmed that I'd arrived at my destination. All I had to do now was find the town library, where I had a meeting with the librarian turned amateur historian—a pleasant fellow with a neatly trimmed brown beard, who furnished me with the details of several elderly local residents, including a lady who "remembered the War."

"She doesn't have a telephone," he told me as I thanked him and took the piece of paper with the names and addresses, "but she's almost certain to be at home. You can't miss the house. It's the last house but one on the left as you leave town, going east. It's one of the old wooden houses, and you'd be forgiven for thinking that you'd already left Międzyrzec, as those old houses are virtually out in the countryside."

I decided to start at the far end of town, with the old lady. Everything was as my bearded friend had said: the ugly apartment blocks and equally unattractive family houses (presumably built hastily after the war to rehouse those whose homes had been destroyed) gave way to what looked like small wooden farmhouses, with fields and meadows behind them stretching away into the distance.

I drove slowly in an effort to ascertain which house was the last but one on the left-hand side before leaving town. I was fairly sure it was a run-down wooden house with peeling green paint, set back from the road. I drove past just to check, but I'd been right—there was only one more house beyond the one I'd instinctively picked out. I turned the car around carefully and doubled back, pulling up on the grass verge by the side of the road. Chain link fencing some six feet in height surrounded the property, and the only way in—from the roadside, at least—was through a gate, which was locked. There was a bell, but no intercom. I pressed the bell and waited. After a minute or so I pressed it again, not sure if it was even working.

After a couple more minutes, the front door of the house opened with a creaking worthy of an old horror movie, and an elderly grey-haired woman peered out apprehensively. I waved at her and after a moment's hesitation she waved back. Then she went back inside and shut the door behind her. I was taken aback and nearly rang the doorbell again, but then the woman reappeared, pulling a woollen shawl over her shoulders. I smiled at her reassuringly as she made her way slowly and painfully down the porch steps and across the front yard towards me.

"How can I help you?" she asked through the fencing.

"Hello, my name is Frank Johnson," I told her. "I work for *The History Magazine* in London, and I understand from Dr. Lipinski that you remember the time when there was a ghetto . . . " I never got to finish my sentence. The old lady had been observing me with amicable curiosity, but now her face crumpled and she started sobbing uncontrollably, tears streaming down her face and gathering in her wrinkles. I was mortified and started to mumble a hasty apology, but the woman raised her hand in a conciliatory gesture.

"I'm sorry," she managed to say. "I'll take some medicine for my nerves. Please come back in an hour and I'll tell you all about the ghetto." I smiled at her as best I could and nodded my head vigorously. "The gate will be open," she added, trying unsuccessfully to stem the flow of tears with a shaky hand.

"I'll come back in an hour," I told her.

There was really nothing constructive I could do in an hour, but I didn't want to make the old lady any more uncomfortable by sitting outside her house, so I drove back into the town centre, parked up and sat in my car. There was no decent pub to speak of and there was no point in getting a cup of tea, as I knew from my experience of Polish hospitality that I'd be having tea and cake at the old lady's house whether I wanted it or not.

I'd interviewed survivors of trauma before, and I'd had interviewees cry during interviews, but never before I'd even started. I'd always imagined

Polish peasants to be a hard breed, taking history's worst cruelties in their stride and not shedding much in the way of tears for themselves, let alone for the plight of an ethnic minority that shared neither their religion nor their cultural traditions. If nothing else, the old lady should provide some good firsthand material for *The History Magazine*—provided she was able to pull herself together and wasn't totally nuts.

After half an hour of sitting in the car, going through my notes and interview questions, I got bored and decided to drive back to the old lady's house and see if she'd talk to me a bit earlier than agreed. This time I knew exactly where I was going, so I was able to concentrate less on houses and house numbers, and more on the road itself. It struck me how deserted it was. Despite having only one lane in each direction, this was the main road heading east from Warsaw, all the way to Belarus; and yet my car seemed to be the only vehicle on it. Not even an old peasant on a hay cart in sight. Perhaps an accident somewhere further up had stopped the traffic, but that would explain the lack of cars in one direction, not both. Perhaps all the other drivers knew something I didn't. . . I chided myself for letting my imagination run away with me. But as I pulled up alongside the chain link fence, I couldn't shake the feeling of unease.

The gate was open, as promised. I wondered if I should ring the doorbell anyway, to warn the old lady of my imminent arrival, but I didn't want to bring her all the way out in the cold again, so I slung my bag over my shoulder, locked the car and let myself in, closing the gate behind me. As I headed across the front yard to the rickety old house, a chill breeze stirred around me, whispering in the unmown grass and rustling the leaves of the sapling trees that had seeded themselves and sprouted unchecked on either side of the stone slab path. Although only a dozen or so metres separated me from the old lady's porch, I paused to zip up my parka. As I did so, the breeze grew stronger, making a high pitched sound as it weaved its way through the eaves of the house. Unexpectedly it died down, and the air around me was as still as the proverbial grave. Then a sudden gust of wind—this time blowing from the direction of the field behind the house. Urgent, angry almost, the wind brought with it something else: a sound—human, yet unearthly; a cry or moan—distant, but so heartfelt and full of despair that, despite the warmth of my down anorak, I shivered.

I made my way to the back of the house and looked out over the field that led away to a swampy patch of land, and ended in a stream or river of some sort—obscured by tall grasses and reeds. Beyond the line of water, a wasteland of browse and bushes stretched away to a railway track, and then further, to a dark tree-line on the horizon. A mist was rising from the marshy land and, as I peered into the miasma, I thought I saw something: a flash of blue against the grey and brown. The wind blew in my direction again, and this time I was sure that the sound I heard was a young woman weeping.

"Hello!" I called out.

"Hello?" The voice came from behind me, making me jump. "Young man!"

I'd forgotten all about the old lady and my interview. She must have seen me out of a window, and was now holding open the back door, gesticulating for me to come inside. "You'll catch your death of cold!" she chastised gently. I noticed a slight frown crease the woman's already furrowed brow as I threw a last glance back over my shoulder before entering the house. Apart from that passing shadow on her face, my interviewee was a different person from the one I'd left sobbing her heart out almost an hour earlier. Calm and collected, she smiled at me in a warm and friendly manner. When she spoke, her voice was clear and steady.

In no time I found myself sitting in a worn armchair in a small parlour, nursing a glass of black tea in an elaborately engraved silver-coloured holder.

"I'm afraid I don't have much to offer you," said my hostess, holding out a plate with four different types of homemade cake. "You said you wanted to know about the War. I'll tell you everything I remember."

Her name was Bronislava. She was born in Międzyrzec and lived with her mother in an apartment block near the town centre. Her street was mixed Polish and Jewish. Not all of the Jews spoke Polish, but most of the Poles spoke at least some Yiddish, and it was normal for children from the two ethnic groups to play together in the street. Bronislava's father had died when she was little and, as her mother was out cleaning for some of the town's more affluent residents during the week, the little girl spent most of her time at the house of her best friends Esther and Mindla, so that her friends' mum was like a second mother to her. Bronislava and Esther were nine when war broke out; Mindla was a couple of years older. For a while not much changed, but slowly rationing and other increasing restrictions meant that hunger and fear crept into all their lives. Esther and Mindla's family was ordered to wear armbands with the Star of David, along with all the other

Jewish residents, but at this point violence against the Jewish community was incidental rather than systematic.

Then one day, German soldiers with dogs and guns, and auxiliary Ukrainian militia, came marching into Bronislava's street. They swept through the houses, pulling out Jewish families, beating them and leading them away. Bronislava and Esther were playing with the other children. Mindla was out running an errand. When Esther's mother heard all the commotion, she came running out to the two girls, grabbed their hands and tried to pull them away from the shouting soldiers. The three of them were caught and shoved along behind the other Jews. Amid the blows and kicks that rained down on them from all sides, Esther's mother tried to shield the two girls as best she could. Then Bronislava's mother, who had been sewing at home that day, spotted her daughter out of the window across the road, and came running out, shouting that her child was Polish. Somehow she managed to fight her way to Bronislava, and yanked her away from Esther and her mother. Bronislava screamed and grappled with her mother. She tried to go after her best friend, but her mother scooped her up and ran back to their building.

The old woman spoke in a dry, dispassionate, almost robotic way, which I would have found a little disconcerting had I not known that she'd taken some kind of tranquiliser especially for the occasion. She spoke of street roundups, summary executions and coldblooded murder. When she told me about a hyped-up Ukrainian militiaman, in the service of the German military, ripping a baby apart with his bare hands, her voice wavered, and I realised that even with whatever drugs she'd taken, she was making a valiant effort to keep it together.

Sometime after Bronislava's Jewish neighbours had been taken away, the German army took over the building in which she and her mother lived, and the remaining residents were evicted. Some of them moved in with extended family elsewhere; others were forcibly re-housed with other Poles.

"We were lucky," Bronislava told me. "My mother had cousins who lived on the outskirts of Międzyrzec—in this very house. Out here things were quieter. The Germans raided the farms to make sure that the peasants weren't hiding any livestock or reserves of grain over the allotted ration quota, but it was easier to grow some vegetables here and occasionally buy a few eggs from a neighbour who'd managed to hang on to a hen or two. My mother and I helped out in the house, and my mother still took on the odd cleaning or sewing job, so we got by somehow. We were hungry, but we weren't starving . . . Would you like some more tea?" I shook my head and she carried on.

"I quickly discovered that there was no love lost between our cousins and the family next door, and the reasons for this became clear soon enough. I know one shouldn't speak ill of the dead," Bronislava frowned, "but there is no other way to speak of those monsters. The farmer was a mean-spirited and violent drunk. His wife was a greedy, spiteful and malicious gossip, and their son, although slimmer in build than his bloated, overfed parents, was a vile combination of the two of them in both temper and habit. As soon as they laid eyes on my mother and me, they hated us with as much venom as they did the rest of our household.

"I asked my aunt how it was that the next door neighbours were fat and well dressed, while the rest of us were constantly patching up the tatters that hung off our emaciated bodies. And how was it that, when German soldiers carried out their 'inspections', they tore through all the houses—including ours—shouting, kicking things over and showering down blows on anyone who didn't get out of their way fast enough; and yet, when the same soldiers went next door, they joked and chatted with the owner, got drunk with him, and came out clutching food or a bottle of vodka, or sometimes a watch, a piece of jewellery.

"*We don't speak about it*, my aunt told me. *Just make sure you stay away from them.* Well, being told to stay away from something usually has the opposite effect on little girls, and—despite the horror of those times—I was no different. I spent all my spare time playing in the field at the back of the house and watching the neighbours' property. Then, one evening, my curiosity was rewarded.

"That day, a German patrol had swept through the street, looking for food and valuables. They were in a filthy mood, as nobody had anything left. They trashed our house and hit my uncle across the face when he was unable to give them anything of interest. Finally they went next door and left several hours later, singing and laughing. I figured they wouldn't be back again that evening, so I risked venturing outside.

"The sun had just gone down, but a strange light lingered. It was magic hour, and the field and marshland beyond it glimmered golden-blue. The peculiar light brought out all the blues and purples in the field, so that the cornflowers glowed like luminous azure eyes in the grass. I looked over the tumble-down bit of fence that separated my cousins' land from the neighbours', and my heart skipped a beat. Out in the neighbours' field, a brilliant swathe of bright blue shimmered in the shadows. At first I thought it was mist rising from the damp grass. But it was too solid to be mist and, when it moved, I realised that it was a human figure.

"As quietly as I could, I headed towards it. The figure was small and slim, and I finally worked out that it was a girl—a girl in a blue coat. And then it dawned on me that I'd seen that coat before. The girl turned suddenly, as though sensing my presence. She froze for a moment, then started to run back towards the neighbours' house.

"*Wait!* I clambered over a rotted piece of fence and gave chase. As the girl fled, the hood of her coat came down, and a flurry of matted black tresses flowed out behind her. Despite how thin she now was, I was almost sure. But how could it be? How could someone I'd grieved for every day for three years be alive and fleeing from me through a field that was rapidly turning murky grey?

"The girl was evidently weak, but she had a head start, and I realized I wouldn't catch up with her before she reached the neighbours' house. Desperate, I took a risk and called out. *Mindla? Mindla, wait!* She heard me and stopped dead. She turned towards me slowly, her whole body shaking from the exertion of running barely fifty metres or so. She was emaciated—skeletal almost—no longer the chubby-cheeked twelve-year-old that I'd loved and looked up to, but a gaunt teenager with haunted, hollow eyes. Abruptly magic hour ended, and we were in darkness. We stood facing each other, trembling. Then a small gasp escaped Mindla's cracked lips and, as I rushed towards her, she slumped into my arms.

"From then on, Mindla and I met every night at the border of the two properties in which we were reluctant lodgers. I learned how Mindla had returned from the bakery on that day to find her mother and sister gone. The Polish family next door told her that it wasn't safe for her to stay in the street as the Germans could return at any moment to look for stragglers. She managed to get to the factory where her father worked, but all the Jewish workers had been taken away. So she hid in a series of attics and basements in Międzyrzec, moving on when each hiding-place became unsafe. Finally there was nowhere else to hide, so she left the town one night with a young Jewish woman and her fiancé. They'd tried to survive in the forest, hiding in a hollowed-out tree trunk by day and scavenging for food when night fell, but when winter started to draw in, the cold and hunger became unbearable. They came across another group of Jews trying to survive in the open, who told them that a Polish peasant was taking in Jewish girls for payment. Mindla knew she wouldn't survive winter in the forest, so she decided to take a chance. She still had a couple of gold coins that her mother had sewn into the lining of her coat when enemy soldiers first entered town, so she followed the instructions given and made it to the peasant's house.

"*The man told me to give him everything I had,* Mindla explained. *In return he would hide me and feed me . . . But now he says there isn't enough food, so I only get a bowl of soup and a piece of bread a day. During the day I lie hidden behind straw on a kind of shelf above the animals, at the back of the house. That way the Germans don't see me when they come. Sometimes the soldiers stay for hours, drinking homemade vodka with the man and his son. I have to lie very still. I get cramps in my legs, and sometimes bugs crawl on me.*

"Mindla told me about two other Jewish girls who'd been hiding in the peasant's house when she arrived. They'd fled their home village of Rudniki when the roundups started, but the rest of their family had been taken away. One day the peasant and his son came for the sisters in the middle of the night, and Mindla never saw them again. When she asked what had happened to them, the peasant's wife told her to mind her own business, and the peasant said that a relative of theirs had come and taken them away. But Mindla must have had doubts as to the girls' fate because she kept returning to them in our conversations.

"I told Mindla that I would ask my mother if she could stay with us. *No,* said Mindla. *I won't put your lives in danger.* I related our conversation to my mother, and she said that Mindla was right; we didn't have the privileges that the next door neighbour had—unlike his house, ours got searched from top to bottom—and, in any case, there were no hiding-places in our house. So Mindla and I met outdoors, sometimes in the pouring rain. I lived for those meetings. I put aside what little food I could, as did my mother. We didn't tell my cousins what I was up to. The fewer who knew, the better. Sometimes my mother caught me sneaking out at night. She was very afraid for me, but she didn't stop me.

"One night Mindla was late to meet me. Finally she appeared, looking paler and more frightened than normal. She usually managed a wan smile and a few words when she saw me, but this time she was withdrawn and silent. It took me a while to get her to admit what had happened. The farmer had become tired of hiding her and feeding her. He said that he wanted payment. *I said that I'd already given him everything, and he said 'Not everything.'* Mindla cried as she told me that the man had tried to force himself on her. She was only saved because her screams brought out the man's wife, who called her 'an ungrateful little whore,' and dragged her husband back to bed. I don't think I fully comprehended what Mindla was telling me—at twelve I was very naive about the ways of the world—but I knew that my beloved friend was in trouble and that I had to do something. *Let's run away together*, I told her. *Let's go right now—tonight.* Mindla looked at me with love and sadness. I've never seen such sadness in anybody's eyes. *We can't run away*, she told me. *There's nowhere to run.*

"That night I had a terrible nightmare. Mindla was standing by the marsh at the bottom of the field. She was only in her underwear. She reached out to me and at first I thought that she had that same sadness in her eyes, but as I drew closer, I saw that her eyes were gone." Bronislava paused. I had been engrossed in her recollection, and the sudden silence startled me. I looked at her, but she avoided my gaze. She turned away and pretended to blow her nose, but I could see that she was wiping her eyes.

"The next night Mindla didn't come," she finally said, then fell silent once more. I waited in vain for her to speak. After what seemed like a long time, but was probably only half a minute, I finally asked her what had happened.

"I waited for hours," she said. "It was raining and very cold. Eventually my mother came out and found me by the fence, soaking wet. I contracted pneumonia and nearly died." Another pause.

"What happened to Mindla?"

"She was never seen again."

"Well, what do you think happened to her?"

"I don't *think*. I *know* what happened. They killed her. The farmer and that son of his. As soon as I saw my Mindla's blue coat stretched over the grotesque body of that woman, I knew that they'd killed her."

"You saw the farmer's wife wearing Mindla's coat?"

"Yes. When I was well enough to get out of bed, I looked out of the window and saw her parading around shamelessly in it. It had always been too big for Mindla. I remember, she'd seen that coat in a shop and fallen in love with it. That was just before war broke out. She persuaded her mother that she'd 'grow into it' and eventually her mother gave in and bought it for her. But Mindla never grew into it. Instead of filling out like other girls her age, she'd been starved and the coat always hung off her. But it was too small for that awful woman—she couldn't even do the buttons up, and yet she strutted around in it as though Mindla had never existed. God knows why she wanted it—it was tattered and badly worn, but it was a pretty colour, and the woman was greedy.

"I flew out of the house before my aunt could stop me, and I confronted her. I asked what she'd done to Mindla. The woman shouted at me to mind my own business. Her husband came storming out of the house and told me that if I didn't shut up, he'd make sure that something very bad happened to me.

"The next thing I knew, German soldiers came storming into my cousins' house. They beat up my uncle and tore up the floorboards in the kitchen. The next door neighbour had told them that we'd hidden grain under the floor. They didn't find anything, and the farmer got a clout round the ear hole for making them waste their time, but he'd made his point.

"I didn't confront him again until the war was over. The communist authorities weren't interested in the wild accusations of an adolescent girl—or her mother. In any case, the farmer was a man of influence. He had grown wealthy on the suffering of the unfortunate souls he had exploited and, although the other residents on the street viewed him with distaste and went out of their way to avoid him, he didn't care. He now drank with the NKVD, and, when the Soviets left Poland to the Polish communists, he drank with the chief of police. It was made very clear to me that if I continued with my accusations, things would end very badly for my mother. By the time the communists were overthrown, the farmer and his family were dead. The man and his wife died of natural causes, but not until they had buried their only son. It's said that he was drunk and—for some inexplicable reason—wandered out onto the tracks beyond the field at the back of his parents' house, where he was hit by a train." The old lady paused, and I thought that she'd finished her story. I tried to think of something appropriate to say, but after a moment's hesitation, during which she seemed to be sizing me up, she carried on.

"Sometimes I dream about her," she said. "Sometimes, especially in autumn and in early spring, when the mist rises from the marshy ground, I see her walking along the ditch at the far end of the field. Mostly I just hear her crying . . . " The woman broke off, tired and sad. I could tell I wasn't going to get much more out of her. She fixed her rheumy eyes on me, and seemed to wait for my full attention. I placed my glass of tea carefully on the table and returned her gaze. Something in her tone changed, became more urgent, almost pleading. "I've waited fifty years to tell her story to someone who would listen," she finally said. "To someone who could tell her story to the world and . . . right the wrong."

I lowered my eyes and finished my honey cake, weighing up whether or not to tell my down-to-earth editor the story of the girl in the blue coat. As I sipped the last of my tea, I already knew that the 'ghost story' wouldn't make it into my research notes . . . I know what you're thinking, but, in any case, it wouldn't have made a difference; my boss dropped the Międzyrzec story. It wasn't that he was unhappy with my report—quite the contrary; I'd managed to find two credible eye witnesses of the so-called 'ghetto liquidations,' during which the Jews who had been rounded up or enticed out of hiding with promises of immunity were robbed, beaten and murdered, or herded onto trucks and driven to the local train station for transportation to the gas chambers of Treblinka and Majdanek . . . No, my research had been thorough, as ever, but the ghetto liquidation story was abandoned in favour of the Chelmno death camp; aerial photography had uncovered a hitherto unknown mass grave in the nearby forest, and my boss was keen for *The History Magazine* to be the first publication outside Poland to cover the find.

And so I forgot all about Międzyrzec, and the old lady, and the girl in the blue coat. Until fifteen years later—when I was working as a war correspondent for Reuters in war-torn Iraq. I'd been stationed with the US regiment I told you about for over a month. We'd been lucky: the territory that came under our patrols was fairly quiet, and the worst thing about the posting was the heat and the desert wind. No matter how carefully you covered up, you could always taste sand in your mouth, and the grit would irritate your nose and make your eyes run—despite the shades we all wore virtually around the clock.

Then one night I saw her—the dead girl from Międzyrzec. She stood in the mist at the bottom of the old woman's field, looking at me with eyes of death and sorrow. The cold blue-grey of that Polish landscape couldn't have been further from the blistering yellow of the desert into which I awoke, and yet no amount of burning desert dust could dispel the horror I felt. That day the convoy I was travelling with drove into a trap—a double whammy, if you like—of a landmine and a car-bomb driven by a suicide bomber, who died on the spot, along with five of the soldiers who'd become my friends over the past few weeks. Nobody escaped without injury; some of us lost limbs, one young man from Idaho lost an eye, another boy lost part of his jaw. I was lucky; I escaped with shrapnel in my knee and cuts to my back and arms. But it shook my confidence in my indestructibility—for a while, at least.

With all the blood and guts and horror of the aftermath of the attack, I forgot about the girl in the blue coat once more. But she came back. Whenever I became complacent, whenever things were going a bit too well, or when I simply forgot about my own mortality, she came back. Don't get me wrong, people weren't blown up around me every time I dreamt about her, but each time reminded me of the unpredictability and cruelty of the world we live in; of death which will one day come for all of us, and of the fact that she's still waiting—waiting out there in the cold, the damp and the dark for her story to be told . . . And I've been dreaming a lot lately.

I see I've rendered you speechless. Well, I'm sorry. Like the old lady in Międzyrzec, I've waited many years to tell that story. I realise it doesn't quite fit with the image of the tough old reporter that we've created together, but you must promise to allow me to tell it to the world as I've told it to you today. You know it now. And, believe me, if either of us is to have any peace in this world or the next, then it must be told. Promise me.

"His words, not mine." The ghost writer looked his publisher straight in the eye. "So you see, we have to keep it in. It's what he wanted." It was a plea more than a statement.

"Nonsense!" the publisher scoffed. The writer's sentimentality and inexperience were starting to annoy him. Perhaps it had been a mistake to give the Johnson gig to someone so young. "Don't you see? A supernatural yarn about a dead girl goes against everything else you've written. It's out of character, it's completely inconsistent with the rest of the book; it will alienate our readers and ruin Johnson's reputation."

"You don't understand . . . " the writer implored.

"But I do understand. I understand that including a drugged up old man's fantasies in what is to be his legacy to the world would not just be *unfair* to Frank; it would be a total violation of the trust he placed in all of us to tell his story." The publisher studied the writer closely. The young man's face had blanched and he was starting to sweat. "Look," the older man's voice softened a little, "Frank Johnson was hard as nails. Not a fanciful bone in his body. If he'd been in his right mind the last time you saw him, he'd never have said what he said. He was a tough, unshakeable war correspondent who did a dangerous and responsible job, and did it well—you know that better than anyone. Now his reputation is in our hands. And there's no way this publishing house is going to destroy his legacy for the sake of some crazy story that he told you in his last days, high on morphine."

The writer had lowered his gaze to his hands, which were clasping and unclasping in his lap like the death throes of a beached fish. When he raised his eyes again, the publisher was shocked to see in them a look of desperation and—perhaps—fear. When he finally spoke, his voice shook, and for a moment the publisher had the worrying notion that the writer was going to burst into tears.

"You don't understand," the young man practically begged. "I've . . . seen her."

"What? . . . Who?"

"The girl." The publisher stared at the writer uncomprehendingly. "The girl in the blue coat."

"What do you mean? Where?" The publisher wasn't sure what disturbed him more: the writer's evident breakdown or the fact that he now found himself alone in a room with a madman.

"In my dreams . . . Nightmares." The writer looked down at his now motionless hands. "She walks along the ditch at the bottom of a field. It's cold. It's lonely. When the wind blows in my direction, I can hear her crying. And then she looks at me . . . I see her every night . . . Her eyes are like death. Full of betrayal and sorrow that can never be healed. Grief not just for her own short, painful existence, but for all those whose bones or ashes lie in unmarked graves. I can't stand her eyes. The desolation in them gets inside you. It makes you wish you were dead. Makes you wish you'd never been born . . . " The publisher was too stunned to react and, after a moment's pause, the writer carried on. "I don't know how Frank Johnson lived with it . . . He was a . . . strong . . . man." The writer raised his eyes once more, but did not meet his boss's incredulous gaze. His attention was focused on the window at the far end of the office, behind his listener's back, where something—a gust from the air-conditioning unit perhaps—caused the reinforced textile strips of the cream-coloured blind to stir and rattle softly against the glass pane. He added quietly, "I'm not . . . that . . . strong . . . "

ANNA TABORSKA *(b. London, England, 1969) studied Experimental Psychology at Oxford University and went on to gainful employment in public relations, journalism and advertising, before throwing everything over to become a filmmaker and horror writer.*

Anna has directed two short films (Ela *and* The Sin)*, two documentaries* (My Uprising *and* A Fragment of Being*) and a one-hour television drama* (The Rain Has Stopped)*, which won two awards at the British Film Festival, Los Angeles, 2009. Anna has also worked on seventeen other films, including Ben Hopkins'* Simon Magus *(starring Noah Taylor and Rutger Hauer).*

Anna worked as a researcher and assistant producer on several BBC television programmes, including the series Auschwitz: The Nazis and the Final Solution *and* World War Two: Behind Closed Doors—Stalin, the Nazis and the West.

Anna's feature length screenplays include: Chainsaw, The Camp, Pizzaman *and* The Bloody Tower.

Short screenplays include: Little Pig *(finalist in the Shriekfest Film Festival Screenplay Competition 2009),* Curious Melvin *and* Arthur's Cellar.

Recently published short stories include: "Buy a Goat for Christmas" *(*Best New Werewolf Tales *Vol.1, 2012),* "Etude" *(*This Hermetic Legislature: A Homage to Bruno Schulz, *2012),* "Tea with the Devil" *(*Strange Halloween, *2012),* "Cut!" *(*The Screaming Book of Horror, *2012),* "Rusalka" *(*Exotic Gothic 4, *2012), and five stories published in* The Black Book of Horror, *volumes 5-9 (2009-2012).*

Anna's short story "Bagpuss" *was an Eric Hoffer Award Honoree and was published in* Best New Writing 2011, *and her story* "Little Pig" *from* The Eighth Black Book of Horror *was a runner up for the Abyss Awards 2011 and was picked for* The Best New Horror of the Year Volume Four *(2012).*

Poems include "Mrs. Smythe regrets going to the day spa" *(*Christmas: Peace on All The Earths, *2010),* "Song for Maud" *(*No Fresh Cut Flowers, An Afterlife Anthology, *2010) and three poems in* WHAT FEARS BECOME: An Anthology from the Horror Zine, *2011.*

Anna's debut short story collection will be out in late 2013.

Anna recently adapted Thana Niveau's story "Antlers" *(*Death Rattles, *2011) into a short screenplay and is currently trying to raise the money to film it.*

You can watch clips from Anna's films here: www.imdb.com/name/nm1245940/

Commentary on "The Girl in the Blue Coat": *I wanted to explore how powerful emotions can live on long after the people who experienced them have died, thanks to the power of storytelling. The ideal vehicle for this type of narrative* seemed to be the 'story within a story' format, so that's what I experimented with in "The Girl in the Blue Coat".

Mindla's story was told me by an elderly lady I interviewed for the BBC while working on a television series about Auschwitz. My interviewee's husband, also present at the interview, added that the local peasants had seen "Death walking up and down the ditch" in which Mindla's body had been dumped. I decided to make Mindla's story more 'western' and 'Gothic' by changing Death to the familiar trope of the restless spirit of a dead girl whose body has not been found. In reality, Mindla's partially clothed body was found in the ditch at the bottom of the peasants' fields, but not the bodies of the two Jewish girls also mentioned by my interviewee.

The town in the story is real (I simplified its name, which is actually made up of two words); its history and fate are real.

My interviewee's story wasn't used in the BBC series. It has haunted me ever since, as have the stories of many of the other 100 or so people I interviewed at that time. I don't really like to revisit those stories, but some of them have been keeping me awake lately.

NORTH AMERICA

BURIAL GROUNDS

NICK ANTOSCA

I

THERE ARE HUMAN BONES BURIED IN THE WOODS OUT BEHIND
our house.

By *our house*, I mean my family's, the one where my sister Jess and I grew
up. People hunted in those woods, but we didn't. My father once found
someone's hunting dog out there, its right front leg detached from its heaving body by a shotgun blast that had tattooed a nearby sapling with
buckshot. Some hunter must have accidentally maimed his own dog and
left it for dead. My dad carried the dog home, bandaged it, made a deathbed
for it, and, after he realized it wasn't going to die, named it Finch.

My father had a quiet, thoughtful way about him and a fondness for
family customs, like the elaborate breakfasts he prepared for us every
Saturday morning. He was a vegetarian except on Thanksgiving. He was also
an environmental engineer. When I was seven, he gave me a telescope, and
I would wake in the middle of the night and watch the moon.

Really, my dad was my only friend except for Daniel Autland, the son of
our nearest neighbors. Daniel and I liked to dig for treasure in the woods—
often we buried the same treasure we would later dig up, just to have
something to discover. Hood ornaments, toy cars, Star Wars action figures,
and a few of Jess's dolls, anything. "Look!" one of us would yell. "This must
have been hidden here for *years!*"

Daniel was braver than I was, predisposed to be the leader, the admired
rather than the admirer. He had a constant urge to climb trees—but only
high, dangerous trees, up which I was afraid to follow. Sometimes he would
not come down and I would go home alone. "I'm leaving," I would call up

to him, and his voice would float down from a hackberry tree or honeylocust, strangely peaceful: "I'm staying."

Sometimes, in turn, I think he was nonplussed by things I did. Nothing spectacularly strange—I was just inclined, as a boy, to play the game people often call "doctor." We didn't call it "doctor." We called it "brothers."

Like all children who play this game, we knew it ought to be secret.

Daniel's family, the Autlands, were the only people nearby like us. They didn't hunt either. The father, a gentle, bronzed geologist who fascinated me in ways I didn't understand until later, liked to go bird-watching and take long hikes beside the rocky creek that snaked through the woods. Sometimes he took Daniel with him, and my sister and I might go along too, three-legged Finch hobbling after us. To us, Mr. Autland was like an uncle. His hair and beard were pecan-brown, with a touch of ginger.

Like my father, Mr. Autland had moved his family to western Maryland to escape the concrete clamor of Washington, D.C. The two men had become friends. The summer I turned thirteen, Jess came out of the woods one day crying. She was nine. A storm had pounded the countryside the night before. Everything was wet, flattened. Jess was hugging herself. She told my dad a monster had come through the woods, whispered to her, grabbed her. Then she recanted, saying she'd only fallen and hurt herself. Jess had an imagination that way.

She was holed up in her room, inexplicably sulky, when I went outside the next afternoon. Another storm was boiling. It would break around nightfall, I figured.

Wandering along the edge of pignut hickories and chinquapins, I encountered Daniel's dad just leaving his own yard. I could tell he was about to set off on one of his walks, and I was hoping he'd invite me along with a sweep of his big arm, as he often did ("*Come* on, Evan and Jess, tag along. *Come* on, Finch."), but he seemed reluctant. So I asked the only question I could think of—"Where's Daniel?"—and he jerked his thumb in the direction of the house, saying, "He's got the flu. So do I, keep your distance." He hurried off into the grey and dripping woods.

After a moment, I began to follow.

The patter of water falling from branches and the moan of wind gusting up once in a while concealed the sounds of my passage. He moved quickly, his big dark ginger head ducking under low branches, his shoulders hunched.

For a long time, maybe forty-five minutes, he walked along the creek. His hands were jammed in his pockets and he didn't pause, as he usually did, to look around.

Then, ahead of us, crashing disturbed the undergrowth. He stopped, I crouched. Something was coming toward us, moving parallel to the creek from the opposite direction. I thought of Jess's monster—*it whispered to me, and then it grabbed me.* After a moment, my father appeared through the trees.

He saw our neighbor, but not me. Mr. Autland took a step back, and my father crunched toward him. His hair was wet and he was out of breath. He came to the edge of the steep creek bank and stood over the man, looking down at him.

"John . . . "

"Jess told me," said my father. Dad was a big man. His voice carried. "Now you tell me. What did you do?"

"I didn't do anything," said Mr. Autland, raising his palms as if to ward off a cloud of hornets. He took another step back. Now he was standing in the shallows of the swollen creek. He said, "Please."

"The police," said my father. "I'll get the police."

"John, I didn't do anything,"

My father, still panting, said, *"Alan . . . "* He began to descend the creek bank, steadying himself against the rocky incline with one arm, and our neighbor stretched out a hesitant hand like he was declaring a boundary—and touched my father's shoulder. My father reacted as if this were an electric jolt: a bearlike noise came from him, and his arm lashed up from the bank—there was something in it, a rock—and cracked Mr. Autland across the skull.

He toppled backward into six inches of creek, staring straight up, blood streaming from the gash. Slowly he sat up—blinking—stunned.

There was a moment then—I saw it in my dad's face—where things could have gone either way. Then dad walked into the creek.

"I can't help it!" Mr. Autland yelled.

My father beat him with the rock until a place in the front of his head caved in. Then he knelt over the body watching the water carry red pulp away. I was gripping a tree branch. A little rain had begun to fall and the wind was picking up.

I heard barking, crashing, in the forest behind me. Instinctively I shot to my feet. My father, hearing the noise, looked up and saw me. His horror must have mirrored my own. Finch limp-hopped happily out of the beeches, fur leaf-covered, and came to sit at my side. I sprinted.

Simultaneously, thunder exploded to the west, terrifying the dog, who took off in a different direction. I became aware that my father was chasing me. That monster voice calling my name didn't sound like his, though. My feet would not stop. He tackled me.

He flipped me over on the wet leaves and grabbed my shirt like he was begging for mercy. "Evan," he said. "I shouldn't have done it. I wish you didn't see. But your sister. He—"

My father broke off, looking up into the rain, which was falling harder. Then he looked down again. "If anyone finds out, our family—do you understand? I'll go to jail for the rest of my life. Our family will not exist anymore. Do you understand?"

Blinking away rain, I nodded.

He got to his feet, letting me up.

"Do you understand?"

I nodded my head. He caught his breath in his throat.

"I have to bury him."

Then he said nothing for a moment, looking around, and I guessed his thoughts—he didn't want to send me home, fearing I might break down at once and tell everything—but he also didn't want to have me witness the burial.

"Find the dog," he said finally. "He bolted the other way."

I nodded.

"Will you do that?"

"Yes."

Watching me, he backed away and then began to run in a different direction. I realized he was returning to the house to get a shovel.

Instead of going after the dog, I went back to the creek and hid in the trees. A humming dusk had come, and the real beginning of the storm was gathering close by.

My father came back with the shovel, which he dropped. He waded into the creek. With a groan, he hauled Mr. Autland's body up by the armpits and at length began to drag it through the wet woods. I followed at a distance.

In a rocky, low grove, maybe a hundred yards away, he laid down the remains. I ducked and flattened myself to the earth as he retraced his path to pick up the shovel again. Then he returned and for an hour, two hours, in the rain I watched him fight the mud and make a stony grave. And that was the end of Daniel's father.

When it was done, I fled. The storm was brutal now. Thunder chattered and snapped. I waited in our backyard, streaked with dirt, shaking. Finally he emerged from the dark.

"Did you find the dog?" he said.

"No."

We went inside. Finch was there, happy, his fur puffy from being blow-dried. He barked at us. My mother gawped.

"Where have you *been*?" she said. "Are you crazy?"

"Just horsing around," my father said, hiding his face behind a towel, rubbing violently. I went in the bathroom and stripped for a warm tub.

Through the door I heard my mother say, "I think we should take Jess to Dr. Wells. She's acting so strange and she won't tell me why."

With a hitch in his voice, my father said, "No, no, I'll talk to her."

The police brought dogs to search for Mr. Autland. They combed the woods for two days, then widened the search to nearby communities. But the storm had protected us. No scent was left to find.

His widow and his son came to our house one night a couple weeks after the disappearance. My mother had invited them over, made them dinner. Daniel seemed to be studying me with resentment and confusion. He didn't understand why I'd withdrawn my friendship, why now, of all times.

"I'm so sorry," my father told the widow who didn't know she was one. Then my father gripped Mr. Autland's son by his scrawny shoulders. "Daniel, I'm sorry."

My mother sensing, I think, the weirdness of his condolences and believing that strong optimism was called for said, "Margaret, they'll find him. You'll have him back soon."

The evolution of dad's alcoholism was so incremental. It didn't fully dawn on anyone until he was diagnosed with diabetes. By then, he and my mother barely spoke, and my sister was a ghost. I never found out what he'd told her about that day.

The divorce surprised no one.

Jess went with our mother and I stayed with him. I cared for my father during those years, the last years of my adolescence. I searched the car for hidden bottles before he left for work; I reminded him to take his insulin.

He moved slowly like an accident victim with invisible injuries, and he needed company. "Come sit in here with me," he would yell from the glassed-in living room, "while it rains." Unusual weather made him restless. "Don't talk," he'd say firmly, once I had come. "Let's watch the rain and not talk."

He never went in the woods again.

I loved the man and I did my best for him. But during all those years, the five years I lived there afterward, we rarely met each other's eyes.

II

Almost ten years after Mr. Autland disappeared, when I was twenty-two and a senior at Appalachian State, I came home in late April for a funeral. Jess's funeral. She'd been visiting my father and gone driving late one night, gotten into a one-vehicle accident. Married her car to a tree. My childhood friend Daniel Autland showed up at the funeral.

He was twenty-one now, taller than me, with chestnut ginger hair and a deep reserve in his light eyes. When I saw him, something inside me tried to hide. It was the first feeling I'd had in a week besides grief. "I know what it's like losing someone," Daniel said to me after the funeral, laying a strong hand on my shoulder. It was the first time we'd seen each other in several years. He had gone off to Harvard.

We were standing on soft new grass on the landscaped lawn of the funeral home. I was smoking a Parliament. Daniel, a mirror of his father, shoved tanned hands in the pockets of his black suit and said, "How's your mom?"

My mother had been at the funeral, of course. Gripping my father's hand with one arm and mine with the other, crying. Her new husband stood tactfully a few feet off.

"Not so good," I said. "I just don't know."

"Christ," said Daniel, looking up at the dazzling, almost-May sky. "Jess. I remember when she was this tall, you know? And the three of us used to go out walking with dad."

"I remember that, too," I said.

"I'm going to put the house on the market," my father told me the next morning, trudging around the kitchen, looking for a spoon. We were the only ones at the house. His body had become shorter but fleshier, his eyes hooded and sad. He was fifty-six. "You won't mind, will you? Do you want some oatmeal?"

"I hate oatmeal, Dad."

He took his bowl out of the microwave and rummaged through the cupboard in search of brown sugar. The doorbell rang and I went to get it. Daniel Autland was there, wearing aviator's sunglasses and peering through the screen, shielding his eyes to see in.

"Hey," I said. He came in tentatively, taking off his sunglasses and folding them with one hand.

"I just came by to, well—first, to say hello again, properly," he said. I noticed a single bead of sweat trickle discreetly down his forehead. "I don't want to bother you, is it all right?"

"Yeah, come in," I said, ushering him down the hall into the sun-filled living room. My father, I'd thought, would be eating in the kitchen, and for his sake and mine, I wanted to keep him and Daniel apart. But there he was, sitting on the living room loveseat, the bowl of oatmeal balanced on his knees as he stared inscrutably out the sliding glass doors at the yard.

Finch was sitting at his feet, an old dog now, frost-muzzled.

"Hi, John," said Daniel gently. "I'm sorry I didn't give you my condolences yesterday. I know it's been quite a few years, but if there's anything I can do—really."

Some process was taking place beneath my father's face—the muscles there trying to take natural shape. To Daniel, this probably looked like grief. "Thank you," said my father. "Thank you. I do appreciate that."

Daniel glanced awkwardly at me, seemed about to clear his throat and say something important—but then, as if forcing himself to wait, only leaned forward and scratched the dog's muzzle. Finch was nearly blind, and the touch took him by surprise. He shivered, leaking urine all over the rug.

Outside on the deck, I lit a cigarette while Daniel stood beside me, arms folded, surveying the trees. I'd said I wanted to smoke, but mostly I just wanted to get Daniel away from my father.

"Let me get one," he said, and I gave him a cigarette, lit it for him. His cheekbones looked like Roman architecture.

The woods around the backyard were silent, thick.

"Yeah," I said, "so you're home why?"

"Oh, you know," he said, raising his eyes to the sky, "I took the semester off. Spent a few months out by myself, climbing. In Alaska."

"Alaska."

We both gazed up at the burning blue sky.

"I hardly know how to say this," he blurted, "so I'll just get right to it."

"Yeah?" I said.

"I was wondering something about my dad, actually. From the distant past, you know, ten, twelve years ago."

"Ah," I said, my stomach withering.

Daniel sucked in his lower lip with a hissing sound, shoved his left hand in his pocket and tapped away cigarette ash with his right.

". . . You know, it's been ten years and we never found out anything about what happened to him—I'm wondering if there were things we didn't know, if they had something to do with his vanishing. If they *are* true, and they're the reason for whatever happened to him—if he deserted us, maybe, from shame or something else—I'd want to know that. I'd want the truth."

"Yeah," I said. "Of course."

He killed the cigarette under the heel of one of his black oxfords, the same shoes he'd worn to the funeral. Then he looked up at me—his eyes were an unnatural light blue, like pieces of ice held up to the sky—and I felt something being offered, even while a comparable thing was lifted out of me.

"I need to show you something," he said.

In his house, which felt both sparer and smaller than I remembered, the curtains were half-pulled and light like thin, cold broth filled the rooms. My memory had preserved it as a place of warm clutter.

"Your mother around?" I asked.

"No."

He led me upstairs, to a hallway I hadn't seen in years. At the far end, he stopped by a closed door.

"For a long time we kept this room like it was," Daniel said, "in case he came back. Then after a few years, we packed things up. Everything's still in there."

He started to open the door, then paused again.

"I found these when I was going through the desk," he said. "At the time, I guess I didn't let myself really think about it, thought it was odd, that's all."

He led me into the room. It had been his father's study. Two tall windows admitted wistful sunlight. Dust, like a thin dry snowfall, covered the floorboards. Cardboard boxes from a produce section stood stacked against one wall. Against the opposite wall hulked a massive, cherry-wood, roll-top desk.

Daniel approached the desk as if it were a sleeping lion. He rolled up the curved face of the desk to expose a cemetery of old envelopes, letters, odds and ends. He fished around for a thin cream-colored envelope and, finding it, removed its contents: a few photographs.

"Here," he said again, handing them to me. "These."

The photographs showed Jess at eight or nine years old. She was in this room, Mr. Autland's study. Behind her, I could see the roll-top desk, and on it, bathed by a lamp's glow, a soft mountain of books and letters.

She wore a red summer dress, a child's dress, and was laughing. In two of the pictures, she held something, a neatly halved rock—a geode—that Daniel's dad must have given her. Its shy violet crystals caught darts of light. There was nothing menacing about the pictures. Nothing except their existence.

But there was something, something else that tugged at me. Suddenly I realized what it was: I'd never seen that red dress. She was wearing a dress he had given her.

"Where did these come from?" I said.

That red dress. Looking at it, I felt something like vertigo. This was a secret passageway. A trapdoor of my family's history, built by Mr. Autland, hidden from us.

"I don't know any more than that," Daniel said. "I found them when I was going through things."

I gave them back. I didn't like looking at my sister's face in the pictures; there was something awful about her happiness. At her funeral, she'd had a closed casket. He returned them to the envelope, set it on the desk.

"Let's go," he said, "I—"

His voice cracked, a branch broken.

"—I don't like to come in here much."

I nodded. "Yeah, okay."

He held the door open for me. We stepped into the hall and hesitated, neither of us ready to leave the house, feeling there was more to say.

I followed him into his room and on the bed. The room was small, cluttered with the vestiges of his youth. Stacks of action novels, photos of his father smiling. Posters of mountains with highest peaks.

He pulled over a chair from his desk, sat down facing me, a foot away from me.

"If this is true," he said, "if he really did these things, I'm glad I know." He looked at his hands—slender but strong hands, veins and tendons elegant under the skin. He rubbed them together slowly, as though trying to summon something.

"When I was in Alaska," he said, "I thought about him. I was climbing Denali. In February, it gets sixty below. You get to these places, these freezing, ice-cold, empty places, and you'd think it diminishes you, but no. I was"—he sighed, as if leaking time—"I was on the Kahiltna glacier. That time of year it was only me, alone."

He brought his knuckles to his mouth, pressed them thoughtfully against his teeth. "I sat down on this field of ice, it looked like the moon covered in snow. Near me there was a couloir, and every few minutes a thin, ghostly avalanche would slide down it, wouldn't make a sound. If you got caught in one of those, you'd just vanish."

Daniel and I regarded each other, just a foot or so between us, so close I could see my warped reflection in his pupils.

He said, "Where'd he go? What happened to us?"

I kissed him. There was a strenuous, disorienting moment, the blood going to my head, as he did not react, did not resist. Ten seconds, fifteen, and then slowly he removed back and settled into the chair, ending it, whatever was happening.

Blood was pushing at the insides of my temples. I wiped my mouth. "Sorry," I said.

He seemed out of breath. He wiped his mouth too, absently, as if unsure what to do, just following my lead.

I could not break his gaze, could not look away from him. At that moment, I saw his father in him, in the curve of his jaw.

It's possible, I guess, that I slept sometime during that night. If so, however, I dreamed that I was lying beside Daniel Autland in a state of excruciating wakefulness.

Every thirty minutes or so—that is, every eternity—he would slightly rearrange his limbs and, in a clear, unhappy voice, say something like, "It's too late for a walk," or, "The storm will last all night." When I closed my eyes, I saw Mr. Autland's grave being covered with rocks.

Dawn approached. I felt detached, a little delirious. His heartbeat seemed separate from him, maddening and curious, and at dawn I slid my hand over and touched his back, felt his heart slamming against its cage like it wanted to leap into my hand.

The feeling. The intimacy of it.

"You know, I feel good about it," he said suddenly. I thought he was talking in his sleep again, but he went on in a clear, alert voice: "Let's go get breakfast. I feel okay now. I did the right thing."

"I know what happened to your dad," I said.

A long silence passed before, in a groggy yet somehow more awake voice, he said, "What'd you say?"

"My dad; he killed him. We buried him out in the woods."

"Huh?"

"It's true."

"What?" he said, sounding annoyed. "Why are you saying that?"

"I followed your dad into the woods that day," I said. "I saw my dad fight with him, then bury him right before the storm. Remember? There was a thunderstorm the day he left you all."

Daniel said nothing. Didn't move.

"My dad killed him because he molested Jess," I added.

An explosion happened beside me, as if a giant fishhook had yanked him upward from bed by the spine, so he stood staggering backwards on the rug, his arms out as if to keep balance.

Daniel whispered, "What the *fuck* are you saying? *What are you talking about?*"

I sat up. Suddenly it all felt too slow, as if I'd been drugged. My brain recoiled from the importance of things. I couldn't understand what was being asked of me.

Ten, fifteen minutes later, he dragged my father out of bed, threw him on the floor. It was dawn.

"Stop," I pleaded. "You'll hurt him."

My father lay stunned, tangled in bed sheets, moving his arms like a crab turned on its back.

"John, wake up," Daniel said. "What did you do to dad? Wake up. I'm asking you a question."

Still my father just flailed around until Daniel seized him by his faded blue pajamas and hauled him up, deposited him *back* on the bed's edge, where he sat, bouncing slightly, like a life-size doll.

Daniel bent forward, hands on his knees, to stare my father in the eye. "Did you kill my dad?"

My father did not look at me.

He said, "Yes."

A blow to the solar plexus caused him to double over, silent, shoulders curled in pain. "You lived next door for ten years after you killed my dad?" said Daniel. "How did you kill him? Where is he?"

I said, "I already told you all that stuff."

Daniel gripped my father by the back of the neck, causing his head to jerk backward and his shoulders to clench.

"I want to hear it from you, John," he yelled.

"Leave him alone," I said.

He gripped harder, his face contorted, and my father's mouth opened in a pitiful *O*.

"Where, is, he, *buried*?" Daniel yelled.

"In the woods," choked my father.

"The woods are big, John. *Where* in the woods?"

I toppled the bedside table, sending a lamp crashing to the floor. "Stop!" Daniel turned to look at me, still gripping my father's neck. "I'll show you," I told him. "I'll take you there. Right now."

III

Daniel strode behind me, carrying two shovels from our garage, his face set and grim. The early morning air was cool, damp, almost chilly.

I turned to him once and said, "I am so sorry."

He said, *"Don't."*

We came to the bend of the creek where the murder happened. Something in my face must have given it away, because he said, "This is it?"

"He's not buried here."

Daniel said, "That's not what I meant."

I started off again, through the woods. The last time I'd gone this way it had been raining and I was thirteen.

He followed close behind.

"Listen," I glanced back, "Maybe you don't know this, but my dad paid for your college. I don't know if anyone told you that."

I said, "He didn't mean to kill him."

"Is this the place?"

"Almost." I trudged on. "He confronted him about Jess. And your dad—he hit him. My dad was defending himself."

"Don't talk."

"We had to keep it a secret." I ducked under a sharp branch. "Imagine what would have happened to our family if my dad went to jail."

"Evan. . . ."

Birds cried out, irritated by the early-morning intrusion. The burial grove wasn't far at all—not like I remembered. I came to the parting of the trees, the low, rocky grove. I said, "This is it."

"Here? Where?"

"Under those rocks right there. And then dig."

He threw me a shovel. "You help," he said. Slamming the blade of his shovel under the largest rock, he began to pry it up. His clumsy, bandaged hand made things difficult, but after a moment or two, the rock tumbled over. "Come on," he said, and I joined him, kicking and prying rocks away. No point in delaying.

Once the rocks were gone, he began to dig. Now he was sweating. Little red blossoms appeared on the white surface of his bandage. Shovelfuls of dirt arced through air, breaking against rocks. "How far down is he?"

"A few feet."

He pushed me away. "I'll do it," he said. He dug awkwardly, unmethodically, dislodging massive chunks of earth and flipping them aside. The shovel struck a root of something and he chopped through it. Soon he was standing in a hole more than two feet deep.

"Keep digging," I mumbled. Birds screamed around us.

The shovel scraped something yellow and solid. Daniel gave a cry and threw the shovel aside, fell to his knees, clawed dirt with his good hand. He exposed a curved bone that looked like a squat, monstrous butterfly: a pelvis. In its center, a belt buckle. The removal of more earth revealed the contorted spinal column. Then the flattened rib cage. Then the caved-in skull.

He stopped. We stared at the half-exposed skeleton. It looked too small and frail, and I couldn't picture Mr. Autland's flesh, his personality, wrapped around it.

Still kneeling, Daniel put his hands on the skeleton, groping from one place to another as if he wanted to touch everything at once. He felt the broken edges of the skull. He whispered something.

Then he looked up at me. The rage was gone from his face.

"He was here the whole time," he said, crumbling dirt between his fingers.

I looked away, at the trees. Then, quickly, I looked back at him. "It destroyed my dad."

Daniel shook his head, as if it were unbelievable that I should say such a thing. He stood, climbed out of the hole. "My mother will have a breakdown," he said.

I grabbed his arm. "What do you mean?"

He stared at me. "When I tell my mother, she's going to break down."

I had not really thought through the fuller implications of what was happening.

"Then what?" I demanded. "Then what?"

He knocked my hand away. "What do you mean, 'then what'? She'll be in shock, that's then what."

"No," I said. "I meant what will you do?"

Daniel still didn't comprehend my question.

"What—are you going to do—to my *dad*?" I asked.

His face turned mask-like, merciless.

"I won't lay a finger on the man," he said. He started toward the woods, but I grabbed his shirt.

"Are you going to call the police?"

He shoved me, hard. I staggered backward and he started walking away.

"Wait. He's an old man—he can't go to prison. His diabetes—*Daniel*."

I caught him at the edge of the rocks and seized his shoulders. "Get off me," he said, spinning, facing me, the anger back in him, malice there too.

"Go to the house," I pleaded. "Kick him, hurt him, beat him up. He'll get on his knees and beg. Anything."

Daniel stabbed his finger at my chest. "I don't want *revenge*."

"Prison would kill him," I repeated. "Please. He's sick, he's been sick for ten years, that day poisoned everything."

Daniel turned away.

I grabbed his shoulders and yanked him back, yelling, "Listen to me—"

I saw his shoulder rotate suddenly and then I felt the blow, the skull-rattling impact against my left cheekbone, and *then* I recalled seeing his arm coming up, his fist sailing toward me. White light, crimson splinters.

As I toppled, I got a fistful of his shirt. Then we were in the grave. Bones crunched under us. My head struck a rock and I clawed at his eyes. I said, "Don't." He tried to get to his feet, but I ripped him down again, face-first, by the neck of his shirt, and this time his teeth crunched against rock. He spat blood. "I hope it does kill him," he said. It was almost slapstick how we both tried to get to our feet while stopping the other from doing so. His bandaged hand was a handicap. I kicked his legs out from under him.

He arched his back, face contorting as if something had given way inside him. Broken rib, maybe.

"Don't try to get up," I said. He tried to get up. I set my forearm against his throat.

"He—should—suffer—too," Daniel croaked.

"He *has*," I said. "He *has.*" He squirmed under my arm. Still—*still*—trying to get up. I put all my weight into my arm.

"We all have," I said. Blood sputtered from his mouth onto my arm. His bandaged hand pawed at me. He tried to get the other arm up, but it was pinned. "I can't let you go, I'm sorry," I said. A bubble of blood formed on his lip, trembled, delicately burst. I pressed down on his throat. Something crunched. "I'm sorry about this, I'm sorry, I'm sorry… "

His eyes strained to escape their sockets, protuberant goldfish eyes. With detached horror—as if I were watching someone *else* do this to him—I actually saw blood vessels breaking in the whites of his eyes. Earthquake fissures.

I'd never seen anything like that.

How long did I stay like that, with my arm crushing his windpipe? Two minutes, maybe. Three, maybe. Four. Five.

After a while, his eyes looked like red marbles, just floating there in his head.

I fell off of him, collapsed against the side of the grave. My chest was heaving.

"I'm sorry!" I cried. "Not my fault!"

I buried my face in my hands. My heart felt like a broken arm. I got the shovel and began to fill the grave again.

Exhausted, nerves bludgeoned down to nothing, I reentered our back yard. The house looked different. When you see something change over time—a child grow up, a parent get old—you don't quite notice.

Now I realized that our house had fallen to ruin.

The deck was discolored, warped. A streamer of cobweb, flecked with insect sarcophagi, hung from the porch light.

I crossed the grass and went inside the house, into the living room, which was empty. "Dad?" I said. He wasn't upstairs in his bedroom, either. I went in the bathroom, undressed, and stood under the cold blast of the shower, mind fading in and out.

Maybe a storm would come.

Mat the forest down.

Wash away the blood.

Afterward, in my own bedroom, I threw what clothes I could into a suitcase along with a bottle of vitamins and a little silver charm my mother had once given me. I neatened my bed sheets and smoothed out the pillow which still bore the impression of Daniel's head.

Then I went downstairs, dragging my suitcase. It thudded on each step.

Perhaps because I was clean, all the sweat and dirt showered away, I smelled it only then: breakfast. Oil, bacon, herbs, fried grease.

Leaving my suitcase in the hallway, I walked into the kitchen. My father sat hunched over the table, a big breakfast laid out there. He had cooked himself omelets, waffles, a plate of bacon.

He looked at his food. Something seemed different about him.

I stood a while, quiet, before he spoke.

"I'm ready to go." His voice was quiet.

He'd changed into a green-gray sweater and ancient jeans—his old outfit for hiking. Watery red veins showed in his eyes. I saw him just as I'd seen the house: aged, diminished.

"Go?" I said.

"Yeah," he said. Relief in his voice. "I'll turn myself in. It's been a long time coming. Where's Daniel? We'll all drive over together."

"Daniel's gone," I said.

A crease formed in his brow and he rearranged his silverware.

"What do you mean? Did you—show it to him?"

"We dug up the grave. He saw it."

His mouth did something funny. He didn't look at me. "Well, where is he now?"

"He's still there," I said. "He's. He's."

Suddenly it seemed as if another heart was beating in the room, a huge heart panicked and pulsing.

"Well," said my father slowly, "when is he coming back?"

I didn't answer.

"Because I'm ready to go, Evan."

"No," I said. "It—isn't necessary."

Neither of us spoke. We could not look each other in the eye; it seemed for the longest moment absolutely crucial to avoid doing so.

"He was going to turn you in," my voice broke in.

His hand jerked, an involuntary spasm, and a silver knife clattered on the floor. Slowly he sat back from the table and looked directly at me.

We met each other's eyes.

His face was unfamiliar to me. It was the face of a man approaching the end of life and knowing that his salvation had passed. Because to give himself up now would mean condemning me.

"I'm leaving," I said. "Going back to school."

"Good." My father nodded. "Good, I understand."

I went into the hallway and retrieved my suitcase. As I dragged it to the front door, I heard him clearing off the kitchen table, dumping dishes in the sink. I stepped onto the porch. I closed the door behind me.

NICK ANTOSCA *(b. New Orleans, Louisiana, USA, 1983) is the author of the cult novels* Fires, The Obese, *and* Midnight Picnic *(winner of a 2009 Shirley Jackson Award). His fiction and journalism have appeared in* n+1, The Paris Review, The Daily Beast, Hustler, Nerve, Film Threat, The New York Sun, The Barcelona Review, Bookforum, *and* Interview. *He has also written for the TV shows* Teen Wolf *and* Last Resort.

Commentary on "Burial Grounds": *I used to live in a house very much like the one described in the story. I'd always find animal bones out in the woods. Some of them are still stored away in my parents' house.*

MOONRISE ON HERMIT BEACH

NANCY A. COLLINS

THE DREAM STARTED LIKE IT ALWAYS DID: WITH HIM TRYING TO clean the old man's blood from his hands.

He was standing knee-deep in the surf, desperately trying to wash the dark stains away. As he sobbed and cursed, he looked out to the horizon and saw the moon rising from the ocean, like the eye of some great beast. It was then, as always, that he realized that he was not alone.

Just as spiders can sense every movement in their web, so dreamers, in their way, are aware of everything that occurs in their dreams. That is how he knew, as he always did, that someone was standing on the shore, watching him, without actually looking over his shoulder. The knowledge brought with it a dread far sharper than any he had ever known, even in Vietnam, not because he was being observed, but for fear of *who* might be observing. Slowly, relentlessly he turned toward the shore, his eyes streaming tears of horror, as the moon rose like Aphrodite, casting its light upon the watcher on the shore. But before he could glimpse the watcher's face, his head seemed to burst asunder, destroyed and splintered by his own terror.

He awoke then, as he always did, with his heart pounding against his ribs like an angry fist, and a stillborn scream in his throat. But this time, unlike all the others, the telephone beside his bed was ringing. As he picked up the receiver he glanced at the clock radio. It was just before dawn. He could not make out the number on the caller ID, but he instantly recognized the voice in his ear, although he had not heard it in four decades.

"Lloyd's dead. Check your email."

Twenty minutes and a hastily brewed cup of coffee later, Gilbert Tread-well—better known as Gil—found himself seated at his desk, logging onto his laptop. As he pulled up his email, he saw that there was a message waiting for him in the inbox. The sender was identified as Lloyd Blanchard, and whatever the email contained, it was not meant for his eyes only, since an electronic carbon copy had also been sent to Hoyt Herndon. The subject heading simply read: **Forty Year Reunion.**

Although the body of the message itself was blank, there was a file attached. He clicked on the attachment and an image suddenly filled the screen. He gasped, his breath hanging suspended in his lungs for a long moment as his brain fought against the impossibility of what he was seeing: a photograph of a painting of the moon rising over the ocean as seen from the beach. And standing in the foreground, knee-deep in the surf, was the figure of a man, bent over as if washing his hands in the waves.

The last time he was in Treasure Beach was over twenty years ago, when he moved his parents out of the area following Hurricane Hugo. Although he knew better, part of him still expected to find the streets strewn with palm fronds and the telephone poles tilted like the Tower of Pisa. Even though the vast majority of the local businesses and restaurants that had been such a part of his childhood were long gone, the underlying bone structure of the town remained intact. The wide sidewalks, broad streets, one-storey commercial district, and associated boardwalk that he remembered so well were all still there, providing a sense of continuity from one generation to the next. The biggest change, however, was that the ocean that had once been visible from the town's main drag was now hidden away behind a solid wall of condominiums and high-rise hotels.

For half a heartbeat he imagined he could hear his mother, dead for seven years, softly sobbing in the backseat as he drove both her and his father away from their dream home, never to return. Even though he had found them a nice little place up in the mountains, just outside of Asheville, where they seemed to adapt, they were never quite the same after that. His parents had dreamed of retiring at the beach, not the mountains, and no matter the view atop the Great Smokies, it could never be their dream.

His parents had grown up in the Piedmont, working for Hanes and R.J. Reynolds, back when textiles and Big Tobacco ruled the state like feudal kings. Neither one of them had graduated high school, but back then you didn't need a diploma to drive a delivery truck or sew labels into under-wear. They worked hard and saved their money throughout the year, so that for two weeks every summer they could escape the blistering, mind-melting heat of the North Carolina interior and vacation in the southeastern coastal resort town of Treasure Beach, situated on a large peninsula that extended between the Cape Fear River and the Atlantic Ocean.

During the off-season, Treasure Beach's population barely numbered five hundred souls, but during the summer it literally swarmed with tourists, most of them families identical to his own, eager to escape the drudgery of their workaday world for the sun and sand of the coast. During those long-ago summers, he was free to cast aside the fact he was a truck driver's son, dressed in the factory seconds his mother brought home from her job at the mill, and remake himself into someone more interesting. He liked to tell the other kids he met on the boardwalk he was captain of the baseball team and the son of a junior-executive. He knew better than to give his father too big of a promotion, because of the simple fact no one would believe a senior vice president would be renting a cottage in the dead cen-ter of Treasure Beach. In a community where most of its citizens walked around in nothing but swimsuits, towels, and flip-flops, the easiest way of figuring out where somebody stood on the social totem pole was not the size of their vacation home as much as its location. Since the Cape Fear River was to the west and the Atlantic Ocean to the east, these were the preferred points of the compass. The oceanfront property was the most desirable, of course, and that was where the wealthiest families tended to congregate. Those who were considered up-and-comers had cottages that faced the river, and enjoyed breath-taking views of the setting sun. And since it was a good twenty-minute slog in either direction from the bungalow his par-ents rented every year, there was only so much social climbing Gil could pretend to.

As he waited at the town's solitary traffic light, he quietly watched the most recent generation of tourists, dressed in thongs and sunblock, make their way towards the beach, like scantily clad pilgrims on their way to Mecca. Suddenly a memory rose, unbidden, of his mother, resplendent in her Capris and matching tank-top, her hair tied up in a kerchief to protect it from the sea breeze, barefootin' the Carolina Shag with his father while a live band played on the boardwalk. It was the only time he ever saw his parents as they must have been before he was born. The fact that he had been embarrassed by them at the time filled him with shame decades later.

But then, there was much about his final summers in Treasure Beach to be ashamed of.

The aptly named Dyer's Funeral Home was on the far end of Treasure Boulevard, beyond the cluster of eateries and beach shops that catered to the tourists. He parked his car in the shell lot provided for mourners and by the time he made the front door he had already sweated through his dress shirt. As he tugged at the dampened Windsor knot cinched about his neck, he realized that this was the first time in his life that he had worn a suit within the city limits.

Gil heaved a slight sigh of relief as he stepped into the cool, shaded quiet. The place was small, with a single foyer that served as a sitting room for two separate viewing parlors. There were a couple of sofas and wingback chairs occupied by people his age and older, all of whom looked vaguely familiar but he could not easily identify. A hand-lettered sign propped up on an easel in front of the larger of the two rooms read: Lloyd Blanchard Service.

As he looked around the foyer a man with close-cropped, graying hair, dressed in a quietly expensive suit, rose from one of the chairs and walked over to him, holding out a hand in greeting. Gil glimpsed a flash of gold as a Rolex slid out from hiding under his jacket cuff.

"Glad you could make it, Gil." The voice was the same one that had told him of Lloyd's death three days before.

"Hoyt," he replied as they exchanged handshakes.

The other man took him by the elbow and steered him toward the viewing room, all the while speaking in a low, steady tone of voice. "You open the email?"

"Yes. I'm not sure what it means, though."

Hoyt's grip on his elbow tightened, causing Gil to wince. "Don't give me that bullshit. You know damn well what it refers to."

"Now isn't the time for that," he said, shrugging himself free of the other man's grasp. He looked about the viewing room, expecting to see a casket. Instead, there was an urn sitting next to a large blow-up of a recent photograph of the deceased. The Lloyd Blanchard that grinned at him was not the same one he had hung out with all those long, lost summers ago, although Gil could see the ghost of the boy he had once known haunting the older version's eyes.

They had met while playing a round of Putt-Putt on the boardwalk when

Gil was six and Lloyd was seven, and had become fast friends by the time they got to the windmill. Although their friendship never extended beyond the confines of summer and the beach, it was real, nonetheless. Unlike himself, Lloyd actually lived at Treasure Beach year round, as his father was the town sheriff. Whenever Gil returned to Treasure Beach with his parents, Lloyd was always there to greet him, and they invariably picked up the thread of their previous year's adventures with the thoughtless ease of childhood.

That said, he had not seen Lloyd since 1977, the summer he was discharged from active service. Despite his better judgment, he had accompanied his parents to Treasure Beach, more as a favor to his mother. Lloyd was finishing up law school at Wake Forest, and had just married his first wife. He insisted on taking Gil out for drinks 'for old time's sake.' It was then that he noticed his boyhood friend had developed a drinking problem. They spent an awkward hour reminiscing over a pitcher and shots at the old pool hall, careful never to mention the one thing they dare not speak aloud—until Lloyd had one boiler maker too many and leaned forward to whisper: *"Do you ever dream about Hermit Beach?"* It was the last thing Lloyd ever said to him, for he promptly stood up and left the bar, never to see or speak to his old friend again.

"How did he die?" Gil asked, staring at the urn. "The papers said something about a boating accident?"

"He was probably drunk," Hoyt replied with a sigh. "He took that sailboat of his out on the ocean, down around the Point. They think the boom caught him when he wasn't looking and broke his neck. He was dead before he went in the water. It was a couple of days before his wife called the cops looking for him. By the time they found him, the crabs had been at him, so I reckon she decided there was no point in an open casket. Or any casket at all, for that matter."

Gil's stomach tightened as his mind flashed onto the image of hundreds of tiny fiddler crabs swarming dead flesh like so many soldier ants. But the corpse in question was not his friend's.

"Where was he found?"

"Hermit Beach," Hoyt replied in a tight, clipped voice.

Gil spent the next hour sitting beside Hoyt in one of the wooden pews in the funeral home, listening to a paid minister eulogize Lloyd Blan-

chard. He learned that in the decades since they last spoke, Lloyd had succeeded in becoming an attorney, briefly clerking for a city judge in
Wilmington before returning to his hometown to practice law. Somewhere
along the line he and his first wife had a couple of kids, got divorced, got
married a second time, all while fixing speeding tickets, drawing up wills,
and handling business contracts for the fine people of Treasure Beach. He
had become a pillar of the small community, a fixture amidst the constant
shifting sands of tourists and retirees, just like his father before him, Sheriff Blanchard. He was praised as a loving husband, devoted father, doting
grandpa, good friend, and dedicated sportsman, who died doing what he
loved.

After the service, Hoyt followed him out to his car, just as Gil knew he
would. They stood there, sweating in the afternoon sun, staring at one
another for a long moment, waiting to see who would say it first. Gil finally
broke down and asked the question.

"So, you reckon it really was an accident?"

Hoyt pulled a linen handkerchief from his breast pocket and used it to
mop the sweat from the back of his neck. "What else could it be? You're
not thinking it was a suicide, are you?"

"You got the same email as I did," Gil countered. "What I want to know
is where did he find that painting?"

"That's easy enough to answer," Hoyt replied. "Come with me."

The art gallery was located in the beachside commercial district of Treasure Beach, in the middle of a strip of restaurants and souvenir shops
that catered exclusively to the tourists who stayed in the motels along the
main drag. The sign hanging outside the storefront was made from a piece
of driftwood and said *The Hermit's Gallery*, while a banner in the front window proclaimed: 'Grand Opening!'

The interior was small and devoid of fixtures, save for a counter where the
cashier stood. The walls were covered with dozens of oil paintings, all of
them folk-art landscapes. While some of the pictures were on stretched can-
vas, most appeared to have been painted on pieces of plywood, heavy
poster-board, or, in one case, the blade of an oar. All of them bore the ini-
tials 'A.C.' in the right hand corner. Next to each painting was a tag with its
title and price, which started at two thousand dollars and went up from
there.

The only picture in the gallery that wasn't a painting was a large black-and-white photograph of a short and spry old man seated on an up-ended wooden cable-spool, dressed in nothing but a pair of ragged shorts and a hand-woven straw hat. His skin was dark from years spent out in the sun, and his arms and upper body were surprisingly muscular for a man of his apparent age. His bushy hair and full beard, bleached white by the sun, made him resemble a gnomic Ernest Hemingway. The old man smiled at the camera, his left eye closed in a permanent squint. A plaque attached to the photo-portrait read: *Alvin Crocker a/k/a The Cape Fear Hermit 1906-1972.* With a start, Gil realized he had not seen the old man's face anywhere but his own mind in forty years.

"May I help you, gentlemen?"

Gil turned to find the gallery owner—a slender woman in her early forties, with cat's eye glasses and dangling ear-rings shaped like dolphins—standing behind them. "Yes," he replied, trying to sound far more casual than he felt. "Are all these paintings by the same artist?"

The gallery owner smiled and nodded. "These were all done by the Cape Fear Hermit, Alvin Crocker, who lived on the beach back in the Fifties and Sixties. He was something of a local celebrity, in those days, some said the second biggest attraction in the state next to the battleship *North Carolina.* He'd been a hero in the war—he was awarded the Silver Star—but then moved to Treasure Beach in 1955 and became a beachcomber. He died in 1972, under mysterious circumstances. Folks back then called him a hermit, because he lived by himself out on the Point, but I guess nowadays he'd be called a hippie. Scores of people visited him—even Ava Gardner went out to his camp once—but all Alvin ever really wanted was to get back to nature and paint his pictures."

Gil glanced over at Hoyt as the gallery owner explained things they'd both known since the third grade. Hoyt's mouth was set in a scowl as he stared at the artwork. If the gallery owner noticed his disapproval, she didn't show it.

"He lived a nearly self-sufficient lifestyle for almost two decades, surviving without electricity, even during hurricane season. He fished and crabbed for his meals, and spent what little money he had on the few things he couldn't scavenge for himself. My grandfather used to run the A&P here in town, and Alvin would trade his paintings for toilet paper and kerosene for his lamp. Turned out to be the smartest thing Grandpa ever did. About five years ago an art collector came down from New York, looking for examples of The Hermit's art. Turns out he's the new Grandma Moses! Luckily,

Grandpa had a soft spot for ol' Alvin, and couldn't bring himself to throw his stuff out. He sold a chunk of what he had to that art dealer and retired to Wrightsville Beach. We decided to open a gallery and sell the rest of the collection ourselves."

As he listened to the gallery owner's spiel with half an ear, Gil allowed his gaze to travel over the paintings on display. While clearly the work of an untrained hand, there was a naive energy to the compositions and unexpectedly vivid use of color that made them compelling. The subject matter seemed to be divided between depicting the marshlands and native wildlife of the Cape Fear River basin, and the windswept dunes and rolling surf of the seaside. After a couple minutes of searching, he finally located what he was looking for, hanging in the far corner of the gallery.

"What about this one?" he said, pointing to the picture Lloyd had photographed. "What can you tell me about this painting?"

The gallery owner peered over the top of her glasses at the title card. "It's called *Moonrise on Hermit Beach*. It's thought to be Alvin's last painting. It's unusual because it's the only one he ever did that showed a human figure. It's been suggested that it might even be a self-portrait."

"How can you be sure it's him?" Hoyt snapped. "You can't see his face."

The gallery owner blinked, taken aback by such inexplicable vehemence. "Well, um, there's no real way of knowing for *sure*, of course. But since the figure is gathering his nets, which is how Alvin did his fishing, it is widely assumed that's who it's supposed to be . . . "

"What makes you think he's pulling nets?" Hoyt countered, his eyes shining with barely-concealed disdain. "You can't see *what* he's doing."

"Well, what else *could* it be?" the gallery owner replied, pushed to the edge of politeness. She then turned back to smile at Gil. "You seem to be quite taken with this piece, sir—are you interested in purchasing it?"

Gil smiled sadly and shook his head. "I'm afraid it's got too many zeroes for my check book."

"I'll take it," Hoyt said suddenly.

"Are you *sure* about that, sir?" the gallery owner asked in surprise.

"I know what I said," Hoyt growled as he took his wallet from the breast pocket of his suit. He plucked his platinum card out and waved it at her. "Ring it up."

"Of course, Mr. Herndon," she replied, glancing at the name embossed on the bottom of the card. "It'll take me a few minutes to wrap that up for you . . . "

"Don't bother," he said tersely, literally yanking the painting from its place on the wall.

Although clearly perturbed by Hoyt's brusque behavior, the gallery owner still managed to keep her smile in place. "Well, I'm *certain* you'll enjoy it . . . "

"*Enjoy* it?" Hoyt spat. "Hell, woman, I'm gonna burn it! And then I'm coming back and buying everything else y'all got and building myself a big ol' bonfire on the beach! Alvin Crocker wasn't a 'local celebrity'—he was a filthy old crazy beach bum, plain and simple! And the sooner folks realize that, the better off Treasure Beach will be!" With that, Hoyt stuck his purchase under his arm and stormed out of the gallery, leaving Gil to retrieve his credit card from the flabbergasted gallery owner.

"I'm sorry, ma'am," he said apologetically. "He's been under a lot of stress lately."

"Well you can tell Mr. Herndon that if he thinks I'll sell him another painting, he's crazier than poor Alvin ever was!"

He found Hoyt standing in the parking lot of the funeral home, holding the picture he'd just purchased at arm's length, as if trying to decide whether to destroy it right then and there.

"Are you really going to burn that thing?" Gil asked as he handed Hoyt back his platinum card.

"I'm sure as hell not going to hang it on the wall, now, am I?" He unlocked the trunk of his gray BMW and hurled the artwork inside as if it was nothing more than a spare set of jumper cables. "You're not headed back to Asheville, are you?" he asked. "That's a hell of a round trip."

"I hadn't planned on staying this late," Gil admitted, shielding his eyes against the setting sun. He had a four hundred mile drive ahead of him, and was not looking forward to it in the least. "I reckon I could get a room at one of the motels . . . "

"I wouldn't hear of it!" Hoyt said, giving him a companionable slap on the shoulder. "You'll stay with me! Besides, you know all the motel rooms are booked up for the season—that's one thing that never changes around here. I'll throw some steaks on the grill and we can toast Lloyd with a few drinks. Sounds good, don't it?"

"Yeah," he agreed, staring at the ten thousand dollar painting lying in the trunk of Hoyt's car. "Just like old times."

The Herndon vacation home sat on the beach like a grand dame spreading out her skirts, taking up as much space as she liked, the neighbors be damned. Hoyt's grandfather, who made his money in the furniture business in High Point before branching out into construction and real estate development, built the original two-bedroom cottage that served as its core during the Depression. Over the decades, as the family's fortunes grew, the cottage had been regularly added to and updated, until it boasted three stories, six bedrooms, four and a half baths, an elevator, and a maze of interconnected decks and balconies facing the Atlantic. As Gil parked his sedan alongside Hoyt's BMW in the garage underneath the beach house's north wing, he could tell by the amount of sand the wind had blown onto the carport floor that the vacation house had not seen visitors for some time.

"You'll have to excuse the house," Hoyt said, as he unlocked the front door. "My fourth wife doesn't care for Treasure Beach; she prefers Palm Beach. She keeps after me to sell the old place—but I just can't bring myself to put it on the market."

As Gil crossed the threshold, his heart skipped a beat at what, at first, looked like a crowd of ghosts arrayed to greet them. It took him a moment to realize they were nothing more than chairs and sofas shrouded in dropcloths. Hoyt snatched away a few of the sheets, revealing better furniture in his disused vacation home than most people have in their main residences.

Gil walked around the living room, pausing to study a photograph of a thirty-year-old Hoyt and his sixty-year-old father deep-sea fishing on a charter boat, smoking cigars as they toasted the camera with bottles of Mexican beer. "How's your dad?" he asked idly.

"Senile," Hoyt replied sourly. "Mom's not much better. They're in a retirement community in Arizona that specializes in Alzheimer's patients." He emerged from the kitchen with a bottle of twenty-one year old Glenlivet in one hand and a pair of cut crystal lowball glasses in the other. "This is a far cry from the Purple Passion the three of us used to swill under the pier, but it will have to do," Hoyt said as he set the tumblers on the coffee table and dispensed a generous amount of Scotch into each. "To Lloyd."

"To Lloyd," he echoed, raising his glass in somber toast.

Gil sat on the deck in the gathering darkness, listening to the sound of the surf as Hoyt busied himself with the grill. Despite how the breakers and the smell of salt-air brought back memories of people and times long gone and best forgotten, there was no denying he, too, had missed the beach as much as his parents.

"What do you think Lloyd meant by sending us that picture?" Gil asked.

"Lloyd was a friend, but he was also a drunk," Hoyt replied as he removed the steaks from the grill and dropped them onto a platter. "For all we know, he attached the wrong file."

"Yeah, but how did he send it in the first place? He'd been dead for at least two or three days when it popped up in my mailbox."

"He must have scheduled it to go out on the fortieth anniversary," Hoyt replied with a shrug.

"Yes, but *why*? I hadn't seen or heard from him in thirty-five years. Why *now*?"

"We'll talk about that after we eat," Hoyt said as he set the food on a wooden picnic table bleached gray by exposure to sand and salt.

Gil silently took his place, spearing one of the porterhouses and dropping it onto his plate. As he cut into the meat, there was a thin trickle of blood. Without willing it, his mind flashed back to that night, all those years ago. He looked up to find Hoyt staring at him, and he did not have to ask to know that his friend's mind had traveled to the same place.

Later, when the steaks were no more than gristle and the Glenlivet a third gone, Hoyt and Gil sat side by side, staring out in the direction of the ocean.

"They say he's come back," Hoyt said around his cigar.

"Who?" Gil asked, pretending he did not know.

"The Hermit."

"That's impossible."

"People boating off the Point at night say they've seen his hut on the beach. I know for a fact the real one is long gone—knocked that sumbitch down with a bulldozer myself when I worked for my daddy's construction company."

"Do you think someone's rebuilt it as a shrine?" Gil suggested. "Maybe that gallery owner or some other art lover?"

"Anything's possible," Hoyt said with a shrug. "The federal government bought that land after Hugo wiped out the marina and fishing pier we built out at the end of Point Road. They decided it was more useful as a coastal barrier and wildlife refuge than a vacation retreat. The old trail to the beach is still there, but that's about it." Hoyt stared at the glow of his cigar for a long moment, as if debating to continue. "I haven't told anyone this, but Lloyd called me before he died. He got it into his head that those paintings being discovered had woken up the old man's ghost, and he was haunting the beach. Told me he was going to sail out to the Point and see the Hermit."

"That's insane."

"That's what I told him," Hoyt sighed. "But he didn't listen. And the rest you know. But assuming there *is* a ghost—which is utter horseshit, of course—why the hell would Lloyd want to have anything to do with it?"

Gil shrugged. "Maybe he just wanted to finally get a good night's sleep?"

He waited until Hoyt dozed off in front of the mammoth flat screen TV in the living room before sneaking out to his car. As he drove through town, his was the sole vehicle on the road. One thing had definitely not changed since his boyhood: Treasure Beach rolled up its sidewalks every night at ten o'clock. As he headed down the narrow two lane blacktop known as Point Road, Gil's mind turned toward the Hermit.

He could not recall the first time he saw him. As far as he was concerned, the Hermit was as much a part of the scenery of summer as the pelicans and the saltwater marshes. It wasn't until he turned eight that the Hermit registered as being 'different' from the other adults who wandered the beach community in nothing but shorts and straw headgear. He remembered seeing the old man walking along the side of the road, a gunny sack slung over his bare shoulder, wearing sandals made out of old rope and the rubber tread sliced from a tire. He was burned browner than any white man he'd seen before or since, with skin like a well-seasoned catcher's mitt. His father would always wave when he saw the Hermit on the side of the road, and the Hermit would always wave back, as if returning a salute. Once, when his mother wasn't in the car, his dad actually stopped and offered the old man a ride to wherever it was he was going. The Hermit had merely smiled and shook his head, thanking him all the same.

Sometimes his father and uncle would rent a small outboard and head down to the Point, where the mouth of the Cape Fear River met the sea, returning with redfish, sunburns and more than a few empty beer cans. When Gil turned ten, he was deemed old enough to be included in the outing, if not the drinking. As they sat in the bobbing boat, he saw the Hermit digging for clams on a small strip of beach. He asked his father why the strange old man lived by himself out on the Point, without electricity or running water. His father shrugged and said the Hermit had single-handedly saved his platoon by overtaking a Nazi machinegun nest, and that General Patton shook his hand, as if that explained everything. His uncle chimed in, then, saying he'd heard that the Hermit had ended up in Broughton, the state mental hospital, after the war. That made sense, as a man would have to be crazy to stay out there in summer heat, surrounded by mosquitoes, poisonous snakes and alligators, not to mention the occasional hurricane. Still, his uncle said, the Hermit wasn't a bad sort; he was friendly to anyone who came around his camp. As his father and uncle resumed their fishing, Gil stared at the distant figure of the man who had killed a dozen Nazis and shook Patton's hand as he sat on the beach, patiently mending his nets.

Two years later, he was hanging out with Lloyd and Hoyt in front of the Burger Bar, the fast-food shack next to Burt's Surf Shop. To his surprise, the Hermit walked up to the order window and handed the owner a handful of change.

"Where does the Hermit get his money from?" he asked aloud, not really expecting an answer.

"I hear he panhandles down on the boardwalk on Memorial Day and Fourth of July," Lloyd replied. "He also sells some paintings and stuff to the tourists."

"That codger makes me sick," Hoyt said sourly. "I hate his guts."

Gil frowned, puzzled by the animosity in the other boy's voice. "What's he done to you?"

"That hobo's squatting on our property."

"Your family owns Hermit Beach?" Gil was genuinely surprised. All he knew at the time about Hoyt, who he had recently met through Lloyd, was that his family owned one of the big oceanfront getaways and came and went from Treasure Beach whenever they liked, not just a two-week window.

"Yeah, my grandpa bought it up during the Depression," Hoyt replied. "I wish my dad would kick the old man off the Point, but he won't on account he's some kind of freakin' war hero. My old man said Eisenhower shook his hand."

"I thought it was Patton?"

"He could have shook Mickey Mouse's hand for all I care," Hoyt snarled. "All I know is that he's just a smelly dirty old weirdo keeping my dad from making money. Who cares who the bastard shook hands with?"

Gil didn't really know why Hoyt should care about his daddy making money, since they were already rich. But since he enjoyed the benefits of hanging out with someone who always had more than enough pocket change, he acquiesced to his friend's peculiarities.

Over the next five years the three of them roamed the arcades along the boardwalk together, playing skee-ball and pachinko, sneaking cigarettes under the pier, and keeping a weather-eye out for girls sunbathing with their bikini tops undone. But as each summer ticked away, stripping away more and more of their boyhood, they started becoming increasingly restless. They were in that dangerous age where they were too old for Putt-Putt, but too young to enter the local bars, dance halls and pool rooms. This, of course, did not keep them from getting their hands on alcohol or tobacco. Lloyd, in particular, had a knack for jimmying open liquor cabinets.

To be fair, they were not the first to harass the old man. There were stories going around for years about how the Hermit had a small fortune hidden away in his shack. It was obvious bullshit, of course, but that didn't keep the rednecks, drifters and white trash from finding their way to his camp and ransacking it. It was no secret where he lived, and easy enough to find, if that's what you wished to do.

It was Hoyt's idea, of course, to give the old man a hard time. And since Hoyt was the one who paid to get them in the movies and ponied up for Putt-Putt and the pinball machines, he was the one who called the shots. They were fifteen the first time they made their way out to the Hermit's camp. They went out during the day, after making sure the old man was in town, doing what passed for his shopping. They were still too young to be bold enough to venture out into the wilderness at night, much less confront an adult face-to-face, even a fringe-dweller like the Hermit.

They rode their Stingray bikes out to the end of Point Road, which dead-ended about a mile from Hermit Beach, then set off down a trail carved out of the dense maritime forest that covered the vast, undeveloped acreage of the Point. They eventually found themselves where the Cape Fear River met the Atlantic Ocean, separated by a mere spit of sand the length and width of a football field. To the west was marsh grass, which waved and soughed in the constant breeze like wheat on a prairie; to the east were dunes covered in cordgrass and sea oats, beyond which was a shore covered in sea shells and patrolled by a living carpet of tiny fiddler crabs. Overhead osprey, ibis and pelicans glided on the wind like living kites, their distant cries barely audible above the ceaseless boom of the surf.

On the edge of the clearing, its back to the tight-knit wall of salt-stunted live oaks and twisted juniper trees, stood a shanty built of unnotched logs, chinked with big wads of clay from the nearby river and fists full of Spanish moss from the surrounding forest. Its steep roof was made of discarded scrap lumber, and the door was fashioned from a large piece of plywood scavenged from a work site. Painted across it were the words: KEEP OUT and, below it, PLEASE KNOCK. Surrounding the shack was a jumble of empty tin cans, lengths of wire and coils of old rope, odd bits of lumber, and a multitude of old buckets for rainwater.

Hoyt stood and surveyed the camp, his hands planted on his hips. "What a shithole!" he growled in disgust. "I told you he was nothing but a moocher."

Near the shack was a small, carefully tended garden comprised mostly of tomatoes, cucumbers and squash. Hoyt went over to it and snatched one of the tomatoes from the vine and hurled it at the side of the shanty, where it exploded with a satisfying *splat!* Hoyt laughed, pleased by the result, and plucked another, hurling it at Lloyd. The tomato burst against his chest.

Lloyd clutched at his rib cage, like he was playing a part in *The Green Berets*. "You got me—!"

This triggered a ten minute food fight between the three teens, as they gleefully demolished the Hermit's garden, hurling tomatoes at one another while stomping the cucumbers and other vegetables into paste. Before they left camp, Hoyt systematically kicked over the makeshift rain barrels. On the way back to where they had stashed their bikes, they laughed to imagine the look on the Hermit's face as he returned home to find his fresh water ruined and his summer garden destroyed. Lloyd laughed so hard he peed himself.

That was the first, but far from the last, raid they made. Over the next two summers they descended on the old man like adolescent locusts, taking the plywood door from the shanty and tossing it in the marsh, throwing his fishing nets up into the trees, and every bit of deviltry in between. Although Gil only spent two weeks of the year at Treasure Beach, he knew that Lloyd and Hoyt continued to harass the Hermit off-and-on throughout the year. However, it wasn't until 1972—the summer he turned seventeen—that they finally worked up the nerve to go out to the camp after dark.

The first couple forays were relatively minor mischief, such as throwing stones at the Hermit's shack while howling like banshees. But once they realized the old man was unwilling to leave the safety of his shelter to confront them, they escalated to more egregious vandalism, even using his cast-iron cooking pot as a urinal.

Their final trip to Hermit Beach was a couple of days before the end of his summer vacation. The plan was to sneak up on the old man while he was asleep and carry him in his sleeping bag to the edge of the marsh and throw him in the water; nothing worse than that.

They entered the Hermit's camp just after midnight, armed with nothing but flashlights and the heedless cruelty of adolescence. The embers from the old man's cook-fire had long since died, and they could hear the sound of snoring coming from the shack. Lloyd moved the plywood door aside, careful not to make any noise for fear of waking the Hermit. Although the interior of the ten-by-ten enclosure was dark, Gil could see the Hermit in the middle of the sand floor, curled inside his sleeping bag.

Working in silence, save for the occasional snort and snicker, the trio carefully lifted their slumbering victim by the corners of his sleeping bag and slowly maneuvered him out of the shack. To Gil's amazement, the Hermit continued to snore, no doubt exhausted from a long day of clamming and crabbing, not to mention knocking back some home-made pruno. However, as they neared the bank of the marsh, Hoyt abruptly stumbled in the darkness, dropping his end of the sleeping bag and sending the old man tumbling onto the ground.

The Hermit woke up swinging, screaming and swearing at the top of his lungs. He wasn't even making words, just shrieking and growling. Realizing their prank had failed, Lloyd and Gil let go, guffawing as the old man struggled to untangle himself from the sleeping bag. However, Gil's laughter quickly ended as he saw the glint of a blade. Whatever Alvin Crocker, veteran of Bastogne, thought had him surrounded that night, it wasn't a trio of dumb-asses.

Gil grabbed the Hermit's wrist, trying to wrest the knife from his grip. Hoyt and Lloyd had finally stopped laughing and were now shouting, both at him and the Hermit. All Gil could see was the old man's face, inches from his own, his eyes showing white and his teeth bared like a Doberman's. If Gil did not get control of that knife, he was going to find it in his gut.

Even after forty years of replaying it in his head, he still did not know how it happened. One moment he was fighting for his life, the next the old man was sliding off the blade, wailing as he clutched his belly. Stunned, Gil looked down and saw that he was the one holding the knife and that both of his hands were coated with blood and sand. He cried out then, like the child he could no longer be, and rushed toward the beach, where he waded out into the rolling surf, sobbing as he tried to wash away his crime.

When he returned to where he had left the others, he was horrified to find that Hoyt and Lloyd had dragged the fallen Hermit out into the marsh, forcing him face-down into the brackish water. Lloyd was kneeling across the old man's legs, while Hoyt had his foot on the back of his neck. The old man stretched forth one wildly grasping hand—perhaps the one that Patton had shaken—as if reaching for salvation, before finally going limp.

"*What are you doing?*" Gil shouted as he grabbed Hoyt by the collar of his t-shirt, yanking him away from the Hermit's motionless body.

"I *had* to do it!" Hoyt explained, as if it was the most logical thing in the world. "The old fucker was going to say we tried to murder him!"

"Gawd, Hoyt, you didn't *have* to kill him! We could have taken him to a hospital or something!"

"Nearest emergency room's in Wilmington," Hoyt said as he straightened his shirt. "That's thirty miles from here. There's no way he could have made it that far in the back of my GTO. And there's only *one* doctor in Treasure Beach, and he knows both Lloyd and me. I don't know what *you* got planned for after high school, Gil, but there's no way in Hell I could get into Duke with something like this hanging over my head. He was dying anyways from that sticking you gave him. *You're* the one who cut the old man; I just put him out of his misery is all."

"This has *got* to stay between the three of us," Lloyd said urgently. "If it gets out, we're in fucking *trouble*, you got that? I'm not talking 'black mark on your permanent record' or chewed out by your old man trouble, either. They'll send us to the death house, for this, Gil."

They fell silent then as the enormity of what they had done settled upon them like a mantle made of lead. They picked up the sleeping bag and returned it to the shack, but not before Lloyd used it to wipe his finger prints from the piece of plywood that served as its door. As for their victim, they left him laying face-down in the muck of the marsh, his mouth and nose stuffed with mud.

It was three o'clock in the morning by the time Gil returned to the unfashionable bungalow in the middle of Treasure Beach. His dreams that night were filled by the sound of roaring surf and the sight of a rising moon. After he awoke the next morning, he spent the rest of the day helping his family pack the car for the return home, all the while expecting Lloyd's father, Sheriff Blanchard, to pull up in his squad car and put him in handcuffs. But the sheriff never arrived. Nor were the State Police waiting for him when the family's station wagon pulled into the driveway in Goldsboro.

It wasn't until a week later that Gil's father noticed an item in the *News and Observer* about Alvin Crocker, decorated war hero and self-proclaimed hermit, being found dead in the marshland near his camp on the Cape Fear Point, known as Hermit Beach. According to the paper, Crocker had been dead for at least three days before he was found by a local fisherman. Since the corpse was badly decomposed, the county coroner was unable to determine exactly how he died. In keeping with his status as veteran and Silver Star recipient, his body was to be interred at the National Cemetery in Wilmington, with full military honors. His father said it was a shame, and his mother clucked her tongue in pity, and then turned to the sports page.

Gil's sleep became increasingly fitful. He became plagued by a recurring nightmare that found him back at Hermit Beach, washing his hands in the surf. His appetite suffered and he began to drop weight—enough that it made his mother start to fret. And still the police did not come.

Then, six months after the Hermit's death was reported in the newspaper, Gil received a package in the mail, postmarked Raleigh. Upon opening it he discovered twenty-five thousand dollars in neatly stacked and banded hundreds. He remembered what Hoyt had said about his grandfather refusing to sell the land he owned to developers because of the Hermit. No doubt Hoyt had sent him the money as a token of thanks for helping his family break the barrier between well-off and stinking rich. For the first time since that night on Hermit Beach, he knew exactly what he had to do and, within forty-eight hours of receiving the cash, he opened a savings account and joined the Marines—the same branch of the Armed Forces in which Alvin Crocker had once served.

His mama cried when she found out what he'd done, but there was no going back. He'd turned eighteen the month before, and would be graduating high school in another three. There would be no returning to Treasure

Beach that summer, or the three after it. And in the chaos of the final years of the Vietnam War, he was able, for a time, to block the old dream with newer, fresher nightmares.

As for Hoyt's blood money, he never spent a dime of it on himself. Instead, in 1982, ten years after the event on Hermit Beach, he emptied his savings account in order to buy his parents a two bedroom cottage in Treasure Beach, less than three minutes' walk from the ocean. During the seven years his parents lived there, he never once visited them, always finding excuses to stay away, as the ocean triggered the dream.

But now, here he was—headed back to Hermit Beach. He told himself he was crazy. What did he expect to find there, after all these years? The shack was long gone, and the only evidence that Alvin Crocker had ever existed at all was a bunch of over-priced paintings and a simple soldier's tombstone. If he had any sense at all, he would turn the car around and drive back home to Asheville. But still he pushed onward, like a filing drawn to a magnet.

It had been forty years since the last time he drove down Point Road, but very little had changed. To the east was the Atlantic and a few forlorn concrete pillars that were all that remained of what had once been a marina and fishing pier before Hugo wiped it off the map in 1989. To the west was the marshland, protected by a dense, knotted wall of red cedar, live oak and wax myrtle that formed a barrier against the salt spray and harsh winds coming off the ocean.

Gil parked his car where Point Road dead-ended. It took him a few minutes of shining his flashlight along the side of the road, but he eventually found the break in the thicket that was the trailhead to Hermit Beach. Although he had hiked the path many times before, this was the first time he had ever made the trip alone. Through the darkness, he felt as if he was traveling down a long, leafy throat. After a few minutes he became aware of sounds, both above and below him on the trail, as if something was keeping pace with him. He flicked the beam of his flashlight at the trees that surrounded him, the branches of which curled inward like clutching fingers.

As he drew closer to the marshlands, he was set upon by a cloud of mosquitoes that hovered about his head like a halo. He waved them away, only to have them fly into his nose and mouth. Half-blinded by the living veil of insects, he blundered forward, only to abruptly find himself standing in the open. As he stared up at the star-filled sky, he could hear the sound of the surf hidden behind the dunes, as constant and steady as the breath of a slumbering giant.

He swung his flashlight where memory told him the Hermit's camp should be, but all he saw was an unbroken wall of salt-twisted live oaks and junipers. He let out his breath, shaking his head at his folly. Of *course* there was nothing there. Alvin Crocker was forty years in his grave, his shack long since reduced to kindling. Lloyd's bizarre email aside, it was obvious the only ghost to be found was his own guilty conscience.

But as he inspected the patch of ground that had once been the Hermit's encampment, Gil suddenly felt the hair on the back of his neck go up. He was being watched; he was certain of it. Although he feared what he might see, he forced himself to turn around. As he did so, the beam from his flashlight fell upon the silhouette of a man, standing atop the dunes.

Gil gasped aloud and the flashlight dropped from his fear-numbed fingers, plunging him into darkness. He scrambled to pick up the flashlight and retrained the beam on the dunes, only to find the figure had disappeared. His mouth tacky as glue and his heart fluttering like a hummingbird, Gil climbed the sandy hummock.

The surf rolled against the shore of Hermit Beach with the insistence of a hungry cat greeting its owner. The sand was littered with bushel baskets of sea shells, shining wet and bright like so many tumbled stones. Upon a closer look, he saw an army of fiddler crabs rushing back and forth along the edge of the water. As he played the flashlight beam along the shore, searching for some sign of the figure, he spotted what looked like an outboard boat pulled onto the far eastern end of the shore, partially hidden behind a dune. The dread he'd felt earlier quickly dissipated as he realized what he had thought to be a ghost was merely a fisherman who had put ashore for the evening. As he moved closer to the boat, a man's shape stepped out from behind a nearby dune, blocking his way.

"I'm sorry if I frightened you, mister," he said with an apologetic chuckle. "But you gave me a bit of a start, too . . . " His smile abruptly disappeared as the flashlight beam revealed who it was standing before him.

The machete blow was so swift, Gil barely had time to realize he'd been struck before his belly opened and spilled his intestines onto his shoes. He dropped to his knees like a felled steer, staring down in dumb amazement at his exposed bowels, strewn before him like gory party streamers. Truth to tell, he was not so much surprised that he was being murdered, as at whose hand was doing the killing. As he gazed out toward the ocean, he saw the full moon looking back at him, like the eye of some great beast.

The second blow, this time to his neck, severed his jugular and trachea, and all but separated his head from his shoulders. As he collapsed onto the ground, the fiddler crabs came skittering forward to claim him, covering his face with a living veil of chitin.

H oyt dropped back against a nearby dune, wiping the sweat and blood from his eyes with the back of his arm. He hated killing Gil. He really did. But he would not have been pushed to such extremes if Lloyd hadn't decided to grow a conscience so late in the game.

Of the three, Lloyd had always been the weakest link—but it wasn't until the Hermit's Gallery opened that he snapped completely and became obsessed with that damn painting. No, not obsessed. *Frightened.* That's when he started calling him up in the middle of the night, drunk as a skunk, going on about how the old man had come back from the dead and was haunting Hermit Beach. That's when Hoyt knew he had to get rid of the damn lush before he started blabbing.

It was easy enough to do. Lloyd had told him that he was sailing out to the Point to catch a glimpse of the phantom. All Hoyt had to do was take the launch from his yacht to where Lloyd was anchored, and, under the guise of helping him keep watch, make sure he got properly sloshed. Once Lloyd was eye-rolling drunk, he simply came up behind him and hit him as hard as he could with a belaying pin, then tossed his body overboard. After that he wiped down the pin, hopped back into his launch, and boated back home, with none the wiser.

As for whatever was supposed to be spooking Hermit Beach, if there was a spirit, it did not make an appearance that night to Lloyd. Still, it *was* something of an eerie coincidence that his body was found on the fortieth anniversary of the Hermit's death. Of course, Hoyt had no way of knowing that Lloyd had scheduled that damned email to go out on the same day. Yet it did serve the purpose of luring Gil back to Treasure Beach. And as much as Hoyt disliked the idea of eradicating yet another childhood friend, there was no denying that Gil *was* as much a loose end as Lloyd. The last thing he needed was to find himself in his seventies and charged with murder due to a death bed confession, simply because Gil was afraid to meet his Maker unshriven. It was better to get rid of him now, while still in decent enough physical condition to do so.

All he had to do was plant the idea of going to Hermit Beach to check out the 'ghost' and then pretend to get pass out-drunk and wait for Gil to leave the house. After that it was an easy boat ride from his beach house to the Point. Once there, all he did was sit around until his victim arrived so he could take care of business.

Now it was time for the dirty work. Once he reduced Gil to easily maneuvered pieces that he could stow in the large cooler in the launch, all he had to do was call the towing company (which he owned) and send a truck out to pick up Gil's car and haul it to the salvage yard (which he also owned), where it would be promptly fed into the crusher. Then everything would be taken care of—nicely and neatly, although far from tidily. He removed Gil's wallet, car keys, and ring, then stripped the clothes from the body. Hoyt knew he had to move fast—dawn came far too soon that time of year, and fishermen were notoriously early risers. It would not be long before someone would come cruising past the Point on their way to the open ocean. But even with a freshly sharpened machete, the butchering was far from easy, and soon he found himself covered head-to-toe in gore.

Hoyt decided that since he was mere yards from the ocean, he might as well make use of it, and waded out into the surf to clean himself. Then he would take his yacht out into the Atlantic, where he could safely dispose of Gil's remains in the Gulf Stream. After that, he might cruise on down to Palm Beach and surprise his newest wife to make sure she wasn't fucking the cabana boys like the last one did. As he plunged his hands into the waves, he was reminded of the painting he had bought that afternoon, the same one that had triggered Lloyd's slide into madness. Hoyt prided himself on being a pragmatic man, with no time to waste on flights of fantasy. Hell, he didn't even dream; or if he did, he never remembered them. But there was something about that painting that irritated him from the moment he saw it. Once he was back at the beach house, he was going to make good on his promise and burn the goddamned folky thing.

As he straightened up, something in the back of his mind whispered that he should turn around, even though his instincts told him that to do so would mean not only the end of his life, but of his reason as well.

He was still struggling against the urge to turn and face the horror he was certain awaited him on the shore when something, drawn by blood in the water, leapt from the surf and grabbed Hoyt by his left arm, pulling him beneath the waves. Hoyt screamed as an eight-foot bull shark sped off in the direction of deep water, dragging him along behind it like a child's pull-toy, sea water filling his lungs in place of air. The last thing he saw, before drowning, was the shark swim away with his arm.

Alvin Crocker silently watched as the last of them disappeared beneath the waves. He raised his gaze, as if in thanks, to the moon that spilled its light equally upon the just and the unjust, the dreamers and the dream, the living and the dead, and then turned and headed back over the dunes to his shack.

NANCY A. COLLINS (*b. McGehee, Arkansas, USA, 1959) has authored numerous novels, short stories, and comic books, including* Swamp Thing. *She is a recipient of the HWA's Stoker Award and the British Fantasy Society Award, and has been nominated for the Eisner, World Fantasy and International Horror Guild Awards. Best known for her ground-breaking vampire character, Sonja Blue, which heralded the rise of the Urban Fantasy genre, her works include* Sunglasses After Dark, Knuckles And Tales, *and the* Vamps *series for Young Adults. Her most recent novel is* Magic and Loss, *the third installment in the critically-acclaimed* Golgotham *urban fantasy series. She currently resides in Wilmington, North Carolina, with her fiancé, Tommy, their Boston terrier, Chopper, and an indeterminate number of cats.*

Commentary on "Moonrise on Hermit Beach": *The story comes from the true-life mystery surrounding the death of Robert Harrill (1893-1972), aka the Fort Fisher Hermit, who lived—and died—on the banks of the salt marsh that separates the Cape Fear River from the Atlantic Ocean. I have taken a certain amount of poetic license with the story—Robert Harrill was considerably older than the Hermit in my story, never served in the military, and wasn't a painter—but other than that, the truth is not much stranger than the fiction you're about to read. Robert Harrill was less a hermit, in the traditional sense of the word, than he was a proto-hippie and philosopher. From 1955 until his murder in 1972, he maintained a subsistence existence, squatting in an abandoned concrete bunker on federal prop-*

erty, without electricity or running water, living off the bounty of the land, the occa-sional odd-job, and spare change from the thousands of visitors who came to his campsite to listen to him philosophize on man's relationship to nature. He even played host to actress Ava Gardner on more than one occasion. During the seven-teen years Harrill spent as a "hermit," he eventually became one of North Carolina's most popular tourist attractions. However, his fame also attracted unwelcome atten-tion from thieves and vandals, many of whom believed the old man kept a secret cache of money in his bunker. News of his death in 1972—only recently reclassi-fied as a homicide—shocked and saddened the multitudes of tourists who vacationed along Carolina Beach and Kure Beach, and had come to view The Fort Fisher Hermit, as he was called, as much a part of the scenery as the ocean and the river. Despite initial reports that Harrill had died from natural causes, it has been an open secret that he perished at the hands of a group of young men, believed to be the sons of prominent citizens in the local community. Rumor is these boys—now grown men—are still around.

GOTH THING

D. E. COWEN & DANEL OLSON

(Sometime today or tonight in Huntsville, Texas)

A COLLECTION OF HALF LIVING BLACK LIPPED FACES MOVED INTO the Old Main auditorium noisily, chains on their chests and bottom cheeks jangling. Professor Daniel J. Glasscock felt like it was more of a visitation than a class. Though the summoning of this dark brood was on his account, he shuddered watching them come in.

They were a gathering of dark tattoos and pearl piercings, with sparkles on the tips of their tongues from the gold studs impaled on them. All of them wore shades of black—from faded black, to dark black, to shiny patent-leather black to studded black with thick zippers that seemed to open into their chests. The young women wore large torn fishnet hose and mid-thigh charcoal skirts. Their faces were all white—cold paleness imitating an abandoned corpse. Some of the women were dressed in black vests with netting across abundant cleavage. Those more anorexic relished the lean and fainting look; as if they were trying to blink out of existence like the lines of an old television set being turned off. They would get thinner and thinner until they simply ceased to be.

At the end of this migration of the abominable, a small handful of corpulent women found their way to the last few open seats. They excreted jewelry from their bodies and had manufactured hair that somehow seemed to rise up on top of their heads. The housewives.

Every semester since he started these classes, *hausfraus* buxom and plump from surrounding wealthy suburbs signed up to audit his class. They wanted romance. They wanted to hear about sensual vampires who seduce the understimulated and unadorned, flying them from their dull lives and freeing their souls. They wanted to hear about the vampires and werewolves who rescued lonely women. All wanted to meet a true blooded supernatural creature, that dark guest who came to class and claimed their lives, and gave a monstrous love. That love more devouring than their beer stained, T-shirted husbands, who ignored them on football Sundays, could ever give.

It was three years before when he first performed his debut lecture on Gothic fiction in this former chapel. He was originally booked in a small classroom near the school's maintenance shop across campus, but so many signed up for the class it migrated here. He was agape when he saw the 150 wander in.

The dean made him teach it. The horror movies actually repelled Daniel, and the Goth students were equally frightening. Crow's wing hair, kohled eyes and pancake makeup all seemed a subterfuge for wearing extremely short black skirts and piercings in their tongues only to give better blow. Black torn stockings, or even worse, tight black jeans with links and silver rings and studs, must be crazing a strict father or mother who made the students go to church too many times a week when they were girls. He had no idea this would become the most popular class on campus, forcing him to teach it several times a day. The website one of his students designed helped manage the questions and host the readings. That took time for content, but with his class load, Daniel was assigned a graduate student to do that. The genius of the site was the chat room one of his best students put together for him. *DrGoth.com* soon grew beyond the boundaries of the school.

The website had become a scandal only when a legion of bored housewives trolled their way in, and unexpectedly, absurdly, bared their opera-diva chests. Several major social media sites wanted to buy it then, but Daniel had put the copyright in his name and had bought the domain names too. Soon the university claimed it belonged to them. The student who wrote its script also argued ownership wanting to rename it *"AGOGG 24/7—Awesome Gothic Odd Girls & Grannies"*. Attorneys had been hired. Lawsuits filed. Newspapers had reported. And Daniel just kept on teaching, biding his time until the legal morass finally settled, and mercifully a sabbatical arrived.

The research sabbatical was to be carried out, at the dean's insistence, in Transylvania—literally, the "Land Beyond the Forest", the fabled place of witches' sabbaths and sacrifices, devil-corrupted maidens, and, of course, vampires. Perchance the dean was hell bent on punishing Daniel somehow after the website tussle; possibly he sensed Daniel would come under baleful influences, and perhaps he wasn't wrong.

So six months following the sabbatical granting, Daniel found himself in the feudal prince Vlad Dracul's home city—Sighişoara, Romania—a place where hardly anyone seemed to be walking about, either day or night. Idly waiting for a train at evening in Sighişoara, Daniel chanced to befriend what he had never believed in, a creature truly supernatural. A young gentleman approached—thin, lightly bearded, aristocratic, and attired in a red-speckled inky robe. No one else was heading north to Cluj, and no one else disturbed the professor and the stranger until at last the northbound train pulled into the station. Out of the corner of his eye, Daniel noticed in the reflection of the station lights against the ticket counters' glass doors, that Daniel stood alone. Though young in the light, when the gentleman turned his head, half shadowed, Daniel could see ancient lines of weary foreboding. This gentleman was an old creature. He called himself fallen; life had become "his unlife". The gentleman spoke to Daniel for two hours about the Gothic life of death. Holding Daniel's slate-colored eyes with his own nearly black ones, the Romanian paced and recited poetry, apparently of his own invention, under the sulphurous glow of the train station lamp:

In the souls of those who sit in the dark
so much desire and unfulfilled thirst

In those who sit, and wait and whine and beg in the dark
I enter
so they will no longer want
empty, lonely, pining, unfulfilled.

It is why they never turn on the light
when I enter

It is why they leave the window unfastened
and doors unlocked
allowing me to consummate in the shadows of open rooms.

No shouts, no screams, no cries
for there is nothing to fear in my giving darkness.

The stranger with the waves of dark glossy hair continued,

She is supple
she is soft
she is eager,
her want equal to the cold heat
of need in my ancient veins

I sense the warm flow
of fresh life
in the lines of her neck and breasts

In joyful agony
her body releases
into me

Soul long inhibited
life long hidden
by the chastity of her barren sun,
she is spent to make me full.
She goes into the void
satisfied.

Daniel didn't know whether to clap or run, but he did realize one amazing thing: whether demented or not, this man's hunger could be recorded and analyzed, could form the writing end of this so far fruitless sabbatical and possibly the next, as well as the bloodspring for a new book of photographs and text on living vampires—even a nature film he would narrate of vampires stalking, courting and eating. Why not steal the title for the thing right here? It was so appropriate . . . *The Gothic Life of Death.* What *The Vampire: His Kith and Kin* did for Montague Summers in 1928, or *In Search of Dracula* for Raymond McNally & Radu Florescu in 1972, or *Vampires, Burial, and Death* for Paul Barber in 1988, or *Our Vampires, Ourselves* for Nina Auerbach in 1995, or *The Science of Vampires* for Katherine Ramsland in 2002, this study would do for Daniel right next year. He could leave the little university and scolding dean behind, along with a droning ethics investigation, and head his way to Cambridge, Oxford, Princeton, Harvard, or Yale.

There had just been one consideration the tall gentleman asked to complete the arrangement. A few women each term. A ruby juicy handful of American women who would enter his space freely and of their own free will. A few volunteers for the banquet. In America, the stranger had read, young women would write and pledge marriage to serial killers serving multiple life terms. America was the land of equal opportunity for all monsters. Daniel considered this business for almost two minutes, and had to allow for the sense of it. Besides a stairway to higher academe built by the habits of this unsparkly fellow, he had just found the way to keep classes thrilled with expectation, the romance running high. No woman, however wayward, would ever consider dropping the course now, when Daniel could promise bringing in a real vampire, the wildest animal of her own night fantasies. The cloaked gentleman, who called himself Archangel, pricked his own finger and touched Daniel's skin.

"*This will give you my power over the ones I desire.*"

Daniel felt a stinging on his skin and burning in his veins. He shook it off and got up to leave. Unsatisfied, the gentleman kept a fixed pleading gaze on Daniel.

"One more thing. I am tired of these shadows. I need to smell the freshness of a new world."

Fearful of the next request, Daniel asked, "What else can you want?"

"Teach me about this Internet. It intrigues me."

Daniel sighed, that at least was harmless.

"What is Gothic literature? Is it about vampires? Is it about werewolves? Is it delving into the recesses of the darkest part of a diseased human mind?" Dr. Glasscock prodded the class.

He paused, and then smiled again, taking a small remote control from his pocket. With a single red button he lowered a screen. With a green button he turned on a projector hidden in the wall behind them. With a blue button, he lowered the lights in the room. With an orange button he projected a photograph of the head of a mummified corpse in frozen shriek on the screen. He waited as he heard the usual mixture of "cool" and "gross" and "ewww" blow through them, like wind rippling.

He repeated his question, "So WHAT THE HELL IS GOTH, AND WHY DO WE READ IT ANYWAY?" With a flick of the remote a single red light shone down on him holding a dripping sword he had taken from the prop box he kept inside the hollow of the tall lectern.

Daniel could sense ripples of questions and murmurs from behind him. And then he would begin by walking to the edge of the stage, wireless microphone in hand. From that vantage he could see everything and anything. With his poker face he saw the plump black tops of the front row, dark edges of nipples rising, and up the tight black leather skirts of those in the upper rows. He didn't like to see the ones who were into "cutting", but there they were. He, ironically, did not like the sight of blood so much and the scabs of crosses and horns made him queasy. Goths also tended to have large, dark tattoos just above their pelvic bones and they either wore very low cut black jeans or their heavy chain belts would sag the pants to reveal their lower-backs. Daniel decided that there was only one reason to have a tatt placed there: as a landing strip. Most semesters, he was offered to test his landing gear on at least a sextet of the more entranced of his followers. But now, he pointed the sword at a Gothic Lolita in the front row, all black cupid's bow lips smiling in the red shadows of the light.

"The study of Gothic literature and its psychological meanings is not a study of vampires or werewolves or ghosts," he posed. "They are just dark images to project your true fears. Addiction—the vampire's blood thirst. The sexual predator—the vampire's seduction and destruction of young women. Misogyny—or the hatred of women—the vampire's desire to destroy young, beautiful women. Sexually transmitted disease—the bite of the vampire and the wound of the werewolf; they are really allegories for sexually transmitted diseases. Immortality—the true corruption of the vampire. To be immortal, but *not to live*! The price of the ultimate wish of men is the ultimate corruption of men."

So Daniel went on:

"The story is not as important as the allegory. The darkness of the vampire and blood lust of the werewolf. Insatiable addicts who cannot control themselves and even have no memory of what they destroy in their feeding frenzy."

A sparkled wrist would always rise up. One of the housewives. He knew what was coming. It happened every semester. He looked up and pointed to the hand. He hit the remote and raised the lights to get a good look at the woman.

"I view vampires as romantically tragic figures who just need the love of a good woman to turn them back? Am I wrong?"

The Professor's eyes scrunched, his head tilted like a corgi's.

She hesitantly nodded and then said, "I am a Christian Gothic writer. I live for Christian Gothic romances."

This was a new one to him.

"Christian Goth?"

The woman looked slighted.

"You know, like where in the end the vampire turns good and finds Jesus, who was born in the night-time and rejected too, and preached about cutting off offending arms and treacherous eyes, and who totally ripped a temple! Then the *Chrampire* cherishes forever the woman who turned him into a loving husband."

Daniel exploded.

"Do you have any clue what that means? A vampire is the incarnation of corruption and evil. There are no good vampires. He exists against the laws of God and nature. His blood lust drives him and controls him. Can you imagine the torment a Christian vampire—your *Chrampire*—would go through? To know everything about your existence is evil and corrupt. To know that every time you grew hungry, you hurt someone. . . you killed someone. You violated someone in a blood rape. Do you know the corruption that would instill inside of such a creature? It would corrupt and corrode him. He would become the most vile, evil thing that ever existed. He would carry out his evil with full knowledge of the harm he was doing. He would feel guilt. That guilt would eat at him until it turned him insane. In the end, he might even justify what he was doing believing this Christianity demanded that he seduce and destroy his victims."

It was only after he noticed that spittle was flying out of his mouth onto the Lolita that he stopped, and took a few deep breaths before continuing.

"Let's move on from that sort of silliness."

The woman very loudly stood up and walked out crying, "Jesus was Gothier than thou," and then spoke something about having him fired.

"They can't fire me," Daniel yelled, "I have tenure."

Charlene DeBovier was deadened. She had finally gotten the girls to bed and had gone into the spare room where the computer was hooked up; locking the door she would not be disturbed. Since her walkout from class, there was to be no more reading or homework for *The Gothic Life of Death* course. Why do professors have to go hysterical like that? She was too tired to write one more paragraph of her latest novel *Blacker Lipstick*, but never too exhausted for field research. She was a professional; this was one of a writer's duties. She spent the usual ten minutes pulling out her headset and vidcam, untangling the wires; loading the instant messenger program and then getting online in a tabbed set of browser windows each showing her favorite sites. Charlene then loaded her online music player and video player and was ready. Very ready. Another fight with her husband; another day dragging the kids to school and back. A PTA meeting. Her only pleasure was knowing that while she listened to this set of undersexed mothers argue over the upcoming Christmas cotillion for the PTA, she could feel her nipple ring rubbing against her bra and smiled thinking how shocked these leaders of a private Christian elementary school would be scandalized to know. They would not know arousal if a large tongue went down on them while sitting in the front pew of a church naked.

Charlene liked to think in terms of secret scandal. That was her online life. She had put together multiple online personalities all over the Internet: MySpot, Wahoo 180, MyPlace, Shutter, Blogland. All different and all aimed at attracting the attention of lonely men and a few women she could tease and taunt online, leading them on with suggestions and near invitations; always keeping them far enough away never to upset her real life or real name. That, she protected.

To one set of her lapping dogs as she called them, she was the HunstvilleGirl. A sweet thirtyish housewife in a bad marriage desperately looking for sexual abandon. To another she was DarkandSassy, a provocative seductress who openly solicited hanging tongues and photos of engorged pantspythons, which they were always willing to give her. Charlene's favorite, though, was Demile, a twisted hotty Gothie who just needed someone to tenderly suck her arteries from her breasts while she orgasmed.

She would go through their pages and target four or five, cultivating them like an erotic gardener. Slowly leading them to contact her more and more. First, some gently flirting notes. Then a regular exchange with a few dramatic and charged questions like, "I am just bored trying to decide if I should get online or get out my Trojan *Tri-Phoria* and come to a happy ending . . . so good it will blow my hair back." That one tended to draw out the tongues she could tell were drooling over her. She would get them to begin to instant message her and share their hopes, dreams, disappointments and fetishes.

Dr.Goth.com was the ultimate meeting site for that. For every sweet note she would post on someone's Gothblog, she would get ten back. Each was typical: a stifled, sexually frustrated male acting like a chow-chow salivating at a lamb chop just beyond his leash. She loved it. She knew exactly what made them sweat and got them hard, releasing themselves while she cooed and coaxed through her web mike.

She would also play the sweet, jealous and afraid lover-to-be, questioning every post made by every Goth Girl on their Gothblogs. She would start with little pouting questions about a "wink" or "nudge" or "dude" left in passing. Later, as she dominated their online time, she would get more demanding: throwing online tantrums and shutting them from her email for days then forgiving them if they performed on their webcams.

She loved this play. Her husband, a salesman for a jet fuel distributor, was gone so often she no longer cared if he was in the house or not. They slept in separate beds and even though she missed the sex, she did not miss him or his sex. He fucked like a child slurping ice cream. Sloppy, quick and then over. She could find all the virtual sex she wanted and never have to worry about STDs, stalkers or even commitment. No one knew who she was. No one saw who she really was. She controlled everything and would only occasionally flash glimpses of camera phone photos of herself standing in front of the bathroom mirror. Her breasts, large, but broken down from her teen years of going braless to taunt male teachers, were held up for the photos to keep their shape.

Tonight randomly running through Gothblog pages, she found one avatar she had been slowly grooming—The Archangel. His picture was very realistic. Long wavy black hair with corpse-paint makeup and black lips and eyebrows. His teeth were bared and, of course, pointed. Every person here wanted to be something undead. Vamps and slave bitches—all begging for verbal sex; all playing this game. Charlene thought she was the best, though. She got them to be real and then sucked the life from them. She even talked two men into leaving wives and heading to Des Moines to meet her at a Big Boy diner on the interstate, dreaming of fucking her brains out in a motel nearby. They were to arrive and find an empty table, and they couldn't touch her now. All grist for her writing mill.

Archangel was very subdued, though. He played coy. On occasion, he would allow a webcam shot of himself but only for a moment; as if it were a strain and he would dramatically turn it off and go back to IM. But she knew she eventually could get out of him what she wanted. In their last exchange she had him believing she was having an orgasm while he cut and pasted Gothic poems onto the IM screen. Crazy boy!

Charlene smiled when Archangel responded to her IM buzz. His avatar and text screen popped up immediately.

"Salut Demile"—Archangel

"Hey lover"—Demile

"I was thinking of you. I was willing you to buzz me"—Archangel

"Are you ready to be my slave tonight?"—Archangel

Charlene paused then typed,

"My, my, u are being forward tonight. What's a virgin girl to do?"—Demile

This time Archangel took a bit to respond. Growing impatient, Charlene wrote

". . . . . "—Demile

"Just pondering how I would despoil my willing slave's virginity"—Archangel

Charlene smiled again. She had him! He was in and now she could play with him.

"I'm a little hot, let me take my bra off. Hold a sec"—Demile. Then she changed her IM icon to a camera phone and showed him.

"Take everything off"—Archangel

Hmmm, Charlene thought to herself. Not quite what I thought. Maybe I misjudged him.

This time she flashed a photograph of her substantial ass she had taken holding the camera over her shoulder. "OMG OMG OMG"—Archangel

"Invite me in"—Archangel

A link appeared on her text screen. She held the cursor over it and the browser read nothing. It was obviously a web link, but she was nervous that maybe he was trying to have her download a virus.

"What is this?"—Demile

"An invitation"—Archangel

"To what?"—Demile

"To me"—Archangel

"Are u trying to load a virus?"—Demile

No one had ever sent a link on IM. She did not know you could do that and she knew IM better than anyone.

"Do what I tell you to do, my New World Bitch. I am hungry"—Archangel

Charlene paused. Goth was one thing, being called a gothbitch was over the top. She was a Christian woman.

"Exactly, what I intend"—Archangel

"INVITE ME NOW, AMERICAN WOMAN"—Archangel

Charlene hit the disconnect button on the IM screen and nothing happened. Archangel's avatar changed and became an animated version of itself—eyes moving and lips opening to smile, fangs baring, in repetition.

"INVITE ME SLAVE . . . "—Archangel

The avatar grew larger on the screen. Charlene hit the Ctrl Alt Del buttons in succession but nothing happened.

"I know where you are"—Archangel

"INVITE ME NOW MADAME CHARLENE"—Archangel

She tried to shut down the computer and nothing happened.

"Madame Charlene DeBovier of Huntsville, Texas"—Archangel

Fear grew in her and she was annoyed that she was being aroused by it. No one had ever taken over her computer before. She reached over and turned off her wireless router. Nothing happened.

"INVITE ME *NOW!*"—Archangel

Charlene unplugged the computer from the wall. The screen went blank and she sat in her chair. She'd never seen anything like that before. *Who was this guy?*

The screen flickered back on and the avatar of Archangel was now the background for the screen. The text box was blinking red:

"Please, invite me. It is what you really want."—Archangel

She felt her hand moving to the mouse on her desk and then moving the cursor over the link. Her index finger clicked the left button of the mouse.

Archangel's head began to lift from the screen and approach her as she tried to scream; her throat locked from fear.

Statuesque Archangel grabbed the woman and forced her onto her bed, then ripped into her silent throat. He drained her quickly and let her drop on the bed.

"Certainly no virgin," he said as he re-entered the computer screen, not noticing a big-thighed apparition rising from the woman's body. It seemed to stretch as if waking from a long slumber. A form shimmered into view out of the shadow. Confident in its existence, it floated toward the computer.

The shimmering Charlene laughed and followed Archangel into the screen.

Such a Goth thing, he thought. *Such a cheap, gaudy, goddamn Hammer Studios Goth thing, but it's got to be done. It was part of the deal.*

Prof. Glasscock examined his surroundings on leaving the women's dormitory. The auditorium in Old Main was once a chapel, discontinued when Texas courts finally decided that state universities weren't supposed to make students go to church. The windows were stained glass images of Christ and shepherds and angels looking over Roman soldiers. Vaulted ceilings were still inlaid with gold filigree borders edging rounded corners. The plaster in between revealed once painted shapes of gargoyles, demons and angels in combat, swords drawn, while their leaders at opposite polarities watched. The gaps between the rows of seats mimicked a transept cross that made him uncomfortable to focus on, though he had stood lecturing here many times. Behind the curtains on the stage was the outline of an apse. An oddity for a small university in a small town in Texas filled with Baptists and a few Catholics, where every fourth citizen is a prison inmate, and the "Killer Burger" is served just across from the town's "Walls" prison and active death chamber.

One fixed spotlight beamed directly on him as he sat on the edge of the stage; legs dangling, dispersing shadows across the pews, he nervously swung them while waiting.

The other light was also on the stage where the three female students were kneeling, arms behind their backs, all heads down. They weren't bound, but they might as well have been. Daniel held them there with the gift of the gentleman's blood; the stranger would sense they were held now, and was certainly getting hungry, not pleased by the wait. The young women were each in various states of night garb: one in black underwear; one in a red bathrobe; the last still wearing her midnight-blue blouse, but only a tiny matching thong panty underneath. A fraternity candy store. And if they wanted this, Daniel thought, then who really is to blame? Who is the victim here? Who the villain?   Daniel knew at least one of them had claim to the title of virgin. She would be Catholic. They wait and keep it official when they can, he mused, sincerely touched. But an official virgin is an official virgin and needed here—that is how it is supposed to work for the guest in this necessary *cliché*. The rest were dietary supplements, available if needed.

A vampire's scarlet dream, this gothic mise-en-scène so perfectly staged by night in the space Daniel taught by day. Nothing less than ideal for a devouring, and yet . . . I am not this kind of person, Daniel began repeating to himself. I am not someone who does this sort of thing. *But why shouldn't I be?*

He heard movement on the roof and looked up. He could see ragged shadows on the stained glass. A pair of shadowed wings flickered, or maybe two pairs, behind a white glass angel as if using the form of righteousness to shield its motives as it looked in. *Here are three gorgeous voluptés to bow to your every whim, Vampire,* Daniel thought. *The Hounds of Hell may await you, and me, but in the meantime here are the willing women, dark femmes right off the cover of* Gothic Beauty *magazine, and eager to show full dedication to Gothdom, all to be had for a bite.*

A fist smashed through one small stained glass panel and dispelled Daniel's rationalizing. The glass sparkled like a Tiffany river, swirling in the air until it coagulated in a single lump of color. The fist way above was dark and clawed and lean and sinewy. It had streaks of white running down it. It was not black. More like something that was once white but began to turn after years of corruption. Daniel remembered his stock lecture and thought he really had taught the truth, after all.

The winged shadow at the window tried to pry off the screens covering the larger stained glass through which Archangel's body could enter.

Well at least it should all be over soon. He looked over at the women and could feel their growing panic over a predator's hunger for them.

More shadows moved across the windows, and looking over at the vulnerable women on the stage who seemed the opposite of eager . . . A feeling was seeping into Daniel. His memory of Archangel's arrangement was blurring and becoming vague. His mind was going somewhere else. Pleasure, pressure, urges—a sensation awash with young blood, a sad disgust with himself.

He would resist whatever came, if he had the courage, because no one's really a cad all the time.

Three Goth Girls stared at him. They were already acrouch with fear before this, but now they were paralyzed as the winged shadows began to slam against the window.

Daniel had meant to try to block their minds from recognizing it with a fatherly smile, an understanding look, but his wintry smile lacked the energy to calm their fear.

It was all coming to a horrible end just like the Gothic novels do. Female flesh bitten, broken, and forsaken. But something was changing the formula.

The sounds of the hunter began to fill the air in Old Main lecture hall completely, and had the three women fully in stupors.

Daniel was surprised that the sword he pulled from the prop box in the lectern hollow had any edge to it at all. He never considered it could lop anybody—it was, well . . . something you buy on the last day of the Renaissance Festival because you can't afford the suit of armour. He only used the sword at the start of each term to add drama, especially to inspire his students who would in week three act out the terrors of Ray Russell's mock-Gothic tale for *Playboy*, "The Runaway Lovers".

Archangel had finally given up on the screens above, and flew down outside trying to find a door release below. Daniel was hoping the fiend would pull it back and see if this festival sword could actually chop.

Daniel sucked in a deep breath and pointed the sword at the hole in the door. He stabbed straight into the hole, striking flesh. A jolt ran through him: searing pain as if grabbing a cast iron handle sitting over a flame. Daniel pushed in further until he felt the blade break through the flesh, and a black-nailed hand fall to the floor. Archangel screamed and grabbed the blade with his remaining hand. Daniel slid the blade out from the vampire's torso through the hole, slicing through Archangel's fingers, severing three. They wiggled on the floor as Daniel reeled back into the room. He heard a thud from the other side of the door. A shrill cry vibrated against the heavy door. Something crashed into the door but it held. Another hand reached through the wound in the wood groping for a handle. Daniel brought the sword down one more time. The blade sliced into the wrist and the hand fell to the floor like a dying spider.

The blood was what overwhelmed the professor. It splattered everywhere and it seemed to sear his skin when it splashed on his hands and face. Daniel fell to the floor in pain, writhing for some time before it stopped, either drying on his skin or being absorbed into it because there was no residue left.

Their professor's fall seemed to break the vampire's spell on the women who once called themselves Doom Cookies. They proceeded to run caterwauling to the door, saw the hand and then ran to the windows. There they screamed again and scrambled under seats in the 12th row. As Daniel was trying to recover, their screams, along with Archangel's, ripped into him like ice picks in the ears.

Daniel steadied himself to his feet. He stood up straight and waited to see if he would lose consciousness again. The remaining disorientation had faded and he looked down at the hand again. It had traveled: six feet gone, and heading for the door. Trying to get back to its owner, Daniel knew. That was both wily and touching, but not going to happen tonight.

He looked around. There was nothing to drop on it. The sword he had used was broken when he severed the hand and even if he poked it with the jagged edge, that wouldn't squash the thing. Daniel searched for something large, flat and heavy. Nothing.

So he stepped on it. His heel went down on the hand and he stomped. He did it again and again like he was trying to kill the Devil's own roaches. He could feel little crunches of bone under his shoe each time he did it. Archangel screamed even louder, which caused the ladies under the 12th row to screech in a way that made him think that each time he broke a bone, some cord to Archangel was being severed.

Daniel kept up his attack, alternating feet as one grew tired, until he had pureed the hand. The black blood seemed to have been squeezed out of it. It had stopped moving. It looked like a large white and black asterisk plastered on the floor.

Then he took the remaining jagged edge of the broken sword and poked it into the flesh. The hand began to bubble and then burst into flames, while some of the blood coagulated and formed what seemed to be brown recluses running away as Daniel tried to clomp them, too.

His hands had a burning sensation and Daniel could see the spilt blood there bubbling into his skin. He could feel the absorbed heat beginning to flow into his veins, racing to his heart. Fear struck him dumb. "I'm being poisoned," he sputtered.

Archangel roared in a deep voice, like a phlegm-clogged yell, as if he was running sandpaper through his vocal chords.

The burning sensation inside the professor grew throughout his body. Every inch of him grew warm, but he did not sweat. It was on the inside. On the outside, his skin was still cool.

Daniel moaned as the burning grew and was getting on the verge of being unbearable. "You poisoned me *youwingedfuckingfreak*!" he bellowed at the door.

On top of the burning, he felt a hunger. He wanted one of the women, and the desire to possess and consume was searing him.

Daniel fell to the floor as he felt as if his insides were scrolls burning in a hearth. He rolled on the floor for a few minutes until he noticed the three women peering up at him with an unmistakably sensual mixture of excitement and dread, with their eyes stretched wide and white, wondering if this action figure could really be their professor. They suddenly poked their heads down beneath the seat-backs.

Astonishingly, the pain was lessened with one thought: *It would be better for me to die, than for them to suffer. I have made my choice.* Daniel felt fine again. Better than fine. He got up and felt really strong for the first time in a month. If there wasn't a homicidal angel waiting outside the door, he'd really enjoy a good walk.

It was at this point Daniel experienced several epiphanies. Daniel liked the word epiphany and considered it to be a highbrow term. He felt ennobled and well-read when he used that word, and since it had a semi-religious meaning, he almost felt spiritual when using it. So that was the word that came to mind as he began to realize several spirit truths.

First, the hunger was controlled. Not gone, just controlled. He could turn it on and off and it could not overwhelm him. Useful, he decided.

Second, he realized that Archangel's severed hand had not been crawling toward him like in the movies. It had been actually crawling toward the students. He heard screams from the hiding women as it landed in rows close. I have a weapon in these digits, Daniel realized. I can kill things with those fingers, but not the Goth Girls. No, they shall not be killed. Useful again, he decided.

Third, Daniel came into the knowledge that the spilled blood desecrated the last remaining vestiges of sanctity of the auditorium, going back to the days when it was still used as a chapel. He then heard screams from outside, a woman's screams. *Not useful,* he decided.

Finally, Daniel looked at the sword and the corruption that had overcome it. He could feel that the corruption was connected to Archangel, the sword seemed to tell him his name. He could still feel the weird nature of Archangel's blood mixing in his. Archangel was here to die. He wanted to. Daniel looked at the sword. *It talks to me,* he realized. *That's useful too,* he decided. The blade ignited for a moment and Daniel saw the metal replenish itself. *You have my power. Kill the fallen one.*

Daniel raised the sword and smiled.

Daniel unlocked the doors and let them swing open. The be-handed Archangel was rising to his feet.

Following the mental instructions provided by the sword, Daniel pirouetted clumsily toward Archangel, trying to look like one of those leather clad heroes in the fantasy novels he once read. Despite his ineptness at sword fighting, the sword guided his arms. Wings outstretched and his mouth-face gaping open, Archangel poised at Daniel to strike.

The blade swung round with his last turn; Archangel was still approaching as if he were in a Tarantino film. The blade sliced through the Romanian's neck, leaving a clean line across the base. He stopped and stared at Daniel.

"*Bagamias pula in mata*," Archangel whispered before trying to look down to see what had happened. The line at the base of his neck widened as his head lowered, toppling to the floor. Archangel's headless body stood for a moment, black ooze gurgling from his upper torso.

The head rolled on the floor as his body crumpled. The black bile flowed from Archangel's neck; then small creatures, like some type of formless bugs escaping a burning house. The things scattered across the floor and were gone. Archangel's body and clothes were no longer black. They had become a brilliant white. Cleansed.

The eyes on the severed head stared at Daniel as web lines of glowing red spread over it and Archangel's body. It burst into a bright cold blue flame which dissipated into a shallow outline of dust.

"STOPPPPP. Don't touch His Dark Holiness. Not My Beautiful One," cried a voice behind Daniel. He turned to see a flickering winged specter rushing toward him. It was female, not young but not ancient, with large and drooping breasts losing their fight to stay in a sooty halter top: a phantom in a very short black skirt the color of vulcanized rubber, that accentuated a Liberty Bell ass. A familiar woman in the painful way that an aged succubus is to male dreamers. A woman named Charlene. Daniel remembered her.

She looked at Daniel as if first getting her bearings as to where she was. After a few seconds she began to throw curses at him. Not magical spells, but curses, a boiling stream of bitchcraft. He definitely heard them, and for a moment felt, *It's just like being married all over again.*

He raised the sword and she plunged into it, and halted. The newly reforged Gothic blade penetrated the ephemeral skin of the Gothic bride. *I have its power now, Christian Goth,* Daniel smiled.

She yelled trying to pull herself back. The wound began to spread into a lattice work of broken lines. She flickered and then was gone.

Daniel's eyes circled the place.

Not one of his students was still in church.

I'm not hungry just yet anyway.

D.E. COWEN *(b. Brownsville, Texas, USA, 1957) is a trial attorney by trade and author of a volume of poetry entitled* Sixth and Adams *(2001). David lives in Houston, Texas, with his wife Susan and his two sons. He practices law in the historic city of Galveston, Texas, which has inspired much poetry and photography. His poems have been published in various hard copy and online journals for the past many years including those from George Mason University, Stephen F. Austin University, Sam Houston State University and many privately published journals as well. His poetry was featured in the Canadian Broadcasting Company's Radio journal* Outfront *in a 2005 tribute on 9/11. Thisibelieve.org printed an essay of his in its 2012 collection* On Motherhood *currently available in bookstores. In 2012, CineAction Magazine, Canada's leading film journal, published David's essay review of Danel Olson's* The Exorcist: Studies in the Horror Film *(Centipede Press, 2012). Three short scholarly articles on the subject of zombie films written by David will appear in June Pulliam's* The Encyclopedia of the Zombie: The Walking Dead in Popular Culture and Myth *to be published in 2013 by ABC-CLIO. David has a number of fiction and analytical projects in the works.*

His work as a trial attorney brings a different element to the horror genre: a jaded view of the true nature of humanity exposed countless times in various forms in his cases. David is convinced that if a devil truly exists, he is jealous of the unending capacity of human beings to sink below their status to commit the unspeakable. This fosters a gritty, sardonic point of view reflected in David's writings.

Commentary from D.E. Cowen: *"Goth Thing" began with a trip taken by Danel Olson to Romania, relayed to me in photographs and fascinating recountings of Danel traveling through the inspirational birthplace of modern horror and gothic literature. I suggested to him that he try to pen a story of a professor taking a sabbatical to the mother country for all horrors and in turn he suggested that I do it. Taking up the challenge I produced an entire novel,* The Goth Sabbatical, *a twisted tale of ancient horrors uncovered by a hack college professor more interested in preserving his job and satisfying his sexual desires than the subject of his profession. We decided to collaborate to present a variation of this story in short form as "Goth Thing". Ultimately, the story is about choices and their consequences. Choosing to bask in the darker recesses of one's desires has its pleasures, but the consequences for the soul are sometimes inalterable. While not a good man by any means before his grim sabbatical, the main character Glasscock still chooses to* *wallow in the corruption of tainted blood for the shallow pleasures it brings. His attempt to purge himself of the choices he has made only serves to corrode his humanity even further. Such is the way of all such choices in history from Caligula to Pol Pot and beyond.*

DANEL OLSON, Editor, *(b. Brainerd, Minnesota, USA, 1965) has taught as English professor at Lone Star College in Houston since 1993. His favorite class to teach is Horror, Ghost, & Gothic Fiction. That is where this book will be read with equal fright and delight, and even acted out.*

Recent projects Danel edited include 21st Century Gothic: Great Gothic Novels Since 2000 *(Scarecrow Press, 2011),* The Exorcist: Studies in the Horror Film *(2011, Centipede Press), and* Exotic Gothic 1-4 *(Ash-Tree Press and PS Publishing, 2007, 2008, 2009, 2012). This fifth, most sumptuous set of* Exotic Gothic *you now view marks the 121st story featured in the Series, each tale a kiss on the lips from dusk itself.*

For the print journals The New York Review of Science Fiction *and* Cemetery Dance, *Danel has interviewed writers, and he is a columnist for* The Weird Fiction Review, *introducing promising new fiction & graphic novels. For American encyclopedias and French journals, Danel has written on ancient goddesses in literature and film (from the presence of Kali in the novel* Jasmine *to the influence of Ishtar on modern zombie movies).*

In progress are a new interview with Patrick McGrath, a book on how 9/11 affected American Gothic fiction, as well as The Devil's Backbone & Pan's Labyrinth: Studies in the Horror Film *and* The Shining: Studies in the Horror Film *(both from Centipede Press).*

Danel and his family live in The Woodlands, Texas, where he is often found in a hammock under the giant loblollies, reading a scary PS volume while night falls, the coyotes stir, and his drink vanishes.

For always believing and making this book possible, he thanks Nicky and Pete Crowther, Marcela Bolívar, Apolinar Chuca, Sabrina Sin, Nick Gevers, Michael Smith, Catherine Olson, Morris and Olga Olson, Amy Price, Don Bratland, Dale Townshend, Aliki Varvogli, Glennis Byron, David Punter, Walter Rankin, Bernice Murphy, Patrick McGrath, Jerad Walters, & Universities of Stirling and Dundee.

Commentary from Danel Olson: *Not all of "Goth Thing" is true.*

THE CORONER'S BRIDE

CAMILLE DEANGELIS

IT IS AN EXPERIENCE KNOWN TO ALL WHO SLEEP, TO BE CALLED OUT of a dream by a voice which cannot be traced upon revival of the waking faculties. The voice may be that of one in the household who denies any attempt to wake the sleeper, or it may belong to one who is very far away, even beyond the grave. In my case, it was a voice completely unfamiliar to me, though it spoke as if it knew me all my life.

Once my chores were finished and before the children arrived home from school, it was my habit to go out into our little back garden with my needlework and revel for a while in the bright afternoon. As I grew drowsy in the dappled shade of the elm tree, the sounds of the city faded and my embroidery hoop fell to my lap. One day, indulging myself in this manner, I heard the voice. It was not Mariah's—how could it be?—but it spoke with the same easy affection:

Have you ever known a finer day, Nora? The sun rims everything in gold. Oh, I do wish I could feel that breeze on my face. You're so fortunate to be possessed of all your senses.

This strange remark roused me somewhat.

Look, Nora, a hummingbird! They say hummingbirds move so quickly they live outside of time. Perhaps I am a sort of hummingbird myself now.

I woke fully then, darting glances to either side as a clamor of childish laughter and scurrying footsteps sounded on the pavement beyond the side gate. I was alone in the garden, apart from the hummingbird dipping into the honeysuckle upon the lattice.

My uncle is not the sociable creature he once was, in happier times, so it was a pleasant sort of shock when he brought an old college chum home for supper. Charley introduced me to Dr. Cutler with a warmth and vigor he hadn't shown for months, and I could tell they'd already passed an hour or two in the tavern. The children stared at the two men in fascinated silence, their chicken croquettes forgotten in the excitement. This was a side of their father they seldom saw.

Old jokes and reminiscences can be rather tedious when one cannot share in them, but they allowed me to observe our companion, who seemed ever more amiable as the evening went on. Dr. Cutler answered Charley's questions about his travels through Europe and the Caribbean, and spoke fondly of two sisters, one of whom had died of cholera. The three siblings were visiting their uncle, a prosperous merchant in Havana, Cuba, when the outbreak occurred. Dr. Cutler's voice caught on the name *Annabel*, and the look on his face stirred something I kept buried in my heart.

A few days had passed since the dream-voice in the garden, and from then on even the most ordinary occurrences had taken on a tinge of unreality. When Dr. Cutler regarded me warmly in the midst of one of Charley's rambling anecdotes, I thought it was merely the candlelight indulging my feminine optimism. Charley had always been kind to me, and I loved my niece and nephew almost as if they were my own; but I was weary of overlooking that portion of the household income which furnished the liquor cabinet, and wearier still of strangers mistaking me for Charley's wife. I did not wish to watch the children grow up and go away, slouching into middle age with only my melancholy uncle for company.

I put Kitty and Little Charley to bed, observing with detached curiosity the haste in my own movements. When I returned to the table Dr. Cutler said, "I hope you'll pardon my imposing on your family supper, Miss Dobbin. There is plenty to eat at home, but I am starved for laughter."

My uncle took out his tobacco pouch and filled the bowl of his pipe. "I wonder how that new job of yours affects your appetite."

His friend laughed. "If it did, I should look for a position for which I were better qualified."

"We neglected to mention, Nora, that I once persuaded Magnus to sneak me into the morgue, so I might look at the cadavers. Of course I'd been to plenty of funerals, but I had need of one—good and spoiled—for a story I was writing."

"Charley!" Our guest cast an apprehensive glance in my direction.

My uncle lit his pipe and shook out the match. "I never watch what I say in Nora's company. She'd consider it an insult."

"Is this true?" Dr. Cutler asked, and I smiled by way of an answer.

Two weeks earlier our friend had been appointed city coroner. Dr. Cutler and his sister were visiting an aunt in Mount Airy when the post became available, and upon his appointment they'd taken a house in the same neighborhood. Now I knew for certain there was no Mrs. Cutler.

"Next time you must bring your sister." Charley's jovial tone signaled, for me at least, that he'd sufficiently drowned his sorrows. But by the look on Dr. Cutler's face I saw my uncle's remark, however generous, had been ill judged.

Soon afterward Charley saw his friend into a cab, and when I passed him a candle the look on my face betrayed me. He fell into an armchair with a sigh. "Don't be ridiculous, Nora. What kind of life would you have, with a husband always getting called away in the middle of the night to interpret a murder scene? It's not as if he's practicing medicine anymore. There's nothing noble in it; the life in question is already lost."

"And you call yourself his friend! The writing of sensational tales of blackmail and revenge—now *that* is the most noble of professions, is it?"

Charley slumped in the chair and rubbed his eyes. "I'm sorry, dear. You know I only said those things out of selfishness. Magnus is the best of men, and I won't say or do anything to prevent you knowing him better."

I laid a hand on his shoulder—*pax*—and took up my candle. Once I'd dressed for bed I stared into my mother's looking-glass, to survey myself as objectively as I was able. My face was by no means unpleasant to look upon, but I'd never been a great beauty; I had faith in my own intelligence, yet I couldn't see how anyone outside my immediate circle knew I possessed it. Hope is sweet, and it is tempting to take too much.

*T*here, now, said the voice. *It was not easy, but I arranged it.*

"What do you mean?"

In a city this size they might've gone for months without a chance meeting. And I know my brother: he would've kept on thinking 'I must look up old Charley Dobbin', and you'd both have been worn and gray by the time he got around to doing it.

"Your brother . . . Dr. Cutler? Magnus?"

My, you are *sleepy.*
"Annabel. Am I dreaming of Annabel?"
You'll see. Oh, do say we'll be friends, Nora . . .

"There's never been a better time to view this collection," Magnus said as we went up the steps of the surgeons' museum. "The new acquisitions are incomparable."

The Mütter was rarely visited by anyone outside the medical school, and he'd arranged to give us a private tour. Charley was sure to touch something ghastly—or *say* something ghastly—and if I felt ill at ease it was for this reason only.

We were alone in the museum. In tall glass cases we found skeletons suspended, some of which still wore the elaborate trappings of the vascular system, preserved through a sort of curing process and dyed a livid red. There were shelves upon shelves of unnatural protuberances, and faces without even a skull to cling to.

Magnus approached a horizontal case, which housed a massive and very ancient corpse. "Now here is another of the great new marvels I mentioned to you: this poor lady was discovered when one of the older burial grounds was overturned in the name of civic progress. It is believed she died of yellow fever in the epidemic of 1792. Through the decomposition process, the fatty tissues of her body have been turned to a substance which is very like soap."

My uncle opened his mouth and I immediately held up my hand. "If you're going to ask if we can use her to wash with, Charley, for Heaven's sake, spare us."

He rolled his eyes as if I were the childish one. "Actually, I was going to ask our esteemed guide if the lady hadn't lost her teeth before she passed from this mortal coil. Certainly they're missing now?"

"Very good, Charley. It may be that they neglected to bury her with her false set, or perhaps she hadn't any." Magnus regarded the remains in the glass case with something akin to tenderness. "We call her Mistress Leidy."

I raised an eyebrow. "That isn't her name?"

Magnus smiled wryly. "It's the name of the doctor who brought her here."

Once we'd made the acquaintance of Mistress Leidy, Charley went in another direction, pulling faces at the wax models and making notes in the little black book he carried in his pocket. Magnus approached a case of foetal skeletons, including a specimen I could not decide whether to think of as one, or two. Beside these tiny sets of bones a group of their fellows slept in jars with eyes shut tight.

For a moment I turned away, and resolved to think of something ordinary. "I thought your sister would be joining us, Dr. Cutler."

"I'm afraid this isn't Margaret's idea of a pleasant outing." Magnus pointed to a pair of conjoined foetuses, nestled forever in a false womb of glass and preserving fluid. "Particularly in light of such specimens as these." He sensed my hesitation, and at the same moment we lifted our eyes from the babes in the jar. "They were twins," he said. "I don't believe I've told you that. Everyone was surprised to hear it, even when they were small. Margaret is dark and Annabel fair. Temperamentally, too, they were very different, but always they were each other's greatest ally—as all sisters should be, though seldom are."

I'd thought I was long past wishing for a sister to ease my loneliness in the world, but just then I felt a flicker of the old longing.

"I hope you and Margaret will be great friends, Nora. These past two years she's lived in a sort of twilight: eating little, taking pleasure in nothing. I see a spark in you, and I hope it will kindle her."

I felt the heat rising in my cheeks. "You have a faith in me I can't possibly have earned, Dr. Cutler."

"Let me be the judge of that. Will you come to luncheon tomorrow?"

Tell him you hear me. Tell him I remember the frog he hid in my pinafore. It was the voice of the garden. It had whispered in my right ear, and when I turned sharply to meet it I found a little patch of fog on the glass, already fading by degrees.

"Miss Dobbin?" I felt his hand on my wrist. "Are you all right?"

"Did you . . . " I pointed to the spot on the glass where the breath-fog had been. "Do you see that, Dr. Cutler?"

"I promise you," he replied, with only the trace of a smile. "They didn't move."

We continued on to the next display. Here was Hyrtl's collection of skulls from across Central and Eastern Europe, each carefully labeled—ink on bone—with name, age, place, and cause of death. There were nearly a hundred and fifty in all, and displayed together they made quite a gathering of faceless faces.

Such a morbid place to start a courtship!

This time I didn't turn when I heard the voice, and I heard her laugh ever so softly. Magnus regarded me with concern, and I resolved to test him. "It is very quiet in here, isn't it?"

Just then we heard the soft sound of a page turning. Charley stood before the plaster death-cast of the famous Siamese Twins, licking his pencil-tip before he resumed his scribbles.

Magnus regarded me with a brief, fond look, then glanced at the wall of skulls. "It ought to be."

If I'm to marry a man who spends his days in the company of the dead, well then: when he comes home in the evening he's bound to appreciate me all the more.

But first I had to make friends with his sister. Magnus held onto my hand after he'd helped me out of the carriage. "Before you meet her, I just want to say ... that it will take time to get to know her. I know you'll be patient, Nora."

Margaret did not greet us at the door, and Magnus showed me through the downstairs rooms with an air of apology. "The house came fully furnished. It won't quite feel like ours until our own furniture and trunks arrive from Richmond." Luncheon was ready, but he showed me his study while we waited for his sister to appear.

This room was much more comfortable than the gloomy chambers we'd passed through to reach it. A family portrait hung above the desk, and as I studied it the rest of the room seemed to melt away. Margaret and Magnus were seated on a garden bench beneath an arbor of wisteria, and Annabel stood beside her brother with her hand resting on his shoulder. Both sisters were beautifully dressed, their eyes lit with intelligent good humor; they were so alike that if the artist had painted Margaret with blonde hair, or Annabel brown, they would have seemed the same person. "I had the portrait sent ahead. We sat for it in Richmond, and it was completed after Annabel's death."

"I'm very glad you have it to remember her by," I said, and he replied with a grateful smile.

"My sister never set foot in this house, and yet I feel her presence here every day. When the curtains are drawn in the middle of the afternoon I can almost hear her demanding I open them and let the light in." He laughed quietly. "Annabel was never more herself than when she was making demands, even petty ones like opening the draperies." Then he turned to the doorway, and I followed suit.

There Margaret stood, pale and unsmiling, dressed in a black gown that might have belonged to her grandmother. "My apologies for keeping you waiting," the woman said stiffly. How could this be the luminous dark-haired sister of the family portrait? It seemed quite impossible that she and I were the same age.

Magnus introduced us, and we went into the dining room. They'd hired a cook, and the bouillabaisse put my simple soups to shame. I couldn't take much pleasure in the meal, however, when Margaret only moved her spoon through the fragrant stew, gazing at the food as if it disgusted her, and made responses to my friendly questions which were uncivilly brief. I began to fear an attitude of patience might entail my waiting forever.

Little Charley stood at the back door, his nose pressed to the windowpane. "There's a blonde lady in the garden."

Kitty followed me to the door, and when I opened it she clutched at my skirts hoping for a peek at the stranger. "Stay here," I said. "I must go and talk to her."

"Who is she, auntie?"

"I don't know. She must have wandered into our yard by mistake." I closed the door behind me and went slowly down the steps into the garden, my heart fluttering in its cage.

The girl turned from where she'd been admiring the white climbing roses, a perfect bloom still cradled in the palm of her hand. The afternoon light made a halo of her already golden hair, and her eyes shone with the enthusiasm of one who will never take another sunny day for granted. "I knew it. I *knew* you would see me. Dear Nora!" She dropped the rose, took my hands and pressed them.

"Your hands," I whispered. I could feel the bones and sinews in each of her fingers, the blood coursing in her veins.

"It's *your* doing," she said happily. "You have made me over."

She was as real as I was. I could hold out a finger and trace the curve of her cheek, flushed as if she'd walked a good distance to be here.

"I'm so sorry I haven't let you get a word in edgewise, but you see it was so difficult to reach you. I had to go on talking until I knew you would answer. Just as I couldn't show myself until you had eyes to see."

"Eyes . . . to see?" But I *did* understand, and she gave me a knowing smile as she let go of my hands and looked around her.

"This is a lovely garden, an absolute oasis. I must admit I never much cared for 'the City of Brotherly Love.' I was only here once, to visit Magnus at the university, but once was enough. Oh, but I love your little kitchen plot over here. Parsley, thyme, feverfew . . . you are so practical, Nora."

I felt the children's eyes on me, and I turned and saw their faces hovering between the mullions. I waved, then flicked my hand at the wrist. *Run along.*

"You're very good to them," Annabel remarked.

"And you're very generous with your compliments. I can't quite see how I've earned them."

"I've seen more than you think." She paused, looked to the window and waggled her fingers, and the children's faces vanished from sight. She went to the bench beneath the elm tree, the green shadows dancing on her gown of robin's-egg blue, and I seated myself beside her. "I know you and Magnus have only just met, but I've *always* had a sense of these things, even from the time I was a little child. I used to dream of the girl he'd marry: strong and capable, but with a keen imagination. It was *you*, Nora. I dreamed of you and me and Molly all together, dancing barefoot, telling riddles and laughing uproariously at our own peculiar jokes. I knew we'd love you as we loved each other, so that it would never feel as though Magnus had been taken from us."

"I don't know what to say, Annabel."

Again she flashed that conspiratorial smile. "Tell me you will be my sister."

I could promise no such thing. "It's strange to hear you call Margaret by a pet name."

"Why?"

"She was very cold to me when we met. I'm afraid she doesn't like me."

"Don't fret about that. Molly doesn't like anybody anymore." Then, almost as if she'd forgotten I was there, she went on, "She never listens to me. She *never* listens."

On Saturday I packed a picnic basket with roast beef sandwiches and a jug of lemonade, and we took the children to Wissahickon. When our carriage pulled up to the park entrance we found Magnus waiting. "I must pass on my sister's regrets," he said as we disembarked. "She is not well."

"I'm beginning to think your sister is a figment of your imagination, old man," my uncle said.

"Charley! How could you say such a thing, after all he has suffered?"

Magnus strode into the forest beside me. "I'm sure she wishes she *were* a figment of my imagination," he said, and smiled as if to smooth it over.

We spread our blanket upon a broad rock beside the rushing water to enjoy our meal, and afterward we went for a walk along the lip of the gorge. At this distance from the water we could better hear the birdsong, and the children ran ahead along the shady track, peering at toadstools and leaping for low-hanging branches. Charley dawdled behind us, swinging the empty picnic basket and swiping at shadows with a long stick he'd found in the grass, wearing the long face of a disappointed child. Magnus glanced over his shoulder at my uncle and said softly, so Charley wouldn't hear, "He told me it's been three years since he lost his wife. When I first met him again I would have guessed as many months."

"The first year was the hardest," I said. "It seemed like we had a flock of Spiritualists in the dining room nearly every night, singing hymns and squinting for shapes in the dark."

Magnus kept his eyes on the ground as he walked. "That isn't the Charley I knew."

"We are none of us the people we used to be." Casting a glance over my shoulder to be sure my uncle was still at a safe distance, I described the events which presaged Mariah's death: the bizarrely nonchalant announcement over breakfast that her father, dead two years, had been to see her late the night before—her attitude of resignation, which chilled our blood—the fever, and the fulfillment of her own horrible prophecy. "I have always believed in eternal life," I murmured. "But I also took it for granted that there would be enough companionship in Heaven to last them 'til the rest of us arrived."

For a while we walked in a pleasant silence, but his next remark unnerved me completely. "Do you believe in spirits, Nora?"

It was as if he *knew*. I took a moment to compose myself before answering. "That's a peculiar question coming from a man of science."

"Oh, I don't think so. It's preposterous to consider science as an inhuman pursuit, as most scientists do. A human being, with all his yearnings and complexities of thought and motive, has nothing in common with a piece of worn-out clockwork." The afternoon light, filtered greenly through the canopies of the ancient oaks, danced across his face as we walked. "When you observed the foetal remains at the museum, did it occur to you to wonder whether those ill-fated creatures possessed, for a time, any souls of their own?"

"Of course. I believe there was a soul attached to each and every one."

Magnus nodded, and when he spoke again it was almost dreamily. "I held her hand at the end, and I could feel the change in her fingers as she left her body behind. In that moment I knew it for what it was—a piece of clay, which some divine artist had molded into a shape of temporary beauty." He paused to face me, and when he reached out to draw a leaf from my hair he let his fingers hover at my ear. "And what do you suppose becomes of the soul, when the earthly shell ceases? Does it fly to that place you call Heaven, and there's an end to it?"

"I take it . . . " I hesitated. "I take it that's not what you believe of your sister."

"Annabel was restless," he replied. "If there is such a place as Heaven, she wouldn't stay there long."

Once again Annabel lured me into the garden, and I left the children in the parlor with their schoolbooks. "Tell me about your life," I said. "It seems as if your brother is always talking around you, so that I learn more from what he hasn't said."

"Where do I begin?" she asked laughingly. "It was much too short, but I pride myself on having seen things other girls couldn't have fit inside a hundred years. Papa never kept us to any one place for long, you see. Most of the time, when he left on business, we came with him, and had our own adventures."

"Tell me about your travels, then."

"When Margaret and I were fifteen he took us on the Grand Tour. Paris was my favorite, of course. Magnus was studying at the Faculté de Médecine and we stayed for a full month, going to the opera and taking our morning coffee at a café just opposite Notre Dame. It was the happiest time of my life." Then her pretty expression darkened with regret. "Papa passed away soon after we returned to Richmond."

"I'm sorry for your loss," I murmured.

"But I won't talk about that," she went on, as if she hadn't heard me. "I want to tell you about Paris. One day we went inside the cathedral and I stood inside a pool of colored light on the old stones, and I thought . . . "

"What did you think, Annabel?"

As she replied she closed her eyes and lifted her face to the sun. "I thought, 'someday when I die, I want to be swallowed up by the light, all the little glimmers of red and blue and gold and violet. I want dying to feel just like this.'"

"What did it feel like?"

She opened her eyes again. "Not like that."

"Did it hurt?"

"I don't remember."

The backyard was bordered by three high walls of handsome old brick, which were obscured by lush and tangled climbing vines, and suddenly this favored place felt terribly confining. "I'd give anything to go to Europe."

"One day you'll go. Magnus will take you."

I sighed. "Oh, Annabel. I wish you wouldn't speak of things that might never happen."

For a moment she paused to consider this remark. "Then *I* shall take you." She pointed to the little yellow door that opened to the alley between the yards, and I laughed outright.

"Is it that easy?"

"It is for me." She took me by the hand, opened the door—it did not groan on its hinges as it did every other time—and I beheld, not the ordinary weed-choked alley-way, but a shimmering void, colorless and utterly magnetic. Annabel regarded me with shining eyes. "Shall we?"

I nodded, and together we stepped into the blank.

Paris was everything I'd hoped for, and more. I stood in the pool of colored light on the ancient flagstones of the cathedral—smiled to watch the old men savoring their steaming cups of coffee under the red awning of Annabel's favorite café—gazed up at shop windows teeming with gilded treasures. The Arc de Triomphe loomed up before me like a pop-up in a storybook, and I watched elegant men and women in open carriages pass beneath the chestnut trees of the Champs-Élysées. I ran like a child down the cobblestoned streets, through crowded markets and gloomy alleyways, and after a time it occurred to me that I never could've covered so much ground on my own two feet. I couldn't smell the flowers—nor the fish—for sale in the market stalls; not a single person caught my eye, or pardoned himself as he hurried past.

I turned to my friend, who'd been watching me all along with a look of faint amusement. "We aren't really here, are we?"

"This is Paris, as I remember it. You cannot see anything I did not."

"Then this is the Paris of seven years ago?"

Something caught my eye, and when I looked over Annabel's shoulder I saw three young people crossing the square inside the shadow of Notre Dame. As I ran to join them she called my name, the warning note unmistakable, but I didn't hesitate. In another moment the sun was gone, and I was following the Cutlers down a rain-slicked street, the light of the gas-lamps gleaming on the wet cobblestones. I wished to see their faces, and in a twinkling I found myself in step beside them. The girls were beautifully dressed in silk gowns, bonnets and capelets, and I knew they'd just come from the opera house. A church bell tolled eleven o'clock. The living Annabel turned to her brother, and laughed. "Truth, or truth?"

My heart clutched as Magnus grinned. He was so young. "Truth," he said.

"Which of your sisters do you love best?"

Margaret stopped short, and stared at Annabel as if she'd just sworn allegiance to a fallen angel.

"Really, Annabel." Magnus cast her a disdainful glance. "I can't believe you'd ask such a thing, even in jest."

Her eyes glittered as no diamond ever could. "In life, we may be either truthful, or polite." If she'd noticed how deeply she'd hurt her sister, she gave no sign.

"Then I choose to be polite." Magnus took Margaret's hand and tucked it under his elbow, and they went on walking for another few steps. It was a gesture of kindness, of solidarity, but it shocked me as no other revelation had thus far. Magnus *did* have a preference, in his secret heart. Annabel knew it, and now Margaret knew it too.

I watched the tears well in Margaret's eyes, and she broke from her brother and ran down the street. He turned to Annabel with a look that chilled me even further. "How could you?"

The lamps winked out, and I felt myself being lifted out of the past, carried away toward a little yellow door. This time I traveled alone, but I heard her voice in my ear. *I asked you not to go there, Nora. If I didn't know better I'd think you didn't trust me.*

Margaret wanted none of my company, but Magnus refused to see it. When he invited us to supper she'd hardly acknowledge our presence at her table, if she ventured from her bedroom at all; and when he wrote me that she wished to pass the afternoon with our needlework I knew it for a kindly falsehood. Still, I came with my sewing-basket on a rainy day, and applied myself to my piecework while the clock on the sitting-room mantelpiece loudly ticked away the seconds.

A quarter of an hour passed before I resolved to speak. "That is a beautiful ring, Miss Cutler." I'd noticed it at luncheon: a heavy, ornate piece of jewelry fashioned out of a dark and smoky sort of metal, and crowned with an oval of malachite.

Margaret laid down her embroidery hoop and covered the ring with her other hand as if embarrassed, though I saw no sign of it on her face. She murmured a thank-you but did not meet my eye.

"It looks as if it might have a secret inside—like a ring I saw once in a book. The hero had lost a great battle. He could either be captured by the enemy, or drink the poison from his ring, and . . . "

As I spoke she slipped the ring from her finger, tucked it in her apron pocket, and resumed her needlework. This time she made no answer at all, and I would have preferred the sticking of a thousand pins and needles to the silence that followed.

At last Margaret laid down her needle and cleared her throat. "I'm afraid I've been very rude to you, Miss Dobbin. I apologize. But you must see that we can never be friends."

I laid my hand over my thudding heart. "I wish you'd tell me what I've done to offend you, so that I may offer an apology."

"It's nothing you've done." Margaret rose from her rocking chair and drew back the curtain to look out at the rain. "He is trying to replace her. It will not do."

"I don't understand."

"You know all about Annabel. I know he's told you."

"Yes, of course he has. Annabel was his sister. *Your* sister."

"Then you do understand."

"I'm afraid I don't. It may come to pass that Magnus asks for my hand, but I can't see how he plans to replace a sister with a wife. There can be no replacement."

"Annabel would beg to differ."

"Your sister is dead, Margaret. She cannot have an opinion on the matter." I spoke without thinking, but as soon as the words had passed my lips I felt a certain coldness in the pit of my stomach. Had she heard what I'd just said? Would she consider it a betrayal?

Margaret turned from the window and smiled at me for the first time. It was a hard, cold, ugly smile, a gargoyle in the flesh, and that night the recollection made me shiver in my sleep.

"I can't stay here," I whispered as I fumbled for my sewing basket. "I must—I must go home now. Please pass my regrets to your brother."

The next time Annabel appeared in the garden, I almost didn't want to go. I felt as if I owed her an apology, but when I thought over what had happened in Paris I didn't see that I'd done anything to regret.

As I came down the steps she smiled as if nothing were strained between us. "There's one more place I must bring you," she said. "This time we travel in the present." Again the alley door yielded to her hand without protest, and she took my hand as we passed into empty space.

We landed on a grassy hill overlooking the sea. To the north-east, the dusty roads of a sunbaked colonial town were laid out before us. There wasn't a cloud in the sky. Seabirds wheeled above a quiet harbor. I looked around me, and found stone markers punctuating the tall grass. "This is Havana?"

Annabel nodded, and moved a few paces beyond where I stood. "There. That one is mine."

Her name, and nothing else, was done in black paint on the rough gray stone. As memorials went, it was terribly crude. "Why is there no epitaph?"

"Too expensive." She glanced at my face, and laughed. "Magnus told everyone he'd have a proper stone made someday, but I can't imagine he'll ever get around to it, being so far away now." I could see the wind whipping through the tall grasses on the crest of the hill, yet it did not touch the golden tendrils that fell from her intricate arrangement. "He'll never come back," she said. "He promised he would, but I know him better now."

"Please don't say that, Annabel!"

"Why shouldn't I? You're only saying I shouldn't because it's the proper thing. This is the way of it, Nora: you die, and in a little while they forget you."

"I've never forgotten," I replied warmly. "Nor has Magnus—nor Margaret. You are always in their thoughts."

Annabel smiled as she held out her hand. A large opal pendant lay in her open palm. It was a very old and very beautiful piece of jewelry. "This is for you," she said.

"Oh, but I . . . "

"Don't argue, Nora. I want you to have it." She came to me and fastened the clasp at the nape of my neck, and her hands lingered there for a moment. She looked into my eyes.

"Thank you," I whispered. She wanted me to be grateful, and I complied.

For a short while I ruminated on her tombstone, fingering the opal on its chain, until a marvelous thought occurred to me. "Could I see the others?"

She lifted an eyebrow. "What others?"

"Mariah. My mother. My father. My little brother." Everyone I had ever loved.

"I don't know."

"Where are they?"

"I told you, Nora. I don't know."

"Don't you ever see others who've . . . passed?"

She shook her head, and took my hand. "Let's go. Give me your tidy little garden over this horrible place any day."

That Sunday Magnus asked if I would go with them to morning services at Christ Church, and I couldn't bring myself to make an excuse. I climbed into the coach, and without a greeting Margaret stared at the amulet I wore around my neck. It hadn't occurred to me that she might recognize it—foolish, foolish me!—and so I'd worn it as I had every day since Annabel had given it to me.

"Lady Berringsley's amulet!" She lunged forward and tore it from my neck, the clasp on the old silver chain giving way with a snap, while Magnus looked on open mouthed. In a twinkling his sister became completely unfamiliar to us both: her colorless cheeks were flushed to a deep crimson, her cold eyes were alight with rage, and her bosom heaved with an emotion I'd never suspected she could feel. "Where did you get this?" she shouted as she clutched the amulet to her heart. "I put it around my sister's neck the night she died. She wore it to her grave. *Where did you get this?*"

Magnus overcame his initial surprise at his sister's outburst, and attempted to soothe her. "Margaret, my dear. You must calm yourself now, and accept the truth of what I've been telling you all along."

I began to comprehend him, and felt a cold trickle down the back of my neck.

"Annabel lives," he whispered, and met my eye as his sister cast her face against the side of the coach and began, violently, to weep.

I waited in the carriage while Magnus brought Margaret into the house. A few minutes later he came out again, and in a glance we agreed that church services were now out of the question. "Really, it isn't necessary to see me home, Magnus."

Still he directed the coachman to my address, and settled into the seat opposite as the carriage sprang into motion. "Please, Nora: don't put a distance between us. Now more than ever we should have the world to say to each other. There's so much I need to ask you—so much I need to know."

"How is Margaret?"

"I've put her to bed."

I kept my eyes on my folded hands. "I hope she will make a swift recovery."

He drew the amulet out of his hip pocket and offered it to me. "I can't," I said. "I wouldn't dream of keeping it now."

"She did give it to you."

In silence we regarded one another.

"Please—at least hold onto it," I said at last. The carriage turned onto Market Street, and the foundations of the new City Hall came into view. "Who is Lady Berringsley?"

"A character from childhood. Every day for a year or two when they were eight years of age, Margaret became the Countess de Foix"—here he smiled at the excessive Frenchness of the sobriquet—"and Annabel was Lady Berringsley. One day Annabel would conspire to murder Molly for her fortune, then the next day they'd both die of the pox, and so on—always thinking of increasingly melodramatic ways to do away with themselves. Years later we stumbled upon a curiosity shop in Montmartre, and Father bought trinkets for each of them to give the other. Then for a time the old game renewed itself." Pensively he ran his thumb over the shimmering milk-white stone. "They were never happier than when they were playing Lady Berringsley and the Countess de Foix." He paused, and I braced myself for what I knew must come next. "You have seen her?"

I nodded.

"And how does she appear?"

"Just as she does in the portrait above your desk."

"As solid as a living creature?"

Again I nodded. "She's taken me by the hand, and shown me places across the sea." I told him of our visit to the Paris of seven years gone, and of the little burial ground on the hill above Havana.

By this time the carriage had drawn up to the house. "I don't understand," he said. "Why does she come to *you*, Nora, and not to her own sister?" To my relief, he didn't expect me to answer. "They fought just before Annabel fell ill. Margaret was kept out of the sick room, and they never got the opportunity to forgive each other. She used to take one of Annabel's dresses from the wardrobe, lay it out on the bed and fall asleep beside it. Sometimes I'd find her clutching the sleeve . . . as if she were clutching a hand."

I shook my head. "When will it end, Magnus?"

He glanced up from the amulet. "What do you mean?"

"It's as if she can't bear the thought of you living your lives without her." Of course it was true; how hadn't I seen it before? "It's been two years now. Will you give up the mourning? Will Margaret?"

Magnus looked at me sadly, but did not answer.

"She took me into her memories," I went on. "I was there that night in Paris. She asked you to choose between them. Even now, she's asking you to choose." I gazed at him, willing him to understand, but he couldn't meet my eye. We may have had the world to say to each other, but there were certain things he might never be ready to hear.

"The lady's in the garden again." Little Charley glanced at me, then turned his face back to the kitchen window. "You aren't going to talk to her?"

"Not this time, dear."

"Why not?"

"She confuses me."

"Does she tell riddles?"

"No, Charley. It's something else. Something I can't quite explain."

"She's still out there. I think she might stay for a long time."

I turned to him sharply. "What makes you say that?"

"She keeps looking up at me. Now she's waving for me to come down. Should I?"

"No!" I spoke more forcefully than I'd intended, and it pained me to see the children wince. "Please—Charley—come away from the window now. Both of you, go into the parlor, and I'll bring you a bite to eat."

That night, when pictures came welling up out of the darkness, I couldn't shut them out. There on that sun-parched hillside over Havana I turned into a tiny speck, tunneling deep into the earth and through the coffin-lid. I saw the dirt crumbled in the creases of her gown—her hands folded over the thing that had been her heart—her face as cold and elegant as Diana in marble. Then I watched her lips part and a worm slither out, disappearing again beneath her ruffled collar, and all at once I found the evidence of decay she hadn't wanted me to see. The golden hair grew brittle and colorless. The lovely face shrank from the teeth, and fell away. I pressed my fingers into my eyes and stifled a shriek.

Then I heard a delicate but unmistakable cough, and the horror of the grave receded into the corners of my room. I sat up, clutching the bedclothes as if to conceal my pounding heart. "Who's there?"

At the foot of my bed was an old armchair retired from the parlor. It was now occupied by a sort of silhouette: black through and through, yet with a shape and dimension that played at human form. "It's only me, you goose," the shadow said. "I've missed you terribly, Nora."

"And I you," I replied, but the falsehood lodged in my throat like a stone. Had she read my innermost thoughts? Was there any place where I could be safe from her?

The shadow leaned back in the chair and crossed its arms. "Then why didn't you come into the garden when I waited for you? I'm beginning to suspect you don't care for me anymore."

"It isn't that. But you know I don't belong with you, Annabel."

The shadow made a sound of derision. "As if I belong here, without ever having the chance to marry and bear children?" The room grew colder as her anger mounted. "You don't belong with me. Hah! Who are you, to say you don't?"

I glared into the darkness. Who was she, to imply I did? "You said you were my friend."

"And you said you would love me as a sister. You and Margaret are very alike, you know. You'll despise me for saying so, for you disliked my sister the moment you touched her hand. But this is the truth, and it gives me pleasure to tell it: you say you want to love and be loved, and then you shut your ears and eyes to the one who loves you most. I offer you the best of a better world, and you withdraw."

The shadow rose from the chair and crept closer, and this time when I opened my mouth it was not to reason with her. For a moment she seemed stunned by the noise, and inched no further. Then there were quick footsteps in the hall, and a light glimmered under my door. As it opened and I heard Charley's voice—somber and concerned—I looked back to the place beside my bed where Annabel's shadow had hovered, and found no one, nothing, there.

In the morning I wrote to Magnus and hailed a newsboy to bring the letter to the coroner's office. At five o'clock he arrived in a carriage with the city emblem, and I showed him into the parlor. He reached for my hand. "She came to me in the middle of the night. She . . . " I couldn't bring myself to use the word *threatened.*

"Can you bring me to her?"

I rose and went out of the parlor, and Magnus followed me down the hall to the back door. "She comes to me in the garden. I didn't see her at first— I only heard her voice."

"She's been speaking to me all along, hasn't she?"

I paused with my hand on the doorknob, and nodded. There was grief in his face, and jubilation, and together they formed an expression I have never seen the like of before or since.

We went into the garden, and I pointed to the bench beneath the old elm. Magnus sat straight, his palms on his knees and his eyes darting to every hopping sparrow and drowsy nod of the peonies. "Close your eyes," I said, "and try to rest. She may come to you then."

He took my hand with a grim smile, and we closed our eyes and leaned our heads against the wooden seat. In time we both must have nodded off, and the next thing I remember he was speaking to the silence. Whatever my former friend was saying to her brother, this time I could not hear it. "Tell me what I must do, Annabel. Tell me how I can give you peace, and I promise you I'll do it."

I wanted to object, but I couldn't bring myself to speak. Annabel would take whatever was offered, and then some. He let go of my hand and I heard him rise from the bench and take two steps down the path beside my little plot of herbs.

I called his name, and when he hesitated it gave me time to rouse myself. The garden door stood ajar, and just as before, the narrow, weed-choked alley beyond it had vanished. Magnus stared into the void with the wonderment of a child. I went to him and he clasped me by the shoulders. "You have done this, Nora. No one else could have made it possible."

"You say that as if it's a blessing." I felt a terrible certainty pressing down on me. This was what Annabel had wanted all along.

"It's the very greatest blessing," he said. "I shall settle all that is unresolved between us, and be back in time for supper." He slid his hands down my arms to clasp me by the fingers. "I'll never forget your kindness, Nora."

"Don't say that," I whispered. "That's the sort of thing you say at a final parting."

He lifted a hand and fondled my cheek with that same determined smile. Then he went to the old yellow door, and as soon as he was through it blew shut behind him. I ran to the door and pulled at the handle, but it was no use.

Leaving the children with Mrs. Mooney next door, I took a carriage to the Cutlers' house half expecting its tenant would refuse to see me. A bright-eyed Margaret met me at the door, wearing a gown of dusky violet that flattered her almost beyond recognition. I stood on the step, struck mute by the change. She spoke with concern but no trace of distress: "He's gone with her, hasn't he?"

I had to believe he would return—believe, for his sake and mine—and when I told her what had transpired Margaret seemed oddly confident that he would. "Supper is ready," she said as she led me by the hand into the dining room, where the table was set for three. "He wouldn't ask us to wait."

She began to carve the mutton. "You said she gave you the amulet, and I believe you. Not that I could return it even if you wanted it again. This morning I took it to a curiosity shop on Cherry Street."

I stared at her in wonderment. Was this truly Margaret—sullen, inconsolable Margaret?

"I sold them both." She smiled faintly to herself as she ate, and I noticed the poison ring was gone from her finger. "And then I went to a milliner's on Eighth Street and bought a new hat." Margaret took another bite, swallowed, and paused to reflect. "I suppose I did it to spite her. Did she tell you I never listened?"

I nodded. "But how could you have known, unless . . . ?"

"I heard her voice in my mind. It filled every idle moment. At times I was afraid my thoughts would never be my own again. But until you showed me the amulet I never thought she was truly speaking to me."

"And now you speak as if the voice were silent," I said.

"Mercifully silent." Once she'd collected the last morsel of potato with the last bite of mutton, Margaret laid down her fork and regarded me gravely. "You once offered me your friendship. Is it too late to accept?"

"Never," I replied.

The smile lit up her face, and she looked more like Annabel than ever. In that way we took our first meal as friends, and when we parted she gave me a kiss on either cheek.

The summer dwindled, and with it our hopes for Magnus's return. I offered the detectives the plainest version of the truth: that Dr. Cutler had been to see me that evening, and had departed by the alley door at the back of the garden. His post was handed to another, and Margaret went to live with her aunt. For the first time in years Charley seemed to turn out of himself, and arranged for one of our neighbors to take up some of the cooking and housekeeping. He understood me well enough to know that I would find no solace in industry.

Now, when I come to Wissahickon, I walk in my own company. The leaves are turning, and I can sometimes smell the woodsmoke wafting up from the riverside inn where the occasional excursion maker still pauses for refreshment. This afternoon, as I trod the path above the gorge, I felt a certain pressure in the palm of my hand, as if someone were slipping his fingers into mine. I stopped and looked behind me, frantic with hope.

But it is just as I said. Hope is sweet, and I have already given in to temptation.

CAMILLE DEANGELIS (b. Moorestown, NJ, USA, 1980) is the author of two fantasy novels, Mary Modern *and* Petty Magic: Being the Memoirs *and* Confessions of Miss Evelyn Harbinger, Temptress *and* Troublemaker *(Crown), as well as a first-edition guidebook,* Moon Ireland *(Avalon). She is a graduate of*

New York University and the National University of Ireland, Galway, and spends enough time abroad that she feels justified in telling people she lives in her shoes. She has two novels forthcoming, one for children and one for young adults.

Commentary on "The Coroner's Bride": This story is an homage to Joseph Sheridan Le Fanu (1814-1873), whose ghostly tales I devoured in the name of "mindful procrastination" while writing Mary Modern for my M.A. portfolio centerpiece. I'm fascinated at the extent to which his fiction drew from real-life experience. The story Nora tells Magnus of her aunt Mariah seeing her dead father actually happened: Le Fanu's father-in-law appeared to his wife Susanna in the same way, and she died soon afterward. The writer never quite recovered from his grief, and because he wrote by candlelight in the wee hours and seldom left the house (and when he did, it was only to peruse secondhand bookshops for occult literature), his neighbors called him "the invisible prince".

I began writing "The Coroner's Bride" during a residency at Yaddo in 2010, on the same desk Sylvia Plath used in the autumn of 1959. I'd originally conceived of Nora as a sort of "occult detective", a female version of Dr. Hesselius from In a Glass, Darkly, and she may yet become that in a future series of stories.

The story was set in Dublin in its first incarnation, but when my friend Sarah came to Philadelphia for the express purpose of visiting the Mütter Museum, I thought it might be fun to set "The Coroner's Bride" there instead. The Mütter, by the way, is even more wonderful than the Hunterian at the Royal College of Surgeons in London. Much of the collection would already have been in place in Nora's time, at the museum's original location at 13th and Locust. Check it out the next time you're in the City of Brotherly Love. And if you make it to Wissahickon Valley Park, think of Poe, who enjoyed and wrote of its natural beauty while he lived in Philly in the late 1830s and early 1840s.

THE STARVATION EXPERIMENT

SHERI HOLMAN

Y OU ARE NOT THE FIRST TO ASK FOR MY STORY. EVERY YEAR ONE OF
you steps off the UN cargo plane with your clipboard and ten ton ship-
ment of rice to find me already here. You think of your time in the war zones
as a radical experiment. Your hands, your heart, your Master's degree in
anthropology will change the world. In a few years, you will return home
tanned and thin, full of sadness and photographs snapped from moving
vehicles, a brush with malaria, perhaps a mild venereal disease. Nothing so
serious you'll need to mention it to your future husband. Perhaps you'll tell
him, instead, about the old woman who had spent her life over here, moving from one refugee camp to another, following the hunger. The
disapproving, cranky old lady who spoke French or Hausa over your head
to the doctors too fast for you to understand. One hot, humid night you
got her drinking (*She had to be eighty, but she could still keep up*, you'll say) and
she told the craziest story. My story, when you retell it back home, will be
what gets you that husband. You'll retell it like a seduction, like my darkness
is your own. You can have whatever boy you want when you kiss him with
my mouth.

I n the summer of 1947, I had lived in Manhattan for nearly a year. I had
come directly after graduating from Sweetbriar College with a sturdy
Samsonite suitcase, a crate of books, and a bit of money I'd saved working
as a doctor's receptionist. Since the very mention of Greenwich Village sent
my mother to her bed for a week, I had taken, instead, a coldwater flat

uptown in the dwindling German district, where my dimes bought me slices of black bread and liverwurst and sour garlicky pickles. Through a family friend, I had landed a job in Midtown fact checking for the *Daily News*. When the weather was good, I would wrap my sandwiches in cloth napkins and eat them on the white marble steps of the Public Library, where I'd watch the men come home from war.

But once a week that first year, I splurged at the 42nd Street Woolworth's lunch counter. The soup du jour and a cup of coffee were all I could afford, but I tried, at least, to make an art of it, composing columns of food criticism in my head: *The reconstituted potatoes of Tuesday's Manhattan clam chowder float in their sanguinous broth like just-lost baby teeth.* I came a different day each week so that I might sample all the fine soups Woolworth's had to offer, and that's how I came to notice the man whose story would become my own. No matter which day I took my seat at the counter, I was sure to find him perched on the far stool, always settled before I arrived, not shackled, as I was, to an office lunch hour. He was tall and very thin and severely handsome in that monkish way men are who have worked through some profound disappointment.

Always, by the time I settled myself, he would be sitting silently waiting, his tie thrown over his shoulder and his battered fedora on the ledge at his feet. When his meal arrived, he would spend a full minute staring at his plate as if memorizing the exact configuration of his meal—the pale turkey at six o'clock, the mashed potatoes at nine, the cranberry sauce at three. Every day Thanksgiving. Then carefully, he would begin to dismantle—the slow, deliberate saw of his butter knife and the precise piercing of tine to flesh, his mouth opening long before he raised his fork to it, opened like an O, like an *Oh*, in surprise that food would find him. As the ripe crimson of the cranberry sauce bled across the border of the potatoes (dusted, I remember with a few eyelashes of dill on top), I would watch him beneath lowered lids. How could he eat so much and remain so thin? Was this his only meal of the day? Was he ill? Was it possible, after all these months, he never noticed the prettyish blonde girl at the other end of the counter, popping oyster crackers like pills and making the most of the free refills of coffee? Over the course of several months, he became the fixture of my week, a man I described to the girls from the office over drinks after work— that man who eats like other men pray. Those were the exact words I used to describe him. He eats like other men pray.

Then one day in June of 1947, as I remember it, he was there when I arrived, but everything was different. Though there were a dozen laughing, smoking patrons between us, I could see the meal before him left untouched. His coffee, undrunk, too. His appearance had altered so radically from the week before, I was forced to acknowledge he might actually have a life outside this department store, plagued with pressures and anxieties beyond what to order for lunch. I thought it impossible he could be thinner or more gaunt, but his skin was drawn tight over his wide planed cheeks, pallid as if he'd been stricken by flu. His unwashed sandy hair sat up straight on his head from obsessively running his fingers through it.

He fidgeted on his stool for some minutes, peering at the other customers with a curiosity he'd never shown before. He lit a cigarette and put it out. At last, he offered his seat to a woman waiting with her whining child and left a dollar bill on the counter. I'm not sure what possessed me swiftly to request my own check and follow him. Certainly I had never done anything so impulsive before, but I had the strongest premonition I had witnessed this man's last supper and I didn't even know his name.

The street was lunch-hour crowded with Midtown businessmen rushing around in their ill-fitting suits, trying to figure out what they were supposed to be buying and selling. My friend was taller than most, and I spotted his fedora just as the light changed for Lexington Avenue. He stepped into the crosswalk, then stopped, lost and confused. As he searched the wall of pedestrians on both sides of the street, businessmen flowed around him like a stone in the river. *I'm here,* I opened my mouth to shout, instinctively stepping forward. *It's me!* For how could we be strangers after all these months of proximity? Surely seeing *me* would be enough to help him with this momentary panic. Yet his eyes looked through me and swung to the other side of the avenue.

I saw her before he did—a woman expertly scanning the street, like a woman at home among crowds of men. She wore a matching gray tweed skirt and jacket, but the fabric was limp and shiny as if rained on and ironed, and the jacket buttons were subtly mismatched. Her dark hair hung to her shoulders and her high cheekbones and peaked nose suggested she might be an Eastern European refugee. I glanced automatically at her narrow wrists protruding from her cuffs, checking for the blue number I'd seen too often tattooed there since the war, but nothing marked her as a camp survivor. As if she caught me staring, she looked my way, and instinctively I recoiled. The whites of her deep-set eyes glowed unnaturally in the Midtown shadows. They were white as porcelain, bloodless as chalk. The shrinking of ocular capillaries that accounts for that eerie brilliance is an unmistakable sign of profound malnutrition, but I would learn that only years later, when the children I nursed in Bangladesh and Biafra turned those same eyes on me.

In an instant I took all this in, you must understand. They found each other at the same time, and she quickly stepped out to where he had stopped. He reached for her hungrily and pressed her to him, and I fought an irrational feeling of betrayal as he kissed her red mouth. They stood kissing in the center of the street, oblivious to the last straggling pedestrians trying to beat the light, or the traffic surging up around them. They fit together like old lovers, and as he kissed her, the color returned to his face, enough that I momentarily forgot my jealousy, so happy I was to see him look healthy. His fingers tangled in her long dark hair; it came away from her temples in thick handfuls.

Jesus! Someone shoved me from behind. *Is he dead?* A taxi making the turn onto 42nd Street had screeched to a stop—there was noise and confusion and then a body sprawled in the street. Shouting obscenities, the cab driver leapt from behind the wheel as I raced to where my friend lay.

Where did she go? I demanded of the crowd that quickly gathered. *Where is the woman he was with?*

What woman? barked the cab driver. *The crazy fuck stepped right in front of my car!*

I placed my head on my friend's chest and through his thick felt vest, I could hear his heart beating. Seeing him up close, he was much younger than I had originally thought, maybe twenty eight. His face had lost that skeletal rictus, his lips were full and swollen and moist from having just been kissed. A few drops of blood slicked his bottom lip from where he— or someone else—had bitten it. Where was that awful woman? She couldn't have run away, leaving him like this? I didn't hallucinate her—her long, dark hair was clenched in his fists.

Klara.

He said her name as his eyes opened, then shut again in disappointment. I was not the woman he wanted to see.

To the crowd, I had become the next of kin, and everyone began barking questions at me. *Was he dead? Should we call an ambulance? Was he insane to walk out into traffic like that?*

Please, he whispered, and this time he was asking me for help. I ordered the cabbie to assist me in getting him to the curb, but he begged—*Please.*

No ambulance. I only fainted. A man passing by shot him a look of disgust. Everyone who served and everyone who suffered at home had had their share of hardship and death, sympathy was in short supply since the war.

"You pass out on your buddies like that?" the cabbie asked. "You faint when you saw a Nazi?"

"I didn't see any Nazis," he said quietly. "I stayed home."

The cab driver turned to me. "You're stepping out with a fuckin' 4-F'er?"

"I don't really know him," I said, forgetting just moments before I thought of him as a friend. But any man classified 4-F who sat out the war was defective. Sick. Weak. Wrong.

"I was a C.O.," he explained, looking at me. "A conscientious objector. I believe war is never justified."

He turned to the cab driver and offered to pay for any damage. The cabbie waved him off with more curses and drove away, happy not to have the cops involved. The scene was over and the crowd dispersed. I was left sitting alone with him on the curb. "Is there someplace I can take you?" I asked. "I'll hail another cab."

He shook his head. "I was hoping the driver wouldn't take me up on my offer. I spent the last of my money on lunch. I don't even have enough for car fare."

I looked at my watch. I was already fifteen minutes past my own lunch hour.

"I could walk you somewhere," I said.

He nodded gratefully as I offered him my arm. Instead of dropping the woman's hair he still held in his hands, he shoved it deep in his pockets and we fell into step headed downtown. With so many young women in line for my job, I was sure to be out of work in the morning. I thought of the coffee mug I'd bought my third day in New York and the half eaten box of Cracker Jacks in my desk drawer. I always ate down to the bottom before looking at my prize and now I'd never know what I'd got.

"I recognize you, you know," he said after we'd walked some blocks. "You always sat at the other end of the counter."

"I never realized you noticed," I said.

"You were always alone."

"So were you," I pointed out. "I suppose your friend doesn't care for Woolworth's."

He turned to look at me. "Friend?"

"If you can call her that," I said with some superiority. "I don't know what kind of friend doesn't stick around to see if someone has been killed or not?"

I expected him to defend her or explain, but instead he returned to silence and we walked that way for a while, cutting west on 33rd Street. In front of the Empire State Building, tourists were still coming to see the spot where poor Evelyn McHale had jumped to her death only weeks before, landing on a UN limousine. I saw her picture in *Life* magazine, her white gloved hand still clutching her strand of pearls, her face lovely and serene as if asleep in the wreckage around her. She was one of five people who had jumped in three weeks and now they were putting a mesh fence around the 86th floor. It struck me that my lunch counter friend's face looked equally peaceful when I found him in the street. I wanted to ask his name then, but I didn't have a chance because suddenly he spoke.

"You saw her, then?"

At first I thought he meant Evelyn McHale, but then I realized he was referring to the woman he called Klara. "What did she look like?"

"What do you mean, *What did she look like?*" I asked, annoyed. "You were kissing her, you should know!"

"Pardon me, what did she look like to *you?*"

It seemed an odd question, but I indulged him. I described her gaunt features and her cheap suit. I remembered a few more details about her shoes and the way she wore her hair. I made mention of how anorexically thin she was, and of her haunting, bloodless eyes. To my surprise, he laughed softly.

"To me, she is beautiful, and nothing like you've described. She is soft and round and her skin smells like peaches on a window sill. She asked me to meet her in New York, but I had finally given up believing she would come."

This was about the time I should have taken leave of my friend. We had walked nearly fifteen blocks together and he was clearly strong enough to get anywhere he needed without my help. My own fantasies of him had carried me this far, but he was a disturbed man. Maybe dangerous. Clearly delusional. But some recklessness kept me walking. We turned on Sixth Avenue headed once again downtown.

"Where are we going?" I asked him.

"It depends on how far you want to walk."

"Until we get there," I answered.

"Then it's a very long ways."

"*W*ill *You Starve That They Might Be Better Fed?*
"The cover of the recruitment pamphlet was a photograph of some waifish European children clutching empty soup bowls, their eyes imploring. Dr. Keys couldn't have crafted his message better to appeal to us at the Civilian Public Service Camps. It was right after D-Day. We were the ones who had the conscience or the narcissism to go against the tide of the nation, of history itself, by refusing to bloody our hands. So instead of joining the army, we healthy men had been assigned to forestry camps and to work as orderlies in psychiatric hospitals. We were the perfect test subjects because we were bored and filled with doubt and, more than anything, needed to prove we were brave."

Because I had seen Klara (he pronounced it in the European way— Klaaara) he decided to trust me with his story. It was troubling, he warned me, and perhaps not fit for young ears, but I waved him off and told him I needed to make sense of what I had seen. I cannot guarantee sense, he told me, but I can at least promise truth. Perhaps you will understand in time.

Out of the hundreds of C.O.s who volunteered, thirty six were chosen as physically and emotionally fit enough to participate in the Minnesota Starvation Experiment. Pugnacious, middle aged, a confirmed atheist, Ancel Keys, the doctor who had worked with the army developing the "K" ration, proposed to chart famine's effect on the human body by starving these men to the point of death. In turn, he was given a warren of forty laboratories underneath the University of Minnesota's football stadium. There, the men would begin a three month control period, consuming 3600 calories daily. Then, at the beginning of the starvation period, their diet would be dramatically slashed to 1500 or less, the standard number of calories Russians ate during the Siege of Leningrad. Their food would be watery soups and boiled potatoes, bits of bread, as much black coffee as they could drink. They would walk twenty two miles every week. After six months of starvation, Dr. Keys would increase their rations to see how most cheaply and effectively relief might be administered.

"It was a raw and rainy Sunday morning, November 19, 1944, when our bus pulled up in front of the football stadium," he told me. "For a year, the thirty six of us were to live in a single dormitory. We were to eat, sleep, and—pardon me—shit together. Hanging over the stadium entrance were two signs: LET EVERY MAN PROVE HIS OWN WORK. And WHATEVER IS SET BEFORE YOU, EAT, ASKING NO QUESTION FOR CONSCIENCE SAKE."

"Why would you agree to such a thing?" I asked. Up until this point in our walk, shame or pride had kept him looking straight ahead. Now he turned to me, trying to make me understand.

"You have to remember, in '44, no one knew how or when it all would end. Dr. Keys looked across the ocean and saw displacement and famine everywhere. And the Russians drawing ever closer to Berlin. Democracy cannot take root where people are hungry, he used to say to us, urgently, as if the future of the American way of life depended on our frail bodies. Then in January, at the end of our control period, four Russian cavalrymen stumbled across a camp called Auschwitz-Birkenau. We were to be starved down to the weight of the living skeletons they found there, so that Doctor Keys might learn how best to save them."

"I've been following the Nuremberg Trials," I said. "They are executing Nazi doctors who experimented on people."

"We were volunteers. We had no idea how bad it would get.

"At first all the men were upbeat. We would help the starving masses of Europe, we would save lives rather than take them. For the first three months we were fed well. We took classes at the University, worked odd jobs in town. We were allowed to date women—anything so long as it didn't interfere with the diet."

"Did you have a girl?" I asked as casually as I could. He smiled at my jealousy.

"I did. She was one of Dr. Keys' nurses. She weighed me every day and checked my hearing and vision. Over the months we became close. But one evening, about a third of the way into the starvation period, I took her to the movies. I couldn't concentrate on the plot, I saw only Humphrey Bogart's dinner. I wanted to take her for a coffee at the department store downtown, but I was too weak to push the revolving door. She avoided me after that.

"Every day as our flesh fell away, we were tested. They stripped us naked and photographed us against graph paper. They made us run the treadmill until we collapsed. When we began I could run at full speed for ten minutes or more, but by the end I managed barely ten seconds. Grown men cried

with shame. They had us breathe into gas masks to measure our oxygena-
tion. They gave us a pin-up of Betty Grable and sent us off to test if we were
still men. In those last months, less than fifty percent of us were."

I did not let my eyes drop when he told me this. I was a modern woman,
living on her own in New York City. The things men did with Betty Grable
were not unknown to me.

Luckily, at that embarrassing juncture, our walk was interrupted by a
young black boy pushing a rolling rack of clothes down the sidewalk. We
were passing through the Garment District where steam poured from the
open windows of the pressing buildings. From inside came the heavy clack
of machines stitching next winter's fashions. My friend wore a vest and coat,
even on a mid-June day.

"Aren't you hot in all those layers?" I asked him.

"I am always cold. I am cold in ways I thought I could only be if I were
dead."

"You're exaggerating," I said. "You are still quite thin. Your body is con-
serving heat."

"No," he shook his head slowly. "I am dying in chunks and clots. Like toes
black with frostbite, you'll have to carve them away. I still marvel to see
bustling life when I know how few calories separate us from apathy and
pure animal instinct. The Experiment exposed me for what I am."

"You are a good man," I said to him. "I used to tell people you ate like
other men prayed."

He took my hand. "You really were watching me? Enough to talk about me
to others?"

For the first time I understood how great a part this man had played during my first lonely year in New York. I had few friends and no men ringing
me for dates. I had only my soup du jour and my fantasies of him. Perhaps
I had conjured that cab to hit him to keep him from leaving me.

"When I slipped these pumps on this morning," I said leaning lightly
against him, "I didn't expect to walk the length of Manhattan."

"I've tired you," he said. "I have grown so restless over the years I lose
track of how far I've gone."

"Never too far for me," I assured him. "But I could stand a snack if we're
to keep going. I have seventy five cents left over from lunch. Enough for two
coffees and a slice of pie."

His story had carried us all the way downtown to Greenwich Village and
we found ourselves up the block from the black semi-circular awning of

Café Reggio. I made a swift internal apology to my mother, and suggested we rest there before walking on.

"I can't allow you to pay for me," he said.

"Then I'll order a slice for myself and you can watch," I said.

He held open the door for me. Inside, the walls were painted a deep glossy red and marble cherub heads hung from the picture rails.

"I like to watch," he said.

"**K**lara," I forced the subject, after we had ordered, and true to his word, he followed every bite of chocolate cream pie to my lips without ever taking a taste for himself. "Did you meet Klara during the Experiment?"

"By the time I was down to 109 pounds, I didn't care about women any-more," he admitted. "I didn't care about religion or philosophy, right or wrong. I cared only for food. I cannot begin to describe the gnawing pains of an empty stomach. Or the lethargy that turns instantly to fury if a meal is even minutes late. Our lives revolved around our trips to the mess hall. We began to 'soup' our food as we called it—mixing everything on our plate into one gray-green mess and soaking it with hot water, to stretch it fur-ther. I would shake on enough salt and pepper to form a crust. Every mouthful I chewed twenty times. At the end, I would lift the plate to my mouth and lick it. Dr. Keys and his assistants were there to record every psychological break. He nearly expelled another man for eating an orange peel."

"How horrible," I said, finishing my last bite of crust.

"By the eighth month, I began hoarding cookbooks. I stole them from the University library and out of trash cans. I licked the pages of *Your Frigidaire Recipes, 1939*, until the color came off on my tongue. Its glisten-ing salads and compotes and fruit laden cream cheese gelatins. Its sweet pink hams. Dr. Keys made us keep a journal. In it we were to record our pri-vate thoughts and dreams. I began to dream of eating human flesh."

Slowly I set down my fork. He saw my alarm and reached across the table. "Please don't reject me now. I have been more naked with you today than I have been with anyone since Klara."

"Klara," I echoed.

"If you hadn't seen her, I might still believe she was a dream. I wasn't sure even then. The night she first came to me had been a bad one for the C.O.s. One of the men we looked up to, who had always been the least quick to anger and held the deepest beliefs in the value of our sacrifice, was chopping wood for some elderly women in town. They knew better than to offer him dinner but he smelled it wafting from the open door. Harder and harder he swung the ax, until at last he brought it down on his own hand, chopping off three of his fingers. Keys was convinced it was no accident and was determined to dismiss him for hunger psychosis. We all pleaded for him. I can still hear him begging. *Please don't expel me. When the war is over, what will I tell people I did?*

"That night I left the dormitory where the other men slept, wrapped in coats and blankets. I crept to the bathroom to put my mouth under the faucet. My belly was already swollen from all the water I drank trying to feel full. My ankles, too, had ballooned with edema. It hurt to put weight on them. I was a broken man. I had come into this experiment idealistic and proud of my pacifist beliefs, but hunger had stripped me of all other appetites. I cared for nothing beyond my next meal. Where was philosophy? Where was idealism? Humanity was a construct. As I railed against this hollow man in the mirror, I caught a glimpse of something moving in the shadows behind me. Two bright white eyes watching me from the hallway.

"'Is someone there?' I asked.

"A woman's voice whispered my name. The nurse I briefly dated had not spoken to me in months, it couldn't be her. I followed the voice down the long, catacomb hallway connecting the laboratories. Around each corner, I would catch a glimpse of ankle, a lingering hand.

"'Who are you?' I whispered. 'Where are you leading me?'

"'Call me what you like,' she said. 'I was last called Klara, when I was in Russia.'

"'You are Russian?' I asked. 'How did you get here?'

"Her voice was everywhere and nowhere, husky and accented.

"'I have lived in India and China,' she said. 'I was a ballerina in the Ural Mountains between the wars. Lenin took our food and starved our farmers. First my father died, then my mother. There were five children. When my youngest sister died, we had no choice. We distinguished between *liudoedstvo*, people eating, and *trupoedstvo*, corpse eating. The latter was horrible, the first unthinkable. Until we thought it.'

"Down the hall, under the football stadium, I heard children crying. Khleb, khleb. Bread, bread.

"'Why are you here?' I asked, stopping my ears against the murmuring dark.

"'The Americans came into my country after the revolution to save us poor peasants from starving—they gave us millions of dollars, millions of bags of rice. Yes, you saved a few, but the one you really saved was Lenin who eventually made a fine feast for us. And because you saved the Bolsheviks, we got Stalin and his labor camps, Stalin and his genocides. Now there is another war and more relief. But the War is never over'."

My friend was telling me his story, but really, he was using me as an excuse to relive it. His eyes came to life as he described reaching the end of the dark hallway. A woman waited, white and naked, her healthy flesh gleaming in the dark. Her long, black hair snaked over her breasts which she held out to him like loaves on a platter. She stretched out her hand and invited him into a cold, empty laboratory.

"I made love to her like a dying man," he told me. Inside her, he was eating chicken on a college picnic, prying wing from greasy breast. He was stealing pie from the pantry; he was dribbling milk down his fat baby chin from his mother's swollen tit. Making love to her was more real than anything that had come before and he feared would ever come after. "I had never lost myself before," he said, "and it was a relief to set down the burden." Yet within minutes of lying with her on the tiles of the laboratory, his stomach began to rumble again. He was once more ravenous. There could never be enough of her.

Now, over our black marble café table, my friend reached for my hand and brought it to his mouth. He placed my fingertips just before his lips.

"*Taste of this,* Klara told me, *and know yourself.*"

"Stop," I said. "I do not need to hear the rest. I have idea enough of what she offered you."

He dropped my hand abruptly, realizing how deeply he'd forgotten himself. "She came to me every night after I accepted her flesh. Every blissful night to help me bear it until they began to feed us again. Then the bomb was dropped and the war was over. We were released. She told me I might find her here, but until today, I never had."

I looked around for our elderly Italian waiter. The café was filled with bohemians, scribbling in their notebooks and drinking wine in the middle of the day. Two women reached across a small table to wipe crumbs from each other's mouths leaving crimson kisses on their crisp white napkins.

"I'd like the check, please."

Back on the street and further downtown, we let the overhead noise of the 3rd Avenue El substitute for conversation. We were closer for all he'd confessed, yet Klara, his nightmare made real, kept pace between us. I thought I saw her around every corner, stepping onto the bus or darting into the grocery. Before I knew where we were, he turned onto the Bowery, the only major avenue in New York never to have had a church built on it. I had heard all about the flophouses of the Bowery, all the drunk men broken by this war or the last or their own jitterbug complexes or just bad luck. But I was unprepared for the dozens of men who lay sprawled on the sidewalks, passed out as if they'd been shot.

"You're staying here?" I asked.

"There's a recommissioned Liberty ship leaving the Port of New York bound for Japan. I'm going over with the Heifer Project to deliver 800 head of cattle. I'll be a sea-going cowboy."

"You're taking cows all the way to Japan?"

"We ship pregnant heifers, so they can be milked immediately. Any family who receives one must sign a pledge they'll give the first of her daughters to another needy family."

"So you go from a stadium full of starving men to a ship full of pregnant cows?"

"Conscience makes strange bedfellows."

He looked at me then and I felt the lurch of my own stomach. He had eaten nothing all day, and I understood now that it had been his final attempt to summon her in New York, to say goodbye. If he were ever well-fed and whole, he would lose her forever. I took his thin, cold hand and drew him off the street into a narrow alley between two saloons. A grizzled man in stained gray trousers slept propped against a wooden beer barrel, another lay face down on the cobblestone street. I didn't care. There was no risk I wouldn't take to fill us both up. I thought about my little flat so far uptown. I saw us lying together on my daybed, the orange chenille bedspread tangled between our legs. After he made love to me, I would cook for him. And when he wanted seconds, I would offer them.

"When do you leave?" I asked, trying to keep my voice steady.

"In the morning. I sleep here with the guys, then ship out at dawn."

"When will you be back?"

"Not until long after you've married a nice G.I. and are working on your third baby."

It was not the answer I wanted and I snapped at him. "You don't know the first thing about me."

"I know you're not the kind of girl to be long satisfied with the soup du jour."

"You're going looking for her, aren't you. Do you think you will find her in Hiroshima? In Nagasaki?"

"Look around you," he said. "These men who understand how powerless we are, how we have become both too big and too small in our own lives. They know it is past time for grand gestures, that the bomb has made corpses of us all."

"If everyone thought like you, we'd all give up and the Hitlers of this world would win."

"Or maybe if everyone thought like me, the Hitlers of this world might never be born."

The Bowery Mission down the block rang its soup kitchen bell letting the drunks know a hot meal was ready. The grandfather sleeping at our feet roused himself and suddenly all my mother's cautions about the appetites of men rang in my ears louder than any bell.

"Do you even believe in God?" I threw at him, angrily. I was young and didn't yet understand one man's surrender would not bring down the entire world. "Do you suffer because you believe you are doing good or because you know only how to reject the life before you?"

He kissed me then, just when I didn't want him to. But he kissed me like a brother, on my forehead. He stood back and touched my hair. Strong, golden hair. I wanted to cry but I wouldn't dream of giving him the satisfaction. His eyes held enough sorrow for us both.

"Thank you for always being at the counter," he said.

To hell with him, I thought, reaching out in that dark, desperate alley. I pressed my lips to his and felt his mouth open above mine. I wanted to kiss him back to life but we were falling together, through the darkest times and across the darkest continents, and suddenly I didn't care which direction we were going—towards life or death—I didn't care if his cropped hair came away in my hands, I had watched and wanted him so long. I would wait and search for him forever as he waited and searched for his Klara because just hearing his story had gloriously ruined me in some essential way. I would taste his restlessness and negation at intersections the remainder of my life.

"No," he shook his head and pulled away. "I can't let you."

I pulled him to me again, but he was done. He spoke in a hoarse, harsh voice, and the whites of his eyes glinted in the shadows.

"Once upon a time," he began, stepping back from me, "A king angered a goddess, so she cursed him with insatiable hunger."

"Enough stories—" I began. He placed his fingers on my lips.

"Everything he ate only made this king hungrier. He tore through all his own pantries and storehouses and fields and hunting grounds; and soon enough, he turned to devour his neighbors' crops and his neighbors' livestock. His daughter who loved and obeyed him, he sold into slavery. She escaped and came back, so he sold her again. She kept coming back until one day she died of a broken heart. So he ate her dead body. *Woe*, cried the king, *I have nothing left, I have consumed everything and everyone*. And he shook his fist at the gods."

This was a pitiless story and I didn't want to hear it. I wished I'd never followed him out of Woolworth's or wasted my day walking with him. I had no job to return to and I quivered with humiliation. Roused by the soup kitchen bell, men poured out of alley doorways and tramped down wooden steps from second floor flophouses. So many of them coming, more than I ever could have imagined.

"The king shook his fist, and in that moment, his fist appeared delicious. He took a bite and tears sprang to his eyes at how good it was."

To my horror, my friend placed his own clenched fist against his teeth and tore away a strip of flesh. I cried out, but the men walked past us, drunk and oblivious. No one saw. No one acknowledged my scream.

"The king ate first his right arm and then his left," my friend continued, holding my gaze. "He ate his feet and his legs. He leaned down and devoured his own torso."

As I watched, incapacitated with terror and disbelief, this man I kissed consumed himself. In a back alley of the Bowery in New York City in the middle of June in 1947. His bodiless head rolled across the cobblestones until even that was gone. He ate everything down to his lips. When at last I stooped and plucked them off the rough macintosh, I expected to find a trail like a snail would leave. Instead, they were still strong and muscled, warm on my palm.

"Then he swallowed his lips," his lips said, "and troubled the world no more."

Overhead, the El clattered past, sweeping bits of dirt and stray food wrappers off the tracks. Pigeons rose up and resettled. I backed out of the alley onto the bright street in front of the Sunshine Hotel. I had spent my last seventy five cents on pie and coffee and now my pockets were empty. I would need to start the long walk home. Around me, more men and even a few women arrived to join the line for the Bowery Mission soup kitchen.

Earlier this spring, before Evelyn McHale jumped to her death, a businessman traveling to Mexico contracted smallpox. He came home to Manhattan and promptly died. The whole city had to be vaccinated, and the lines at the clinics stretched on for blocks. It was April and the weather was fine. I remember thinking how small the world was getting.

I never went back to Woolworth's and I didn't stay in New York long after that. I signed up with the newly established UNICEF and had them ship me off first to Europe then on to Bangladesh, Biafra, later to Rwanda and Congo, and now here, to feed the children he was willing to starve for. In 1950, Dr. Ancel Keys' two volume, thousand page study, *The Biology of Human Starvation*, was released. No one has ever made a more thorough scientific study of famine, and we still use it in our work today. In the book, all the conscientious objectors he used as test subjects were assigned numbers, so I will never be sure which one was him. Or if his data, like some of the others, was thrown out as tainted.

Still, every time I cross a chaotic intersection in Kampala or even a dirt path in a village outside of Kano, I look for him to find me as his Klara found him. I'll go for days sometimes, fasting, craving, hoping my hunger might summon him. It never does. He tried to spare me but he misunderstood the nature of experiments. What we have seen, we can never un-see. What we have heard, we can never un-hear. Some kisses are better left untasted.

You may now pass me the bottle.

It's time to marinate this food for worms.

SHERI HOLMAN (b. Richmond, Virginia, 1966) is the author of Witches on the Road Tonight which won the 2011 Shirley Jackson Award for Best Novel as well as the Independent Publishers' Gold Medal for Literary Fiction. Witches was a New York Times Editors' Choice, and made the Best Books of the Year lists for The Boston Globe, The Toronto Globe and Mail, and PopMatters. She is the author of three other novels also published by Grove/Atlantic—including The Mammoth Cheese, named a Publishers Weekly and San Francisco Chronicle Book of the

Year and shortlisted for the UK's Orange Prize; and the national bestselling The Dress Lodger, *a* New York Times *Notable Book and longlisted for the Dublin IMPAC Award. Sheri is a founding member of The Moth, and you can hear one of her stories—"Rescue Mission"—on its podcast. Having begun her career as a novelist, this is only the second time she's been brave enough to try her hand at short fiction.*

Commentary on "Starvation Experiment": *Early in 1944, millions of concentration camp victims and displaced people across war-torn Europe were starving. With the conflict hurtling to its close, the Allies urgently needed to understand the effects of famine and how best to rehabilitate its victims quickly and inexpensively. American Doctor Ancel Keys, inventor of the army's "K" ration, devised an experiment to simulate famine in the laboratory and chose for his subjects 36 conscientious objectors, drawn from the Civilian Public Service camps. These men who had elected to sit out "The Good War" refused to kill for their country but were willing potentially to die for it—most for their humanitarian beliefs, others to prove their own bravery. For nine months, held underneath the football stadium at the University of Minnesota, these men were systematically starved while being subjected to physical and psychological tests to chart the effects of hunger on the human mind and body.*

As their bodies began to eat themselves, the men grew more lethargic and apathetic, slept longer, lost interest in women and sex—their thoughts turned exclusively to food. Their body weight down to an average of 118 lbs, a few of the men dropped out or were expelled for cheating. One man gave in to hunger psychosis, chopping off three of his own fingers. Before the experiment was over, America dropped its atomic bombs on Hiroshima and Nagasaki and the war came to an unexpectedly swift conclusion. Keys' data would not be properly analyzed and published until 1950, two years after the Helsinki Convention on human experimentation.

I wanted to set my story after the experiment was over and from the point of view of a woman who might have fallen in love with one of these men, as I might have done, and I wanted to move beyond hunger for food to hunger in its sexual and spiritual forms. The story of a king who consumes himself is taken from the Greek myth of Demeter and Erysichthon, whose name means, literally, tearer of the earth.

A GAME OF DRAUGHTS

JOYCE CAROL OATES

HERE WAS A NOVELTY, AND SOMETHING OF A SHOCK: A CHILD IN THE Bog Kingdom after so many centuries.

So tattered was the boy's clothing, so disheveled and sickly his appearance, he was believed at first to be a mere urchin or beggar-boy, or a chimney sweep cast out by his master, in an early stage of lung disease. But the Countess Camilla, drawn by servants' excited chatter, perceived that he was a decent boy, perhaps even well-bred, and decided upon a whim to take him in, and save his life. *For one day my life may want saving, and here is an investment.*

When one of the Countess's retinue observed that taking in a strange child might go over poorly with the Master of the castle, the Countess said haughtily: "You've heard my wish. It's enough to *hear* it, I hope, to *obey.*"

So it happened in June 1906 that New Jersey boy Todd Slade, wandering alone through swarms of gnats into the soft, sinking interior of neighboring Crosswicks forest, found a clearing in queer silvered sunshine, in which gigantic ossified logs lay in jumbled profusion like fallen monuments, and gained himself entry to the mist-shrouded castle at the heart of the Bog Kingdom.

"Your life has been saved, Rat-boy," the Countess Camilla said, not unkindly, "and now you must repay me. What qualities have you? Can you sing, can you dance, can you tell stories?"

When the eleven year old did not immediately speak, being in a state of numbed shock, like one who has been propelled through time and through space bare-headed, exposed and with no protection, the Countess said, "Will you play mute, boy?—and tempt me to forget my good intentions?"

At first, the boy seemed incapable of responding. Then, with the air of one who must react, to save his life, he slowly shook his head—*No*.

"You are not mute, then?" The Countess was both vexed and amused. "Except you don't speak, eh?"

And again the boy shook his head slowly—*No*.

As the Bog Castle lay beneath a dread weight of *ennui*, the inevitable curse of a seasonless and timeless land, it was hoped for a while that the foundling child might provide a suitable diversion for Countess Camilla, who'd had no child of her own. She ordered Rat-boy bathed in her own sumptuous marble bath, in clouds of effervescent bubbles; and surfeited with every manner of sweet and liqueurs, until he grew ghastly pale, and was sick to his stomach—a novelty in the Bog Kingdom, and a particular revulsion to the Countess, who commanded that Rat-boy be taken from her quickly, anywhere out of her sight.

Yet, not long afterward, the Countess commanded that the spindly-limbed boy be dressed in an embroidered silk costume, complete with ruffled white blouse and kidskin boots, that he might perform as her page. "He's but a child and harmless. If he begins to sprout a beard, and hairs in his armpits, the Master will kill him, or castrate him—but not for a while, I hope. In the meantime, our household has been too long empty of childish laughter which is *unpremeditated laughter*." So said the queenly Camilla whose pale golden eyes snapped even when she smiled and whose will was not to be thwarted within the castle walls, except by her brother the Count.

For Countess and Count were not wife and husband but sister and brother and between them there was no deep bond of love but only of the more sinister primordial *blood*.

Once bathed, and his hair brushed and curled, and his frayed and filthy clothing cast away and replaced by a costume suitable for the Countess's page, Rat-boy was attended by the Countess's own servants, and fussed over by certain of the women; kissed, petted, and proclaimed as an *angel-child* by Countess Camilla herself. In her hands she framed his face and peered into his eyes, that blinked with fear; she interrogated him as to his name, and his homeland, and his reason for the journey alone, afoot, through the hazardous wastes of the Bog. But Rat-boy only shook his head, silently; as if he were not only mute but also deaf and dumb; in truth, the frail boy was malnourished and weakened, for the castle food scarcely nourished him.

"What is your name, my little page? Whisper it in my ear."

The Countess pinched the boy's cheeks until a dull flush came. But he had not a word to utter, and shrank from the fierce woman in apprehension. "Where did you come from, my lad, and where did you intend to go? It was not *here*—of course. For *here* is not imaginable from *there*—whichever *there* was your home." The Countess stared into the boy's eyes that fascinated her as the eyes of one *still living*, which she had not seen in a very long time.

"Do you know where you are at this moment? And who is Master here, and who is Mistress? Or have you truly 'lost your tongue'?" So saying, the Countess made a show of prying the boy's jaws open that she might see if his tongue *was* missing, and terrified the child by asking if he should wish to be disburdened of the "slimy useless thing" which, it seemed, he did possess after all, attached to the back of his mouth.

"For if you are indeed mute, my boy," the Countess said, in a reproachful voice, "it may be that you will be required to look the part."

When the Master of the castle returned, he thought his sister's page a rat-faced little whelp who looked familiar but could not recall having seen him before. Unless, in some dim chasm of his brain, the boy lingered as a memory of a meal of no particular distinction hastily and only partly devoured.

"I don't doubt, Camilla, that you've taken Rat-boy in to spite me, and not out of a charitable love for *him*."

The Countess, already beginning to be bored with her Rat-boy page, yet protested that the boy was her pet, and not to be molested or frightened; in any case, not to be tossed out for carrion birds to pick at until she, and she alone, gave the command.

So heavy was the pall of damp and lassitude upon the Bog Castle, the nights were spent in joyless carousing, and the playing of draughts; but, as an elderly bent-backed servant informed Todd, the game was no ordinary game of draughts of the kind played by persons in civilized lands, but a most ingenious and deadly species. For the winner was not only privileged but required to chop off the head of the loser in full view of the assembled court!—which feature the Master had initiated upon his return from the

East some years ago, that the *ennui* of the castle might be stirred. And now all were mad for the game, and had acquired an insatiable desire for blood—the blood of others, that is. "When you hear a bestial roar erupt in the early hours of the morning," Todd was told, in a lowered voice, "it's the response of onlookers to yet another 'execution'. And nearly as horrific a sound to hear, as it is a sight to see."

Todd would have liked to question the man further, but he thought it most prudent to remain speechless. For some reason, it is human nature to speak more openly to one who appears to be mute.

Being of a disposition desperate to survive, and made cunning through desperation, Todd Slade had acquired certain mannerisms appropriate to a mute—signaling with fingers, rolling his eyes agitatedly, grimacing, rapidly nodding or shaking his head when others spoke; in this case, he shuddered, and shrank away in fear. And the elderly servant warned: "You must never consent to play draughts with any of them, my lad. But if you are forced into it, your only hope is *never glance up from the board*. Not for an instant—not for the wink of an eye! For the experienced players have grown fantastically adroit in cheating, and the Master above all. (Master prides himself on playing draughts with any opponent, and acquiescing to his own execution if he loses; but of course, Master never loses.) If they can't clear the board of your pieces legitimately, they will sweep them to the floor or pocket them; and then all that awaits you is the chopping block and the starving reptile-birds. Not even Mistress could save your life—nor would she wish to, as she too is mad for blood."

Todd had played numerous board games with his cousins and grandfather back in the world he remembered of Princeton, New Jersey; in fact, it was his grandfather who'd taught Todd to play draughts—"an English variant on American checkers"—and to play with "both a serious and a playful heart." Winslow Slade had quite enjoyed playing such games with his young grandson, and was surprised and delighted when Todd quickly began to win. The boy's precocity at draughts/checkers was marveled at by those who'd seen him play with adults; but, unfortunately, at about the age of ten, Todd became easily bored by games so restricted by rules as board-games, so that not even his cousins anymore enjoyed playing with him. With dismay Todd recalled his brattish behavior—if he'd lost a piece at the wrong moment he might fly into a tantrum, and send all the pieces tumbling to the floor; sometimes, he cheated by advancing a piece by stealth, or with a sly movement of a finger dislodging one of his opponent's.

"If only I had my childhood to relive!" Todd murmured to himself, crouched in one or another of the castle's damp corners. "I would do everything differently, and not have come *here*."

As the Countess lost interest in the novelty of her rat-boy page, Todd was free to wander in the castle as he wished, so long as he kept clear of those residents who seemed to take offense at the sight of a child, and amused themselves with drunken pranks and torments—seizing Todd by the scruff of the neck, for instance, and forcing him to compete with snarling dogs for scraps of food. (So humiliated, yet bent upon surviving, Todd accepted such indignities with the steely resolution he recalled his grandfather speaking of, at a time when Todd had scarcely paid the old man any heed: *As you are a Slade, you can and will keep your own inner counsel.*)

The cunning child also reasoned that, if his tormenters saw him broken and weeping, they would be satisfied for the time being, and he would be spared another day; and might hope for revenge.

By daring and stealth Rat-boy made his way to the great dining hall where wood fires dispiritedly burned in great, six-foot-high fireplaces littered with bones, and where, through the long, sleepless night, the castle's revelers caroused. (For sleep of a normal kind was, while not forbidden in the Bog Castle, considered déclassé, and a sign of weakness.) It was observed by one of the Countess's female consorts—(such were chosen by the beautiful Countess for their ugly faces and misshapen bodies, for the Countess was amused to appear to great advantage beside them)—that a child of such tender years should be spared such gruesome sights as beheadings, as they might give him "unnatural inclinations"; provoking the sulky Countess to shrug, and tousle her page's hair, saying: "Why, where's the harm in it?—one can't be a *boy*, and *tender*, for very long."

So it happened that Todd Slade was a mute witness to some very coarse behavior among members of the court, and occasional visitors; and to the nightly games of draughts—which, though begun with drunken optimism and noisy bravado on the parts of the players, always culminated in craven terror on the part of the (disbelieving) loser; and in an execution so bloody, and so often mangled, poor Todd hid his face in his hands.

So rowdy were these nocturnal merrymakers, so strident and forced their laughter, the very spiders shuddered in their webs hidden high against the vaulted ceiling of the great hall; and in the bone-littered courtyard outside, scavenger birds stirred in sleep, and flapped their wings, in anticipation of the dawn's bloody repast. Todd's sheltered boyhood had ill prepared him for the brutality of the world—at least, *this world*; he recalled like a dream the customary quiet of Wheatsheaf Lane in Princeton, the way in which his mother and the household staff coddled him, despite his bad behavior; only his father had no patience for him, and now Todd could quite understand why.

In the Bog Castle, Todd shrank from all that he was forced to see, and expected to be "amused" by. His first execution, for instance, was carried out by Master himself, who, being very drunk, with frog-eyes bulging, badly botched the job, and had need to bring the (poorly sharpened) ax down five or six times on the neck of a smooth-chinned castle youth, before the deed was accomplished. Several nights later Todd was yet more astonished and repelled by the spectacle of the fair-haired Countess Camilla!—who, for all her hauteur and scrupulosity, often indulged in draughts with untutored male opponents who offered her no serious challenge and were easily defeated. "My queen conquers all! D'you see?—*all*"—the Countess's voice rang thrillingly.

And then what paroxysms of laughter arose at the sight of the beautiful woman with her mask-like face of blonde perfection, her composed expression, in velvet, silk damask, and ermine robes, glittering with jewels, as she stood like a woodsman with wide-spread legs, to swing the ax with fearsome determination through the air!—and to sever in a single blow the head of a luckless admirer from his body.

And cheers arose drunken and callow as cheers at the Princeton-Yale football game that Todd had several times attended with his family.

But now Rat-boy hid away crouching with the dogs. With the most craven of these, he had made friends; these were creatures bonding in equivalent misery. He thought: "Will I ever escape this hellish place? And if I do, where can I go? For I have lost my way back home."

W hile teaching himself the alphabet, and how to fashion words into logical sequences, Todd once had occasion to peruse some of the very old, never-opened books of his father's library; as something of a prank, meaning to stupefy his father, he'd committed to memory a passage from Anaximander: *It is necessary that things should pass away, into that from which they are born. For things must pay one another the penalty, and the compensation, for their injustice, according to the ordinance of Time.* Todd had not understood this wisdom at the time, though he had felt its implacability.

And, in another of the old, ignored books, a passage of Heraclitus that had made him shudder, for something uncanny and prophetic in its words: *Time is a child playing draughts; the kingship is in the hands of a child.*

Little could Todd have guessed that, one day, his own life would be in his hands, in a game of draughts played where the swampland of southwest Princeton sank into a sort of lightless slough.

It was a distinct advantage that Rat-boy's skinny frame and sallow skin made him seem younger than he was. A casual glance from any adult in the castle would have marked him as no more than ten, and negligible. Children were rarely seen in the castle, though babies were born; but babies did not long survive in the atmosphere of dank rot. But Rat-boy slipped past much scrutiny, for his small size, and muteness; and his privilege as the Countess's page, even if the Countess no longer cared much for him, and had allowed his page-finery to become dirty and tattered. The females of the court, imagining him so young, were careless with their dress and toilet in his presence, as with their speech; for Rat-boy did not seem to matter. A fleshy female with a harridan's face said, with ribald wit: "Rat-boy is but a baby, yet both *too old,* and *too young,* to properly suckle at a woman's breast." Blushing fiercely Todd remained very still as the gathering of females laughed.

Imagining him so young, and mute, the court was the more astounded when one night when the evening's merrymaking was not so strident as usual, the Countess's shy little page spoke aloud at last, in a high, frail, whispery voice—"Countess? May I speak?"

"*May* you speak? What is this? *Can* you speak?"—the Countess was very surprised. "I have healed you, have I? Is that it? My care of my little Rat-boy page has restored his speech, has it?" The Countess thought well of herself for this miracle, as others congratulated her.

In his frail whispery voice, that was near-inaudible, Rat-boy spoke in the Countess's ear: "I would like to play draughts with M-Master."

"Draughts with—*Master*?" The Countess stared at Todd with genuine alarm. "Are you mad? You will lose, and your dear little cabbage head will be chopped off, and flung to the carrion birds; and your Countess is not prepared for that, just yet."

But Master had heard the page's reckless words, that could not so easily be revoked. And through the gloomy vaulted room that resembled, for all its air of febrile festivity, and fires burning in several fireplaces, a vast mausoleum, there were startled exclamations and a scattering of applause, for the possibility of such sport was exciting, or at least carried the promise of excitement, in this morass of *ennui*.

"My page is too young to play draughts," the Countess protested, "and my brother is a master of draughts who can't be beaten, or even held to a draw; so it would be only slaughter, and can't be permitted."

"All things are permitted," the Countess's brother said to her, with a scornful curl of his lip. "All things in the Bog Kingdom are permitted *me*."

The Count was delighted that his sister's Rat-boy page had issued such a challenge, for, over the centuries, he had grown so skilled at draughts, and so ingenious and frequently negligent in his playing, he often played with two or three opponents simultaneously, and had begun to find the game, even with its bloody finale, tedious. So he rejoiced that this evening should at least be *diverting*; for in the history of the Bog Castle, dating back to time before Time, no child was ever known to issue any challenge to any adult, still less one of the nobility. And it struck the Count that there was something treacherous, something uncontrollable, indeed something *unnatural* in the very concept of a child. "For is not a 'child' a being that will alter by degrees, not quite before our eyes, yet in our presence," the Master of the castle mused, "and is not a 'child' an early version, or mockery, of ourselves?—an image of our despoiled innocence and our blasted hopes? Most intolerably, is a 'child' not *one who will replace us?*"

The Count's pallid frog-face brightened in a smile, that revealed jagged yellow teeth as the Count clapped a hand upon Rat-boy's head, in a pretense of genial affection; and said that yes indeed, he would accept Rat-boy's challenge at once, for the evening was unusually slow and dull, and a perpetual wintry rain fell through the bog, and his companions had become cowards who dared not challenge him, or even one another—for there was no fresh blood at the castle, hence no "fresh blood" for the night's sport.

"Could you have spoken all along, Rat-boy? And 'held your tongue' out of cunning?" the Count asked the Countess's page, with a deceptive sort of sympathy; seeing the Countess frown and shake her head just perceptibly, behind the Count's back, Rat-boy shook his head slowly to indicate *no*, all the while grimacing, and twitching his shoulders, to suggest that indeed speech was difficult for him, if not painful.

The gameboard was set up on a stained marble pedestal, in a central position in the vaulted room, several yards from the fire burning without much heat in the largest fireplace. In itself the board was a work of art, or had been at one time, comprised of zebrawood, with squares set individually in place, and painted in exquisite tones of red and black; around the edge of the board, a matte-finished gilding in an abstract design to suggest the Oriental and the serpentine. The draughts-pieces, or checkers, were somewhat larger than Todd had played with as a child, fashioned of carved ivory with serrated edges; and divided, as usual, into two arms, the red and the black.

Unfortunately, not fifteen feet away from the gameboard was the reeking chopping-block, a much-abused stump of log taken from the bog; and the deadly ax itself with its sturdy handle worn smooth over the years and an enormous double-edged blade covered not only in dried and blackened blood but in myriad hairs as well. (This repulsive sight clearly worked to the Count's advantage, as it unnerved the brashest of players, while the Count affected utter nonchalance, as if unaware of its presence.)

The Count led Rat-boy to his chair, and took his place across the board from him, and said in a pretense of sobriety that he supposed the game of draughts as played at the Bog Castle required no detailed explication; but in the event that Rat-boy had forgotten, the novelty of the game was this: "If your army triumphs over mine, you are required to employ that ax—(do look at it, my lad: *do*!)—and with all the strength in you, you must sever my head from my body. You cannot grant mercy because you have not the power: the Bog Kingdom admits of no mercy, even to its masters. Is't understood?—and you promise not to dissolve into tears at being *required to kill* your host and benefactor, who has tolerated your presence here in his kingdom for so long? However, in the event that your army, these red fellows, are defeated," the Count said, with a sly smile, "why, our situation is simply reversed; but that event is so remote and unlikely, we need not waste our time in speculation."

Though this was a feeble sort of wit the hall rocked with malicious laughter; but Rat-boy, poor frightened Todd Slade, sat frozen with eyes affixed to the gameboard. Clearly in his head the admonition sounding clearly *Do not glance up, do not glance up even once.*

A tankard of pungent dark ale was brought to the Count, and a miniature version brought to Todd, to provoke laughter from the onlookers; diverse sweetmeats were served; and the bloody "cannibal sandwich". These dainties the Count nibbled on through the game, wiping his sticky hands on his velvet clothing, while Todd declined to eat at all; though in truth he was faint with hunger.

As the hollow-sounding bell of the castle tolled midnight the game began, with Master allowing Rat-boy the first move, as his army was red; and the idlers of the court, including sulky Countess Camilla and her retinue, drew around. With some hesitation Todd made his first move, taking up one of his first-row pieces; but felt a sudden fear of releasing it from his fingers.

"Come, come!" the Count chided, "—you must let go; there is a time limit for such ploys, beyond which the offense fingers are *chopped off.*"

Then, it was the Count's turn. Fearfully Todd raised his eyes to take in that queer flaccid green-tinted face in which, lurking beneath its ugly exterior, one could almost discern a reptilian sort of nobility.

"Take care!"—the Countess hissed at Todd, with some disgust.

For, in the mere instant required to gaze at the Count's face, and think his melancholy thoughts, Todd's cunning opponent had managed to knock from the board two of Todd's pawns . . .

On all sides the Master's sycophants chuckled. So swiftly had the frog-Count moved, so stunned was Todd to see his army already reduced by two playing-pieces, Todd sat frozen with panic, unable at first to fully comprehend what had happened.

A stern voice admonished him *Your only hope is never to glance up from the board.* So he'd been warned clearly enough, yet like a fool he'd forgotten.

The Count naturally betrayed no awareness of having cheated, still less of his child-opponent's look of dismay.

For some minutes the game proceeded in a more or less normal fashion, though with painstaking slowness on Todd's part, for again he was reluctant to lift his fingers from a checker; and recalled how recklessly he'd played as a boy, trusting to good luck and inspiration to carry him along, as frequently it did, to his grandfather's delight. When the Count asked, in a kindly voice, if Todd would like another sort of beverage, one more suited for a child, Todd knew that he must not be deceived, and look up at the man; he must only just shake his head *no*, but keep his eyes fixed to the board. *I will not be drawn into my own death. I must concentrate exclusively on the game of draughts.*

By contrast, the Count moved his black pieces swiftly, and with a show of indifference, never failing to snap his chin up after a move, that he might beguile Todd into glancing up at him and locking eyes; but Todd clenched his jaws and did not surrender to the impulse.

Concentrate!—his grandfather had once counseled him. *Only in concentration can you succeed.*

So the game proceeded slowly. At one o'clock a number of the onlookers muttered among themselves that the game had grown "tedious"—and they might be up until dawn at this rate. Countess Camilla dared to taunt her brother by observing that it was clear he wasn't half so gifted a player as he prided himself, if a mere child of ten years or so could keep him at bay. "Move for move, and piece for piece," the provocative woman said, "the lord of the manor and the lowly Rat-boy seem to me near evenly matched, neither being sparked by genius."

This rude remark was meant to annoy the Count, as it did; he disguised his vexation by yawning, and stretching, and sighing; and drawing out of his vest a worn leather pouch filled with a sharply poignant substance smelling of bay rum and heat. He dipped his fingers into the pouch, and raised them to his nose: the familiar motion of "taking snuff" in one nostril, and then in the other; as Todd couldn't watch him directly, these motions were distracting; and so he surrendered to the instinct to glance up another time.

Poor Todd!—in that instant the fiend's free hand darted across the board and so blithely removed one of Todd's crucial checkers, which was in a position to guard his back row, that, a second time, Todd blinked in confusion and incomprehension. How was it possible that anyone could cheat with such quicksilver skill?—and such seeming innocence?

Again, everyone laughed. Even the Countess laughed in disgust.   And the Count merrily sneezed, and blew his nose most repulsively into his handkerchief; and urged Todd to make his move—"For the hour is growing late for you, my lad. Soon, it will be your *bed-time.*"

By this time Todd was both demoralized and terrified; his poor red army had been depleted by three pieces, at no cost to the black army; like a crippled old man he sat rigid and hunched over the board; dangerously, his eyes flooded with tears. He had to blink rapidly to clear his vision; but did not dare wipe his face, for fear that his opponent would take advantage. In a mock-kindly voice the Count was saying, that draughts, having little of the subtleties of chess, should really be played in a carefree manner. Wasn't it the quintessence of *childhood*—a game of straightforward simplicity, all its elements visible to the eye, and requiring little ratiocination? "In draughts one may as well move a piece quickly as after deliberation," he said, "for it will make little difference, eventually."

So tense had Todd become, when finally he made his next move, and lifted his fingers from the checker, he saw to his horror that he'd made a terrible blunder—and could not now retract it.

Concentrate!—so Grandfather Winslow Slade admonished.

Never glance up from the board!—so the elderly servant admonished.

As if suspecting a trap, the Count hesitated; then proceeded to leap over not only the luckless piece Todd had moved, but a second; and bore them off this time in honest triumph from the battlefield.

At which the gathering of sycophants and idlers responded with hand-clapping, and murmured compliments to the Master on his prowess.

Sullenly the Countess said, "It was the boy's mistake, not the Count's 'prowess.'"

Now a sickly sort of realization came over Todd, as he feared he'd forgotten the rules of the game. At home, when he'd played so heedlessly with his cousins, he'd often violated the rules, and they had not much minded.

"Come, Rat-boy," the Count said, "my little army is roiling for the kill. And you know, caution is useless."

Todd tried to recall: the object of the game was to become "kinged"—in that way to acquire more power. Being "kinged" had something to do with the back row of the board. This recollection came into Todd's mind like a drifting butterfly, in time to allow him to make his move; and a lucky move it was, as if it had been deliberated.

So hastily then the Count pushed a piece into Todd's depleted ranks, with the obvious plan of acquiring a king in the next move, he committed a blunder as well; which he and Todd saw at the same moment. But by then the Count had released his piece, and had to surrender it.

Or was this a trap?—Todd wondered. His eyes darted frantically about the board.

Yet it seemed not to be a trap. Every sycophant and idler in the vast gloomy space drew in breath, in anticipation. Todd shifted a lone piece into a strategic position that blocked two of his opponent's crucial pieces, and would in the next move account for the loss of one.

"Child's luck. Rat-boy luck." The Count muttered sullenly, like a petulant child. For now he was forced to make his move, and to sacrifice a piece. "Well. I see Rat-boy will be 'kinged' now. But so shall I, soon. And you have postponed your bedtime, it seems, for another hour."

How innocent, how unobtrusive, the Count's stubby fingers, resting lightly on the gilded edge of the board; but Todd knew how swiftly those stubby fingers could move, and did not dare look away.

King! He'd acquired a *king*. He felt an uneasy thrill of elation, though he had but seven pieces remaining, to his opponent's eleven.

Do not. Glance up. DO NOT.

Minutes passed, and, to the disgust of many, a full hour; and when the hour of 2 A.M. sounded the perspiring Rat-boy had but five pieces remaining, of which three were kings; and his opponent had six pieces, of which only two were kings. By this time the raucous crowd of onlookers had quieted and the atmosphere had grown brittle.

"Here is another tankard, brother," the Countess said, with a sly sort of solicitude. "Perhaps it will yield inspiration."

The Count took the tankard from her irritably, and drank deeply, and, with a bluff swashbuckling motion made a move to approach one of Todd's unprotected men from the rear; yet in so eccentric a manner, it must be a trick.

Todd brooded long over the new alignment on the board, yet could discover no logic to it. He saw now how the game mimicked war: there was no logic to it. He started to move one of his kings, then hesitated; started to move the lone piece, then hesitated; and stared, and swallowed hard. Was his opponent planning an ingenious assault, or had the Count plunged ahead blindly, without seeming to see that a sharp-eyed opponent could capture one of his two kings in two or three skilled moves . . . ?

How Todd's head ached, and his eyelids quivered with strain!

Badly he regretted his past life, his heedless child's life, when he had been so headstrong with his family, so cruel to even his loving mother, and a thorn in the heart of his father. No, he had not loved his Grandfather Slade enough, either.

The Count was betraying some apprehension, for he shifted about in his throne-like chair, and wiped at his face with a soiled handkerchief. "Rat-boy," he said softly, "you are perhaps *not a child* at all."

"He's a child, brother! He's just a child. *You* must be prepared to be beaten by a child, in front of witnesses." The Countless laughed in delight, revealing yellow-tinged teeth, that did not detract from her curious mask-like perfection, but rather enhanced it.

After a long minute of deliberation Todd made a move; and the Count made his; and, suppressing a shiver of apprehension, or a little cry of elation, Todd quickly took advantage of his opponent's poor judgment—

capturing *not one king but two* in a spirited hopping march across the board!

Now it seemed that Rat-boy was near to winning the game, unbelievably, against the Master of Bog Castle. All of the great hall grew hushed.

"Well, brother, you are driven to it," the Countess Camilla declared in a voice both exhilarated and fearful. "You and I both—for my fate rests with yours. *Take care.*"

Slowly the Count drew forth his filthy snuff-pouch and, while positioning a tiny pinch of the foul tobacco in one of his nostrils, succeeded in wafting a grain or two in Todd's direction; with the result that the boy's eyes welled with stinging tears, and he could not stop himself from sneezing— once, twice, a third time; and, instantaneously, the wily Count swept Todd's most valued king to the floor.

All of the assemblage reacted with a murmur, though not of support for the Count's crude move; for even a cheater is obliged to act with grace, and to disguise his dishonesty.

Todd saw at once what the situation was, and fought back tears of help- lessness and anger; for he'd been tricked again, and truly unfairly. The Count was like Todd as he'd once been, as a spoiled child; but far worse, since his pranks were lethal.

Yet Todd managed to recover, to a degree, to continue the exhausting game, and in so forthright a manner, no one could have told that the loss of the king had thrown him into a temporary panic. Following this exchange, so warily did the Master of the Bog Castle and the lowly Rat-boy play at their game of draughts, and so cautious were their soldiers of one another, the castle bell tolled 3 A.M.; and then 4 A.M.; at last 5 A.M.—with no sig- nificant change of fortune. *How strange that I am evenly matched with the Devil*—the thought came wryly to Todd.

By this time all but the hardiest of the onlookers had lapsed into drunken slumber. The Countess Camilla had resorted to taking snuff, with her retinue of coarse-featured court women, in order to stay awake.

"Shall we declare a draw, brother?"—so the Countess said, disguising her concern in a jesting voice. "It would not be so dishonorable, you know, but something of a novelty in the Bog Kingdom."

"No. Never a draw."

"But—"

"I said *no*. Never. This Rat-boy is a devil of some sort, from another sort of Bog Kingdom, and not what he seems. But I will beat him—fairly. I promise."

Todd's throbbing head was nodding; his eyelids had grown heavy. He sensed his opponent's weariness as well, but knew enough not to glance up at the Count.

At last the game of draughts ended, in an altogether unexpected way, at 5:21 A.M.; when only six pieces remained on the board, evenly divided between three kings of the red army and three of the black, timidly huddled together in their respective camps.

By this time, so far as Todd Slade knew, all of the vast Earth had been reduced to the shimmering squares before him. Dazed, hollow-eyed, faint with hunger and anxiety, he could recall little beyond the gameboard or the game. All that mattered were maneuvers and counter-maneuvers. In two moves possibly—in three moves assuredly—he might win; yet it was best to be prudent, to take care. If the red king advanced by one more square, then the cornered black king would be forced to move laterally; but what of the other black king, positioned so crucially? There was no end to the game in sight. The game of draughts, Todd saw, was interminable—*it was his life.* And when he weakened, or slid helplessly forward in a faint, it would be his death.

Precisely how the *coup de grâce* was administered by the exhausted Rat-boy page none of the onlookers could have said afterward; nor, unfortunately, can this historian replicate the final moves of the game, though I have set up a small checkerboard here on my desk, to follow the game. According to evidence afterward provided by Todd Slade, the end came at dawn, or what passed for dawn in the Bog Kingdom, when a languid and sickly sun penetrated the smoky interior of the hall; and only a few observers, including the ashen-skinned Countess, were witnesses. The Count, nearly as drained of strength as his child-opponent, and somewhat inebriated, was overcome by a sudden rage against one of the snoring bloodhounds at his feet; and, cursing, gave the dog a sound kick in the ribs, which sent the poor creature yelping and whimpering into a corner... But when the Count returned his attention to the board, to reach for one of his kings, he saw to his consternation that the king had vanished; and his two remaining kings were now vulnerable to being captured.

"What! How is it! Rat-boy has—*cheated?*"

"He has not cheated, brother. I saw nothing."

"But, my king—"

"Your king is at your feet, brother. Where you yourself toppled it."

But was this so? The Count did not dare to look, for fear that his wily child-opponent would cause another piece to "vanish".

The Count clapped both hands to his forehead. His eyes bulged and quivered. For it was clear to him that the game of draughts was all but over, and Rat-boy had defeated him honestly, following the rules of the Bog Kingdom; and there was no way out.

Even in this flush of triumph the wily child knew not to glance up at his opponent's strained face. *Do not weaken, remain calm and have no pity.*

The Countess was swaying, and clutching at her hair that had come loose in the course of the long night, in an attitude of angry despair. "It is over. The game—our game—the Bog Castle—the Kingdom. The Kingship is now in the hands of a child and our long reign is ended."

"The Kingship is in the hands of a child," the Count echoed, as he continued to stare, and stare, at the lone pieces before him of his black army. Piteously, the protuberant frog eyes filled with moisture.

So it was, pitiless Todd Slade jumped two of his opponent's vulnerable kings, and the gameboard was cleared entirely of *black*.

"You must, you know. There is no turning back."

The Countess herself had taken up the heavy ax, to force into the boy's hands.

"You *must*. It is the completion of the game of draughts which you began, on the very hour of your arrival among us."

In this way we come to the blood denouement: for when the spindly-limbed Rat-boy, reeling with fatigue, dread, and repugnance for the terrible deed he must commit, at last manages, with some four or five clumsy swings of the ax, to sever the Count's head from his shoulders, and erase forever the Count's smirking face, the shadowy hall with its gaping witnesses vanishes—and the Bog Castle vanishes—and the Bog Kingdom vanishes through its vast waste stretches; and Todd Slade wakes, his young heart hammering with life, whether in his old bed at Wheatsheaf Lane, or in another place, he doesn't know at once.

He knows only in that wondrous instant that the Curse has lifted, and he is alive—again alive.

JOYCE CAROL OATES *(b. Lockport, New York, USA) has had her life documented in* Invisible Writer, *an authorized biography by Greg Johnson (1998, 492 pages,*

Dutton), and her heart laid bare in the autobiographical, A Widow's Story (2011, 432 pages, Ecco). Publicizing the former, Dutton noted that "Oates's own life was marked by the same chaos, violence, and dark twists of fate that would later beset her fictional characters and create her obsession with what she calls 'the phantasmagoria of personality'. Here is the child born into poverty in the desolate heart of upstate New York; a girl shadowed by emotional terrors; a young woman drawn at an early age into an intensely private world of the intellect and imagination. . . "

That imagination, as The Academy of Achievement would put it, "surprised critics and readers with a series of novels, beginning with Bellefleur, in which she reinvented the conventions of Gothic fiction, using them to re-imagine whole stretches of American history."

Joyce, having written nearly sixty novels at time of press (and contributed to the very first Exotic Gothic), continues to reinvent the conventions from Princeton, New Jersey, where she is Distinguished Professor of Humanities at Princeton University. Her newest works waiting to surprise, seduce, and disturb readers are Daddy Love *(a suspense novel),* Evil Eye: Four Novellas of Love Gone Wrong, Carthage *(a novel),* The Coming Storm *(a book of poems), and* The Accursed, *AKA* The Crosswicks Horror, *the long awaited novel whose shadows you have now lingered in, and which completes her 'Gothic Quintet' begun by* Bellefleur *(1980),* A Bloodsmoor Romance *(1982),* Mysteries of Winterthurn *(1984), and* My Heart Laid Bare *(1998).*

Commentary on "A Game of Draughts": *Might mere pawns in a game of chess conceive of the fact that they are playing-pieces, and not in control of their fate; what would give them the power to lift themselves above the playing board, to a height at which the design of the game becomes clear? I'm afraid that this is not very likely, for them as for us: we cannot know if we act or are acted upon; whether we are playing pieces in the game, or are the very game ourselves.*

FOODFACE

STEPHEN SUSCO

DON COULDN'T PLACE THE ACCENT. IT WAS SO UNUSUAL, SO ALIEN to his ears that, for just a moment, the fact that the words were voiced not by a person but rather his breakfast became merely a minor consideration.

He abruptly recalled a girl in his freshman class up at State College—her first name was an unusual variant of Hannah. Hosannah, or maybe Hallena? It had been many years since he'd last thought of her, but his struggle with this new accent took him straight back. She'd been exotic to his Midwestern sensibility: born in Germany, raised in Japan, and educated in New Zealand. The inevitable teasing had begun from the moment she'd introduced herself. A few of her new classmates had playfully goaded her into reciting well-known quotes of famous movie antagonists. *"No, Mr. Bond. I expect you to die."* She'd handled it well, acquiescing with a self-conscious laugh, a slight flick of her hair. Don wisely managed to hold his tongue as others ran with the joke. He didn't want to risk letting her smile—that wonderfully delicious smile—slip away.

And as a result he discovered, one drunken evening soon after, that although she may have despised the suggestion that she had the voice of a Bond villain, Hauna—*that* was it—thoroughly enjoyed fucking like one.

Funny what a voice can do. How it can turn back the years as if they'd never passed. How it can make you overlook, even if only for the slightest instant, that a plate of bacon and eggs has begun speaking to you.

All things considered, Don's morning usual was a rather innocuous dish: two eggs, sunny-side up, whole-wheat toast lightly buttered, two strips of bacon—extra crispy, if you please—with hash browns to boot. The kind of American staple greasy spoons proudly unload at $3.99 *("Monday through Thursday only!")* with a bottomless mug of flaccid coffee thrown in for free. Plus tax, an easy five-spot covers the tip. Simple, cozy, cost-efficient and Don's usual. He was a rhythm guy. Or at least, he'd *become* one, since he'd lost Jeanette. It'd been his psychologist's idea—quite possibly the single good he'd had over the entirety of their two-year Wednesday afternoon palaver. *"The three R's,"* the shrink liked to say in his practiced tone of monotonous objectivity. Regularity. Routine. Ritual.

Don had always suspected there was a self-help book in the works, and that the esteemed Dr. Richard Redstone had carefully factored brand-name recognition into the construction of his favorite mantra. He'd likely spent hours of his after-hours time contemplating how Oprah would carefully and lovingly caress the alliteration of each delightful initial for her audience of millions.

Notwithstanding his cynicism, Don had adhered to the tenets of the Doc's catch phrase, even selecting the same ripped-vinyl stool at the counter every time, just ahead of the morning rush. And it had helped. Jeanette still lingered, naturally. It had, after all, been twenty-six years of hiccup-less marriage. He was getting by, drinking less, rarely crying anymore. But she was always there, on the fringes of his thoughts.

That hadn't stopped Shannon from trying, of course. She was convinced his clockwork attendance at the diner had everything to do with her. And Don wasn't of a mind to break the truth to her. She was young—embarrassingly so, if he were being honest about it. Well under thirty. She wore her dyed-crimson hair long around the contours of her face, as if deliberately trying to hide details she otherwise willingly revealed to Don each time she leaned against the counter, casually tucking her locks around her ear. She was never coy about her attention—it was her ease with Don that he found most alluring. He watched her with other patrons. He knew it was special. A gift.

Don picked up on the other things—the tattoos, the piercings, the occasional scar blemishing a field of soft porcelain. He was good with details. He was trained to be. But he picked up on the most salient detail of all—these facets were wings, not anchors. She'd absorbed her past, and like an alchemist transformed the moments that likely would have crippled others (and perhaps even herself, for a time) into foundation stones that kept her poised above the crushing surf of existence.

They'd never spoken about these things—not yet. But he knew just the same. He'd spent every day of the better half of his life face-to-face with the shell-shocked, the walking wounded. His intuition, his mid-game analysis, had become sharp. It never took long for him to size up someone's ability to handle the cards they'd been dealt—or that they'd unwittingly chosen for themselves. And he knew Shannon had been through the darkest of tunnels. And that she'd emerged on the other side—renovated, remodeled, and renewed as the Doc might say.

Sometimes he fantasized about her. Innocent things, mostly. Like what it'd be like to fall asleep next to her. To press his face into the rich colors inked into the flesh between her shoulder blades. To drift off there, arms wrapped around her slight hips.

Sometimes the flights of fancy were less pious. It had been a long time. A very, very long time.

This morning Shannon had seemed more distracted than usual. The place had gotten busy unusually early, and she was on her own. It was only after a few flybys that she'd finally spotted the fiver he'd slipped under the sugar canister. She'd casually picked up the sugar and flicked the cash back towards his plate. It had become a game between them—*a regular routine ritual, Doc!*—ever since he'd tried to slip a folded five into her apron pocket when she was refilling another customer's mug. It wasn't until later in the day Don had re-discovered the same bill stuffed back into his coat pocket. From that point on he'd always taken his coat with him to the restroom.

"You ever gonna let me pay?"

"Chuck would can me if I ever let you put down a dime." Then she grinned, leaning in just close enough for him to get a whiff of her scent. Perfume, not sweat. For the morning shift. For him. "I'll be happy to let you pick up the tab, when you decide to take me to dinner."

She'd finally given up any semblance of subtlety. He couldn't blame her. This had been their daily dance for the better part of the past year. Chuck didn't seem to mind. Even lodged in the back, sweating out the broken A/C from dawn till dusk, he still saw and knew everything. Every customer was a first-namer. Every order hit the griddle the moment the bell above the door jangled. No one was special because everyone was. But Don and his comrades—well, maybe they were more special. They never paid. Didn't matter if it was the $3.99 breakfast special (*with bottomless mug!*) or the $17.99 dinner combo platter. It simply wasn't allowed.

Sometimes Shannon's flirtations summoned a rare grin from Chuck's grizzled visage. He was a constant third wheel to the energy flooding between them. Maybe it did him good somehow. Gave him hope, or some such. Don tried not to take it as a sign—and he didn't know Chuck well enough to make assumptions.

Shannon had lingered for a moment—that final moment before everything stopped making sense, before the new voice, with that strangely clipped modulation, that unusually strident intonation, reached his ears.

He noticed the details: her slightly flushed cheeks, the sweat beading her brow.

"You okay?" Her eyes met his quickly, as if seeking a respite from . . . what was that in her face? Restlessness? Confusion?

"Yeah. I guess." She scanned the customers tucking in to their breakfasts, the handful of others surfing their smartphones by the entrance. He'd never seen her anxious. And wasn't sure he should say so.

"Times like this, I bet you wouldn't mind an extra hand." He was leading her, very much aware of the empty ticket slip carousel behind her. She was on top of things. Always was. Something else was troubling her.

"Just one of those days, I guess." She grabbed a full coffee pot and headed for the seating area. He'd just been handed his first brush-off. It felt personal. Because everything about Shannon always felt personal—

Youch. Bet that stings.

Don turned. The seat to his right was empty. Its former occupant must have departed during his brief exchange with Shannon. She had a way of doing that, with her eyes locked onto his. Eclipsing the world.

Nope. Down here, pal.

This time the voice was louder—or perhaps *clearer*. Don instinctively looked "down", which sent his eyes in the direction of his plate. He immediately sensed how silly the action was, but in the sliver of time it took for him to recognize this and start to turn to his left he noticed something about his food: the two eggs were positioned with relative symmetry in the top hemisphere of the plate, with the hash browns pressed into a line around the border. The bacon strips were stretched across the lower half, with the edges curved slightly upwards, completing the goofy yet somehow macabre image of a face. A rather pleasant one, as he considered it—large eyes, broad smile (*extra crispy, if you please!*), and a vaguely hipster-esque unkempt hairline. Not entirely unlike the rudimentary sketch of a Muppet about to break into a goofy mnemonic tune.

But the plate hadn't arrived with the food thusly arranged. Or had it? Chuck had a style with his presentation, a certain *je ne sais quoi*, as Shannon had once jested, that elevated the diner above common fare. What he didn't have was a sense of humor.

Mornin', Sunshine. What's the haps?

That wasn't the voice of a Muppet. Not even close. There was a sharp edge to the timbre, a grating pitch that danced with cleated sneakers across the nerves in Don's ears. He hunched his shoulders unconsciously, as if to somehow ameliorate whatever damage the voice was causing to his auditory sensors—and that reflex prompted without invitation a childhood memory, of a horribly shrill voice emanating from the TV set in his older brother's room, ruining whatever concentration a much younger Don had mustered for some irrelevant homework assignment. He'd snuck quietly to the door of the opposing bedroom—his parents had very strict rules about homework hours—and had silently opened the door to peek inside.

Matthew's brother had always been a genre junkie. There was no movie too cheesily horror-ific or sci-fic-tastic not to merit a screening on the TV/DVD combo his brother had sweated tirelessly on neighborhood lawns to earn. He'd watch movies with the volume down, sometimes late into the night—and sometimes he'd even let Don join him in his bed, always willing to warn him when a particularly grotesque moment was imminent.

That night he'd been watching something new. Something strange. Something, Don wouldn't discern until he was older, so very, very English. There was a goofy odd man, a hippy-looking dude in a long coat that other people were calling "Doctor". The sets were lame, the colors washed out and blurry with each movement of the camera. But the actors were committed, chewing the scenery with beatific enthusiasm.

And then, off-camera, a horribly strident voice began to screech a single word, over and over again. *"EXTERMINATE! EXTERMINATE!"* The actors reacted with magnified shock, backing away in terror as a rather un-terrifying looking machine advanced on them. Its appearance was that of a salt shaker enlarged to the size of a small car, coated with an even distribution of dome-shaped protrusions and topped with several jutting arms—one of which was clearly a toilet bowl plunger apparently designed to intimidate as it jiggled in the direction of the petrified characters.

Though Don would later learn that these were in fact rather ruthless creatures, he let out an unstoppable giggle upon seeing his first Dalek—the low-rent construction and shoddy video, combined with the actors' attempt to oversell the monster's ferocity, was more than enough to trip the fail-safe on his youthful bullshit meter.

But at night, as he lay staring at the ceiling, sleep remained elusive. That voice—that piercing, and hauntingly soulless voice—echoed in his mind.

Whassa matta? Cat got yer tongue?

The voice of Don's $3.99 + tax weekday breakfast special was twice artificial. Like the voice of the Dalek, there was a flat cruelty to the delivery, and the anonymous accent contributed to the unnerving quality. But the syntax it was using—the regional affectation, the urban polish—was clearly put-on. It was an ill-fitting disguise. A skeleton lacking the dressings of muscle or organ, yet draped in flaccid skin. It was, quite simply, wrong. Terribly, terribly wrong. And devoid of the mechanical production of the Dalek's voice—the apparent lack of humanity and empathy—the implication was even more frightening. There was a soul behind it. There was a mind.

There was *enjoyment*.

When the voice came again, there was a slight vibration in the yolks of the eggs, the runny interior quivering against the glutinous outer shell, straining gently outward as if to focus more clearly on Don's own eyes. The edges of the bacon inched slightly higher, the breakfast's smile becoming more pronounced.

She's a doll, ain't she? Shame you never took your chance.

Don glanced up at Chuck, sweating with consternation over his perfect line of pancakes; then at the customer to his left, obliviously scarfing down a heap of chipped beef smothered in gravy; and finally at Shannon, only a few feet away, with that unusually glazed expression in her eyes. None of them had noticed. None of them had *heard*.

Two realizations struck Don in that instant. The first was that the voice was choosing its words deliberately. It was mimicking the speech of the only person Don had ever known—a *real* person, not some hard-boiled fiction character or '50s movie protagonist—who effortlessly and without a trace of irony employed the vernacular of "doll" and "pal" and "what's the haps?" in his everyday life. His name was Terrence McAdams, and he was a petty criminal, a thug and an abuser of women.

And he was the first man—the *only* man—Don had ever killed.

The impossible absurdity of this first revelation was only trumped by the gravity of the second: that the voice Don was hearing wasn't reaching his ears.

Of course no one else heard it. It was originating inside his head.

A stroke, Don thought. *Goddamn it, I'm having a fucking stroke—*

You wish, Bub. You only wish I was a stroke.

The movement on the surface of the plate was gaining confidence. As if loosening muscles that had been long out of practice, the fatty edge of the bacon strips now rippled with precision, tightening and coiling in a nearly-perfect simulation of human lips. The always-perfect sunny-side eggs had taken on a gelatinous quality, a subtle yet remarkable shift mirroring the nuanced layers of a cornea and aqueous humour.

Two colorless eyeballs. Watching him.

"This isn't real. *You* aren't—"

Close yer head, Mack. I can hear ya just fine in here, savvy?

He'd always refused the prescriptions that seemed inextricably connected with the loss of his wife. The offers seemed to come from every conceivable source—not just Dr. Three-R's, and his compassionate friends in Big Pharma. It was as if Don's grief was a powerful transmitter, sending out invisible waves, attracting junk mail and television ads targeted specifically for his need. They knew his hole, and they knew how to fill it. Or at the very least, cover it with chemical camouflage.

Don had resisted that path. He'd crossed paths with too many of the lost souls, the victims twice-over, the fallout of the anti-depressant era. The ones who, seeking an escape from the forest, instead found themselves tangled in a deeper, thornier wood.

He'd fought the allure of the easy fix, the temptation of letting go. He chose the path of fortitude, and determination. Of regularity, routine and ritual.

And yet here he was, at the very end he'd sought to avoid.

My mind. I've lost my mind.

The bacon-smile widened, the sinewy tissues quivering in what Don could only speculate was both affirmation and feverish anticipation. The milky eye-tumors shifted to the side and Don followed them, glancing to his neighbor on his left. Mr. Chipped-Beef. He was hunched over his own plate, sweat beading on his brow, eyes glazed with concentration as he shoveled grayish lumps of congealed gravy and saturated whole wheat bread into his mouth. He barely chewed each mouthful, instead using the next forkload to press the last deeper into his cavity. His cheeks were turning an alarming shade of red.

Dat's it, champ. Down the hatch, fast as you can.

Only then did Don notice the silence that had fallen over the diner. Conversation had entirely ceased, freeing wavelength for the unusually loud *CLINK* of utensils and the wet sounds of feverish mastication. The customers waiting by the door seemed caught up in the same ravenous ardor. Their phones and newspapers and books forgotten, they all stared at the other diners—no, at their *plates*—with voracious anticipation. Some were drooling onto their business suits and bright magazine covers.

Shannon stood at the far end of the counter, vacant eyes locked onto a cherry pie cooling on a display plate. One hand clutched the elbow of her other arm, Ferrari-red nails turning the flesh white.

What's happening? What is this?

The great kick-off. The final chill. An' you got yerself a trackside seat.

Through the serving window, Don could see that even Chuck was afflicted. He'd never seen the cook standing still. His non-stop balletic motion had always been a constant, and a performance to behold. But now he was anchored, muscles rigid, staring down at the bacon hissing—*no, snarling*—up at him from the grill. The perfectly-aligned row of pancakes on the lower heat lay ignored, sprouting tell-tale bubbles—*eyes, eyes to see*—that indicated charring was soon to come. There was no alarm in his eyes. No recognition of his cuisine's sudden animation. Only a deep and consuming *hunger . . .*

OW! Keep it friendly, ya louse!

Don's eyes returned to his plate. The tip of the knife he clutched in his trembling hand had nicked one of the coagulated yolks. The viscous humour was now leaking downward, winding toward the bacon like a lone tear as the strips below slowly wound themselves into a twisted perversion of a smirk.

Aw look, yer makin' me all misty-eyed.

He meant to shove the plate. But Don's numb hands caught the edge of the counter instead, and his violent push sent him careening backwards into another table. Plastic cups and cheap silverware clattered across the floor. All eyes turned to him, alert and startled, as if the sound had shattered the spell that had the entire diner held in sway.

"Don?"

Shannon moved toward him, the freckles he'd always adored now lost in the creases of her sudden concern. Even Chuck had turned, his furrowed brow returned to its usual state of disdainful attention. Don could feel the heat of everyone else's attention on the back of his neck. His face flushed in the realization.

They don't know. None of them—

He was the anomaly. He was the deviant. *Him.*

Don stood shakily, stumbling, pushing through the narrow avenue of chairs and tables toward the bathroom.

H e hadn't eaten in almost twelve hours, so there was nothing to raise but acid-curdled coffee. Don gripped the sink, retching with all the enthusiasm he could muster. For a moment he gave thanks that he hadn't had time to consume even one bite of his food. That it hadn't had a chance to get inside him.

He threw water on his face. Scrubbed it into his rough skin. As if he could somehow expunge the truth screaming like an air raid siren inside his head.

Don stared himself down as one hand slipped into his pocket, fishing out his cell phone. The Doc's number was on speed-dial—he'd made Don program it right there, in his office. *If it ever feels like it's too much, call. Don't wait. Don't sleep it off, don't drink it off. Don't assume that tomorrow will be better. Just call. It's that simple.*

As Don's finger pressed the button, he realized how simple surrender could be. It made him wonder what all the fighting had been for.

The bathroom door burst open, catching his arm, sending the phone skittering across the floor as Mr. Chipped Beef stumbled inside, a meaty hand clamped over his mouth, his eyes wide and reeling. His momentum carried his large frame into the door of one of the stalls, denting the thin metal. The thick fingers of his free hand scrabbled at the handle, yanking the door open. And he threw himself on his knees before the ceramic throne with the enthusiasm of a philandering politician exposed in an election cycle.

It wasn't until Don had collected his cell and re-inserted the ejected SIM card that he took notice of the sounds coming from the stall not three feet away. The splatter of half-digested food evacuating through the guy's maw didn't sound to be anywhere near stopping. The pace in fact only seemed to be *accelerating*, and the shifting modulation of the vomit settling in the toilet was akin to that of oatmeal being continuously ladled into a bowl. Like it was being *filled*.

Don thought of his plate. The words it had spoken. The way it had encouraged the hefty man in his tireless efforts to tamp down his stomach with more food.

He kneeled next to the stall, peering under the lip.

Mr. Chipped Beef hadn't quite reached the throne in time, it seemed. The floor was splattered with pools and clumps of his meal. Far from consideration as the most visually resplendent recipe ever concocted by mankind, the appearance of the puddles of chipped beef in ejecta was remarkably similar to its initial presentation on the man's plate. It clung to his pants in gobs as his body trembled with effort. No longer kneeling, the tops of his thighs had flattened against the floor, as if in a weakened state he was relying on the strength—or sheer weight—of his arms to keep his head over the toilet bowl.

But the sounds—those horrible *sounds.*

There was something just so *solid* about them.

Don tapped on the wall. Searching for the right words. "You okay?"

A new sound rose above the vile heaving of the man's organs, the abhorrent sloshing inside the bowl. A plaintive mewling deep in the man's core. A blubbering cry of desperation somehow squeezing through the flood of bile filling his throat.

Don stood, went to the door, reached for the handle. He hesitated, remembering something Jeannie used to talk about, a concept that had always fascinated her scientific mind. It was a theory, proffered by some famous guy—Schroder? Schrader? Schringdinger? He'd always thought it was bunk, the notion of a cat locked in a steel box with an acid flask that could break any moment and leak lethal gas into the air. The premise suggested that until someone finally opened the box to see if it had cracked, the animal was somehow *both* at the same time: a living cat and a dead cat. That it was *observation* that provided form and truth and finality.

Don considered himself embedded in the center of that unusual paradox, as he grasped the handle of the stall, preparing to open it. *Alive* and *dead. Sane* and *insane.*

He opened the door.

His world settled into finality.

Rejoining the dining room, that unsettling silence had returned—a quietude punctuated only by the jarring sound of mass deglutition. At first it seemed like all the patrons had left. But no, there they were, lined up at the counter, pressing against it in a fervent mob of teeth and tongue.

They wanted to be closer to the source. The kitchen.

Chuck was still back there, sweating in the heat. Any semblance of order had vanished, and every square inch of the sprawling grill was covered with food: bacon, ham, sausage, eggs, batter, hash, French fries, scrapple. It was as if he'd carelessly dumped everything he could grab from the walk-in onto the searing surface. Speed had become the motivator now. The people needed to be fed.

Using a spatula Chuck simply scraped the contents from the heat into a series of large mixing bowls lined up by the ticket carousel. Shannon, cheeks flushed, worked the line, a bowl tucked under her arm. She scooped a ladle into the muck, filling it and simply pouring the contents into the longing mouths of the patrons leaning toward her like baby birds anticipating the fruit of their mother's emesis.

Don inched closer, hearing the word—the same word—rising unbidden from their bodies, an instinctive imperative made solid by voices forceful and urgent.

more. More. MORE.

His plate remained untouched. The egg-eyes locked onto him, roiling with a clearly defined expression of euphoria.

Take a load off. Have a bite.

Don stepped closer. Ignoring the bodies writhing around him.

Why are you doing this?

The bacon-mouth grinned wider than Don ever could have thought possible.

YOU did this. We're your children. You made us. You put us in your food, your water, and the food for the creatures you raised to slaughter. Now didn't your mama used to say—you are what you eat?

Shannon stopped before Don, holding out the overflowing ladle.

Her eyes were an empty brown. Bottomless.

It was inevitable, Chief. Roboration. Renaissance. Revolution.

Shannon's outstretched arm trembled under the strain and her left bra strap had fallen. Strands of hair hung down her face. Up and down the counter, all heads rotated towards Don.

Every revolution's gotta start somewhere, kid.

Open wide.

Don tore his eyes away from Shannon's. It was a painful act, knowing he'd been a fool for not taking advantage of the time they'd had. The time they'd now lost.

As he walked to the door, it became clear what he had to do. He'd been trained to know, after all. How to handle these things.

He reached the door, and turned the lock.

Detective Shore had skipped breakfast that morning. Mary had been feeling sick, most likely she'd picked up the bug that had taken down the kids the weekend before. He made the lunches, got them to school, and made it to the station just in time for the daily briefing. The usual pair of pink boxes from Amy's—"*. . . the best apple fritters in New York!*"—had already been emptied, which didn't strike him as unusual. Not then.

Before he'd even gotten to his desk Shore had received the call. He'd been a regular at Chuck's for over a decade now, mostly because the curmudgeon had a soft spot for cops. But one night the cook had stayed open late for him, and pulled out a bottle of single malt when he began lamenting about an argument he'd had with Mary. Since then he'd get the occasional call—usually about a poker game with Chuck's collection of pals, the whole lot similarly graced with an impenetrable crankiness.

But those calls always came at night. And it wasn't even nine am.

"That guy who comes more than you now. Always sits at number four."

"Detective Breslin."

"Yeah. You might wanna come down . . . "

Chuck had trailed off. Shore could hear his breath.

"Chuck?"

"Something funny. In his eyes. You should . . . "

Again, he heard Chuck's breathing. And then a sudden clatter, as if the handset had slipped from his hand and fallen to the floor.

"Hey, you still there? Chuck?"

The diner wasn't far from the Station. It took Shore less than ten minutes to get there. But what Don had managed to accomplish in that small window of time . . .

He'd gone alone, but wasn't alone very long. The diner's floor-to-ceiling windows needed to be covered while the crew did their work. And it was still rush hour, so the rubberneckers—in their cars, on the sidewalk—tied up the city for blocks.

Don had reloaded. Twice.

But that wasn't the thing that would trouble him the most, as Shore sat at the dinner table with his family later that night. It was the expression on the face of that Armenian guy on the clean-up crew—Haro, short for something none of the other guys could ever pronounce. He'd pushed his mop and bucket into the bathroom as Shore was watching the photographer cover the bathroom stall where they found the last body. He was using a long lens, shooting into the commode from above, his flash capturing every detail of the bowl overflowing with . . .

It was the eyes that struck him. The guy's *eyes*, nestled right on top.

Shore had heard the door open and turned to see Haro staring past him at the open stall. His face looked clammy and pale. And at first Shore had figured he was gonna hurl at the sight of that gore-filled toilet.

But he'd just stood there. Fingers clenching his broom so tightly Shore could hear the wood groaning in protest.

"Need another minute," Shore had said to him.

And it was the expression that had flickered across Haro's face that haunted Shore the most—more than anything else that he had seen in the horror of that morning. He'd see the same look tonight on his wife Mary's face, eyes softly glazed as she gnawed on her sixth leg of chicken. And from a glance at his daughter, a committed vegan—how *annoying* she could be, parading that about—as she polished off her second burger and reached for another. He watched his sons as they shoveled down mouthfuls of mac and cheese, eyes locked onto the quart bowl between them as if they'd need to fight over the rest.

Given time and distance, he'd finally been struck by the truth of that moment.

That if he'd stood in Haro's way for any longer than those first few seconds, he might have gotten hurt. And that the look in the cleaner's eyes, as he stared at the pools of regurgitated food on the floor of the stall, hadn't been revulsion.

It was *hunger*.

STEPHEN SUSCO (*b. Philadelphia, PA, 1971*) *As a screenwriter and producer, Stephen has penned and sold over forty scripts and pitches to major Hollywood studios, and has written for a variety of acclaimed directors and producers, includ-*

ing Mike Nichols (The Graduate), Taylor Hackford (Ray), Quentin Tarantino (Pulp Fiction), Philip Noyce (Dead Calm), and Michael Bay (Transformers). Three of his films—The Grudge, The Grudge 2, and The Possession—placed #1 at the U.S. box office, and two others (Red, starring Brian Cox, and High School, starring Adrien Brody and Michael Chiklis) were invited to premiere at the prestigious Sundance Film Festival.

Most recently Stephen has written Infantry for director McG (Terminator: Salvation) and star Taylor Lautner (the Twilight series), and he is currently adapting a superhero comic series for director Brett Ratner (X-Men 3), a science-fiction novel for director Chris Columbus (Harry Potter 1&2, Gremlins, Goonies) and a TV series for director Gore Verbinski (Pirates Of The Caribbean 1-3).

This year marked his first foray into publishing with a contribution titled "The Drop" to the zombie anthology 21st Century Dead (edited by Christopher Golden).

Commentary on "Foodface": *Flipping through the age-worn pages of an old college notebook, I found the following line, hastily scribbled in pencil: "Guy's breakfast starts talking to him. Problem is, he's a cop." I remember I'd just pulled an all-nighter, cramming for a Philosophy exam, and had stopped at a local greasy spoon just before for some caffeine and refueling.*

Perhaps it's ironic that the exam was regarding Ethics—and yet it wasn't until twenty years later, as I was reading an article this Spring about the use of "Pink Slime" as a ground beef additive, that a subtext emerged.

The pros and cons of a sleepless night, I suppose.

THE GIRL NEXT DOOR

GEMINI WAHHAJ

I

I ALWAYS THINK OF CHRISTMAS IN HOUSTON AS THE LONELIEST time of the year because everyone else is having parties and dinners and if you don't know anyone then you are not invited. But this year, Christmas felt oddly comforting. Our neighbor old Miss Joan was alone without her husband Mr. John, who was in the hospital. With my dad and me pulling along without my mom, it felt like we all shared a kindred feeling, almost a holiday feeling, even without the lights, the tree, and the dinner.

On Christmas Eve I set out determined to make a special meal. I walked the three blocks to Kroger in the morning with borrowed money from my father's wallet and bought groceries for salmon with sautéed bok choy and asparagus drizzled in butter. Since my dad wasn't expecting me to cook all the Bengali meals my mom used to know, I had a lot more freedom to choose what to eat. I cooked all day that day, with the music turned on loud and the kitchen fires hot and sweaty, the oven and stove running at the same time. My dad was out all day working on another property he had bought and I expected him to return only in the evening. So that gave me plenty of time to prepare. I brought out little candles from the cupboard in the sunroom and spread them over the tablecloth.

Then, with a scarf tied over my head, I was dusting the room when I heard a knock at the door. It was Miss Joan, plump and pink-faced, wearing a pretty floral dress. Beside her stood a younger woman just as tall, with the same piercing blue eyes, a startling picture of what Miss Joan must have looked like as a young woman, pretty and lithe in shorts and a T-shirt.

"Hello, Asha, this is my daughter Jill."

Jill smiled a lovely smile and gave me her hand.

"Won't you come in, Miss Joan?"

"No, Asha. We have to go see John in the hospital. We're fixin' to bring him a small Christmas dinner. Then Jill has to drive back to her home in Katy. But I wanted you to have this."

Miss Joan handed me a brown paper bag.

"It's nothing. Just a li'l something."

I remembered Miss Joan's frequent gifts to me for every occasion and blushed, already knowing what to expect. When I opened the bag, there was a card inside with a hundred dollar bill. The card said, "To Asha, Ali, and Sheuli. We love you with all our hearts. John and Joan Lytle."

My lungs felt large in my chest. Over the few months since we'd moved into this house and grown to be friends with Miss Joan and Mr. John, we'd seen the fire truck flashing in front of their house too many times, every time Mr. John fell or collapsed or got sick. And now, finally, they had to check him into a hospital. I had a feeling he wasn't coming back.

"You used to know Sylvie?" I said to Jill, trying to make conversation. But I only thought of Sylvie because I'd thought of death. Sylvie used to live in the house next door to us, on the other side. When she was eighteen, she disappeared. I'd heard all the gossip from Miss Joan—Sylvie's father Mr. Walters moved out yet never sold the house, because his daughter had grown up in it. Ever since I'd heard about Sylvie, I was obsessed with her.

"Yes." Her frank face fell and closed.

"Sorry, I didn't mean to . . . " I blushed. I'd been awkward, but it's difficult to be socially clued in when your parents aren't.

"I didn't know her very well," Jill said. "I went to Regan High. Sylvie didn't go there. She attended a private school."

"Jill is very busy writing her PhD," Miss Joan said, beaming.

"Oh, what is it on?" I asked.

"Paranormal psychology."

I laughed because I couldn't help thinking of Miss Joan's own interest in abnormal things. Jill stared at me. Oops. Another awkward response.

"Sorry, I . . . what made you choose such a *cool* subject?"

"Ghosts." She was smiling at me, so mature and cool, her blonde hair cropped close on her neck. I wanted hair like that, or at least to be able to choose what haircut I could have.

"My mom used to tell me ghost stories. But now she's gone." I felt tears come to my eyes when I mentioned her.

"Gone? Where is she?"

"She left my dad. They . . . didn't get along." I thought how much I missed my mom and also that she had abandoned me when she left my dad. She said she'd left on my account, because he was so mean to me, always shouting at me, about dressing up like a good Muslim girl and all that. Things got bad after we moved to this house. Both my parents started to accuse me of giving up their culture. And then they started fighting. They had a big argument about me one night, and my dad was pounding the wall with his fist and shouting at my mom. The next day, my mom had left, going to my dad's own parents' house because she had nowhere else to go. But she'd left me behind, saying that she was worried my dad might be right after all, and I might be going bad after all! I couldn't believe her. Tears came to my eyes as I thought of her now.

"What ghosts?" I asked Jill quickly to change the subject.

"I thought I saw ghosts in this house, actually," Jill said. "When I lived next door."

"What kind of ghosts?" After I learned about Sylvie, I'd been stealing into Sylvie's abandoned house out of morbid fascination. Mr. Walters had preserved the whole house exactly as it had been before, including Sylvie's room. Her room still smelled of her favorite perfume, Jasmine! I'd taken out a leather diary from her room, and I'd been reading it. I kept thinking of Sylvie's family, wanting to have a perfect family like hers, and then I was dreaming of her all the time, almost like she was a phantom.

"Asha never saw any ghosts in this house," Miss Joan turned to Jill.

"No, never," I agreed. Miss Joan had once tried to scare me by saying that the previous owner of our house, Mrs. Brown, had died *in* the house, but I hadn't seen any ghosts. After all, she died of a stroke, gardening in the back, in broad daylight. Why should she come back as a ghost?

"For a while after Mrs. Brown's death, this house was abandoned. I used to imagine all sorts of hoarders and squatters lived here. I heard sounds," Jill said.

"But not ghosts," I pressed.

"After Mrs. Brown died, Asha, your house was empty for a *while*," Miss Joan said. "The old lady's sons didn't rent out this place for a long time afterwards. And then also, there was just a constantly changing line of tenants for a while, young people with rings up their noses and tattoos on their backs and such, and Sylvie's dad as caretaker. D'you remember, Jill?"

I remembered again how old-fashioned Miss Joan was, and laughed.

"I used to hear a girl cry," Jill said suddenly. "Especially after Sylvie's death, I used to be so terrified! Imagine. Someone my age, someone I'd known, was gone, presumed dead. She was supposed to go to Yale, and all the parents on our street were talking about her, what a star pupil she was. And then suddenly, on New Year's Eve, she disappeared. Her car, her dad's blue Chevy, was found abandoned on I-45. The police thought she must have been kidnapped and murdered, her body dumped somewhere in the state park near Huntsville. You can imagine how affected I was."

"Sylvie had gone to a New Year's party," Joan said. "I remember exactly how we heard. I was out front raking leaves. And then I saw Mrs. Corwin and Annie and a couple of our other neighbors coming into the Walters' house. Sandy, Sylvie's mom, was crying and they were trying to comfort her. It was New Year's Day and I was thinking of taking Jill out for a bike ride. So I hurry over there, across your yard, Asha, because old Mrs. Brown had died by then and your house was lying empty then, and I say, what's wrong? And when they told me, Asha, that Sylvie was missing I never would have expected . . . " Miss Joan clutched her chest, remembering that moment again.

"When my mom came home and said Sylvie's missing I screamed and fainted," Jill said. "I had a fever for a week. They had to call a doctor. My parents were so worried about me."

"In those days people felt a lot of sympathy for each other," Miss Joan said. "It was like we were all connected, like on a cord."

"And then?" I asked Jill.

"I was in a delirium. I used to have strange dreams and talk in my sleep." Miss Joan nodded emphatically.

"She was so sick we weren't able to take her to the doctor's office. We had to call the doctor to the house."

"And at night I would hear voices and moans coming from your house. I would dream about Sylvie every night and imagine her crying and calling me. It got so I even felt guilty to apply to college next year. Mom says if I weren't so guilty I might have put in more effort and gotten in somewhere better than in state. I didn't want to go away."

I shivered, thinking of Jill hearing Sylvie's cries and dreaming of Sylvie like that just after she had vanished. I couldn't imagine what it would have been like to be Jill, to have someone you knew disappear. Suddenly Jill looked at her watch and straightened up.

"We gotta go, mom. I have to head back to my house after dinner with dad."

I said thank you again, and Merry Christmas, and how much I loved her, and hugged them both. When they left, the sky was dark already, a heavy grey behind the bare, reaching trees.

I closed the door to the bleak outside and thought I'd make myself a hot cup of tea before my dad got home. My mom and I used to enjoy drinking tea together. She made tea in a pot, boiling the milk for a long time. Then she would turn off the heat and throw in loose tea leaves. We would light candles and sit on the sofas with our feet up cradling our mugs. Now I heated water in the mug in the microwave oven and threw in a tea bag. I lit two candles the scent of ginger and sat down on the sofa hugging my tea. I started to think about Sylvie's diary, as I often did when alone. My favorite page read, *I gave my dad a watch of the purest silver today. I used all my allowance money and all the babysitting money from last summer. Daddy, I said, you better wear this watch all the time. I'm fixing to, he said. Never take it off, promise me, I said.* I had memorized those words. I wished I had a father like Mr. Walters, so kind and loving. I wished I had a family like Sylvie's.

The next time I looked outside the window, it was darker. The trees with their sad branches were barely visible, moving slightly in the wind. I heard the sound of thunder like the sky was clearing its throat.

It felt good to be inside and safe. But as soon as I sat down, a thousand thoughts came scrambling to scare me. I tried to push them away, but they kept coming back. I thought of my mom and dad. Were they really getting a divorce? What did that mean for me? My body slowed down so that even the weight of the cup was too much. I put it down on a coffee table and my eyes fell on the blue topaz necklace. It had been lying there neglected since the day my parents had confronted me about it. My dad had just found it in my room and my mom thought someone had *given* it to me! That's the kind of girl they thought I was becoming. I'd cried and pleaded with them to believe me it wasn't a gift from some boy, but they didn't. That was the last fight they had before my mom left. I said the stray cat that wandered across all our yards had gotten it. But the truth was, I'd actually taken it from Sylvie's room, along with the diary.

Perhaps my mom had left it there deliberately, as a reminder of my going-off-at-nights issue. I sat up with a start. *Blue topaz necklace.* I remembered the next to last entry of Sylvie's diary. *I will wear my blue dress and my blue topaz necklace from my dad to the New Year's party.* If she had died on New Year's Eve, then she had gone to that party wearing the necklace, but if she never came back how was the necklace still in her room?

I buried my head in my hands and sat still in the dark, thinking, worrying for myself. If my dad married again, what would happen to mom and me? We had no money. Would we be forced to live like charity cases with my father and his new wife? Then I started to worry that my dad wasn't coming home tonight. Perhaps he had forgotten about me and would just leave me on my own. The sky grumbled again and the candles flickered out in the draft.

There was something in the dark room. In the distance, I heard the whimpering of dogs, probably afraid of the thunder. I heard long wails, like the mewling of a cat perhaps, I didn't know. But I sensed that I was not alone, that there was someone there with me. I wrapped myself with my arms and swayed, trembling. It was all around me now, gently, gently circling. I felt myself going mad with fear. Outside, the thunder came in waves, starting with a great crescendo and then diminishing into a rumbling in the background, like jet planes breaking through the sky. The wailing continued. And then there was the sound of rain. I tried to think of something close, someone who loved me and cared for me, whom I could count on. Instead, I thought of myself doing something crazy right now, like walking over to Sylvie's house next door, leaving out the backdoor and across our yard and over into the next door yard.

Every sound and everything my eyes fell on made me afraid, including my mom's painting on the wall of a dark girl bending over a wounded white bird, her face anguished. In the dark, her mouth seemed stretched into a toothless moan, all black inside, and her eyes bored into mine, beseeching. I shivered again. My mom used to tell me stories of the *nishi*, the ghosts from Bengali stories who called you with song and brought you outside the house. If someone called me now, I thought, I would die. I realized now that I really *had* been waking up and walking in the night, as my parents had accused me—because *a voice had called me and woken me*! I'd been going to Sylvie's empty house at nights! Now the presence grew stronger and nearer, except that it seemed to be part of me, the electricity running over my body, making my hairs stand up and picking up my heart like a magnet.

Then I heard the old scrabbling over my head that I used to hear when we first moved to this house, in the attic. I'd never really figured out whether it was mice or squirrels or what. It didn't matter. Whatever it was, the sound grew louder and more frantic, driving me crazy. I stood up and started moaning to calm myself. Then, I am ashamed to say, I started crying loudly. I had lost it.

"No, no, no," I said aloud. "Calm down, calm down, calm down."

There was the sound of thunder again and heavy rain. When I looked out, the windows were blinded. Everything was a wet blur in the dark. A sudden flash of lightning lit up the whole scene, giving me a glimpse of black wet trees shaking in the wind over a sopping yard. I worried that the water in the yard would seep into the low sunroom.

In Houston, rains like this led to hurricanes and flash floods. I had a sense of being unsteady, everything unfixed, as if anything could happen today, as if great harm could come to my family. I started acting superstitiously, not turning my head to look out the dark windows of the sunroom or behind me towards the dark kitchen. I found myself working up to all kinds of fear, moving my body in jerky, nervous motions.

My mom used to say if you were afraid of something you had to go check it out. You had to *prove* it wasn't anything supernatural. I don't know if it was my mom's voice that was guiding me, but something gave me a push suddenly. I straightened up and got out of the sofa.

I found myself moving toward the attic. I stood underneath it, looking up at the cord that hung down in the dark hallway between the empty bedroom that my parents used to share and my own room. The doors to both rooms were ajar, showing dark pools inside. I felt for the light switch in the hall, my hands jerking. A dim sodium bulb tinted the tiny hallway, leaving large sections of it in gloom and casting shadows on the walls.

I smelled jasmine. I looked around with big eyes but there was no one around. Okay, okay. I tried to act normal, as if someone were watching and would tease me later on for being so cowardly.

I started thinking about Sylvie, and once I started the thoughts wouldn't stop. A beautiful young girl in a blue dress and topaz necklace, who had gone to a party with a young friend. If she had been kidnapped and murdered on the road, how did the necklace get back in here in this house? Perhaps the diary was wrong—perhaps she never wore the necklace to the party after all. Sylvie with golden hair, brushed smooth with a pink brush. Sylvie laughing. Sylvie murdered by a stranger on the road. I started to cry for Sylvie.

When I looked up again at the rope hanging down, I wanted to do something brave, like climb up a ladder into the attic. For Sylvie's sake. I pulled on the rope. The door didn't give. I pulled harder, with both hands, bending low and pulling.

Then with a lurch the door came down. I hopped up a few times before reaching the folded ladder and extending it. It came down in a rush of dust and particles, making me cough. Now I was faced with a new worry. Would I be able to climb up? This new fear gave me courage about the other fear, filling me up with a rush of blood. As the air filled with the sounds of wind clusters and dripping rain and thunder, I took the ladder in both hands and climbed, a creak at a time. Since the ladder wasn't fixed, it swayed in front as I put weight on it, and I pulled it back against my body. I thought again of my lazy dad who hadn't even bothered to check out the attic, let alone build a second story and put in a new bathroom as he'd meant to with the house since we'd bought it. Sylvie's dad Mr. Walters used to fix up their house all the time, Sylvie wrote in her diary. I wanted a father like Sylvie's, kind, hardworking, loving, and blue eyed. Mr. Walters still came to their old house every week, to pull out weeds, and mow the lawn, to keep the house intact for his daughter. My dad had struck up a friendship with the old man, and asked him to help out with a few things around our house.

I climbed slowly. The rain gushed on in a constant frenzy, thunder clapping in the background. At last, I was level with the floor of the attic. I could smell dust now, thick and choking. There was a thick build up of solid dust under my palms. I must have had something of my mom in me, the neat and clean and tidy part, because I squirmed at the sight of it. I smelled jasmine again, even closer now. Then I pulled myself up by my knees so that I was crouching on the floor of the attic. Miss Joan had said people lived their entire lives in houses and never checked out their attics. I was curious now. What forgotten things were stored here?

There was a low, bare light bulb with a thread attached to it. I pulled on it. A dim light flooded the sloped, suffocating space. Sandwiched between roof and dust, I crawled on my knees, past switchboards I expected were connected to the gas supply. The scent of jasmine was everywhere now, stronger than in my dreams, stronger than in Sylvie's house next door. I felt again that someone was with me. Something urged me on. Was this what the *nishi* were like that my mom had told me about? I longed for the days when my mom and I were so close, when I could crawl into her lap and listen to a scary story and hold her arm close to me. I kept moving into the room, crawling in the tight space, dust now all over my body. I could hear the thunder and wind lashing outside, and the sound of the rain on the roof was deafening, as if it could burst through at any moment.

There were broken boxes about me with objects spilling out, burst into by animals probably. I sat down cross-legged on the floor, hoping that I wouldn't fall through, and began to look through the boxes. They were full of clothes mostly, old T-shirts and shirts, flouncy nylon skirts, scarves, and petticoats. Naphthalene balls fell out from between the layers of clothes. One box seemed to hold different objects than clothes, underneath a heavy red quilt material that looked like a blanket but turned out to be a multi-colored geometric patterned jacket. I held up the jacket in both hands and murmured, *nice jacket*. Perhaps it was in fashion again. Then I put my hand in the box again and started to pull out what I could reach. Under the jacket were a game of Scrabble, a chess board, paperback novels, and under these, photo albums. There were quite a few albums, square and heavy with brown and red leather covers. I began to look through one greedily. There was a young mother, probably the first owner of our house, with three young smiling sons around her skirt. The yard looked like it might be ours, with pine trees, the sun lighting up the four from behind.

"Little did she know they would turn out to be such selfish people," I muttered, turning the page. After old Mrs. Brown had died, I heard they'd just fought over the house, letting it lie empty, and then rented it out for a few years with Mr. Walters its manager, to fix up things and look after the property when it was empty, before they sold it to my dad to just get the money. Not until I had scoured the last page of the last album did I realize what I had been looking for. I was looking for Sylvie, of course. But there was no trace of anyone resembling Sylvie or her parents in any of the photos. And why should there be? This wasn't their house and these weren't their albums.

I closed the album abruptly. Thinking about Sylvie terrified me, and it was *not* a good idea to be afraid while alone at home on a rainy night. I wouldn't go down that path again. I worried why my dad hadn't returned yet. Bayous often crested in Houston, cars were submerged, and drivers drowned. I put the album back inside the cardboard box and looked away determinedly. My eyes fell on something flashy on the floorboard.

I crawled in my dust covered jeans hungrily towards it, peering at it in the dim light. It was a heavy men's watch with a silver chain link, the kind that my grandfather used to wear in his youth. I felt the chain lovingly, admiring the cross hatch pattern and studying the way each square linked with the next making an expensive piece of men's jewelry. Then I turned over the face to look on the backside. There was an inscription. People in the old days probably etched these watches with inscriptions, like people did with wedding rings sometimes. Perhaps the old lady had given it to her husband, the father of her three sons. I squinted, trying to read the letters, and cursed the low light. Slowly, I shifted and slid on the floor until I was directly under the light again. Sitting tall, I held up the watch to the light and tried again. None of the letters I could make out fit together to spell words. There were big gaps and shadows in between. I frowned to focus better. Then, eventually, after several rounds of trying, I had it, the letters pieced together into words, like a puzzle.

From Sylvie. To Daddy. With Love.

I read it again and again, numbly. How did the watch get here? A stray cat in the neighborhood was pulling things out of the house and spilling them on Sylvie's yard and on ours, but how did the watch make it to the attic? Probably the squirrels or rats or even raccoons that were squatters in the attic had carried it up here. I chuckled, thinking of the line of naughty animals that must have conspired to make such an impossible thing happen and also at my own powers of scientific reasoning. Excited, I arched up like a cat on all fours and renewed my treasure hunt. I could still hear the rain splattering on the roof now, close to my head, and the occasional rap of thunder, but the weather now added excitement to my hunt.

Like a four-legged animal, I moved forward to the deepest recesses of the attic. If my dad had been renovating, I would have asked him to convert this attic into my room, with its bohemian slanting roof. I would have asked him to cut me a skylight up ahead on the sloped ceiling to see the glow on a moonlit night and I would have put my bed right there, at the furthest corner, at the dead end. A pretty twin bed with an orange spread and lots of bright colored cushions. I put my hand against the end wall and realized that there was a secret shelf cut into the wall, planked over with plywood. I started to rip it off with my hands! What the hell—my dad would renovate it all anyway.

Behind the plywood, now half ripped off and half hanging on, there was a long oblong cushion on the floor, of the kind I had seen in Bengali homes only, used to cover the length of a sofa or as a cushion to grab when sleeping. I bent low to look at it, thinking my dad and I could haul it downstairs to use it in the house. But when my face was level with it, I realized it wasn't a cushion at all but wrapped upholstery, rolled up like a carpet. It was a dark color, like deep maroon with a sour smell that struggled with the scent of jasmine. I knelt close now, trying to unroll the material. It felt sticky in my hands, like a sugary bun crusted over. But I got hold of the material at one end and pulled and raised and kicked the thing. It was really heavy, and I thought perhaps it was carpeting or curtains, or upholstery for the couch, something rare and expensive. I thought how I was like my father after all. I loved old houses and everything that came with them. It was odd to think that I had inherited anything from him.

The materials unraveled and fell with a bump. I breathed heavily and felt myself growing hot even in the cool temperature. But I was determined. I bent, supporting my hands on knees, and then started again. With each heave, the cloth unraveled a little and then I had to rest. I felt frantic as one does with long homework or a project that just won't end but you can't let go of. The more I unraveled the cloth, the damper it felt, the crustier and more acrid, but it could have been my imagination, sweaty as I was, mixed with dust and dirt from the attic. I started to hear clattering and thudding, increasing in tempo on the floor, and at some point I realized that the cloth that I was unwrapping was cover for something else. My lungs puffed out with curiosity. Perhaps it was silverware, heavy silver, a family treasure, or a carved wooden chest containing silver coins!

I could still hear the rain pounding on the roof. How different the rain sounded in the attic, frantic and immediate, clapping and stomping, and furious. I had never known such a rain and I had lived all my life in Houston. I pulled the free end of the cloth again and let go, panting and wheezing, kneeling down on my hands and feet to examine what I had uncovered from the bits that were now exposed. I felt with my fingers and stretched my eyes to make out what it was. It felt like dry bone, a medical student's skeleton? Perhaps one of Mrs. Brown's sons was a doctor?

With a snatch, I pulled away the cloth entirely and suddenly the thing it was covering was exposed.

I screamed and jumped up, hitting my head on the roof. Somehow I missed the nails poking through. Out of pure terror, I kept jumping and wringing my hands and wailing for five minutes, all of the things that seem like cliché when you are watching TV. Then finally I put my hand to my cold, beaded forehead and stood or half stood, as straight as the roof would allow, staring at the thing.

What I gazed at in the dim light was the fully clothed body of a skeleton in a blue dress and blue ribbons in golden hair matted with crust, which might be blood, old blood, but golden nonetheless. It was a dusty skeleton with hollowed eyes but the dress and the hair and the blood were all too real, gaudy. *The blue topaz, the blue dress, and the watch from Sylvie to her dad.* I was thinking clearly now, as clear as the Texas sky is after a storm. I was adding it all up. A blue Chevy had been picked up by police by the roadside, Miss Joan had said, but Sylvie's body had never been found. *This* was Sylvie's body, in our attic. No stranger had taken her away, and no one had taken her necklace till I did.

The watch that she had given her father was also in our attic with her, proof that he had been here. The house must have been empty then, after the death of the old lady Mrs. Brown, while her grown sons decided what to do with their joint inheritance.

I heard my blood rushing in the deafening noise of the rain and thunder. I had to call the police. I left the body as it was, without covering it, only stuffing the watch in my jeans pocket. I reached the entrance of the attic and turned around, angling my body to reach the first rung. The ladder swayed away from me and I flailed my legs this way and that, trying to find it. There was the loud rap of thunder again followed by a thud much nearer like a tree falling on the street. There were four loud bangs all around, a sound all too familiar to me, as transformers burst one after another. Then the power went out, leaving me in darkness.

I jumped down from the attic in the dark. Then I felt my way to the kitchen and thumped along the counter until I found my mom's favorite ginger-scented candle. With a shaking hand, I lit it from the lighter gun by the stove, steadying the flame against the drafts from the sunroom door and windows. More than ever, I was aware what an old house it was, full of gaps and cracks open to the weather outside. My heart thumped as I carried the candle into the dining room where the phone stood on a dusty shelf in the corner near the dining table. I had to call the police, now.

When I picked up the phone, there was no dial tone.

The storm must have brought down the phone line as well. I wished my parents had given me a cell phone. I knew Miss Joan wouldn't be home yet. And besides, I didn't dare to step outside the house, not just because of the weather.

"Calm down," I told myself. "It's an old murder. There's no real cause for hurry."

But there was. The pounding in my ears and the monotonous wail of the rain told me there was urgency. There was a dead body upstairs. I wished my dad would hurry back home in the floods quickly, safe.

I thought of the most cowardly thing I could do to put the greatest distance between me and the body of the murdered girl upstairs. I could go to my room and pull up the comforter over my head, but that would make me feel more vulnerable and trapped. I felt better being up, aware. Pulling on my old jacket, I went to sit with my candle in the dark living room, rocking back and forth for warmth and comfort. I must have fallen asleep, half dreaming of my mom, wondering why she hadn't called to check on me, dreaming of Christmas, a beautiful, loving father and mother for a family, just like I used to imagine Sylvie had when I used to read her diary, a white Christmas and a Happy New Year.

There was a knock at the door that brought me to. I opened my eyes and cocked my ear, not sure for a moment what had woken me. Then there were knocks again, three at a time. I jolted up because my dad was back from wherever he had gone, back home safe. I don't think I had ever been so happy to have him back, except perhaps when I was very little and climbed on his shoulders the minute he came home to demand candy from him. I ran to the door like that little girl again. I might even have cried out to him, *Daddy*, but that embarrassing cry was swallowed by the rain.

I struggled with the locks nervously. At last, I threw the door open for my father. When I saw the man standing on the waterlogged porch, it was all I could do not to scream. My face crumpled and I clutched my hands together, ready to cry out. My instinct was to close the door, but instead I stood frozen, as in a dream.

"Hello," old Mr. Walters said, "I came to work on the house." He was a tall stooped man, with blue eyes, checked shirt and jeans tucked in Texas boots, the kind of father I had wanted to have. "Your dad said to come by to check some bad drainage. Tonight's a good night for that . . . "

"He's not home," I said in a thin voice. My eyes burned with tears, but I mustered all of my grown-up mettle to bite down the urge to scream. I'd grown up years in that attic. If I remained calm, I told myself, nothing need go wrong. He would just leave.

"*No?*" the old man had to shout out the words in the lashing wind. His eyes were as blue as ever, bright and shining in the sudden flash of lightning.

"May I use your phone then, to call a friend? I can't go out no more in this weather, can't take no more jobs tonight," he said. He was standing in half a foot of water on the porch, up to his boots and halfway up his tucked blue jeans, soaked through to the shirt. His hair was plastered to his pale, wrinkled face.

"Our phone just went dead," I said. The old man gave me a sharp look.

"Phone dead?" he said.

The lightning done, it was dark around us again.

On a sudden impulse, I brought out the silver watch from my pocket and held it up to Mr. Walters' face.

"Do you recognize this?"

He was a foot taller than me. He peered in the dark, bending his wet face to see.

Lightning flashed again, showing his horrified face. I was breathing hard. My head felt light and airy. The smell of jasmine mixed with wet earth and wet leaves played in my head. The rain played like music in the background. In Bengali they would call the sound *jhom jhom. Jhom Jhom Jhom.*

"Is it yours?" I asked again. I felt feverish, out of my body, my heart pounding both from fear and excitement.

The old man frowned and didn't reply. He shook his head. It was almost as if he didn't understand. Now I too was getting sprayed by the rainwater. Miss Joan's lights were off next door—she probably couldn't drive back from the hospital in this rain.

With a sudden movement, the old man was inside our house, shutting the door behind him and locking it, taking his hat off, pulling off his boots, standing on the hardwood floor in his wet feet.

"May I rest a moment here?" he was saying. "With those roads, I have nowhere to go."

What ordinary words, completely logical. And yet, I trembled. As he spoke, he seemed to be pushing me with his body deeper inside the house. Like a king checked in a chess game, I kept moving inside away from him.

"Yes," I said, shaking inside. "My dad will be home soon."

My ginger candle was giving off a strong, sweet smell. I thought of my mother whose candle it was, and felt stronger. I smiled at the old man.

"My dad will be home soon," I repeated.

"Thank you, little girl," he said.

I kept standing and smoothed my hair, rocking back and forth.

"Please sit down."

He crossed to one of the sofas and did.

The rain died down as abruptly as it had begun. Could I make a run for it? Should I run for the back door?

"Did you . . . "

"Yes?" Mr. Walters asked.

His wet clothes were making the sofa sopping wet. He seemed so calm and harmless, tired, this repairman, so worn out, resting. I felt bad to suspect him. Why hadn't he ever removed the body afterward? Wasn't he afraid other tenants would move in and discover the body some day?

I shook my head. Where were my mom and dad when they really needed to keep me safe from all that they feared? They had abandoned me. Really abandoned me. I started to cry, tears running down my nostrils, making my nose run.

"Are you alright?" the old man asked. A kindly old man, a Southern gentleman. I had always wondered what these kind of people thought of immigrants like us, especially of my dad, who always stood out.

"Why didn't you remove the body?" I asked.

Now he looked at me as if *I* were insane, as if *he* were afraid of being harmed by *me*.

"What body?"

"Sylvie's body," I cried.

Now that the rain had stopped, the silence was deadly. The candle flickered in the dark room. It was chilly, with the wind flowing like a real presence in the room.

"Sylvie?" Mr. Walters said. For a long time, he didn't say anything else, as if he had been shunted by that name, pulled back into a different time.

"Sylvie," he whispered again after a long time.

"Please," I cried in a sudden panic, my grown-up composure leaving me. "Don't harm me."

He stood up and came toward me.

"What have you found?" he growled softly.

He was no longer a kindly old man. His teeth were yellow and parts of his flesh seemed to be coming off, like he was made of paper and plaster and falling apart. His whole skin on his neck and his arms was puckered and marked, like he was diseased. He kept coming, advancing toward me. An old man, but still tall, and strong.

"Sylvie," I whispered. It was remarkable how I felt. I wasn't afraid anymore. I was entirely calm.

"Where?"

"In the attic."

"How do you know about Sylvie, little Indian girl? When is your daddy coming home?"

He had seized me by the wrist. It was quiet, a dark, silent night now. I had bemoaned not having a feast or a family to celebrate it with. Now I would take it all back, all my complaints, just to be safe. I could die, I thought. I could die today.

He pulled me by the wrist from the living room to the kitchen. I followed him without much resistance. At this close range, I could smell him, wet pine cones and earth, and an after-smell, the sour odor of old age. The smell made him more real than the kind, blue-eyed daddy picture I had inside my head. Holding onto my hand, Mr. Walters began to pull out drawers savagely in the dark. He pulled them all the way, spoons and napkins flying out of drawers.

"My dad's coming home," I said. "Before you got here, I called my dad on my cell phone. And I called the police."

If anything, his hold on my wrist became more savage. He reached for the knife drawer. I closed my eyes.

So many changes in a year. This might as well be another. I calculated all the things I was afraid of ever, ever facing. The things my parents tried to protect me from. Addiction. Murder. Rape. After all of that fuss, this was where I had landed. This was what Miss B. in English class would call irony.

I was almost not aware of what he was doing. The old man himself seemed to have slowed down now, calmly looking through the drawer, selecting a knife out of so many haphazardly stacked together. Now there was a new smell—the smell of my cooking, of salmon and bok choy, and soy sauce. What had been flavorful and delicious was now overlaid with a nauseating, acrid smell of heavy spices. It was overpowering. I wanted to trash everything I'd cooked. Everything seemed overdone, like an old man with his veins showing and his body reeking, the stench of overcooked food, the mulch smell of soggy earth. I wanted to push it all back and make it neutral again. Neutral, colorless, mundane.

"Why didn't you remove the body?" I whispered again.

"Where is the watch?" He had a knife aimed at my throat, the wrong edge touching my throat. It felt cold, an uncomfortable pressure.

"It's in my pocket. May I take it out?"

Unlike in a TV crime drama, he let me. I brought it out of my jeans pocket and handed it to him. He was standing behind me, one arm angled around my shoulders and the other holding the knife to my throat. Now he took the watch with the same hand as the knife and dropped it in his shirt pocket.

"What are you going to do?" I asked. I wondered the ways I could be saved—if my dad was back, or Miss Joan, or the power, or the phone line. Could I kick him, make a run for it? But I was paralyzed, I had too much regard for him, I felt too close to him.

He didn't answer, just motioned me toward the living room. I walked of my own volition, with his knife at my throat and a slight push as he walked behind me. His arm felt warm on my neck and I shivered at the touch. He pushed me past the living room, where my dad and my mom used to fight so much that I thought nothing could be scarier, and into the opening that was the hallway between my parents' bedroom and mine. We were standing in front of the bathroom again. The rope to climb to the attic hung low above our heads.

"Up," the old man grunted, motioning.

I shivered in the suddenly cold house. Mr. Walters tugged on the rope and the door creaked open. I stood on tiptoe to reach the ladder. The old man made an irritated sound and moved me out of the way, unfolding the ladder himself. We climbed up, one following the other, as if we were a team. We had to keep the ladder steady between us. The rain had completely died by now, and there was a silence in the attic as we surfaced, as if silence could be heard. I tugged another string, this time to switch on the light in the drafty attic. The unmistakable bundle of the body lay spilled before us. My pulling and tugging appeared to me now like an act of vandalism, violating the privacy of Sylvie Walters and exposing her body, the grisly remains of bones and teeth and mad hair, as if an animal had left the remains of his meal behind.

I glanced back instinctively to check Mr. Walters' face. It was lined and worn and tired, but in the gloom it didn't betray any emotion. He just had this tight, fixed look. I kept looking at him, waiting for the next instruction, or his next move. My heart beat like a slow drum with long pauses in between. I waited for Mr. Walters.

At last, he exhaled a long sigh, "It's been so long since I was in this room."

"Don't you feel sorry for her?" I asked.

Again, he didn't reply. He stared at the body fixedly, one arm still pinning my shoulder to him. It was so cold now, the cold air unbearable. A father without emotion at his daughter's death—I just couldn't fathom it—

and this more than anything else brought me to tears. I shook and my teeth chattered.

"What's wrong?" the old man growled.

He unwound his arm from around my neck and held the knife away.

"You stay here," he said.

I nodded. My heart had taken off racing again, but at the same time I felt relief that the old man was leaving. The hairy warm arm against my skin had disgusted me. After making me sit on the floor and pushing my head down on my raised knees, Mr. Walters turned off the light. Then he disappeared down the ladder.

Here I was with Sylvie all to myself, Sylvie beyond all life, I thought. I'd been so obsessed with her, and now here I had Sylvie, her murdered body next to me. I remembered again an entry in her diary, *I gave my dad a watch of the purest silver today. I used all my allowance money and all the babysitting money from last summer. Daddy, I said, you better wear this watch all the time. I'm fixing to, he said. Never take it off, promise me, I said.*

My eyes felt heavy now and really, what I wanted more than anything else was to close them. But in the next moment, I was coughing and choking. If I had been fool enough to think the old man would just lock me and leave me to my solitude, I was wrong. Smoke climbed up and surrounded me.

"Asha!"

I struggled to wake up. Each stage of coming to felt more horrible, with my mouth dry, my nostrils burning. I sat up instinctively, trying to get as much air into my lungs as possible.

"Daddy?"

"Asha, wake up. Please."

My dad was kneeling over me, half dragging and half carrying me down. I tried to help but I couldn't move. My head was heavy as an ancient temple.

"It's worse down there," he said, lumbering me over one shoulder and starting down the ladder. I received everything in still shots, as if a strobe light were going on and off. It got hotter as we descended. My head felt about to burst.

He struggled with one hand on the ladder while holding me with the other.

"Dad!" I coughed. "I . . . I can't breathe!"

I felt a wet towel around my mouth and face, wrapping me in moisture.

The moments seemed to pass like that, in snapshots. I was only conscious of being carried over my dad's shoulder the way he used to carry me as a little girl.

"You okay, Asha?" I heard at times, and I struggled to consciousness again.

At last, suddenly, there was air. The night breeze wrapped me.

"Are you okay? When I saw the attic ladder hanging, I thought you must be up there. But why my girl would be in attic I do not know." My dad had laid me on the concrete porch and he was kneeling in front of me.

"Daddy!" I would have cried but the sound turned into coughs.

"Breathe! Breathe!" My dad kept thumping my back and forcing me to inhale the air.

"Asha, you burned down the house. What were you cooking?"

"Dad, I didn't do it," I choked. "You don't know what happened."

He hugged me close, telling me it was okay about the dinner being burnt.

"I am not going to scold you, Asha."

He pulled my head to his chest, which smelt of smoke and sweat.

"Please, Asha, I know you think I am a bad person but I am not so bad as that. I will not be angry about the house."

"Okay, Daddy," I said and gave up trying to explain.

We stayed there on the porch for a long time, sitting on cold concrete in the night till the fire brigade came. I was sniffling and coughing, and as I gained more sense I knew that I was going to catch a cold, at the least.

"Daddy," I said, as we looked toward the brightly flashing lights and siren of the fire brigade, which we normally associated with Mr. John next door having another accident, "May I please go to mommy? I really need her."

"Yes, baby," he said.

II

On a cold winter evening like this, my mom and I like to sit on the upholstered red and white couch next to each other, sipping black tea and taking gentle nibbles of biscuits. Our current favorites are shortbread cookies, in a long red tin box. My mom has lit a solitary candle and we anticipate the scents of coconut and warm ginger. The warm scent hits my nose. I nod happily as she returns to her place beside me and picks up her moss colored ceramic cup. These are our newly bought possessions, the black tea in a cute box, the biscuits, the candle, and our matching ceramic mugs.

"Asha?" my mom's voice seeks me out in the dark.

"Yes?" I say softly.

"Do you mind very much, my baby, having to go to community college for a year because of all that happened . . . because of . . . your dad and me?" She pauses. "I didn't put you first."

"No, mom. It's okay." I smile at her, raising the mug in a cheer.

She stands up again and goes to get out chocolate from the refrigerator. My mom doesn't eat much, but she likes her sweets. I feel the shiver of the refrigerator door opening, and the candle flickering in the draft.

My mom reenters the living room, inserting the square of dark chocolate in her mouth. I love my father, I think, closing my eyes. I know I'm supposed to pick sides, with my dad's family insisting that he is a saint who never did anything wrong and my mom really disliking him for all the shouting and banging he's done, but he left us this house after he repaired the damages from the fire. I think that was very good of him.

My mom licks her fingers and we snuggle next to each other again, my head on her warm, thin shoulder and the apple scent of her hair in my face. I close my eyes, yawning sleepily, thinking of Sylvie, and staring into a blank, newly painted space on the wall ahead. I think back to that night last Christmas when I sat alone on the old sofa, with Sylvie overhead in the attic. I don't allow myself to think of Sylvie's father, his dreary, sun-marked face, his eyes glistening in recognition when I showed him the watch. A year ago, they arrested him driving aimlessly in his pickup truck and he freely confessed.

My dad gave me more answers than my mom, perhaps because his need to explain his actions and to make sense of what had happened to us was more—because he felt personally responsible.

My dad said, during one of our meetings together at my uncle's house where he now lives, "Do you understand why Miss Joan didn't hear you when you cried and why her lights were still out when the fire truck came that night?" We were sitting downstairs at the long, cold dining table near a closed window.

"Yes," I said. "Because she was still in the hospital with Mr. John. He had just died. She couldn't return that night."

"Also, Asha?" There was a deep silence as my dad waited and I turned toward him. This was also new between us, the subtleties of our communication, the way we understood each other at times even without words.

"Yes, Dad?" I gulped.

"You know that they might call you to court? To testify?"

I nodded, looking him in the eye, but I felt removed from the room suddenly, floating somewhere in space.

"I'll be okay, Dad," I said bravely.

Then I asked, "Dad? How did she die?" The windows in my uncle's house were always shut but I felt a draft of air run over the hairs of my arms as I waited for his answer. I stretched them out on the table in front of me and looked away from my dad toward one of the color-coordinated paintings on the wall.

"Sylvie and her dad got into an argument out on the street early on New Year's Day morning, the police are saying. He was in a rage because she went to celebrate the night before with a young black man. Then Walters says he started the car and accidentally ran her over as they fought. Or he did it deliberately."

I nodded and then we didn't speak about Mr. Walters anymore.

There is one other bond with my dad that I never have with my mom, even though she is the expert on ghosts. My dad knows about our ghost. After Mr. John's funeral, dad spoke to Miss Joan one day across the fence. She said, "Ali, I never told you but there had been a death in Garden Oaks every winter. We all believed—all the old ladies who still live and who used to know Sylvie—that it was Sylvie's ghost, mad and raging, come to take out her anguish on the neighborhood. We all knew that her presence was still about, we felt it that she was unhappy. I just didn't want to tell Asha that."

"So Miss Joan wasn't just a gossip after all, telling us all those ghost stories."

I grinned when my dad told me that.

"Asha?" my mom calls sleepily.

"Yes, mom?"

"Would you like me to read you a ghost story in Bengali?" She offers this in a voice that says she will soon fall asleep, and her head will abruptly fall like a brick, but she just feels really obliged to do something with me.

"No, thank you! It's scary enough already in the dark," I laugh.

"Are you sure you don't want to hear a ghost story?" my mom slurs, starting to snore.

"Yes, mom," I slur back, and we fall asleep against each other, snug and warm. I hold back for one more instant before giving over to the fingers of sleep. I can't sense Sylvie anymore, no matter how hard I try. I don't think she is coming back this winter.

GEMINI WAHHAJ *(b. Dhaka, Bangladesh, 1970) has a PhD in creative writing from the University of Houston. Her stories have appeared in* Granta, Cimarron Review, Crab Orchard Review, Night Train, Carolina Quarterly *and* Northwest Review, *among other magazines. She won the Inprint/Michener Fellowship in Honor of Donald Barthelme at the University of Houston, an honorable mention in* Atlantic Monthly'*s student fiction contest, and a finalist prize in* Glimmer Train's *fiction contest. She is Associate Professor of English at Lone Star Community College in Houston and an advisory board member of Inprint, a national literary organization based in Houston.*

Commentary on "The Girl Next Door": *It is a modified excerpt from an unreleased ghost novel titled,* The House Next Door.

MARCELA BOLÍVAR, Cover Artist, Volume I, *(b. Curitiba, Brazil, 1986) moved to Colombia in her childhood where she was raised and currently lives.*

Marcela is a graphic designer whose passion for photography, montage and illustration led her to digital art in 2004. Since then, she has developed her own style, a combination of multiple techniques, being painting, drawing and even sculpture in the execution of her digital work, sometimes using geso gauzes, papier maché, plants and cold porcelain for the details. The subconscious, dreams, memories and the sumptuous shapes of flora and nature have been her continual inspirations.

All based on photographs, her compositions undergo a complex process of transformation, assemblage and detailing that brings them closer to a pictographic expression. Her graphic design bachelor's degree thesis, "Mercurio, Azufre y Ceniza"—a photographic and editorial project—was honored with cum laude recognition, and some of the series' artworks were recognized in photography contests, exhibitions, and publications around the world.

You can see her gallery at http://www.marcelabolivar.com/.

Commentary on the front cover composition "Light Sheds Through": *Done in 2007 this image is a visceral take on changes and new things to come. Flesh disappears and new life emerges from it. She embraces this new world and willingly feeds it. This is a self-portrait with additional personal elements added, colored and assembled digitally.*

This image I have to say is very personal; it contains elements and objects that surrounded me at that time. I was trying to reflect and overcome what I felt back then when a lot of things inside were destroying me. It was time to not fear pain anymore, but taste it. Let a part of me die with it. The needle means self-healing: at points I thought it meant some kind of self imposed anesthesia (along with the music) but after years I realized the true words behind it. I now see too how she is keeping her eyes shut not wanting to see all the beautiful colors surrounding her.

I was discovering Gustave Moreau and Franz von Stuck at that time and trying to find my own voice within this photomanipulation craze. The title comes from Anathema's song "Mine is Yours to Drown in".

From the dark all is revealed
Light sheds through

Commentary on the back covers' "Eve of Brilliance": *This is one of my many attempts to illustrate a natural force in a surreal symbiosis, where even kingdom Plantae has a human consciousness aware of its own death.*

Since I've always been surrounded by biology books, scientific illustrations and carefully kept samples because of my parents' profession, I've tried to understand all those countless observations and relate them to my own body and to the unexplainable metaphors I see in nature.

The two images can be read in any order: did first the glowing fruits bloom thanks to the water that nourished them? Or, do they exist to conceive the fish? That is just one of many mechanisms of life and death that attracts me.

The hand pictured is my own.